Praise for Chita Quest

"Chita is a unique, fast-paced thriller that weaves nasty Washington cover-ups with assassinations, international intrigue and air combat, racing from the Potomac to Mongolia and Russia's Siberian steppes. Initially, military veterans will cheer the Callahan brothers' quest to find their fighter-pilot father, who was shot down in Vietnam and disappeared decades ago. Then they'll curse the political elites, who broke faith with those in uniform and intentionally left American POWs behind."

William B. Scott, bestselling author of *The Permit* and coauthor of *Space Wars: The First Six Hours of World War III* and *Counterspace: The Next Hours of World War II*

Walter E. "Buck" Buchanan III, Lieutenant General, USAF (ret)

States:
"Brinn Colenda once again proves himself to be a master storyteller as we watch his protagonist, Col. Tom Callahan, battle forces denying the existence of long held POW/MIAs. While his narrative picks at the nation's scars covering those left behind, it also celebrates the efforts of the dedicated few that continue to search for answers. The fast paced story will keep you riveted as you follow Col. Tom Callahan and his intrepid team as their personal search twists and turns; taking them all over the globe for answers with the help of a surprising set of political allies."

Chita Quest
One Man's Search for His POW/MIA Father

Brinn Colenda

Southern Yellow Pine
Publishing

Published by:
Southern Yellow Pine (SYP) Publishing
4351 Natural Bridge Rd.
Tallahassee, FL 32305

This is a work of fiction. Names, characters, places, and events that occur either are the products of the author's imagination or are used fictitiously. Any resemblance to actual persons, places, or events is purely co-incidental.
The contents and opinions expressed in this book do not necessarily reflect the views and opinions of Southern Yellow Pine Publishing, nor does the mention of brands or trade names constitute endorsement.

ISBN-10: 1940869072
ISBN-13: 978-1-940869-07-0

Author Photo: Roxanne Wride Photography
Front Cover Art: Taylor Nelson
Area Map Page 11: www.istockphoto.com

Printed in the United States of America
First Edition
February 2014

Dedication

To my family for putting up with my eccentricities all these years:

Linda, Jake, Josh, and Cameron

Thank You

The Callahan Saga

By: Brinn Colenda

Cochabamba Conspiracy

Chita Quest

#3 Scheduled for 2015

Acknowledgements

Researching this book was the best part of the *Chita Quest* writing process. I came away with a profound respect for American POWs from our many wars, but especially from the Vietnam War, as well as for the men and women of the Joint POW/MIA Accounting Command.

Along the way, I met some wonderful people who contributed their talents and support.

Deepest thanks:

- To: Terri Gerrell, my publisher, and Lindsay Marder, my editor, for their dedication, professionalism, and positive outlook.
- To: Commander Jim Tritten, USN (ret); Phaedra Greenwood and "my ladies" in our Taos writers group; Michele Magazine; Scott Jones; Stan Harrell; Michael Turri; Johnese Turri; Linda Sonna, PhD; Major Stephen Hundley, CAP; Colonel David Hunt, USAF (ret); MSgt Richard Dickerson, U.S. Army (ret); LTC Chuck Howe, U.S. Army (ret); and the late, great Betty B. Scher.
- To: John Webster and the AN2flyers.org who helped with the flying sequence. I have long been fascinated by the Antonov An-2 Colt—finally, a venue to highlight this unusual aircraft!
- A special thanks goes to authors Hampton Sides, Michael McGarrity, Bill Scott, Rosalie Turner, and Jack McLean for their advice and support.

I read a lot of books preparing for *Chita Quest*. Five of the best were: *Genghis Khan and the Shaping of the Modern World* by Jack Weatherford; *Glory Denied: The Saga of Jim Thompson, America's Longest-Held Prisoner of War* by Tom Philpott; *You are Not Forgotten* by Bryan Bender; *Loon: A Marine Story* by Jack McLean; and *Ghost Soldiers* by Hampton Sides. I recommend them all.

This is a work of fiction. Our team pored over this manuscript countless times. Any errors, factual and grammatical, are mine and mine alone.

Brinn Colenda, New Mexico, February 2014

Prologue
Near the Cambodian/Laotian/South Vietnamese Border
November 1972

The wall of thunderstorms towered out of the troposphere, reaching up sixty thousand feet and still climbing. Colonel (Brigadier General-select) Sean Callahan, USAF, had always thought the thunderstorms generated in the heat of a West Texas summer were impressive, but thunderstorms in this part of Vietnam were truly awe-inspiring...except when flying; then they were terrifying. Like all pilots, Callahan feared thunderstorms, their strength, their ferocity and their sheer unpredictability.

Leading a flight of two McDonnell-Douglas F-4D Phantom II fighters, Callahan was in no mood to dawdle. His mission was clear: help rescue a downed Air Force pilot, one of his own men shot down earlier that afternoon. Now he was surrounded by thunderstorms, climbing to the heavens like the galleries of Valhalla, the seemingly solid walls of storm cells spewing lightning in all directions. Winds slashed at the aircraft as he searched for a way through.

"Fats," Callahan said over his intercom, "can you find us a hole through all this shit?"

"No, sir." Callahan could hear the fear in the voice of his navigator, a chubby lieutenant from Minnesota, inevitably dubbed Minnesota Fats by the squadron. After a few combat missions the moniker had quietly changed to Mike Foxtrot, phonetic alphabet for the letters M and F, with the expected double entendre. Callahan had overheard someone call him a cowardly dirt-bag and now he knew it was true. That's it for Fats, he thought. He's on the next plane back to the States.

"General, are you sure this is a good idea? Maybe we should abort."

"Fats, listen to me, you worthless son-of-a-bitch. There's one of our guys down out there and we're going to go find him. Is that clear enough?"

Callahan checked his wingman, flying in a loose tactical position off the left wing. He punched his mic button. "Two, got any ideas?"

The answer was immediate, as he knew it would be. "Lead, suggest heading two six zero...and lower."

"Roger. Coming left two six zero."

Callahan saw the rip in the wall of clouds. He gently retarded the throttles and let the nose drop slightly as he made the prescribed turn. His muscles tensed as the two F-4s descended through the broken deck of rain, clouds, and lumpy air, carefully working the canyons and valleys within the cloud system, finally breaking out over the mottled green of the Vietnamese jungle. From three thousand feet the jungle stretched out under the clouds to the horizon, with a narrow river slicing through the foliage. He could see occasional fields gouged out of the trees. To the north and west, smoke rose from burning targets, probably trucks that had been hit by the downed Phantom. The locals would be alert, armed, and angry.

Against the cloud background, Callahan picked out the OV-10A Bronco of the forward air controller (FAC) working the area and made radio contact. The FAC directed Callahan's flight to the west, closer to the ill-defined border, while two Douglas A-1E Sandys finished their bomb runs. The broccoli tops of the jungle foliage slipped by under his nose as he eased into a gentle climb.

He expected antiaircraft fire, or small arms fire at the least. "Keep your eyes peeled, Fats." He tapped his rudders and sent his wingman out wider. He maneuvered the formation through the mild buffeting from the rising thermals, anticipating that the FAC would send them in quickly. He glanced over his instruments one more time to ensure everything was working and checked his compass. They were heading west towards Cambodia—he thought—or at least hoped. The border in this area was as crooked as a politician—sometimes west, sometimes northeast. He didn't know where he was except that the Cambodia and Laos borders were close, too close. And he was saddled with an incompetent, cowardly, worse-than-useless navigator.

Callahan glanced at his wingman off his right wing. Bright flashes winked from the trees as strings of tracers reached for them.

2

"Break!" he screamed on the radio as he dropped his wing, rammed the throttles full forward and pulled hard on the stick. Gravity sank him into his seat. His G-suit clenched at his legs and torso as he honked the Phantom around. He grunted into his oxygen mask, fighting the Gs. After about ninety degrees of turn he rolled wings level. Suddenly his canopy exploded as shells slammed into the aircraft. Both engines stopped and angry red lights lit up his panel.

"Eject! Eject! Eject!" he shouted into his mask as he pulled the ejection handle. The Martin-Baker seat exploded him into the air. The wind-blast spun him and he tumbled. His world rotated gray and green around him. The man-seat separator flung him out of the madly gyrating seat. His chute snapped open and he bounced in the harness, leg straps cutting painfully into his groin. The gyrations continued until he managed to pull on his risers and dampen the oscillations. He yanked off his oxygen mask and threw it away. As Fats' chute drifted toward the hills, Callahan looked around.

There! More tracers off to the right. He pulled on the risers and tried to sideslip away from the bad guys. Not much time. He knew that every farmer in a three mile radius was rushing to capture him, following his descent. He looked for a good landing area. Nothing. Damn! He was going into the trees. He clenched his legs together and covered his face as he crashed through the branches. His chute caught and he slammed into a tree. He fought off his dizziness, disconnected, and dropped the last eight feet to the ground.

He tried his emergency radio. Not even static. He ran and kept on running.

As darkness fell, the rains turned into a tropical torrent. His energy was draining away with the chilly downpour. Chest heaving and nearly exhausted, he tried to get oriented. Have to keep moving. Keep moving! Using the rain and the dark of night for cover, he sloshed through rice paddies, jungle, and several small streams. He had started his trek with only a vague idea of where he was, but was certain that he was somewhere well west of where he wanted to be so he headed in what he hoped was an easterly direction towards friendly territory.

For two days and nights he stumbled through the thick jungle vegetation. The trails were steep in places, slippery from the rain, and the daytime heat was debilitating. The terrain was rugged; the declines were short and the inclines long. Exhausted and hungry, he knew he was getting careless but he had to keep moving.

Suddenly he popped out of the jungle into a clearing. Several thatched roofed hooches were in a cluster with villagers milling around. Damn! He ducked back into the trees. Not quick enough. Behind him, shouts, a gunshot. He panicked and ran, stumbling through the ferns and vines.

The villagers were on him in minutes. One man tackled him, then the rest, punching and screaming. Someone shouted an order and the beating abruptly stopped. Four men held him down as another quickly stripped him of all his survival gear. They tied his hands with vines, jerked him to his feet, and pushed and shoved him through the jungle back to the village, where he was instantly surrounded by angry villagers who shouted and hit him with sticks. One old woman punched him in the stomach, a blow that sent him to his knees. That seemed to invite others who jostled and pushed for a chance to strike the hated American prisoner. An ancient man, apparently the village boss, shouted something and the crowd reluctantly moved back. A girl threw one last rock that hit Callahan in the head and nearly knocked him over. The man yelled at the girl, who backed away.

A new group emerged from the woods and joined the crowd. They were Montagnards or "mountaineers," the indigenous tribesmen of Vietnam. Very tough. The Viet Cong had been terrorizing them for years into cooperating. Callahan's heart sank. The leader exchanged words with the village boss; then two Montagnards hauled Callahan to his feet and shoved him towards the jungle.

Again he was pushed and dragged through the thick undergrowth. He stumbled, fell to his knees many times until they were bruised and bloody. The trail led past a grass and bamboo hooch that evolved into a well-camouflaged encampment with a few more Montagnard troops and some women. As Callahan collapsed, the women gathered around him. A few made angry gestures; more made laughing comments, no doubt

4

about his filthy appearance. They poked with sticks, spat on him, beat him. Eventually, the crowd dispersed, leaving Callahan immobile, gasping in pain. Two men stuffed him in a bamboo cage like the ones he had seen on mink farms in Denmark. He tried to make himself comfortable, but soon discovered that was impossible. The cage was designed to prevent him from sitting up or stretching out in any direction.

At sunrise an old crone spat on Callahan and stuffed a golf ball-sized lump of dirty rice through the slats. Before he could pick it up, a detachment of North Vietnamese Army soldiers appeared out of the jungle. The NVA troops pulled him from the cage, pushed him to his feet and shoved him towards the jungle. They prodded him into a dead run. They ran and walked him into the hills for what seemed like hours. Finally they reached another well-concealed encampment even deeper in the jungle.

That night they tied Callahan to a tree. The rain beat down again, turning the camp into a mud bog, and making the cold of the jungle night even more excruciating. They kicked him awake at first light, and the group was back on the move.

They maintained a steady pace through the forest. Enormous trees maybe a hundred and fifty feet high surrounded them. Callahan despaired. Jungle cover and low rain clouds meant no search airplane could spot him through that canopy. He was unable to keep directions straight, though he knew they were certainly heading away from American and South Vietnamese positions. Every day, he was farther away from friendlies. Every day, his chances of escape sank even further.

The trail climbed through the rugged terrain, sometimes so steep that steps had been carefully and laboriously cut into the path. Day after day, the soldiers kept moving into increasingly rugged country that Callahan guessed was the Co Co Va Mountains, paralleling the Laotian border. Thirsty, dizzy, and feeble, he could barely keep up. But he willed himself to keep moving, to stay alive. He stole a drink from a creek even though he knew that ground water in these areas could be contaminated from lack of natural filtration in the porous aquifer. Some hours later, he felt ominous rumblings in his stomach and something foul running down his leg. If they didn't stop soon, he would die.

As the sun set, they came upon a small prison encampment carved into the hillside, surrounded by the jungle, well concealed. Like a Vietnamese version of Devil's Island or Alcatraz: even if an inmate escaped from the camp, the surrounding environment would kill him.

Ironically, the first thing the soldiers did was strip off his aviator boots. He could hardly walk, much less run away.

Confined alone in a small hut with no blanket and a bed that was just a board about a foot wide atop two bricks, Callahan was left alone except for occasional visits from the camp doctor. Between the doctor's rudimentary French and his West Point French plus the little bit of Italian he had learned from his Tuscan-raised wife, they could communicate. The doctor forced Callahan to eat the sticky, marmalade-like pulp of a green, baseball-sized fruit that he had never seen before. A few hours later, the dysentery seemed to be cured.

He was often cold due to the surprisingly chilly rain. Downpours continued for days, making the camp a foul smelling cesspool that stank of pain, of fear. He was fed only starvation rations, occasional rice balls mixed with dirt and vermin, no meat or vegetables. Never heavy, he began to shed weight.

Through cracks in his hooch, he glimpsed eight or ten other Americans in the camp, but he was kept separate from them. He knew exactly what the guards were doing: using standard Communist brainwashing technique. Solitary confinement deprived prisoners of a community of peers so they had no one to talk to, no one to support them, no one to act as a filter for their thoughts or a check on their reasoning. When a prisoner was lead into an interrogation, it would be easier to get him to talk. About anything. And everything. Knowing that one day the interrogator would arrive with his list of questions did not make it much easier to survive in a filthy room infested with bugs and the occasional rat.

His daily task was simple: survive this day, then survive the next. One day at a time. The war would be over for the U.S. military pretty soon, perhaps by spring. All he had to do was survive. That was his job now, to stay alive. He was the fourth generation of Callahans to serve the military of the United States. He was valued. His government would do everything it could to get him back to his wife and kids. This one thought, this central ideal Callahan knew in his soul. His job was to keep the faith and survive for however long it took. His country would rescue him.

Weeks passed—how many he wasn't quite sure. He exercised his body with short workouts of isometrics, alternating with push-ups, sit-ups, and pacing the small hooch for aerobic conditioning. He occupied his mind, imagining an art gallery opposite the plaza in Taos, New Mexico, the dream of his artist wife. He had already mentally surveyed the existing historic property, conducted negotiations with the owners, and completed renovations. He was visualizing the arrangement of artwork when two guards burst into his room, dragged him across the camp, and dumped him on the floor of the largest hooch.

The room was empty except for a rough desk, chair, and a stool. Ah, the infamous interrogation room. He steeled himself for the encounter. The rear door opened and in walked a tall man dressed in unmarked fatigues. Callahan's first impression was how clean and well fed he looked. With a start, he realized the man was Caucasian, not Oriental.

The man sat at the desk and motioned for him to sit on the low stool. Each surveyed the other like boxers before a match. The man took a packet of cigarettes from his shirt pocket and offered one to Callahan who shook his head.

"General Callahan, I am Lieutenant Colonel Alexy Petrovich, Soviet Air Force. I have come a very long way to meet you."

Petrovich spoke in Russian. Callahan remained silent.

"Come, General, I know that you speak some Russian. It would be best for both of us if you cooperated with me."

Callahan answered in English with his name, rank, and serial number.

Petrovich smiled. "Excellent. So you haven't lost the ability to speak. I was afraid that the—how to say—the lack of hospitality shown to you by our socialist comrades would have injured you in some way."

Callahan repeated his name, rank, and serial number, again in English.

Petrovich smiled again. "Thank you, General, but I already knew all that." He opened the dossier on the desk and handed Callahan an official USAF document. "It seems this announcement was a bit premature."

Callahan looked down at the document. His own face stared back out of the official photograph, a face he could scarcely remember: clean, hair neatly cut, in Class A uniform adorned with his wings and medals. Most impressive. It was the official announcement of his selection to brigadier general and included his biography, the name of his wife and number of children, a list of his past assignments and honors. It seemed so unreal.

Petrovich said, "Perhaps you would like to look through this." He handed Callahan the dossier. The folder contained dozens of clippings, covering Callahan's career, his completion certificate from Test Pilot School, even his West Point graduation announcement. More chilling, it had information about his family—a surprisingly detailed genealogy of his White Russian émigré, Chinese-born wife, and worse, photos of his kids.

"So, you can see that we know quite a bit about Brigadier General Sean Thomas Callahan, United States Air Force. Perhaps now we can dispense with the stubbornness."

Callahan, still in shock from the photos, said nothing.

"General, I am sorry that you refuse to speak to me. I regret that my English is not good enough for an in-depth discussion. But I do have someone from my staff who can help. His English is excellent." He turned to the door. "Comrade!"

Through the door walked another Caucasian, wearing unmarked fatigues and a smirk.

Callahan froze, then leapt to his feet. "Fats! You son of a bitch! You—"

The man punched Callahan in the face. The force of the blow knocked him down and blood spurted from his broken nose. He hit the wall so hard that he lost consciousness.

When he opened his eyes again, the man stood over him. "Nobody will ever call me Fats again. Thank you, General, for providing me the opportunity to do that."

The Russian officer motioned to Callahan to sit. He struggled to his knees, took a deep breath, and lurched onto the stool.

"Now, General, shall we begin again?"

***

Between 12 February and 4 April, 1973, 591 American POWs were freed and returned home to the United States to parades and the arms of their families. The name Sean Thomas Callahan was absent from all lists provided by the government of North Vietnam. No explanation was ever provided. No responses were ever received from the governments of Cambodia or Laos. His status continues to be listed as MIA.

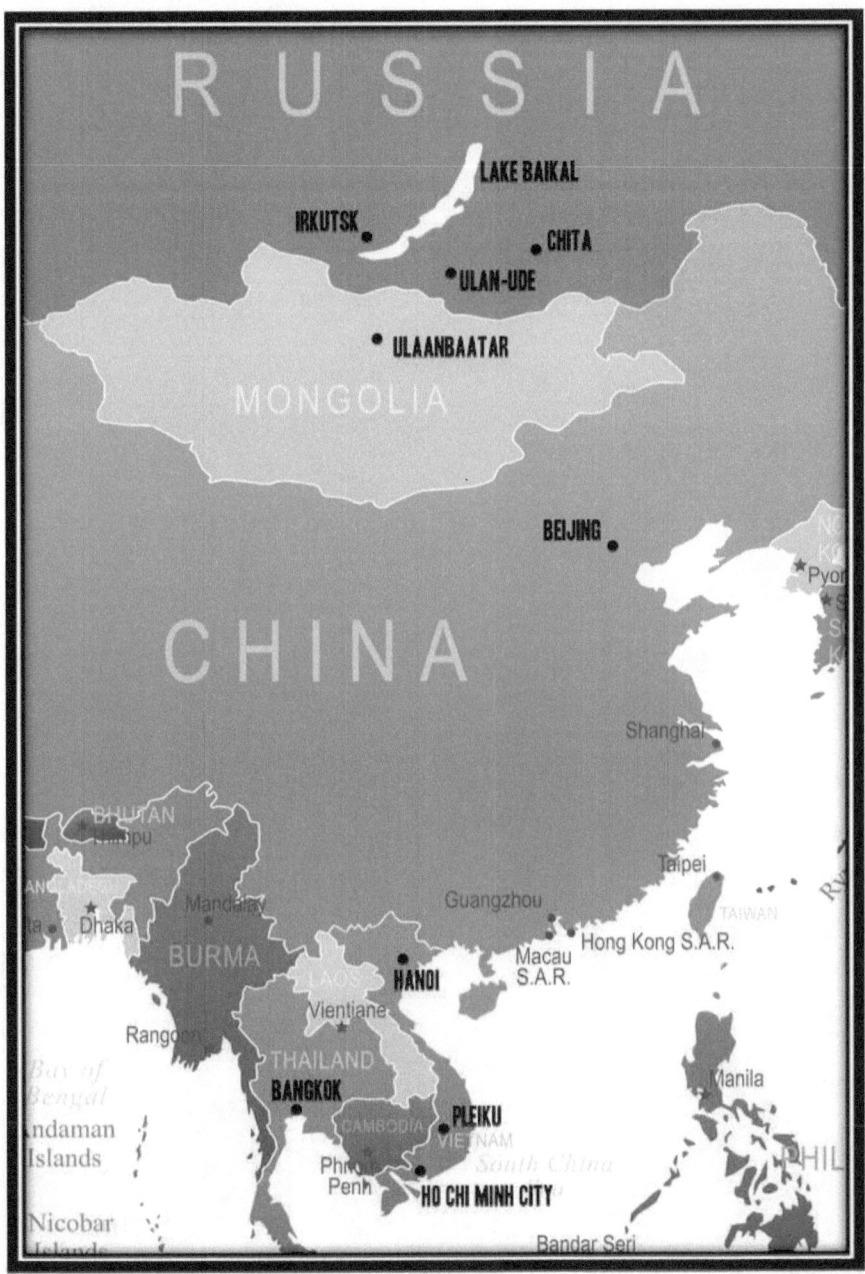

Chapter One
Phú Thọ province, Northwest Vietnam
December 2004

Ron Minor squinted at the temple ruins with a professional photographer's eye. A tall, gangly man in his early forties, he crept around the three sides of the temple where the jungle had been hacked away, checking for the best possible shots.

The ruins were magnificent even after nine hundred years of decay in this steaming jungle. The front of the rock temple was nearly twenty feet high, overgrown with vegetation that sprouted from multiple fissures. Orchids, bougainvillea and other flowering vines that he couldn't identify spread vibrant colors against the jungle green surrounding the walls. Statues flanked the gaping entrance, faces nearly obliterated by age.

The monsoon rains had stopped and the light seeped through cloudy skies to create a sepia aura around the ruins. If he hurried, he could knock this out today before the monsoon clouds closed in again. This shoot would be the perfect ending for his *National Geographic* photo essay.

His interpreter from the Ministry of Tourism, a tiny woman dressed in black, contrasted dramatically with the larger, frenetic Minor in his sweat-stained American flag T-shirt and head wrap, but was as focused as he was on getting a good shot. He explained to her what he wanted done and expressed his need for speed. She spoke rapidly to her assistants from the Ministry of Tourism who shouted at the Vietnamese Army privates to shift the equipment cases. Working fast, Minor set up and took picture after picture. Finally satisfied with close ups, he backed away to frame more shots through the jungle foliage.

He worked his way around the site, focusing briefly on the nearby tea plantation whose expansion had triggered the re-discovery of the ruins. He took a series of long-range photos of farmers preparing the

13

ground to plant new bushes, as background material for the series. The rains started again. Time to pack up for the long drive to Hanoi.

The next afternoon found him in his Hanoi hotel. After a long, hot shower and the first beer he had tasted in a week of driving all over Northwestern Vietnam, he turned on all the lights in the room, settled himself at the desk, switched on his MP3 player, and proceeded to download his pictures into his laptop while classic rock blasted the walls of his suite. He took his time as he clicked through the pictures. He scowled at some and deleted them. He edited dozens of others, cropping here, adjusting light there. He smiled at a few, pleased at the results. Towards the end of his portfolio something caught his eye. He enlarged a section of the photo. Then another.

What the hell?

***

Colonel Thomas Callahan, USAF, strode into his White House office area. Callahan, in his early forties, stood just under six feet and carried his one hundred seventy pounds like an athlete. He was also bleary-eyed and late for work.

Maggie Dawson, his secretary, jumped up and came around her desk to give him a hug. "How is your wife, Colonel?"

"Premature labor. They stopped it in time, Maggie. But she'll be on bed rest for the rest of the pregnancy."

Maggie stood, hands still on his shoulders, and gave him a stern look. "You tell her I said to relax and slow down."

"She's doing everything the docs tell her to. Every single thing."

Maggie nodded. Colleen Callahan, PhD was pregnant for the third time; both the previous pregnancies had ended in miscarriages. This time she had devoted most of her prodigious work ethic to incubating the baby as long as possible. Despite her efforts, she had already been rushed to the hospital twice. This baby had been saved last night only by a combination of quick actions of Georgetown paramedics and a frantic midnight ambulance ride to the Bethesda Naval Hospital neo-natal facility.

14

"The First Lady has called twice and the President once already this morning to ask about Colleen. They both want to see you as soon as we can arrange it. Right now, the President is in conference with the Azerbaijani ambassador." She checked her watch. "Probably for the next twenty minutes. I'll call the First Lady, then let the chief of staff know you're here; he'll call you when the President is free. In the meantime, Porter Nelson is in your office with another visitor." She hugged him again and pointed him towards his office door.

The office was smaller than most Tom had occupied in his career but it was blessed with a window, a White House rarity and a tangible sign to the rest of the staff that Tom was one of the President's favorites. Tom's desk was immaculate, adorned only with a family photo of Tom, Colleen, and their adopted son; two aircraft models, an F-4D and an F-15C were the only decorations. The late morning sun illuminated the two men dressed in casual attire who stood to greet him. The smaller one stepped forward and embraced Tom. "I heard about your night in Bethesda, buddy. How's Colleen?"

Porter Nelson, slender, five-foot-eight, and a Pulitzer Prize winning investigative journalist, was one of the Callahans' favorite people. Tom sagged into Porter's arms and took a moment to gather himself. "Tired. Scared. Not happy." He stepped back and gave a brief smile at his friend. "Staying in bed is not her style. Go see her, Port. She'll be delighted."

"Count on it, *amigo*. This afternoon." He motioned to his guest. "Tom, I'd like you to meet Ron Minor. He and I spent the first six months of 1988 together in Afghanistan with the Russian Army. I've been shot at with him."

They shook hands. Tom leaned back on his desk. "So, what can I do for you, gentlemen?"

"Ron was on assignment for the *National Geographic* for the past month," said Porter. He handed Tom an eight by ten photograph. "He took this picture two weeks ago in the Vietnamese boondocks near the China border."

Tom studied the picture of a temple in the jungle. People wearing black pajamas were working in what looked like a tea plantation in the background. "Okay, Porter," he said, his voice carefully neutral. "I see a nice jungle scene. So what?"

Porter handed Tom another photo, same background but blown up. One of the farmers, taller than the rest, waved at the camera. Odd, Tom thought as he slipped behind his desk, sat, and pulled out a magnifying glass to study the photo.

Porter handed Tom another picture. "And here's the *coup de grâce*."

Tom looked down at the picture on his desk. His heart skipped. The image on the photo was the figure of a tall man, dressed in peasant's black pajamas. He had turned to face the camera; his blue eyes stared out of a deeply tanned, lined face, a face of a man in his late 60s or early 70s. He now stood at attention and was rendering a parade ground perfect American-style salute. His facial features were blurred by distance, but appeared Caucasian.

"I didn't even notice this guy until I got back to my hotel and went through the pictures," said Minor.

"I know where you're going with this, Porter. But there is no evidence to prove that American POWs exist. And the CIA has denied the existence of living POWs to Congress for decades."

"That the CIA would lie to Congress is not exactly a revelation," said Porter.

Tom studied the picture again. "So, playing Devil's Advocate, Ron, how do you suppose this guy would know that you were an American? As opposed to, say, a Frenchman?"

"I was wearing an American flag T-shirt and head wrap, Colonel."

"In Northern Vietnam? How many times were you assaulted?"

"I wasn't trying to be subtle, Colonel. The flags catch people's attention and I get some great war stories."

"Anybody crazy enough to do that is my kind of guy, Ron. Please call me Tom."

He turned to Porter. "I know that you're just trying to help, Port, but these pictures are not evidence."

16

"They don't *prove* anything," said Porter. "They are an indication, a possibility. This should be checked out by the State Department and/or the CIA."

He handed Tom a press clipping. "Here's an article from the *Washington Post* that you may have missed. Last month, a South Korean soldier escaped back over the border from North Korea where he had been working in coal mines since just after the Korean War, fifty-some years ago. That makes nine South Korean POW escapees in the past ten years. If South Koreans can survive, why not Americans?"

Callahan studied the picture carefully, forcing himself to be objective and dispassionate. He could discern nothing to prove—or disprove—that this man was an American, especially an American POW.

"Tom," said Nelson, "I owe you my life. Nothing would please me more than to help you find your dad."

Tom stared at the photos, then tilted his head as he shifted his gaze thoughtfully out the window.

Porter tried again. "If there is one POW, there could be more. If there's more, your father could be one."

Tom settled back in his leather chair and looked at his friend. "Have you shown these to anybody else?"

"I tried to get them into the CIA. Nobody wanted to hear anything about it."

"You tried Robbie Robinson?"

Nelson shook his head. "He's not in-country. And nobody would tell me where he is or when he's coming back."

"He got back from Russia yesterday."

"Really?" asked Nelson, surprised. "What was he doing in Russia?"

"He was following up on some of the information you and he discovered a few years ago." Tom grinned. "And that is all I can tell you, my inquisitive friend."

"*Pravil'no?*"—Really? Nelson's Russian was nearly as good as Tom's. "There were four of us on that little caper, if you remember. And one of us died because of what we found."

"*Pomnyu,*" replied Tom, I remember. "I've been looking over that stuff for three years now. And it's still causing problems between our countries." He studied the picture again, trying to imagine a thirty-year-old version of this man wearing a flight suit, smiling into the camera like so many photos of USAF pilots he had studied, looking for clues about his father. "How about the POW/MIA office near the Pentagon?"

Nelson shook his head. "We tried. The senior guy there, a deputy assistant secretary of defense, is an asshole. He didn't want to hear word one of what we had to say."

"Of course not. The official position of the United States government is that there are no—I repeat—no live POWs left in Southeast Asia."

"Excuse me, Colonel, I mean, Tom, but don't you believe that there are? I mean, your father is still listed as Missing in Action."

"What I believe, Ron, is immaterial. When I got to Washington on this assignment, I made a pest of myself, asking questions, pushing for answers about POW/MIA status. To the point that the Air Force chief of staff told me to cease and desist."

"Your Uncle Harvey told you to stop?" asked Porter.

Tom nodded.

"Wait," said Minor, "the chief of staff is your uncle?"

"Actually, he's my godfather but I call him uncle. He sort of raised me. He was flying my father's wing the day Pop was shot down."

"Whoa!"

"But to answer your question, Ron, my father will be seventy-two next month, wherever he is."

Tom flipped through the pictures again as he thought for a bit. "I have an appointment with SecDef later today. I'll take the photo by the POW/MIA office afterwards and have a chat. I'll get them to see you."

"Thank you," said Minor. "I took the picture. I know it's true. The State Department and the CIA have blocked any credible investigation of the POW question for years. We went round and round with those clowns over at Langley and got nowhere. I think there has been a massive cover-up here in Washington for decades—I don't know

18

why but it has to be investigated and exposed. Porter and I are the guys to do it. And I told them so."

***

Every time Tom drove to the Pentagon he remembered why he hated the building. Squat, gray, and exceedingly ugly, it was much larger than it looked. His father had loathed the place, too. Inside, officers-turned-bureaucrats tried to cope with the winds of political change, a world turned upside down. Former Warsaw Pact countries were clamoring to join NATO; China was now America's largest trading partner. What next?

Ideas once considered crazy were floated, staffers rushed to coordinate, and managers struggled to implement programs, though nobody really had a clear grasp of what was going on around Planet Earth. Most of the Pentagon "detainees," as Tom thought of them, longed for the days of the Cold War when everybody knew who represented what, that we were the Good Guys and those damned Commies were the Bad Guys. So simple. So archaic.

After his meeting in the Secretary of Defense's lavish conference room, Tom wandered down the dreary halls of the dreary building, pausing to look at the artwork plastered along the corridors. He headed for the exit, took the Metro to the Crystal City stop, and made his way to his target. He found himself perceptibly slowing as he neared the Defense POW/Missing Personnel Office (DPMO). He had studiously avoided this particular office all his adult life since his mother had been one of the leading critics of the office and the U.S. government's POW/MIA activities, or inactivity as she put it. Now he found himself curious about what he would find there.

DPMO had been the focal point for many years of the U.S. government's ongoing search for American POWs and MIAs. It was responsible for passing information from the government to concerned citizens via newsletters and its own website. DPMO had become somewhat controversial in recent times, accused by many of inaction, stonewalling the demands of POW/MIA families to investigate reported live sightings, among other things. The current director, Cecil Terry, was an especially unpopular man in POW/MIA family circles. Terry had been the chief aide to the senior senator from California, the chairperson of the Senate Military Appropriations Committee. He was rumored to have secured his appointment as a deputy assistant secretary of defense as partial payback for the senator's vote on an issue near and dear to the Vice President.

Tom found the office itself to be typical Pentagon: standard issue furniture, coffee pot, low tables, bookshelves, the required American flag, and the POW flag, many pictures of troops parading, ships, and aircraft flying the now *de rigueur* Missing Man formation.

"May I help you, Colonel?" asked a dapper USAF master sergeant, standing to greet Tom.

"Good morning, Sergeant Harrell," said Tom, reading the man's nametag and eyeing the five rows of ribbons adorning his chest. Sergeant Harrell had been around the block once or twice. "I'm not sure. My name's Tom Callahan. I'm trying to see what you have about recent live sightings."

"Ah, well, Colonel, Mr. Terry deals with that area exclusively. I am not allowed to voice any opinions on that subject. Mr. Terry's not here right now, but we're expecting him soon if you'd care to wait."

"Thank you." A thought struck him. "My father is listed as MIA. I don't suppose you have any information on him?"

"Brigadier General Sean Callahan, shot down in November 1972? Still carried as MIA. Promoted and carried on the USAF books as a major general. Is he your father?"

Surprised, Tom nodded. "How did you know all that?"

The sergeant smiled and gave a small bow. "Sir, in my prior life, I was an F-15 crew chief. Do you know an Eagle pilot named Brian Callahan?"

"My brother. He's now a professional money-grubber on Wall Street."

"I served with your brother in Asia. He told me about your dad."

"Well, I try to make it an article of faith to thank every aircraft mechanic, air traffic controller, and tanker crewmember I can. Thank you for your service."

"My pleasure, Colonel. Please give my regards to your brother."

"My brother and I haven't spoken in six months."

"I'm sorry to hear that, sir."

"So am I. Anyhow, what do you have that I can look over? Any good photos of Americans running around in the jungle?"

"Your father's file is available if you'd like to see it. All you have to do is send a request through the Air Force Casualty Office. We pull the file, go through it, and you can review it here. Or we can mail it to your office. Where are you stationed?"

"At the White House," said Tom. "And all this bureaucratic mumbo-jumbo takes how long?"

"Usually forty-five days or more. But I think we can probably make it happen quicker if you'd like."

Tom thought that over. "Why do you go through the files, to sanitize them?"

"No, sir. The files are unclassified. We just want to make sure that there is no unfavorable information that might cause the family unnecessary pain."

"Well, Sergeant, I'm a big boy. You can skip that part." He had a thought. "Who else has seen that file?"

Sergeant Harrell sat down and pulled his computer keyboard close. After a minute, he looked up. "According to the computer, Colonel, your mother looks through the file every year. Your brother was here three months ago."

And didn't stop in to see me, thought Tom. The son of a bitch didn't even call.

They were interrupted by the arrival of Cecil Terry. Terry turned out to be a short man, immaculately groomed in a gray tailored suit, gray shirt, and silk tie. His black boots sported two-inch heels, and he wore his hair close-cropped to de-emphasize the receding hairline. He positively radiated the same self-satisfied attitude that was so carefully cultivated in Washington. Tom disliked him on sight.

21

"Mr. Terry, Colonel Callahan would like to speak with you. He works at the White House."

"And to what do we owe the honor of this visit?" asked Terry, glancing at his watch.

"I'm curious about live POWs in Southeast Asia."

"You and every crackpot and conspiracy nut on the Internet."

"Why do you say that?" asked Tom.

"The CIA and the State Department get alleged 'sightings' reported all the time, Colonel. None have been true. Not one."

Tom produced Minor's photo. "Here's another opportunity for the folks at Langley."

With a small sigh, Terry carefully pulled out his glasses and glanced at the photo. "All I see is someone who could be Caucasian in a group of Orientals somewhere in the world."

"This was taken in Vietnam two weeks ago."

"So says the photographer."

"His name is Ron Minor. I met him this morning, introduced by a friend whom I do trust, a journalist named Porter Nelson. The Pulitzer Prize winning journalist, Porter Nelson."

Terry shrugged.

"So you're not even interested in meeting the photographer? You're not even curious?"

"Not the slightest. We hear this all the time from crackpots who want to see their pictures in the papers."

"Well, Minor and Nelson are going to write the article. Somebody will publish it."

"Colonel, I have limited resources. I don't need to spend time and energy chasing ghosts or fantasies of people who refuse to accept reality."

"People like my mother?" Tom asked, aware that his temper was soaring.

"If she thinks her husband is alive after more than thirty years, yes. There are no live POWs. Get that through your head. Now, I have work to do. And so do you, Sergeant."

He turned, walked into his office and closed the door behind him.

The awkward pause was broken by Sergeant Harrell. "Colonel Callahan, your mother lives in Taos, New Mexico, correct?"

"Yes."

"The archives are great at the Vietnam Memorial in Angel Fire, which is pretty close to Taos. They've got more original stuff, especially photos, than we do. Perhaps you can dredge their files."

"That's right," Tom mused. "I've been to the Memorial's chapel, but the archives were closed both times."

"The new Executive Director there is a retired USAF lieutenant colonel named Joe Kozlowski."

"No kidding! I know a Joe Kozlowski from the Academy. Surely there couldn't be two Joe Kozlowskis in one air force. At least, an air force that isn't the Polish Air Force."

They both laughed.

Tom pointed to Terry's closed office door. "Thank you, Sergeant. Now I understand the problem. But this isn't over. And I will appreciate seeing the file."

"I'll bring it over myself this afternoon, Colonel."

***

If suicide weren't a mortal sin, today would be the perfect day for it. Absolutely dismal weather, rainy and miserable, and in about ten minutes Brian Callahan was going to have to attend yet another of the crazy booze and chemical-charged parties that marked another of his firm's successful Initial Public Offerings (IPO). The youngest partner in the company's history, he was ensconced in a corner office in a skyscraper, overlooking Wall Street and the New York City skyline, that perk so coveted by his classmates at the Stanford Business School, classmates he had left in the dust, professionally speaking. Palatial by any standards, his office was tastefully decorated by art he had carefully assembled, part of his investment portfolio, only more tangible than his collection of high tech stocks and possibly more profitable. He bought stocks based on mounds of crunched numbers mixed with flashes of intuition. He bought artwork based on passion mixed with flashes of

23

calculations. The only object in the room not ultramodern, expensive, or a certified work of art was a hand-carved mahogany model of an F-15C Eagle that he had bought after a particularly drunken night in Manila. It was a tangible relic of what he considered his previous life, six action-packed years spent as an Air Force fighter pilot.

He sat quietly, arms folded across his chest, staring into the distance. Dark thoughts wrapped around him like a shroud.

The door to his office opened. "Mr. Callahan, your limo is here," announced his secretary. Brian waved and reluctantly rose from his leather chair. He measured nearly six feet tall, was impeccably attired, and at one hundred eighty-five pounds, was precisely the weight he had carried at graduation from the Academy in Colorado Springs more than a decade before.

The elevator door slid open and he strode across the marble lobby towards the company limousine. He waved off the building's doorman. "No need for both of us to get wet, Freddy," he said as he dashed through the swirling rain to the car and got in back.

"Let's get this over with, John," he ordered the driver. "You know where to go."

As John maneuvered the long black automobile through the crowded, rain-slicked streets, Callahan sat in the dark, staring out into the downpour, letting his thoughts fester. He was tired of this life, or rather, non-life. Making money wasn't living, yet to the people with whom he had to associate here, it was more than a religion. Brian understood passion; he was just not passionate about these non-things anymore. He wanted to feel alive again.

John pulled the limo up to the curb in front of the newly fashionable St. Cyr Club, reserved at great expense by Callahan's company to celebrate the new stock offering and paid for by the unwitting new stockholders. He passed through the brightly lit entryway, past Corinthian leather and chrome sofas and chairs, marble slab tiles and granite counters. He entered the immense party room, took a look around, and sighed. It was exactly as bad as he thought it would be—decorated in the artsy-fartsy style that Callahan associated with people with too much money and too little taste. Expansive walls with clashing primary colors, splashy artwork, expensive flashy furniture, all punctuated by spotlights and rounded out with loud music. Full of the overdressed, overpaid, and over-the-top people that he had come to despise. An ostentatious celebration of capitalism run amuck. So garish that it made Las Vegas look rural and refined.

He asked a waiter for his customary glass of mineral water on the rocks with a twist and slogged his way through the crowd of investors, traders, and stockholders, all guests of the company. It was tough going, everybody reaching for his hand as if he were a rock star on tour. Another stock market killing made for many new friends. At last he reached the far side of the room and found a bit of space to himself. He leaned against a wall and surveyed the scene. The two or three hundred people below him, gyrating on the dance floor or schmoozing in one of the many crannies on the sidelines, represented a staggering amount of wealth. He continued to take in the sights as he counted the minutes until he had fulfilled his corporate responsibility and could depart.

His eyes caught movement as a new woman entered the room and hesitated, standing framed in the door. Tall and exquisite, she wore an elegant satin gown that was tasteful, refined, yet terribly sexy, accentuating her figure. Glossy auburn hair cascaded down to her shoulders, framing her face, showcasing cheekbones only a master plastic surgeon or a Michelangelo could duplicate. Brian could not take his eyes off her. He had seen top-name actresses at Broadway openings that couldn't carry themselves as well as she did, even dated a few. She hesitated, searching for a face in the crowd, then slid through the foyer and glided across the crowded floor. Most of the men glanced in her direction, their eyes lingering for the rear view as she moved across the room. She looked as posh as the surroundings were tasteless. Callahan wondered who she was. The area around him flickered with movement. All he let intrude now was the aura around this one particular female form. He felt a stirring and he was suddenly restless. Without a conscious decision, he straightened up and started on a path to intercept her as she made her way to the farthest corner of the room.

The man she joined was a surprise. Callahan stopped, dismayed that this woman seemed to be spoken for. He was about Callahan's age, thirty-five to forty, and at least that number of pounds overweight. Dressed expensively, he had a huge, unlit cigar in his puffy face. Callahan knew the type. He worked with or against them every day—a B-school grad who had made a quick killing in the overheated stock market and consequently felt that his IQ had gone up at the same rate as his bank account. Damn! She was probably his trophy wife.

The chubby man certainly did not seem particularly glad to see her. He wobbled a bit as he glanced at his watch, then snarled something at her. She said something in a low voice that seemed to infuriate him. He grabbed her arm and pushed her into a nearby alcove. Then he slapped her, spilling his drink, which seemed to make him even angrier.

Brian closed the distance in three quick strides and caught the man's wrist as he raised it to strike again.

"Don't touch the lady again."

"Lady?" spluttered the man. "She's no lady. I'll do whatever I goddamned want to her." He tried to yank his arm away but Callahan held firm.

Brian looked at the woman. Up close she was even more beautiful. She shook her head. Her cheek was red from his handprint and her eyes were bright with tears. "Apparently, sir, she disagrees," Brian said, releasing the man's arm. "Let her go."

"Piss off, asshole." B-School shoved the woman towards the door. "Let's go!"

Callahan moved between them. "She doesn't have to go anywhere with you."

The man dropped his glass and threw a punch. Callahan dodged the blow. B-School stumbled, off balance. Callahan delivered a quick chop to the back of the man's neck and dropped him to the floor. He did not move again.

Callahan looked around the room, spotted the chief of security, and waved him over. "Get this guy out of here," he ordered. "Make sure you get his name and give it to the company secretary. He is never to be invited to one of our functions again. Understood?"

"Yes, sir," said the chief as another guard scrambled to help carry off the unconscious form. "You want him charged with anything?"

"Just get him out of here."

"Don't worry, Mr. Callahan. You'll never see him again." The guards hustled the man away.

Callahan turned to the woman. "On behalf of my gender, I apologize for that idiot."

The woman gave him a small smile. "Thank you. Coming here was a mistake, I'm afraid."

Her voice was low and slightly husky. His heart jumped.

"Look, I'm leaving," he said. "Would you like to come with me?"

Without a word, she took his arm and they made their way out to his waiting limo. Brian opened the door and she slid like water across the leather seat, moving over to make room for him. She sat still, her hands clenched around her evening bag. What to say? Her perfume was delicate, but heady. He closed his eyes and breathed it in. He knew he would never forget that fragrance.

He turned to face her. "I don't know the etiquette involved here…My name is Brian Callahan." He held out his hand.

Her hand was as smooth and exquisite as he knew it would be. "Elizabeth," she said.

A beautiful name to go with a gorgeous creature. It could have been Typhoid Mary or Susan the Psycho and he would still be under her spell. He let go of her hand. "I probably should apologize for intruding in a personal matter but it seemed appropriate at the time."

She sighed. "No, I should apologize to you. I shouldn't have come here tonight. The man you punched out was my ex-boyfriend. He owes me some money. We were supposed to meet before your party but I was held up at work. By the time I got here he had overindulged at your open bar."

"Where do you work?"

"I *was* the manager at a lovely clothing boutique on Madison Avenue which officially closed today."

"Which is why you needed to talk about the money," Brian said.

She nodded and flushed with embarrassment. "Unlike you with your fantastic IPO, my year is not off to a great start."

Brian shook his head. "You might be surprised, Elizabeth." He drew a series of deep breaths. "I had planned to go to an opening at an art gallery this evening—"

Her face lit up. "I love openings!"

"You like art?" he asked, surprised.

Her eyes narrowed. "What is that supposed to mean?"

His face went hot. "I'm sorry." He motioned back towards the St Cyr. "I'm not used to people from that group caring about art."

She looked at him for a moment as if about to challenge him, then seemed to accept his statement at face value. She sighed. "Actually, I wanted to become an artist so I came to the big city. Only I had no talent."

"Then you're in good company," said Brian. "I, too, have no artistic ability whatever." He chuckled. "To make matters worse, my mother is an artist, raised in Italy. She dragged me through every art museum in Europe when I was a kid. I knew more about Botticelli than other kids knew about baseball. But my drawings were awful. Even as a boy, people couldn't distinguish my horsies from bunny rabbits." He gave a little nod. "I am a Salieri with a Mozart as a mother. But I can talk a good game. Hanging out in galleries is my biggest hobby."

"Me, too."

"Great! Then it's settled." He hit the intercom button. "John, take us to the gallery, please."

The drive passed quickly as the two discussed their favorite art and artists. Brian delighted in Elizabeth's depth of artistic knowledge and similar interests. He was stunned at her grasp of printmaking, especially the offset lithography of Frank Stella, something he had only discovered the week before while prepping for this show. After what seemed to him just a flash in time, the limo pulled up in front of a brightly lit gallery. "Here we are. It's new, small, and we hope, intimate and stimulating. Tonight is more or less a grand opening, the first show since we bought the place."

"*We* bought it?" she asked.

"I have a modest interest," Brian said with a grin, "just enough to ensure that I will get an invitation to every show. Plus it's a tax break and I get to hang with fellow art lovers. Like you, for instance."

"You didn't know I was an art lover when we met."

He waved his hand in the air, "Details, details." He grinned again, almost giddy. "This is a big night for me. And I'm delighted that you're here to share it."

As they entered the gallery, newly-refurbished with African pau rosa hardwood flooring, high ceilings, full spectrum track lighting, and brightly colored artwork, Brian was acutely aware of Elizabeth's hand on his arm. Her eyes darted around the room, trying to take it all in. Brian thought that either she was a superb actress or she had an artist's soul.

"I've never seen this gallery before," she said. "The lighting, the colors, the space…it's exquisite."

"And here is the man responsible," said Brian, beckoning over a small, nervous-looking man wearing an Armani tuxedo with a pink Cecil Brunner rose boutonnière. "Elizabeth, this is Moises Epstein, one of my favorite people on the planet. Moises, this is Elizabeth."

"*Enchanté*, my dear," he said with a slight bow.

Brian was surprised at the lack of activity in the gallery. He saw only a few people, apparently caterers, setting up.

"What's the matter, Moises? Where's the staff?"

"Oh, Brian," he almost wailed. "Bobby called. The van with the extra staff has been stuck on the other side of the tunnel for an hour. A truck stalled, can you believe? They may not ever get here. Tonight's going to be a disaster!"

"Calm down, Moises. How many people do you expect?"

"Probably two to three hundred, and they're going to start arriving any minute now."

Brian looked at Elizabeth. "Care to dive into a swamp of art maniacs? You know, walk people through the place, make them feel at home, schmooze them, as it were. Hold down the fort until the troops get here?"

Her eyes widened. "Are you sure? I'm really just a novice."

Brian laughed. "I know better than that." He grabbed a wandering waiter. "Mineral water with a twist for me. And for the lady...?"

Elizabeth said, "Better make it two."

Moises gave Elizabeth a copy of the program and quick summaries of the guest artists and their works while Brian helped organize and energize the caterers. As customers wandered in, Brian happily worked the crowd, feeling alive again. To his surprise, he discovered that this was his element. He reveled in this chance to be an active rather than simply a passive owner. He watched Elizabeth in action, effervescent as she discussed art with the patrons.

By one in the morning the gallery was empty of visitors and the artists had wandered off to their favorite haunts, leaving just the staff.

Brian gathered up Elizabeth and Moises and embraced them both. "Moises, another triumph, my friend. And Elizabeth, you were great."

Moises agreed. "Elizabeth, you were wonderful, dear. Thank you. You simply must come back."

"Oh, no, Moises. It was my pleasure. Thank you for letting me help."

"Any friend of Brian's is always welcome."

Embarrassed, she asked, "Have you known Brian long?"

"Two years. Brian's one of the good guys, even if he is straight. And such a tush!" He rolled his eyes.

Elizabeth giggled. She slid sideways to get a better view of Brian's backside. "Yes, I see that now. Thanks for pointing it out." They both laughed.

"Thank you, again," she said. "I had a fabulous time."

As they walked to the car, she took Brian's arm again. He felt a surge of emotion at her touch. They settled into the limo and he gave the driver Elizabeth's address. "So," he said, settling back into the leather seat, "Moises and I had a chat. He wants to hire you as his assistant."

She met his eyes. "Moises wants to hire me?"

"Well, I asked him and he said yes."

Elizabeth turned away.

"What's the matter?"

After a moment, she said, "Brian, I get propositioned all the time."

"Yeah, I can believe that. But you can be assured that Moises at least won't be hitting on you." They both laughed. "This is not a proposition. It's a serious job offer. You know art better than most people. More to the point, art is important to you. Patrons, potential customers, can tell. You were great tonight."

She looked out the window at the passing buildings, then turned back to him. "I have just extricated myself from a painful and unhealthy relationship. I have no intention of making that mistake again. Nor do I intend to flit about the city doing one night stands."

"I know this small nunnery on Long Island where you could stay."

"Hmm, a boutique nunnery? That might be just the place!"

"Nah, the artwork there is too eighteenth century for a contemporary art maven such as yourself."

They laughed again.

"Tell you what, Elizabeth. Let's try this. You need a job, Moises needs an assistant. You agree to work at the gallery until our next show in three weeks, paid in advance. Just try us out."

She paused, considering his offer. "No strings attached?"

"No strings attached."

"No expectations?"

"No expectations."

They shook hands. She dazzled Brian with a smile. "I can't wait to start."

Chapter Two
The Washington Post, Washington D.C.

Porter Nelson and Ron Minor sat in the executive conference room of *The Washington Post* office, trying hard not appear too impatient as the man who sat at the enormous teak table across from them slowly read through a stack of notes, photographs, and evidence. Nelson tried not to shout "Hurry up, damn it!"

He crossed and uncrossed his legs. "These pictures suggest that Americans were left behind in Vietnam—either by accident or on purpose. Either way, it's a great story. This stuff is hot, Pete. You should move on this."

Peter K. Haloran, assistant editor of *The Washington Post*, studied the photos and glanced through the type-written notes scattered on the conference table. "We've seen this kind of material before, Porter," he said. "It's only interesting if you have proof."

"I'm telling you, I was there. I took that damned picture," Ron Minor protested, face going red. "I'll stake my reputation on this."

"That's fine for you, Mr. Minor, but I'm not staking mine. These days, photos are easily faked."

"Goddamn it, I have the negatives here in my briefcase. You can have anybody you want verify that they're the real thing!"

Haloran took off his wire rim glasses and slowly polished them with a silk handkerchief. "Okay, Porter, old boy, why are you so intent on publishing this?"

"I don't suppose you were in Vietnam were you, Pete?"

"Not me," he said with a smile. "I dodged the draft after I lost my grad school deferment, holed up in Toronto with a hot little Canadian chick. Came back in '74 after President Ford declared amnesty." He raised his coffee cup in salute. "Thank you, Uncle Jerry."

Nelson wasn't surprised. Most of the editors he worked with were proud of having avoided the draft and still disdained the military. "While most of our American POWs were imprisoned in Hanoi, some of them ended up in Cambodia, some in Laos."

"Nobody is interested in rumors of old men holed up in the jungle any more."

"They should be. And who says these are rumors? There are simply too many improbable sightings and stories. The more the CIA and State Department deny these stories and refuse to investigate, the more we journalists need to investigate on our own. That's why this is so important."

Haloran chuckled. "The late, unlamented, Ronald Reagan had one great expression for situations just like this. 'Trust but Verify.' I trust you, Porter, but get me some verification of American POWs in Vietnam and we'll talk."

"It gets better, Pete. There is evidence suggesting that some POWs even ended up in Russia. And may still be there."

Haloran swept the papers and photos into a pile and handed them to Nelson. "I have a great idea, Porter. Let's print your half-baked story, with no facts to back it up, mind you, and accuse Russia of hiding live American servicemen. That lunatic president of theirs is just looking for an excuse to start a war. Maybe he could he use this."

"The storyline is there, Pete. After WWII, tens of thousands of German POWs were herded east to Siberia, never to be heard from again. Americans were interned there as well. How many, nobody knows. Some came back. But maybe some didn't."

"Do you really think the Russians would do something that stupid?"

"You said it yourself, the Russian president is a lunatic! Jesus Christ, Pete, why don't you ask Solzhenitsyn what he thinks about the Siberian 'workers' paradise?" He stopped and took a deep breath. "But we digress. What about Ron's Vietnam picture and our story idea?"

Haloran drummed his chubby fingers on the oak table as he thought things over. "I'm going to make some calls. But don't count on anything coming of this. The Vietnamese are our friends now, with lobbyists and everything."

"Great. Another special interest group on Capitol Hill, buying our politicians."

As they stood waiting for the elevator, Porter said to Minor, "That son of a bitch. He hasn't changed a bit. Little brain, little balls. Hell, with more editors like him, we wouldn't even need a First Amendment. No paper would ever print anything controversial."

"You've known him a long time?"

"Since the first Reagan Administration. That bastard holed up in a Beirut hotel, drinking Dubonnet cocktails with Air France flight attendants, allegedly reporting on the Mid East war. I, on the other hand, was in foxholes all over Afghanistan with Russian Spetnatz units, getting shot at by very angry *muhajadin*."

Minor laughed. "Sounds like he's smarter than I thought."

Nelson shook his head, then laughed. "I don't really like Dubonnet. And now my Russian's so good that I swear better in Russian than I can in English, so I win." Nelson mashed the down button again.

"Can't Callahan get the information he needs about POWs from the CIA?" asked Minor. "He works for the President."

"Not as simple as that."

"Why not?"

"I used to trust our government like you, Ron. And at the macro level, I still do. But hidden within that vast living, pulsing organism are factions and groups that have their own agendas, pursue their own goals for their own reasons. Sometimes there are conflicts, massive conflicts."

"The usual bureaucratic turf battles—like State versus the CIA?"

"That and a whole lot more. These are two powerful and capable institutions. When threatened, they will react with all the means at their disposal. The phrase 'national security' takes on different meanings between those two organizations, and even—no, especially *within* the organizations. My friend, Robbie Robinson, who spent twenty-plus years in the CIA says there are some very scary people squirreled away in the Langley catacombs, working on who knows-what, protecting who-knows-what. Compartmented out the wazoo."

"Sounds like you don't think much of the CIA."

Nelson fixed him with a hard stare. "Ron, a few years ago, I was a regular hard-working naïve journalist like you. Then Tom Callahan saved my life. And I helped him save his reputation as well as a whole

34

lot of lives. Along the way, we found out some shit that you wouldn't believe. That's the stuff he's working on now. That's why I'm a confirmed cynic about our government."

"What kind of shit?"

"No, no, no—you'll have to read my book—which will be published decades after hell freezes over. To protect my heirs and stuff."

"What does that have to do with the CIA?"

"I know some very good operators in the CIA, people who are honorable and competent. It's the Corporate Mentality of the CIA I have problems with." He turned to face Minor. "Right now, the CIA is in a terrible mess, mostly of its own making. It simply does not do its job well." He ticked off points on his fingers. "It missed the first Soviet atomic bomb, the Chinese invasion of South Korea, Saddam's invasion of Kuwait, Soviet missiles in Cuba. Hell, they couldn't even kill Castro. Along the way, it did some pretty nasty stuff. No, my friend," he said as they entered the elevator. "It's a left hand, right hand thing. The CIA has compartments within departments, people pushing on ropes, people pulling on ropes. Not my favorite organization. And neither is the State Department."

As they exited the building, Nelson said, "Look, I scored a parking place right in front of the building. Just like in the movies." He pointed to a dark blue Lamborghini Gallardo coupe, gleaming in the sunlight. "Hop in, I'll take you home. It'll make both of us feel better."

"Whoa, nice wheels, Porter."

"Yeah, driving fast cars is one of my favorite vices."

Minor looked doubtful. "You're not going to do a Jeff Gordon on me now and race out of town, trying to break the sound barrier?"

"Nope, I am a strictly law-abiding citizen." Nelson laughed. "Well, mostly, I mean. These days, I do my racing on supervised courses." He slipped the sleek auto into the early afternoon traffic and headed west on L Street. "I've written some articles on race driving. When I picked up this baby last year, I drove the Lamborghini test track in Italy. Callahan even got me into the Special Forces anti-terrorist defensive driving course at Fort Benning. They taught us how to crash barricades, how to look for suspicious driving, how to avoid bad guys, and most importantly, how to get away."

"No kidding! I bet that was a kick."

"Yeah, I went with Callahan's wife."

Minor's eyebrows shot up. "His wife?"

Nelson nodded. "Yep. Colleen used to race motorcycles back in Australia before she married Tom. She got to take the course because of her position with the World Bank." He chuckled. "She's a hell of a lady."

Minor sank quietly into the luxury that is Lamborghini as Porter maneuvered the sleek automobile through traffic. "Oh, man, this feels really good, Port. How do you stand it?"

They made their way west for several blocks. In his mirror, Porter noticed a sedan accelerate and weave through traffic to move up on his right side. Way too close. The rear window was down and a passenger sat in the back seat.

The passenger aimed a rifle. Both side windows in the Lamborghini exploded. Nelson felt a bullet whiz by his face. Jesus! He glanced at Minor. He was slumped over, jaw shot away. Blood everywhere.

Holy shit! Nelson popped the clutch and slammed the accelerator. The car lunged forward—forty, fifty, sixty mph. The superb Italian machine accelerated rapidly as he swerved around slower traffic. Nelson just had to hold it together long enough to escape. He slid the car around a corner. Then another. He shot across Washington Circle, horn blaring. South on 23rd Street. Traffic flashed by.

He swiveled his head. The other car was gaining. The sedan must have one hell of an engine. Certainly not stock. More shots. His rear window was gone. Wind and noise swirled through the car. Bullets punched holes in the windshield. One popped the dash. Whoever was driving the other car knew what the hell he was doing.

He floored the accelerator, took another corner. Too fast. Horns blared.

Where were the cops? He needed a plan.

Ah! Half the cops in D.C. were stationed between the Capitol and the White House. He spun the wheel back onto 23rd Street and headed south, tires squealing.

He scanned the area ahead again. Cars everywhere, blocking his way. He darted through open spaces, banged off a green Chevy van and nearly hit a bicycle deliveryman. The sedan was right on him.

Using a D.C. Transit bus for cover, he spun the wheel in desperation, tires smoking in a classic 180-degree turn. He stomped the accelerator, reversing back up 23rd. Caught by surprise, the pursuers reacted too slowly. Nelson accelerated away. He whipped the Lamborghini the wrong way onto G Street. Weaving through the oncoming traffic, he clipped one fender, then another. South on 21st to Virginia Avenue. He roared towards the Mall. The sedan lost ground and started to fade in his mirror, then disappeared into traffic.

Nelson snapped his head around towards the intersection. Two cars crossed in front, too close to miss. He screamed as the Lamborghini bounced off the first into the second and careened across both lanes. Throwing off pieces of metal, the car slid up onto the sidewalk and smashed through the window of a florist shop. Glass shattered, metal snapped. The air bag exploded into his face and chest.

Blackness.

Two hours later, Tom Callahan maneuvered his government sedan as close to the crash site as the rush-hour traffic would allow. He parked with his right wheels on the sidewalk, turned on his emergency flashers, got out and locked the car. He hadn't gone six feet before he was challenged by a D.C. cop. Tom showed his White House credentials and got a gruff acknowledgement from the officer as he waved Tom through the cordon. Police cruisers were parked everywhere seemingly at random; photographers were documenting physical evidence, and cops were measuring and interviewing. Porter's car was still wedged in the florist's display window.

Tom caught a glimpse of Robbie Robinson's craggy face through the crowd of emergency personnel and on-lookers. Robinson had been a CIA operative for nearly twenty-five years. But he'd asked too many questions and made too much fuss about certain internal CIA operations before being forced by the Agency into an involuntary "medical retirement." Tom trusted Robinson's judgement and more than once had trusted him with his life.

"Hi, Robbie," he said as the men shook hands. "Thanks for the alert."

"I picked it up on the police scanner. Not many dark blue Lamborghini Gallardos in town. Had to be Porter."

"How's he doing?"

"He's banged up, but he'll make it."

The police parted the crowd to make way for a wrecker. Tom and Robbie watched as it attached itself to the ruined Lamborghini and eased it from the store window.

"So what do you make of this?" Tom asked.

"This was no ordinary carjacking, Tom. There were lots of shots fired up and down the roads around here. At least ten hit the 'ghini. One took out the passenger, a guy named Ron Minor. Dead on impact. These shooters were serious players."

"Any guesses who they were?"

Robinson shook his head. "Nondescript sedan, either a Ford, Chevy, or Dodge and either gray, blue, or white, depending upon which eyewitness you choose to believe." He sighed. "I got to see Porter before the ambulance hauled him away. He was in and out of consciousness. He kept saying 'Get the briefcase, get the briefcase.'"

"And?"

"I got here while the tires were still smoking and the cops were still taping the area off. There was no briefcase." Robinson looked over at the wreckage, then back to Tom. "Do you know why the briefcase would be so important?"

"Nope." Tom had a thought. "He and Ron were working on a story about a CIA/government cover-up of Vietnam POWs. Maybe they had the pictures and storyline in the briefcase."

"Of course!" said Robbie and smacked his forehead. "Jesus, we need to get somebody to Porter's townhouse to secure his computer and any working notes."

Robinson made two calls. In less than fifteen minutes, he got a call back from his D.C. police contact. "The cops say Port's house was burgled and trashed. His computer's gone."

Tom kicked at a stone. This was getting out of hand.

"Who else knew about this story and the photographs?" Robbie said.

"You, me, the director of the Joint POW office in the Pentagon. Porter told me that he had an appointment with an editor at *The Washington Post* this afternoon."

"All pretty high level contacts," said Robinson. "You know, Porter said he had been knocking on doors at the CIA and State Department..."

Oh shit. Tom searched Robbie's face. *He's thinking what I'm thinking.*

***

Brian Callahan was determined to see Elizabeth as often as possible. He could tell that she had been bruised, literally and figuratively, by past relationships so he was careful to arrange meetings that were always business oriented and always in public places.

Lunches were the obvious answer. Raised mostly in Europe and Asia, Brian had always made a point of searching for the unusual and undiscovered bistros around the city where the quality of food was the main event, not where you sat or with whom you were seen. He had accumulated a list of restaurants still not quite famous for the freshest seafood, the most exquisite sauces, the most authentic ethnic foods. He unleashed an avalanche of culinary knowledge on an unsuspecting Elizabeth, determined to show her another side to New York City.

Food, business, and art were the topics of conversation.

As they continued into the second week, the formalities began to drop away. Elizabeth became less wary of his intentions and began to relax in his presence.

For his part, Brian bounced out of bed every morning, alive again with the happy conviction that he was scheduled to have lunch with a

39

beautiful, charming woman. He had never experienced the sheer pleasure of such a nimble-witted beauty whose interests coincided so closely with his own. He was astonished at the range of her interests, her sheer passion for life and especially for art. Even as she hid her past, she exposed her mind, her heart. Van Gogh, Degas, Matisse, Calder, O'Keeffe, Pollock, to name a few, were waypoints in the train of discussion as the two talked for hours about their favorite, and least favorite, artists and schools of art. Even when they disagreed, it was a pleasure to hear her viewpoint. Brian found himself up late, studying art books, and practicing conversations with her in his head as he ran his morning three miles.

Late Saturday evening of the second week, Brian lingered at the gallery with Moises and Elizabeth, finalizing details of the upcoming show. Things were on track and optimism ran high. Artists were signed up, advertising bought, catering arranged. Interest was up: the gallery was on a roll. Moises locked the doors. Brian flagged down a cab and all three squeezed into the back seat. After dropping Moises at a club, the cab splashed its way through the impossible late night traffic of New York City and arrived at the front of Elizabeth's apartment building to find a minor flood from a backed up storm drain.

"Please wait here," Brian instructed the driver, "I'll be right back." He got out on his side and sloshed through the ankle-deep water. He opened Elizabeth's door and, ignoring her protests, scooped her up, and carried her to the apartment steps.

"Brian, your shoes are ruined," Elizabeth pointed out as they rode up the elevator to her floor.

He shrugged. "No need for both of us to get trashed in the rain."

"You, sir, are a true gentleman."

"A Callahan family curse, I'm afraid," he said, wiping his face with his handkerchief.

"It's worth a gold star in my book."

"I'd prefer a goodnight kiss…"

Her face showed her disappointment. Realizing his mistake, Brian said, "A gold star would be just fine. In fact, I would be delighted with a gold star."

"That's better," she said. Then she smiled. "For that you get a goodnight kiss."

Brian moved slowly, afraid she might change her mind. He cupped her face with both hands and softly stroked her cheeks with his thumbs, marveling at the texture of her skin. His lips brushed hers, then back again very softly. He looked into her green, hazel-flecked eyes.

"Goodnight, Elizabeth. I had a lovely time."

By the Friday before the big show, they were friends. Their lunch was long and pleasant and Elizabeth had more than her customary single glass of wine.

"I stopped by the set of *Artsy/Fartsy* this morning."

"Really?" Artsy/Fartsy was the nickname of the more properly named *Contemporary Art in the 21st Century,* a new PBS series headlining contemporary art that was sending ripples through the American art scene. The series was headquartered New York City.

"One of the directors is quite a *fashionista.* She used to be one of my regulars at the boutique. We had a nice chat. She gave me a tour of the studios and a copy of the script for their next show. I gave her some of our gallery brochures."

"Great move! Brilliant!"

"She said she would stop by next week to have a look."

"You have a flair for marketing, Elizabeth. Another of your talents emerges from behind your cloak of secrecy." Brian wanted to hug her. Instead he waved down the waiter and ordered another coffee.

Watching him take a sip, she asked, "Are you a teetotaler, Brian?"

"Right now I am," he admitted. "I am slowly recovering my health. Eventually I will imbibe again." He took a deep breath. "I once had a serious love affair with cocaine."

"Really?" she asked, surprised. "How did you deal with it?"

"I didn't. My older brother and his wife dragged me out of a nightclub and put me in a clinic."

"Are they social workers?"

"No, he's an Air Force officer and she's an economist."

"You're not serious?"

"Oh, I'm serious. My brother is quite possibly the best fighter pilot in the Air Force, a man with two MiG kills in the Persian Gulf War. So naturally he's strapped to a desk in Sodom-on-the-Potomac. In the White House to be precise. Colleen is a super-grade executive with the World Bank."

"Well, I certainly didn't see that coming."

They ate in silence while she quietly considered his story.

She put down her fork and looked up at him. "I grew up on a ranch in Oklahoma," she said.

He chuckled. "I have a hard time seeing you roping cows, dressed in Versace."

"Oh, but I did. And I was the barrel racing champion of Jefferson County, Oklahoma. I stayed there as long as I could stand it, then migrated north to the big city of Stillwater. I took art and art history classes at Oklahoma State until I ran out of money."

She paused for a sip of wine. How marvelous it was to watch her, enjoying the delicious food, so unlike many of the women he had known in this city, women who existed on yogurt and diet pills to maintain their anorexic figures.

The cool air in the restaurant was having a fabulous effect on her nipples. He made a heroic effort to keep his eyes somewhere north of her gorgeous décolletage. "Would you like to have dinner with me at my apartment Sunday?"

"So we're finally getting to the etchings line? Somehow, Brian, I thought you'd be more original."

He shook his head. "No, no, it's really about food. I love to cook." He paused. "Yeah, okay, I do have some art at my place, no etchings, though."

"But, Brian, more food!" she sighed. "I must have gained ten pounds over the past three weeks."

"No, you haven't. Your figure is still perfect."

She looked at him and smiled. "So, you have been looking."

He shrugged. "Guilty."

"Well, Mr. Callahan, I must say that you are a man of your word. You haven't made one risqué comment, even once made a hint of a pass at me."

"Just because I haven't, doesn't mean I wouldn't like to."

"If you had, I wouldn't be here." She leaned back in her chair as if to get a better view of him. "Even your eyes are under control, always looking into my face instead of at my chest."

He laughed. "Not always," he said, affecting a leer at her bosom. "At the Air Force Academy, it's called 'keeping your eyes caged', meaning staring straight ahead. It's a modest talent of dubious utility."

"Well, I appreciate your talking to my eyes instead of to my boobs."

He took her hand and gently caressed it. "Elizabeth, the past three weeks have been the best three weeks I have spent in this damned city. I look forward to our lunches and our business meetings more than anything else. Just seeing you makes my entire day."

She nodded and smiled.

"Moises says he can no longer function without you. He can announce your official appointment at the opening tomorrow night, which will be a smashing success due to you. Then you simply take Sunday afternoon off and come over in the evening for an Italian dinner. Nothing special, no big deal. And no strings."

"I was hoping you'd ask."

***

Brian Callahan looked up from his dinner preparations and mentally ran through his checklist again. Everything was complete. He glanced at his watch. It was precisely ninety-six seconds past the last time he looked. *Brian, damn it, relax.*

The intercom buzzed and he heard her voice, husky and sexy even through the speaker. "I'll be right down," he replied, ripping off his apron. He popped a bottle of Dom Perignon, took a chilled glass from his refrigerator and carefully poured.

With glass in hand, he rode the elevator down. The doors slid open and there she was, wearing a cashmere sheath dress that fit her like a second skin, smiling just for him.

"You look smashing," he said.

He handed her the champagne, with a slight bow. "For you, *signorina*."

"*Grazie, signor*," she said as she stepped into the elevator. She sipped it, then leaned into him, placed her hand behind his head, and pulled his face to hers.

Recovering quickly, Brian kissed back.

"If I had known you liked champagne that much, I would have given you some weeks ago."

"I've wanted to do that since the night we met."

Brian pushed the STOP button. "Once more," he said, and took her into his arms.

As they parted, he said, "I will be sure to keep cases of Dom Perignon on hand any time you're in the neighborhood." She laughed as he pushed the button again. The doors slid open to his private foyer.

"Very nice!" she said as they crossed to his penthouse. "And what is that heavenly smell?"

"Dinner cooking, my lady."

"Well, Mr. Callahan," she said, taking his arm, "it's time to show me this alleged art collection of yours."

He opened the door to his apartment. She gasped at the great room with its twenty-foot ceiling, one wall entirely glass showing a vast expanse of Central Park and Manhattan skyline. Sculptures, vases, tapestries, and paintings everywhere.

"Brian, this is like living in a gallery!"

He was thrilled by her reaction. "I picked this apartment because of the size and the lighting. These pieces just have to be displayed."

"The view's not bad either," she said, peering out the windows. She spun around on one foot and gestured at his paintings. "But the art is fantastic."

"I'm glad you like it. I'm in my Southwestern period. It's not held in high regard here in Manhattan, much too provincial for my high-tech contemporaries." They walked slowly through the apartment, hand-in-hand.

Remington sculptures, Nambé vases, and Navajo rugs helped stage the paintings by R.C. Gorman, Robert Redbird, Jennifer Cavan, Michael Hensley, Harvey Johnson, and others. Elizabeth seemed entranced.

"Is this a Sylvia Avenius Ford?"

"You know her work?"

"Only what I've seen in magazines. She's a member of the naïf school of art continuing Henri Rousseau's *nativo* influence. This is a primitive southwest scene. Colorful, entrancing, gorgeous. I love it."

She slid over to a large painting of a female skeleton with elaborate makeup, flowers in her hair, wearing fancy European clothes. "Is that a *La Catrina*...?" She edged closer. "It looks like a Diego Rivera. Brian, it can't be an original!"

"An early work. I certainly hope it's original. You wouldn't believe the insurance premiums I have to pay."

"Oh, my God! Is this really a Georgia O'Keeffe?"

He nodded. "She lived in New Mexico, near Taos where my mom lives now. Mom got this years ago. She gave it to me for a graduation present from the Academy."

"And a Chagall!"

"Yes, obviously not Southwestern, but a particular favorite of mine. My mother is Russian, though born in China. She has a certain affection for Chagall, champion of the rural Russian. My brother has one as well."

"Brian, your collection is magnificent. Some of these pieces are museum quality!" She turned back to study his face. "Yet, it seems so personal."

He reached for the champagne bottle. "You now know my secret and I now know how much you love good champagne. And now that I know your weakness, you will never see the bottom of a champagne glass again."

"That sounds lovely."

Callahan's wristwatch alarm went off. Still looking at the Chagall, he automatically reached into his jacket pocket, took out a vial of pills, popped one into his mouth, and took a quick swallow of his mineral water.

Surprised, she asked, "So you're a pill freak?"

"No, no, it's not a pill, it's medicine, tetracycline in fact."

"What for?"

"It's a prostate thing."

"Ah, that's why the no alcohol. Anything else?"

"No drugs. No women. I've lived like a monk for the past eighteen months. Nothing but work and sleep since I got out of rehab." He blushed and cursed himself.

"Men?" she asked.

He shook his head. "Nope, I said I lived *like* a monk, not *with* a monk. And no gerbils or chickens, either. Strictly work. Very boring."

"Do you do anything else besides the pills?"

"What? I'm supposed to flush my prostate once a day..." He felt his face redden. "Oh, you meant anything else I don't do?"

"How?"

"How what?"

"How are you supposed to flush your prostate?"

His face reddened still further. "Never mind."

"Well," Elizabeth whispered, "Maybe I can help there."

He laughed. "You're really something." He touched his glass to hers. "Before dinner or after?"

Chapter Three
The White House, Washington, D.C.

The Secret Service agent slipped into the ornate conference room. Tom Callahan looked up in annoyance. Monday morning meetings were not to be disturbed except by the President. The agent's body language screamed that he didn't want to be there as he edged his way around the enormous walnut conference table. Callahan knew whatever was coming was coming for him and that he wouldn't like it.

Eyes on the floor, the agent crouched and whispered, "Sir, your wife went into labor and they can't stop it this time. She's being transported to Bethesda."

Oh, God! It's too soon. Too soon. Tom exploded to his feet and almost knocked the agent over as he sprinted towards the door.

"Get my car ready!" He ran through the doorway and down the hall, fighting panic.

The black Suburban limo screeched to a halt in front of the building as Callahan flung himself through the door and down the steps to the driveway, beating the Marine sentry to the door handle.

"Bethesda! And fast!" he almost screamed, knowing his orders were unnecessary, that the driver knew what to do. Callahan had to try to regain control, be back in charge of this situation that was wildly wrong. His mind was racing. So was his pulse. All he knew was that his wife and son were in mortal danger and he was helpless. The cars on the road were there to impede him.

He willed them out of the way. He grabbed for the car phone. "Get me the Bethesda commanding officer." The admiral was on the line within seconds.

"Colonel, your wife has gone into premature labor with major complications. She's being prepped for a C-section right now."

"How long?"

"She'll be in the operating room in less than ten minutes."

"We'll be there in twenty..." He hesitated, "Admiral, and the baby?"

47

"He is clearly in distress. That's all I know at this point."

Two D.C. police cars appeared out of nowhere to lead the convoy in its race through the city streets, sirens screaming. Callahan's mind careened along with the caravan in a jumble of emotionally charged fragments: the two previous miscarriages, Colleen's tear-stained face after each one, the weeks of depression, the joy in her eyes when she learned that she was pregnant again. Watching her be ultra-careful in her diet, her exercise, bed rest, trying in every way to make sure that this baby would make it. She had done everything right. It just couldn't go wrong again.

He was terrified for the first time in his life. He was a key advisor to the most powerful man in the western world, and yet, he couldn't control what happened to the people he cared about the most. It took every bit of self-control he could muster, every bit of his training as a fighter pilot to keep from screaming. He rubbed his throbbing temples and wiped the sweat from his forehead as he scanned the horizon for the telltale tower of the naval hospital.

Another Marine was waiting to open his door as the limo skidded to a stop in front of the hospital. Callahan sprinted up the steps, three at a time. He recognized the commanding officer and another of his wife's doctors.

"They're still in the operating room."

"Where?"

The doctor pointed.

Callahan ran through the hallways into the dressing room, throwing off his jacket and tie. Technicians had his baggy green hospital clothes ready. He ripped off his clothes and threw on the greens, scrubbed, and followed a doctor into the operating room. Colleen was on the table, unconscious, the center of focus of everybody in the room. All Tom could see of her was part of her face.

The baby. Wet. Bloody. Tiny. Very tiny. Stillness gave way to small, jerky movements. Tom's heart leapt. *He's alive!* But quiet, too quiet.

The nurses readied the baby for his trip to the nearby neo-natal ICU. Tom gently stroked his wife's damp cheek and whispered,

48

"Sweetheart, I'll go with our son." He squeezed her unresponsive hand. "I'll be back as soon as I can."

He had to will himself not to charge down the hall. He paused at the door and forced himself to take several deep breaths before he pushed open the door.

Electronic monitors were everywhere. Another baby was already there, wires and tubes connected, with a nurse hovering nearby.

Beyond her, Tom saw his son surrounded by people clad in green cloth. All he could see of their faces were their eyes, eyes that never left the baby. He was reassured by their aura of cool competence, the intensity of their actions. He had met one or two of them and knew that these people were some of the best in the world at what they did, exquisitely trained and unbelievably dedicated. This particular unit had saved babies born as early as twenty-three weeks gestation. He did the math. His baby was right at the ragged bottom edge of that range.

The size of the incubator dwarfed his newborn son. His face was partially covered by a bandage holding the tube of a high frequency respirator through his nose, delivering dozens of tiny puffs of oxygen each minute to keep the immature lungs open. Other wires and tiny tubes were attached on the arms and legs. Adhesive patches were placed on the baby's chest, abdomen, and legs to keep the tubes clear. He knew the machines, he'd read the literature and knew the drill. Monitors, doctors, nurses, respiratory therapists, all working to save his son.

Tom's mind registered the irony of the situation. Here he was, Tom Callahan, military advisor to the President of the United States. Tom Callahan, a self-described techno-addict, a man who surrounded himself with the newest and coolest technology advances and toys. He now sat surrounded by the world's best technology available to keep human babies alive, reduced to a mere spectator, machines preventing him from even holding and comforting his own son in the boy's terrible fight for survival.

As the hours passed, Tom prayed for the baby, prayed that the pain of his son could somehow be transferred to himself. He marveled at the spirit of his son, struggling to simply breathe, fighting against all odds for his life. Refusing to give up. A quiet pride grew at the stubbornness of the boy, refusing to die quietly. "Hang in there, champ," he whispered. Gradually the baby's movements became less. His systems were starting to shut down; the lights were going off.

He could no longer control the tears that slipped down his cheeks. He sobbed quietly into his hands. His wonderful son would never grow up, never play soccer, run through a forest, or laugh with his mother. His son would never leave this room alive. And these machines would only prolong the event, not prevent it. There was no escape.

Tom felt the presence of someone. He looked up. Tom could read the doctor's eyes.

"My boy's not going to make it, is he?"

"Sir, there are just too many things not working right."

"He's in pain, isn't he?"

"Colonel, it's just a matter of minutes."

Tom looked back to his son, the eyes now closed. "The boy needs to be at peace."

Tom squeezed his eyes shut in a massive effort of self-control. He took a deep breath, then stood. "I need to hold him. To say good-bye."

The doctor nodded to the nurse who began to gently unfasten the wires and take out the tubes. She wrapped him and, with tears in her own eyes, handed him to Callahan.

He took the tiny bundle and held his son for what he knew would be the first and only time. "Hey, sport," he whispered. Tom unconsciously rocked the baby as he walked around the small, now dimly lit room. "Did you know that your mother wanted to name you after me?" He shifted the nearly weightless tot to his other shoulder. "No, you didn't? Well, now, that would make you Thomas Patrick Callahan the Second. But I think you're more like your grandfather, my dad. He was a fighter, a real warrior. Just like you."

Tom made another turn in the crowded room. "Yep, you're a Sean all right. Tell you what, pal, let's make you Sean Thomas Callahan. What do you think? Don't want to disappoint your mom, now do we? And I think your Grandma would approve, as well." Tom slowly paced the room, "Let me tell you about your family." He murmured softly into his son's ear. He continued around the room, tears tracking down his face, reluctant to give up his baby.

Finally he faced the doctor. "Sean was a fighter, wasn't he?"

The doctor covered his own eyes, then said in a soft voice, "Yes, sir, he gave it everything he had."

The nurse took the tiny bundle. She carefully unwrapped the baby and showed Tom how to gently flatten the tiny hands to make handprints, the only physical memories the Callahans would have of their son. She started to swaddle the body.

"No, please let me do that." Tears streaming down his cheeks, Tom carefully lifted the tiny body and wrapped the blanket around it, tenderly embracing the boy. He laid the body back onto the bed, leaned over and gave his son a last kiss. "Thank you, little man, for coming into our lives. I only wish that you could have met your mother. But I'll tell her what a fighter you were, what a champion you turned out to be. That I promise you, son." His voice broke. "*Vaya con Dios, mi amor.*"

He looked up at the doctor. "I have to tell Colleen." He took a deep breath. "Don't let them cut him up, doc."

"Sir, there is no need for an autopsy."

Callahan took a last look, then squared his shoulders, and began the longest forty-yard walk of his life.

Chapter Four
The White House - Washington, D.C.

Tom Callahan found himself staring out the window. Again. He looked down at the classified document on his desk and had no idea what it said, even though he had already read it twice this morning. He kept thinking of little Sean and how he missed the boy. Colleen was devastated. Tom had thought he could find refuge in his work, but it wasn't helping.

His phone buzzed. The President's secretary said, "Colonel Callahan, the President would like to speak with you. Could you come up, please?"

"On my way."

Tom passed down the corridors and made his way to the Oval Office. He was not kept waiting more than thirty seconds before he was ushered in to see The Man. The President came out from behind his desk and offered his hand. "Tom, the First Lady and I would like to express our condolences."

"Thank you, sir."

The President looked at Tom closely. "You look terrible. We agreed with your wishes to not attend the funeral services in order to keep them low key, but you need to go home and spend whatever time it takes to heal."

"Mr. President, I have too much to do."

"Nonsense. Take some time off. Attend to your family." He laid his hand on Tom's shoulder. "Do what you need to do to take care of your family."

"Mr. President," protested Tom, "I—."

The President frowned. "This is an order, Colonel. Take some time off. I don't want to see or hear from you for at least a month. Is that clear?"

Tom nodded.

"Good. I'll call the World Bank and speak to them about Colleen. You just go. Thirty days minimum. If you need more, call my chief of staff."

Tom returned to his office and just sat there, all energy drained, numb.

The intercom buzzed. "Colonel, there is a Lieutenant Colonel Davidson calling from Hawaii."

Perfect timing. Angela was one of his favorite people. A classmate from the Academy, someone he could always count on. Angela was one of the top C-130 pilots in the Air Force, decorated for special ops work in the first Persian Gulf War. She was currently assigned in Hawaii with the Joint POW/MIA Accounting Command. JPAC was the agency responsible for recovering and repatriating remains of American service members lost in its many wars.

"Hi, Angela," said Tom. "Good to hear from you."

"Hi, Tommy. What's the matter there, Colonel? Too much paperwork? You sound awful. How's Colleen doing?"

It hit him again, harder this time. He couldn't hide the catch in his voice. "We lost the baby."

"Oh, Tommy, I'm so sorry."

He fought to regain his composure. It was taking longer each time. He wasn't healing. "What did you call about?"

"Tommy, I don't think this is the time."

"Let's hear it, Angela."

A pause. "Tom, we're about to launch on a mission to Vietnam. I think you should know that this time we'll have several digs going at once. One an OV-10, one is an A-37." She hesitated. "And one is an F-4D up near the Cambodian-Laotian border northwest of Pleiku, shot down at the end of 1972. You said you wanted me to call you if anything like this ever came up."

He nearly dropped the phone. The memory—or was it a specter?—of his lost father was thrust into the open wound of losing a son. The seething emotions were too much for his stressed out system.

"Tommy, are you all right?"

He fought for control—and was losing. "Bye, Angela."

He sank his head into his hands and sobbed. He cried for his son. He cried for his wife. He cried for his father. And his mother. For his whole family. Life was so fragile.

He had to act—anything to dull the pain.

He looked at the phone for a long while. Finally he reached out, picked up the handset and dialed a New York City number. "Brian, this is Tom, your brother."

**

Brian Callahan sat brooding as he stared out the apartment windows. He wondered again how life could take such mysterious turns. Just when things seemed to be smoothing out, *Bam!*—something strikes from nowhere. How was he going to explain this to Elizabeth?

His moodiness was interrupted by the buzzer of the downstairs doorman. "Miss Elizabeth's on her way up, Mr. Callahan."

Brian buzzed back. "Thank you, Ali. Another gold star for you, my friend." He automatically opened the refrigerator and deftly poured a flute of Dom Perignon, still a continuing joke between them.

Brian watched her come through the door and again felt the room brighten simply from her presence. He idly wondered just why that should be.

She took the champagne and softly kissed him on the lips. "Thank you, handsome." She stopped and looked closer. "What's the matter, Brian?"

He took her hand, led her to the couch, and then took a deep breath. "My brother, wife, and adopted son are coming up this evening."

"This evening? Why such a rush?"

"They lost a baby ten days ago and he wanted to get the family out of Washington for a few days."

"Oh, how terrible!" she said. "Was this baby news to you?"

He nodded, thinking how distant he was from his family. He hadn't seen his mother in over a year, his only sister in two. "I didn't even know Colleen was pregnant."

"This is the man who saved your life by getting you off drugs?"

Brian nodded.

"I'd like to meet them," she said, voice soft and tentative.

"What do you mean 'like to meet them'?" he asked, confused by her reaction.

"I'd like to thank them for helping you, but I understand if you don't want them to meet me."

"What in the world are you talking about?"

"In case you don't want them to find out about me."

He shook his head. "No, that's not it, Elizabeth." He took a deep breath. "It's just that my big brother and I have been on the outs for a long time. It might get tense."

"Why?"

He looked at the floor, then met her eyes. "I made a pass at Colleen."

Her eyes widened. "At your brother's wife? *You*?"

"What do you mean 'you'?"

"I mean you, Mister Straight Arrow. You. Even Moises sometimes calls you Sir Galahad behind your back."

"No, no, my brother is Sir Galahad. I always figured myself the Sir Gwain sort, more dashing you know or, I guess in this instance with Colleen, maybe the Lancelot type."

"What happened?"

"I was high and tried to jump her bones."

"Tom stopped you?"

"No." He shook his head. "Colleen kicked my ass. She's one tough lady."

"Have you apologized?"

"I stumbled through one this afternoon. But, Elizabeth, I betrayed my own brother, or tried to, anyhow. I was so humiliated that I couldn't even face him. I can't imagine why he wants to come here tonight."

"Brian, these are the people who tracked you down and put you in rehab. They love you and deserve your thanks." Elizabeth took his hands and kissed them. "Tom wouldn't have called, if he didn't want to see you." They sat quietly for a few moments. She kissed him gently again as her eyes searched his face. "Why, Brian? Why would you make a pass at your sister-in-law?"

He wanted to tell her. Everything. She was smart. Intuitive. And even if she refused to believe it, he valued her opinion.

"Because I was lonely. I was jealous of what they had together." He took a deep breath, "And because, up until now, I thought she was the most incredible woman I had ever met." He looked her in the eyes, "Now I'm not jealous anymore. I have what Tom has."

It was her turn to blush. "Are you sure you want me to be here when they come?"

"Absolutely." He took her in his arms. "Funny that you should ask me that tonight. I've been carrying this around for days." He pulled a small velvet box out of his jacket pocket and handed it to her.

She hesitated, then took the box and opened it and gasped. "What a beautiful ring!"

"Well?" he said. "Any more thoughts that you'd care to share with me?"

"My first reaction was that it could put out someone's eye. This looks like it belongs in a renaissance museum."

He laughed, delighted. He took her in his arms and softly said, "That is exactly right. *Renaissance* means rebirth. We'll celebrate our rebirth together, with new lives."

***

Colleen Callahan watched the elevator doors open into Brian's private foyer. She was exhausted and her arms ached from carrying a sleeping Michael Andrew Callahan. Her husband carried three suitcases, and Ali the doorman had two more and a child's car seat.

Brian met them and took a suitcase from Ali. He motioned them all inside where they were surprised to meet what Colleen thought was a stunning, if nervous, woman. "Tom, Colleen, this is Elizabeth. Elizabeth, this is my brother Tom, Colleen, and little Mikey."

"Oh, he's adorable," Elizabeth said in a whisper, as she crouched down to get a better look at Mikey.

"He is when he's asleep," said Colleen with a smile. "The rest of the time he is going about a hundred miles an hour."

"We'll put him in the guest room," said Elizabeth. "I had Ali bring up a roll-away bed this evening."

Colleen noticed how Elizabeth took charge. Even as tired as she was, Colleen could see how Elizabeth knew her way around the huge apartment; that her decorative touches were everywhere in the previously all-masculine home. Clearly, she was not just a casual girlfriend.

Brian fussed around his guests, throwing off nervous energy that Colleen found irritating after the hectic trip from D.C. "Brian, relax," said Colleen. "We're hungry, not helpless. Hand me the wine and I'll open it."

It was her favorite Australian red. She knew that Brian had gotten it just for her. A touch so typical of Brian. She began to relax a bit.

"Tom, why don't you help Brian fix us some dinner while I get to know Elizabeth."

"Yes, dear," they chorused and beat a hasty retreat into the kitchen.

Colleen opened the bottle like a professional sommelier, poured two glasses and passed one to Elizabeth. "I haven't had much of this for a while."

Elizabeth leaned forward, met her eyes. "Colleen, I'm so sorry about your baby."

Colleen felt the familiar stab of pain in her chest. She closed her eyes and visualized the tiny body in the miniature casket, buried in the acres of headstones at Arlington National Cemetery. She had promised herself that she wouldn't cry any more and knew she wouldn't be able to keep that promise. She took a long sip of her wine and swallowed hard.

"Wonderful music. Mozart is it?" she asked.

"Thank you," said Elizabeth. "Symphony Number 40 in G Minor, one of my favorites. It's my sole contribution to the night's festivities. I prefer orchestras. Brian's all about opera." She rolled her eyes and they laughed together. "You'll love dinner. Brian's been working on it for an hour. He's a great cook."

"So's Tommy. God bless the Italian nannies that raised them."

Colleen took a sip of her wine and let it dance in her mouth. "We haven't heard a word from Brian in over a year. He's been lonely. I think that's what got him in trouble. Brilliant, but he thinks too much."

Elizabeth nodded. "He feels too much as well. What I've seen is a warm, loving man with a few lapses in his past."

"Like the rest of us. How did you meet?"

"At a gala celebrating another stock market victory. Brian decked my ex-boyfriend."

Colleen laughed, nearly spilling her wine. "I met Tom in a bar in Sydney. He punched out *my* ex-boyfriend." She laughed again. "Must be a Callahan thing."

Elizabeth continued. "I was there to wring my money out of that son of a bitch."

"Really?"

"Does that surprise you?"

"After our time in Washington, hardly anything surprises me anymore."

"I arrived in New York four years ago, ready to take on the world," said Elizabeth. "Then reality struck. I tried painting. I tried writing. Eventually tried modeling with no particular success. I couldn't get a shoot. Then one day, I stumbled on a job in a boutique." She shrugged. "Not what I expected, but I did get to play artist with mixing and matching clothes for the idle rich. That's how I paid my bills for the past three years."

Colleen slowly swirled her wine glass.

"Let me tell you something, Elizabeth. I have known Brian for over ten years. I have never, and I mean never, seen him date a woman for more than two weeks. The fact that you are here tonight means that you are someone special to him. That makes you special to Tommy and me."

"Do you mean that?"

Colleen nodded.

Elizabeth jumped up from the couch and disappeared. She was back in less than a minute. With a shy smile she held out her left hand.

"Oh my!" said Colleen. "That is one beautiful ring!" She took Elizabeth's hand and studied the ring. "He proposed?"

"This afternoon."

Colleen looked back to the ring, then chuckled. "Tom proposed to me after two weeks. We were married one month and one day from our first date."

"Today is our five week anniversary. I guess that makes me a slacker."

They both laughed.

"Brian was concerned about this reunion. Afraid it might be awkward or get nasty with Tom."

Colleen shook her head. "If it gets that way, it won't be because of Tommy. When their father was shot down, Tommy assumed the role of father figure for the family. When Brian got hooked on coke, Tommy worried himself sick. We had to get Brian in that clinic for Tom's sake as well as his."

Tom and Brian re-entered the room. Tom bent over the back of the couch and nuzzled Colleen's neck. She thought how wonderful he was to try so hard for her.

"Dinner is ready, ladies," he announced

"Tommy, Elizabeth has something to show you."

Blushing now, Elizabeth stood and flashed her left hand. Tom looked at the ring, back to Colleen, then back to ring.

"Wow! Now this is a stunner! He took her hand. "Good grief, that ring must weigh two pounds!" He wrapped his arms around Elizabeth, lifted her up in a bear hug, and whirled her around. "I don't know about my mother and my sister, but as far as I am concerned, anybody that my wife approves of and my brother loves will have to work pretty hard to get on my bad side."

Elizabeth flushed. Brian said, "Thank you, both."

"Hey, we're family," Tom said, smiling for the first time that evening. "Warts and all."

Tom relaxed back into his dining chair and watched Brian and Elizabeth clear the dinner dishes. It had been quite a while since he had experienced such a lovely evening, far too long. Brian and Elizabeth were clearly pulling out all the stops. Tom had forgotten what a lively sense of humor Brian possessed. And this Elizabeth, with her agile mind and stories of growing up in rural Oklahoma, was an extraordinary match for him.

Brian reappeared from the recesses of the kitchen. "Port anyone?" He produced a tray with glasses and a bottle of fine Portuguese port. He decanted four glasses with a flourish, then presented Tom with a large humidor.

"And to accompany your after dinner port, we have a selection of fine cigars for you to choose from, Colonel. What would you prefer, sir? We have Honduran, Dominican, Mexican, Tampa, all rated over 91. Or, since you've behaved so well tonight, something exceptional, some lovely Havanas."

"Brian, have you lost your senses?" asked Elizabeth, shocked, "Offering an advisor to the President of the United States a Cuban cigar? Oh, Tom, I apologize."

"No problem, Elizabeth. I kind of expect this sort of thing from my baby brother." Tom stretched and turned to Brian. "You said something about Havanas? Do you remember Pop smoking Montecristos? I can still remember the aroma."

"As long as it isn't one of those *gigantes*," sniffed Colleen.

"What's the matter with them?" protested Brian.

"It just looks obscene to me for a man to stick one of those enormous things in his mouth and puff away."

Brian laughed. "Colleen, haven't you heard, sometimes a cigar is just a cigar?"

She shrugged, "It is so *déclassé.*"

Brian said, *sotto voce* to Elizabeth, "An Australian speaking French is like me driving a submarine." Then louder, "Colleen, you've been spending too much time with my brother. I hope he's not speaking French at home."

"Mostly Russian and Spanish to Mikey, sometimes a little Japanese to help keep me current."

"Okay, okay, enough talking. Montecristo it is," commanded Tom, determined to get his cigar.

"On the balcony, boys," ordered Colleen. "Let's not stink up the apartment. Elizabeth and I will go check on Mikey."

The men went through the motions of clipping and lighting the cigars. "Tom, you could do me a favor."

"What's that?"

"You and Colleen, be witnesses at a wedding tomorrow."

Tom laughed. "Man, once you make up your mind, you don't fool around, do you?"

"Hey, look who's talking, Mister-Nice-To-Meet-You-Colleen-My-Name's-Tom-Let's-Get-Married."

Tom chuckled. He took a deep draw on his cigar and carefully blew three perfect smoke rings. "On one condition."

"Yeah?"

"Mikey gets to handle the ring bearer role."

"Deal," said Brian. He shook Tom's hand. "Thanks, man."

Colleen and Elizabeth, now with jackets, appeared on the balcony, port glasses in hand. "Have you men solved the world's problems?" teased Colleen.

"Better than that, sweetheart. We're going to be witnesses at a wedding tomorrow."

"Good show!" Colleen hugged Elizabeth. "Well done, well done, both of you. This is wonderful!"

Brian raised his glass. "Here's to doing better on the family stuff in the future."

Tom glanced at Colleen. "That's part of why we're here, Brian. We really ought to tighten up the family. We're scattered all over the country, and the world, if you add in Colleen's family in Australia." Tom took a long pull on his cigar and was silent for a moment. "When was the last time you saw our mother? Or our sister? Do you ever think about Pop? Elizabeth, when was the last time you were in Oklahoma?"

Brian was quiet, Elizabeth leaned against his shoulder. Neither answered.

"See, that's what I mean. We're all so damn busy that we don't have the time or the energy to think about people we love. Even worse, to actually be with them."

"Tom, I think you should go to Vietnam," interrupted Colleen.

Tom blinked in disbelief.

"You've been talking about it for years," she said. "And the President of the United States just gave you a month off. Said you could go anywhere you wanted."

"Really?" asked Elizabeth.

"So why Vietnam?" asked Brian.

"Angela Davidson called to say she was leading the excavation of an F-4D shot down in late 1972, near where Pop was supposedly shot down." Tom looked at his brother. "Brian, it might be his plane."

"Tom, Vietnam is littered with F-4s. Why this one and why now?"

Tom turned away and studied the skyline, trying to formulate his answer. After a moment, he turned back to the group. "I am tired of not knowing what happened to our father. I cannot believe that he would stay away voluntarily. He is either being held against his will or he's dead. We have no evidence either way. All that we know is that he was shot down. His backseater got out. Why not Pop?

"Where is he, then? Where did he go? Why didn't he show up on any lists? Because he was a general? Did he piss off his interrogators? Did they kill him in Hanoi? Did he just die someplace in the jungle?

"I want to know—no, that's wrong. I *need* to know. Our family was ripped apart and *I just don't know what happened!*"

He found that he was breathing hard and his voice cracked. He reached for his wife. "You're right, Colleen. I have a chance to do something. If it's still okay with you, I'll go."

***

First up in the morning, Elizabeth finished grinding the Jamaican Blue Mountain coffee beans and started the coffee maker. Michael Andrew Callahan made his initial appearance, shyly approaching Elizabeth.

"Well, look who's up. And so early," she said, bending down on one knee to look the boy in his luminous Latin eyes, with what she thought were the most gorgeous eyelashes. "My name is Elizabeth."

"Most people call me Mikey," he said. "I hate it. It's for babies and I'm a big boy, almost five!"

"What do you want to be called?"

"Mac! 'Cause that's the 'nitials of my grandpa and great grandpa in 'Stralia. They died 'fore I was borned."

"I always wanted a nickname, too. My mother wanted a little lady, so she insisted people call me Elizabeth all the time."

"What did you want to be called?"

"Lizzie." She paused. "I know, why don't you call me Lizzie?"

"Call me Mac."

They shook hands, Mac looking very serious.

"Do you know my mommy?" he asked, climbing up on the barstool.

Elizabeth nodded.

"Mommy's sad."

"Why is she sad, Mac?"

"Because she had a baby and he died. I don't know why she needed another baby, she's already got me."

"Maybe she's so happy that you're her son that she wants to give you a baby brother or sister to show how to grow up."

Mac thought that over. "I could be a good big brother."

"I'll bet you would be, Mac," said Elizabeth, handing him a cup of orange juice.

"I know lots of stuff to teach a baby." He drank his OJ. "Maybe it's okay if Mommy does have 'nother baby."

"What would you like for breakfast?"

"My daddy makes me breakfast."

"Well, I'm probably not as good a cook as your daddy, but I'm awake. Maybe you could help me."

They were busy making pancakes when Tom appeared.

"Mornin', Daddy. I'm making breakfast with Aunt Lizzie."

63

Tom kissed Mikey on the head then tousled his hair. "No, Mikey, her name is Elizabeth."

"Not to me. We shook hands, didn't we, Aunt Lizzie?"

Elizabeth winked at him. "You bet, Mac." She took a deep breath. "Tom, do you think Brian could go with you?"

"Where?"

"To Vietnam."

"What?" said Tom. "Hold on, Elizabeth, you're getting married today. He can't go with me. You've got a honeymoon to take."

"He wants to go with you. He could help you a lot, too. And we could do the honeymoon after you get back."

"Did he tell you that he wanted to go with me?"

"No, but he listened to what you said last night. It struck a nerve. He really wants to go with you. I can tell."

"Well, it's crazy."

"What's crazy?" asked Brian as he entered the kitchen. He gave Elizabeth a kiss then hugged Mikey. "Hiya, pal."

Mikey squealed with delight as Brian swung him up over his shoulder. "Aunt Lizzie told Daddy that you want to go with him on a trip, Uncle Brian. Where are you going, Daddy?"

Tom looked at his brother. "It sounds like Uncle Brian and I are going on a plane ride to a place called Vietnam."

Chapter Five
Taos, New Mexico

Tom Callahan drove the rented car up the hairpin turn that marked the end of the Rio Grande Gorge and crested the hill, anticipating the panorama that he never tired of seeing. To the north and east, snow-capped Sangre de Cristo Mountains; to the west, the gray sagebrush and green junipers of New Mexico's nearly flat high desert that Tom insisted on calling "America's *altiplano*" like the one he knew in Bolivia. Slicing through the *altiplano*, he could see the jagged edges of the gorge, extending off to the north towards the Rio Grande's headwaters in Colorado. He caught a glimpse of movement through the sky. Two jets took shape—a flight of F-16s from the New Mexico Air National Guard, heading back to their base in Albuquerque, call signs "Taco." He smiled to himself at the irony of F-16s over Taos—with its amalgam of artists, aging hippies, and expatriate Hollywood actors, one of the most anti-military cities in the country, perhaps just after Berkeley.

He used the back roads that only the Taos locals knew, to by-pass the tourist traffic milling around the Plaza, and pressed northward. At the intersection known to all *Taoseños* as "the blinking light," he turned right onto NM Highway 150 towards his mother's house in Arroyo Seco. Taos Mountain, home to the famous Taos Ski Valley with some of the best powder skiing in the country, was almost dead ahead. As he approached Middle Road, he leaned over and poked a sleeping Brian.

"Hey, wake up. We're almost there." Just past the Poet's House, he spotted the pine tree-lined driveway that lead to his mother's house.

"Too bad Mom's in Europe. It'd be nice to see her," said Brian as he stretched.

"I think it's better that she doesn't know what we're up to until we know something," said Tom. "And I still think coming here is a waste of time. Joe Kozlowski already sent us most of the pictures and information from the archives."

"Maybe unnecessary for you, Tom, since you've probably read every word ever written about POWs and MIAs, but I haven't. This'll be a quick review for you and a graduate level course in Vietnam War casualties and politics for me."

"Yeah, little brother, but this unnecessary side trip cost you a day—and a night," Tom leered at Brian, "of your honeymoon."

Brian lightly punched his brother on the shoulder. "Something that I learned at the Stanford Graduate School of Business is that you want the raw data in your hands to get the real feel of a situation or a company. A lesson that you must have overlooked during your stay there. This'll take only a few hours. Then we can hit the ski area. How great is that? At any rate, we're only staying here tonight. We'll be in Hawaii in two days. Relax, man. We're on New Mexico time now. *Carpe mañana* and all that."

The Callahan compound was a beautifully landscaped five-acre parcel with colorful irrigated gardens, koi ponds, a waterfall, and walking trails, capped with a rambling southwestern-style stucco home sited to take advantage of the sweeping views and the natural light so critical in the workspace of an artist.

The men opened up the shuttered house, full of memories. Tom found Brian standing in the doorway of his old room.

"Mom hasn't changed anything since the last time I was here," Brian said, a catch in his voice. "I haven't even returned her calls for almost a year."

Tom said, "She's been waiting for Pop for over thirty years. She's willing to wait a bit for her son."

Brian nodded. "When we get back from Vietnam, I'm going to invite her to stay with us in New York. She's waited long enough."

***

They walked around and checked out the house, paused in the back yard to take in the stupendous view of the high desert, sagebrush-covered terrain leading up to the Taos Ski Valley. After a long argument over which of their many favorite Taos restaurants to visit, they headed back into town for dinner at Antonio's, just off the Plaza.

Over his blue corn chicken enchiladas and *posole*, Brian asked, "So, did you make contact with the President's chief of staff?"

"Yep. He said go for it. He warned me to be careful, then offered to make some back-channel calls. I declined. This is an unofficial, private citizen trip. The fewer people know about us, the better."

Brian nodded. "I'm still impressed by how quickly you got me recalled to active duty. Especially as a major since I left active duty as a captain. How the hell did you manage that?"

"I told you," said Tom, "it was the chief of staff's idea. He thought that it'll be easier for us if you are an officer, especially if you get sick or something goes wrong."

"Hey, what can go wrong? Or is there something that you're not telling me, Colonel, sir?"

"Sure, there's something I haven't told you. You need another haircut, Major."

"Now I know why you really wanted me on active duty," Brian grumped.

Next morning, they drove back through Taos. They turned left at the Plaza and took Highway 64 over the pass to Angel Fire. Waiting for them at the Early Bird Café and Bakery was a balding, short, heavyset man with a quick smile whom Tom introduced as Lieutenant Colonel Jozef Kozlowski, USAF (retired).

"Great to see you again, Koz," said Tom as the men embraced, followed by ribald comments about receding hairlines and expanding waistlines.

"Koz, great to meet you," said Brian. "Tom's kept me away from almost all his Academy friends. I want you to tell me how he really acted at school. Everyone else just says what a superstar he was."

"Oh, he was a superstar, all right. But I do have a few stories you might enjoy hearing."

As the men ate their breakfast, several townspeople stopped by to say hello. Tom judged that the ever popular Kozlowski had settled into village life.

A man with close-cropped, graying hair came into the Bakery, saw Kozlowski, and made a beeline to the table. Koz introduced him as Bill Palmer, retired CIA station chief in Prague, currently a village councilor.

"Koz has told me a lot about you, Colonel. Heading up to the Memorial?"

"Yes, we're going to go through some records Koz found for us. Then we hope to hit the slopes this afternoon."

"I hear you're heading to Vietnam," he said. "Just what do you expect to find?"

Surprised, Tom looked at Kozlowski. Koz shrugged, "Hey, it's a small town, Tom. Word gets around."

Especially if you tell everybody you know, thought Tom.

"We saw a recent photo taken in Vietnam with a Caucasian—"

Palmer interrupted, "So you think there are live American POWs abandoned by our government?"

"Perhaps. Perhaps not. But I want to look for myself."

"Oh, a real Rambo, huh? Most people don't want to see the past turned over again and again."

Tom just stared at the man. "Not that it's any of your business, but asking questions doesn't mean I'm anti-anybody. I want better answers. Too many people are willing to accept corporate answers at face value. I'm not."

"You're spitting in the eye of my agency, mister. How the hell did a communist like you ever make colonel?" Palmer demanded, then stalked out of the building.

The men looked at each other in surprise. "A communist?" asked Brian. "A *communist*?" Brian laughed so hard he got the hiccups.

During the short drive to the Vietnam Memorial, the men watched as the majestic white wing-like structure of the Chapel emerged from the ridge overlooking the Moreno Valley. It reminded Tom of the little white bones he'd found inside sand dollars he had collected along the seashore when he was a kid. His dad told him they were doves of peace. Tom told the same story to Mikey.

Begun by Dr. Victor Westphal as a memorial to his Marine son who had been killed in Vietnam, the Memorial was now a New Mexico State Park. The extensive archives contained battlefield photos, testimonials, pictures of the young men who'd died during the conflict, and hundreds of maps of Southeast Asia, most donated by veterans themselves. The walls of the reading rooms were covered with maps and pictures of young men and women. The atmosphere was somber, clearly a place for reflection.

Both Callahans were sobered by the archives and photos, especially the documentation of the number of MIAs captured near the Cambodian or Laotian border who still were unaccounted for. Brian was mesmerized by the archives and quickly went through the two boxes of source documents that Koz had separated out for him.

As they left for the ski area, Brian said, "Thank you both for indulging me. I had no idea that it would be such a moving experience. Every American ought to visit this place."

"It's an honor to work here," said Koz. "It's a healing place for many people, especially veterans and families of the fallen."

***

It was a classic northern New Mexico winter day. Earlier, the sun had been bright, the day cold and crisp. Now, low clouds were rolling in from the northwest, in the darkening skies over Wheeler Peak. The temperature was slipping and the breeze picking up.

As they shuffled through the ropes towards the chairlift, with the awkward club-footed stance of snowboarders everywhere, Koz said, "One more time, Tom. Try to keep it under Mach two coming down the hill."

"I'm always in control on the mountain," protested Tom.

"Hey, Tom. This is me, Koz. I remember you way back when, buddy. I've seen you scream down the slopes with your hair on fire." He shook his head. "Don't forget, I visited you in the Academy hospital after they put your leg back together. And I mean the second time."

Brian laughed as they settled into their seats and pulled down the safety bar. "That's the kind of stuff I wanted to hear, Koz!"

"Those days are over," said a chagrined Tom. "I'm a dad now. I need my knees for teaching soccer. On a snowboard, my knees are nice and secure, locked in the bindings with no place to twist. When I fall, I can just roll back up onto my feet, especially in powder."

Brian shook his head, "Call me a traditionalist. I'll stick to skis."

Koz pointed down at a small pond passing underneath the chairlift. "Most kids here snowboard because of the competitions, rail-jams, and especially the end of the year pond skimming. It's a great place, lots of fun."

"What's pond skimming?" asked Brian.

"You surf your snowboard over the water in a pond. If you make it to the other side, you're still dry. If you don't it's a cold, cold bath."

"You've actually done this?" asked Brian.

"Twice. Once I made it, once I didn't."

Brian shook his head. "No wonder you two were friends at school."

Tom glanced up the mountain. Visibility was deteriorating as the snow pounded down. The towers of the lift sloped up rapidly and disappeared into the clouds. The wind howled through the lift cables and the chairs swayed in the gusts. It was measurably colder.

Suddenly, the unloading platform sprang at them through the thick snow. Tom quickly raised the bar. The men slid off the seat, and coasted down the ramp. Tom peered around in the gloom, looking for a place to sit while tightening his bindings. The lift operators were huddled up, trying to stay warm in the wind and swirling snow.

The next two chairs disgorged groups of inept snowboarders who stumbled and crashed their way down the off ramp. One ran into Tom and three others fell directly in front of Brian. As Tom bent down to help one up, a bullet exploded past his head. Then another. Two snowboarders went down, screaming.

Bullets whizzed by, breaking the sound barrier right over Tom's head. He felt two more thump into the downed snowboarder at his feet.

Uphill he saw three men on skis wearing ski masks and carrying automatic pistols.

"Shooters!" he yelled. "Scatter! Scatter! Go!"

He spun on his board and ducked behind a tree, slicing through the snow, desperate to gain some speed. "Split up!" he shouted. Brian veered left, Koz right. Two shooters followed Tom; one went after Brian.

Tom headed for the trees. He hucked himself over the lip of the ski run and crashed into the forest. Trees flashed by as he rode the moguls in the glade. He wove through the trees. Branches slapped his helmet and goggles. Bullets whacked into trees around him. He avoided openings and only narrowly missed the boulders in a lava bed as he skimmed the tops of the bumps.

One of the shooters crashed into the boulders. One down. One right behind him.

The trail narrowed abruptly. Steep incline to the left, mountain face to the right. Shit! The terrain suddenly flattened out and Tom decelerated. His speed continued to bleed off and the shooter closed in. Tom spotted an opening in the trees to his left. Very steep. Suicide to try it. He took a deep breath and launched off the edge just as the skier fired.

Tom crashed through the trees. Brush grabbed at his body. He fell and rolled, frantic to regain his feet. Back up, he swerved too late to avoid a tree. The impact knocked him down again. He rolled upright, left side completely numb. His breath came hard. He was sweating, really sweating from the exertion.

The snow and wind in his face and the noise in his ears increased with speed. His heart raced, his thighs burned as he pounded down the mountain in a gut-wrenching, adrenaline-pumping run. Intense as any air-to-air engagement.

He had one killer at his six and in firing range. The flat light made it hard to see very far. He hit a rut and flew through the air, tumbling, snow in all directions. He hit hard and bounced up, spinning as he frantically searched for a landing. He stuck it, nearly fell again, then accelerated.

Like an aerial dogfight, he was in a tail chase for his life, except here he didn't have chaff, electronic countermeasures, or his vaunted flying skills. He'd have to use trees, boulders, dips in the terrain, anything and everything. Real nap of the earth stuff. He smiled through clenched teeth. Not even one mistake. Stay up and stay ahead.

He worked the terrain, using the trees for cover. At every turn, he picked out his line. Conditions were difficult; they didn't feel good to him but it probably didn't feel good to the other guy either. The new snow muffled all sound except his own labored breathing and the wind rushing past his helmet. Plus the occasional gunshot.

He looked for the steepest terrain he could find—speed was life. Skis were faster than snowboards and he needed speed here. He ducked through the trees to get off-piste. He spotted a narrow chute and skidded his turn to cut back into the opening.

He saw tracks leading off to the right and turned to follow. Too late he saw it was a cliff jump for the locals. He blasted out into the open air, faster than he'd expected and forty feet up. Off balance, he started to tumble. He tucked and did an awkward flip, desperate to spot his landing. After an eternity, he crashed at the base of the cliff, powder exploding in all directions. His momentum pulled him down the steep face, smashing through the snow. He twisted to get his feet down below his head and tunneled through the deep powder. Back on his feet, he sucked in his breath and made quick turns to control his speed until the cliff finally flattened out. He stole a look up the slope. No shooter. Tom straightened up and let his board run to maximize his speed downhill. He was exhausted, thighs quivering and on fire.

The trail merged with another and he automatically glanced uphill. There was the damned shooter! *How the hell?* Tom tucked and hurtled down the hill. He made a tight, screaming-ass turn around the final corner. Directly in front was the snowmaking pond.

Only one choice. He tucked lower, flattened his board with the tip up, and rode over the water, surfing to the other side, then rolled down the incline, popped his bindings and scrambled into the trees.

He saw Brian coming around the corner slightly behind the shooter, who reacted to the pond too late and did a spectacular face plant into the icy water. Still in his skis, he flailed around unable to gain his footing, while his waterlogged clothes pulled him down. He struggled, then went under.

Brian skidded in a classic hockey-stop, kicked off his skis and plunged into the frigid pond. He grabbed the panicked assassin and smashed his face twice, then pushed his head under water and held it there.

Tom ran out of the woods, "Don't drown him," he shouted. "We need him to talk." He looked up and saw people standing around. "Call the cops!"

Several uniformed security officers ran up, clumsy in their heavy boots. "Hey, what's going on?"

"There was a shooting up at the summit. This is one of the guys. There are two more somewhere on the hill. Tell Ski Patrol to watch out. These guys have automatics."

Brian and Tom dragged the assassin out of the pond and watched unsympathetically as he coughed and vomited water. Three local cops arrived, accompanied by a Colfax County deputy sheriff.

The cops began to sort out the mess. Ski Patrol reported four snowboarders were shot; one dead, three injured, two critically. Kozlowski had watched the shooters follow Tom and Brian and then ran back up the hill to administer first aid. At least one of the injured owed his life to Koz's quick actions. Neither of the other shooters had been located.

After a brief spat over jurisdiction, the deputy sheriff cuffed the struggling prisoner and loaded him into the police car for the long trip to the county jail in Raton, an hour and a half away.

Tom and Brian followed the cops back to the station where Brian changed out of his wet clothes. They spent half an hour being interrogated before Kozlowski arrived and announced that a second snowboarder had died from her wounds. Before they could explore this any further, the Chief's phone rang. He took the call in his office and came out with a stricken look.

"That was the state police. Deputy Brown's car was found abandoned and full of bullet holes by an ice fisherman on the other side of Eagle Nest Lake. Brown's body was found in the ditch. The prisoner escaped."

After providing the cops with their contact phone numbers and e-mail addresses, the Callahans were allowed to leave. As they got back into their car, Brian turned to Tom. "Why did somebody try to shoot us? And why at a ski resort? This isn't a James Bond movie. They could have shot us at breakfast someplace."

Tom wasn't sure but Bill Palmer's words echoed in his head: There are lots of people who don't want the past stirred up.

Chapter Six
Joint POW/MIA Accounting Command
Hickam Air Force Base, Hawaii

Tom and Brian stood in the parking lot and, in typical pilot fashion, paused to watch a C-17 on final approach to the runway where both men had landed many times. Tom sighed, "Whenever I get near a runway, I'm always reminded that somewhere in the world, there's some lucky guy taxiing out cleared number one for takeoff and it's not me."

Brian laughed and slapped Tom on the back. "Tough being a colonel, huh?"

"Being a desk-warming colonel is not what I had in mind when I joined up," said Tom. "My last flying assignment was in Bolivia. When we got stationed in Washington, I had to buy a plane in order to get some stick time."

The men entered the JPAC Headquarters building where they were met by uniformed security officers who politely but thoroughly scrutinized their identification before notifying the deputy commanding officer that an active-duty colonel was in the lobby. Colonel Tony Arnold, U.S. Army, turned out to be a tall, thin officer with bright blue eyes and an infectious grin. "Good morning, Colonel Callahan. Major Callahan," he said as he offered his hand.

"Thank you for your time, Colonel."

"No problem, Colonel. We try to make ourselves available whenever families of MIAs show up." He held up a thick folder. "I have your father's file, if you'd like to see it."

"If it's the same as the one in the Pentagon, we've already gone through it. Angela Davidson has told me quite a bit about JPAC, but my brother isn't as familiar with your operations. What we're interested in is to see what goes on here and just get a feel for what you're doing in the field."

"Fine, sir. I love to show off our facilities. Just follow me, please." The men left the headquarters section and entered into the working areas.

"Our mission is 'Until They are Home' and we take our mission seriously. We try to be as accessible as possible. For example, we have our JPAC website that, among other things, lists a toll free number that is staffed with linguists for most countries where MIAs are believed to be located: Vietnam, Laos, Cambodia, China, and Russia. We want leads. And those leads are investigated and followed.

"As you probably know, there are thousands of MIAs, way too many. Our numbers change periodically but in the most publicized section, the Vietnam-era MIAs, there are about fifteen hundred in Vietnam, more than five hundred in Laos, and about eighty in Cambodia. Another four hundred twenty-five were lost over water off the Vietnamese coast. Most of these MIAs were Air Force, and mostly pilots. We also have about eighty-one hundred Korea MIAs and something like seventy-eight thousand WWII MIAs."

Brian interrupted, "I saw on your website that your people are identifying about six MIAs per month, to date about thirteen hundred."

Tom laughed, "My brother is the consummate number cruncher, Colonel. Never met a number he didn't like, or remember. What we would like to see is how you accomplish those identifications."

"Certainly, gentlemen. I'll cut to the chase, shall I? I will take you through the identification sequence and introduce you to the teams here, though most are in the field right now." He led them down the well-lit hallway. "We start with the general research function. Our first level of research is the Identification Team—IT—made up mostly of analysts and linguists who research archives in Vietnam." They entered a set of bright rooms, tables with maps, walls with maps, books lining the wall. At one table, two middle-aged men dressed in Hawaiian shirts sat poring over papers. "Here are two of our IT personnel, Ron Ford and Toby Trujillo. Ron is a historian, and Toby is one of our senior researchers."

"Thank you for your work, gentlemen," said Tom, as they shook hands. "It gives us all hope."

Trujillo noticed Brian's interest in the stack of papers on the table. "Major, we're putting the finishing touches on this package, a possible MIA from the Korean Conflict." He handed a thick folder to Brian.

"Pretty thorough analysis from the looks of this," Brian said after a quick examination.

Trujillo beamed. "Thank you. We'll forward our findings to the next stage in the process, a Recovery Team, or RT. The RT will follow up on our leads, conduct interviews with witnesses, then conduct terrain surveys for safety and logistical concerns. The IT's work dictates where future recovery operations take place."

Colonel Arnold nodded. "Then the Recovery Teams, RTs, are deployed, typically ten to fourteen people, including a team leader, an anthropologist, medical personnel, and a linguist. The teams deploy approximately ten times per year with missions lasting thirty-five to sixty days, depending on the location, terrain, and recovery methods. Right now there are two recovery teams in Cambodia, one working on an F4-E crash and one on an F-105 crash site, in addition to the teams in Vietnam."

They bid farewell to Trujillo and Ford and continued on the tour. "Here is our jewel, the Central Identification Laboratory, the world's largest forensic anthropology lab. Among other things, this is where we attempt to construct a biological profile from skeletal remains."

"Like on the television show *Bones*?" Tom asked.

The colonel laughed. "We get that a lot. Are you a fan?"

"It's the only TV program my wife and I watch."

"Well, it's sort of like that, though the TV show is sexed up a bit and in real-life things happen much slower. But we can use a biological profile to either help identify remains or narrow them to a short list of individuals. The forensic anthropologist assigned to the case in the lab is not the one who completed the recovery in the field. This helps prevent any bias from entering the identification process."

Several tables were covered with bones, several more with personal effects. Arnold said, "Rings, watches, and combs are valuable in identification and are also invaluable mementoes to the remaining family members. We try to return as many of them as we can." He sat at a computer terminal and brought up some files. "In this case the teeth are crucial. Not much left except a skull. Dental records for Korea and Vietnam have been computerized. Even in a very hot fire, tooth enamel survives."

Tom nodded, "The man buried in the Tomb of the Unknown Soldier at Arlington as a Vietnam-Era Unknown Soldier was from my squadron at the Academy, though some years ahead. He was ultimately identified by a tooth and some bone fragments, wasn't he?"

"True. One of our goals is that there will be no unknown soldiers in the future." He pointed at the table with the skull. "Our forensic anthropologists use methods to create legally defensible identifications. We treat each dig location like a crime scene to maintain a chain of custody." He smiled at Tom, "Yes, just like on the show. In many cases, we don't have much more than this to work with. The soils of Southeast Asia are acidic, tough on even hard tissues and bones. Remember these remains, as well as aircraft, have been embedded in the ground for thirty or forty-plus years.

"Any remains found by our Recovery Teams are flown back here and are met at Hickam by a joint service honor guard. The ceremony is short, sweet, and dignified." He indicated the array of computers and lab-coated workers, "When we have a possible ID, and before we go public, we meet with the family and go through our logic. The family is free to hire an outside independent review. As we say on our web site, the families deserve every tiny little thing that we can give them. These men went to war and left a hole where their lives should have been."

Tom was impressed. This facility and these people were even better than Angela had led him to believe. "Tell me about live sightings," he said.

"Well, we investigate. We try to see if there are POWs held against their will. We've sent investigators into Hanoi, Peking, and Moscow to see if there are or were collaborators."

"Any success?"

"Almost invariably the 'live sighting' is a European in a place where Europeans or Caucasians are not normally seen. Or a deliberate falsification."

"Almost?"

"Sometimes, we cannot confirm, or deny, the sighting. We simply do not know. Again, I want to stress that we are serious about our mission."

"Thank you, Colonel Arnold. I can see that. If, in the future, I can be of any help, please let me know."

***

The ringing of the phone shattered Tom Callahan's sleep. He groped in the dark, only to knock the damned thing to the floor. Finally he found the receiver. "Hello?" he croaked.

"Good morning, Tommy," he heard his mother's voice say.

"Mom, where are you? And what time is it?"

"I am in New York where I should be, helping Colleen and meeting Elizabeth. Tom, you should have called me about the baby."

Tom took a deep breath. "I thought it better if we kept it quiet. There was nothing anybody could do."

"Colleen told me you named him after your father."

Trust his mother to get right to the point. "It seemed like the right thing to do at the time, Mom. He was such a fighter..." Tom choked up at the memories of his little man fighting to breathe. "Just like the stories you told me about Pop."

She paused, then said, "Your father was the most stubborn man on the planet." She paused again. "Colleen tells me that you're on your way to Vietnam."

So much for keeping the secret from his mother. "Yes, ma'am," he said. "Mom, I just have to try."

"I understand, son. What are your plans?"

"I don't know. I'm going to try to gain access to some of the records, some of the higher-ups, and see what happens."

"That doesn't sound like you to not have a plan all worked out, Tommy, with every detail checked."

"I know and I don't like it. But I only have so much time. I'd rather be working in Vietnam than in an office in Washington. Maybe something will fall into my lap."

"Can you fly to Vietnam through Bangkok?"

"Of course."

"Your father and I have a great friend there. He went to business school with your father. He's very important now, a retired vice admiral. Part of the last military government, Foreign Minister, if I remember. Stop in to see him. My guess is that he can get you an audience with anybody you need to see. I'll send you the details in an e-mail." A long pause. "Tommy, bring him back to me," she said with a choke in her voice, "one way or another." Then she was once again all business, "Let me speak to Brian."

Tom stumbled out of bed and knocked on the connecting door to Brian's adjoining room. "Mom's on the horn."

Brian took the phone. *"Privyet, Mama,"*—Hello, Mother. He listened, nodding. "Yes, Mom…Yes, Mom…Thank you, Mom. This means a lot to me."

He set the phone in the cradle and covered his eyes for a moment. Turning back to Tom, he said, "She says she thinks Elizabeth is marvelous."

"Well, she is marvelous. And you should be on your honeymoon, not here."

"What? Let Don Quixote Callahan go tilt at Vietnamese windmills without his faithful Sancho?"

"You make this sound like some kind of fraternity road trip!" Tom flared.

"Jesus, Tom, calm down. Don't get all lathered up. He's my father and this is my family, too. You remember Dad more than I do, but he is still my father, and I need to fill that hole with something; a funeral, a memory of this trip to find him. Something. We're in this together. Elizabeth and I have lots of time for a honeymoon later."

***

Tom checked into his hotel and collapsed onto the bed as he contemplated the dual curses of jet lag and approaching middle age. He dragged himself to his feet, plugged in his computer to check his e-mail, and found the expected message from his mother: the admiral would be returning to Bangkok that evening for a dinner meeting with Tom. He forwarded the information to Brian, now winging his way to Hanoi alone.

He checked the time, then stripped and dressed for a run. Two hours later, after his run and a swim in the hotel's massive pool, he returned to his room. As expected, the phone light was blinking. Tom retrieved the message, then checked the clock again. A quick shower and a change of clothing helped him feel a bit more human.

The Thai government limousine was exactly on time. The short drive allowed Tom only a glimpse of the beautiful city, but what he saw fascinated him, and he wondered why he had never been there before.

The restaurant was as ornate as any restaurant he had ever seen. He entered the grand foyer to find a distinguished man, mid 60s, whose demeanor had the look of a man used to exercising authority. Clearly Admiral Shinawatra.

Tom smiled, pressed his palms together, and bowed his head in the traditional Thai "wai" or greeting. "*Sawat-dii, khrap,*" he said.

The admiral returned the greeting and smiled as he shook hands. "Thomas, it has been a long time. I remember you in diapers. You've grown a bit since then." They both laughed. "You look very much like your father."

"Admiral, I always take that as a compliment."

"It was meant to be a compliment. But you have your mother's eyes."

The maître d' led them to a private booth with a view of the restaurant's lavish private gardens. The waiter hovered, waiting for the order.

"Are you ready to try something exotic, cobra blood for example?" asked the admiral with a smile.

Tom took a deep breath. "Sir, I've lived in Japan, but this is my first time to Thailand. I will follow your lead."

The admiral laughed and said something in Thai to the waiter who disappeared. "I've ordered us an array of Thai food, a smorgasbord if you will.

"When I was with your father at Stanford, he took me home to meet your beautiful mother. She introduced me to Italian food. And I taught her tempura. A fair exchange, don't you think? A delightful East-West trade. Plus," he added, "I was lonely and your parents were very kind. In the 1960s, people in your country weren't so accommodating to foreigners, especially Asians. Thought we were all Japanese. The hatreds of the world war weren't yet healed. My English wasn't very good and the work at the business school was difficult."

Tom nodded. "That I can believe. It was tough enough for me in English. I can't even imagine how hard it would have been in Thai."

The admiral sipped his drink, his eyes focused in the distance, lost in thought. "Failing at Stanford was, as the saying goes, not an option for me. I would have been shipped back here and court-martialed. Probably shot for disgracing my country." He smiled. "I didn't do so badly in my career, thanks to your father's help."

Three waiters arrived with trays of delicious, spicy-smelling food. There was much bustling about as many small dishes were placed on the table.

"Relax, Thomas. There is nothing poisonous here, no *fugu* like in Japan. Nothing so dramatic." The admiral carefully explained each dish and its ingredients. Here was a man who took his food seriously. As they started their feast, he said, "I don't suppose I could interest you in a woman after dinner?"

Tom choked. "No, thank you, sir. My wife would have various parts of me embalmed."

The admiral nodded. "You are an honorable man in your quaint, barbaric, Western way, just like your father." The admiral continued his culinary discourse while Tom listened attentively, filing away as much information as he could. He thought that this would be a wonderful vacation spot to bring Colleen, though keeping Mikey away from the exotic animals and poisonous snakes might be a bit tricky.

"You don't remember much about your father, do you?

"No, sir. But I try." Tom closed his eyes, remembering. "When we were growing up, I was the oldest, and I had to keep the other kids' hopes up, the memories alive. Mom told us stories about Pop. We always

82

had a seat at the dinner table set for him, like he was coming home late from work. We celebrated his birthday. And all the kids' Christmas presents were always signed 'from Mom and Dad.'"

The general sat there, thinking. "Your father was one of a kind. When I think of your father, I remember one event that summed him up. In our second year at Stanford, we were allowed to take an elective course. Since we were all very serious, dedicated professionals, everyone scrambled to cram in another finance course, or another management course. The first day of classes, in strolled your father, dressed in jodhpurs and riding boots, straight from the Stanford stables. He had decided to take polo. It was classic Sean."

Tom laughed, delighted. That description exactly fit the mental image he had of his father. "Mom told me about her trip here while Pop was on leave from Vietnam."

"Yes, my late wife took her jewelry shopping."

"Mom still has some of those rings. And some of the paintings. She says it was one of the best weeks of her life."

"Your mother is one of the most generous and warm people I have ever met. Never a bad thing to say about anyone. I know she was criticized for hosting Asians in her house back then. And your father was a brave and honorable man. I like to think that I became a better man for being your father's friend."

"Admiral, I think you became my father's friend because of the man you are."

The admiral stared at Tom for a minute. "That was an exceptionally kind thing to say. Such a diplomat."

"I really wish people would stop calling me a diplomat. I'm a fighter pilot, please." Tom grinned. "And, sir, I am my father's son. Judge for yourself if I'm blowing diplomatic smoke up your tailpipe."

The admiral pushed back from the table and motioned for the waiters to clear the dishes.

After they departed, he turned serious. "Details, Thomas. Tell me everything."

Tom filled him in, beginning with Ron Minor's photograph, and both the shootings.

The admiral sat quietly, intent on Tom's stories. "Do you know who these shooters were?"

"No, sir. I don't even know that they are related. Or why either of the shootings took place."

The admiral thought a moment. "It seems there may be a group, or groups, that do not like the idea of someone, anyone, poking around in this area."

"But why? Surely there can't be any harm in the truth."

"How long have you been working in the White House? You should know that isn't true anywhere." The admiral shrugged. "Organizations are like people; nobody likes to be proven wrong or caught in a lie." He lapsed into thought, then said, "I will make some inquiries here in Bangkok and a few calls around Asia."

"Admiral, I don't know what to say."

"Don't say anything, then. Find your father. Or find what happened to your father. I do not believe the stories put out by your CIA. I hear things."

"What kind of things?"

"Things. Like POWs who were not repatriated. Remember that anything happening in Southeast Asia is of concern to my country. We have records from Cambodia and Laos that might prove useful. I also have many contacts in China who do not believe your government's official position. The Chinese are very nervous about this new Russian president. Even our Vietnamese friends are not happy with Moscow right now. You will find some receptive ears in Hanoi."

"Any particular ears, Admiral?"

The admiral shook his head. "Give me another few days, Thomas." He handed over a folder. "Here is your ticket to Hanoi. I'll get information to your hotel when I have something. If you need to contact me or need any help, get in touch with the naval attaché at our Embassy."

Chapter Seven
Thai Airways International Flight TG 682

Tom Callahan watched out the window as the Airbus 300 began its descent into Hanoi. The city spread out in all directions, sprawling across the flat countryside, hemmed in on the east by the Red River. He imagined the gun emplacements of thirty-plus years ago when Hanoi was the most heavily defended city in the world and tried to envision attack corridors that his father might have used.

As the aircraft turned on to final approach, Tom picked up the lights of Hanoi's Noi Bai Airport, a "joint-use" field in U.S. military parlance, meaning that it shared runways with the Vietnamese Air Force. In fact, the airport had originally been built as an air force base and was home to the 921st Fighter Regiment that had vanquished so many American aircraft during the war. It had also served as the departure point for the repatriated American POWs in April 1973. Tom had a Jeppesen chart of the airport in his briefcase with all the statistics: largest airport in North Vietnam; twenty-eight miles from downtown; parallel concrete runways, 11R/29L and 11L/29R. Having all the facts didn't make him feel any more comfortable. His father may have tried to bomb this field or at the very least flown MiG Combat Air Patrol while the F-105s tried to bomb it.

He walked through the new ultra-modern, and most important, air conditioned terminal, picked up his luggage, made his way through customs, and walked down the tunnel to the reception area.

"Tom, over here." Tom easily picked out the blonde Angela Davidson and his brother from the Asian crowd. He shook hands with Brian and hugged Angela.

"Looking good, Angie baby."

"Thank you, Tommy," Angela replied. "Eric sends his regards as well as his condolences."

Tom nodded, accepting the regrets. Eric Davidson was one of his oldest friends who had been dragged along on a blind date, set up by a much younger Tom Callahan when they were both on the Academy ski team. Eric and Angela had been an instantaneous match.

"Having you here is a surprise, Angie. Did Brian drag you all the way out here just to see me?"

"Oh, no. This was my idea. It's my way of getting to see your hotel. It's supposed to be the best hotel in the country, legendary even."

They exited the air-conditioned terminal and were immediately assailed by the smells, heat, and humidity of Hanoi. It had to be at least ninety degrees and eighty percent humidity, even in the relatively cool and dry winter. If it's like this in the winter, he thought, it must be a sauna in the summer, maybe even worse than D.C. That was hard to believe.

The hotel limo, a vintage black Mercedes sedan, was parked along the curb. The driver neatly arranged Tom's luggage in the trunk and eased into the swirling traffic. Tom was fascinated by the street scenes. The city was swarming with people—"teeming" would be more accurate. Very much like the scenes in Bangkok that he had just left, with more than a dash of French colonial architecture thrown in. They were swept along in the frenetic pace of people, bicycles, scooters, mopeds everywhere, roads congested, traffic lights universally ignored. The overhead wires, the collage of bright colors, and the mixture of native and western dress reminded him of La Paz, Bolivia. Only the palm trees lining many of the streets and the different mélange of languages that shouted at him from neon billboards showed that he was in Asia.

The Hotel Sofitel Metropole Hanoi proved to be as elegant as the Internet photos proclaimed. Embraced by immaculate exterior gardens, the pristine white exterior of the French colonial main building gave way to a cavernous marble foyer with an enormous chandelier high overhead.

Angela said, "I've been dying to come here. I can't even imagine how much it costs, but I'm sure it exceeds the government per diem rate."

"I'm not on per diem, Angela. I'm here on my own nickel."

"Even worse."

Tom greeted the desk clerk, "My name is Callahan. I have a room reserved."

The young man checked his computer. "One minute, *monsieur*," he said and disappeared into the back room, emerging with a dapper-looking gentleman whose nametag announced that he was the manager.

"Good afternoon, Colonel Callahan," he said with a heavy French accent. "We have taken the liberty of upgrading you to a two bedroom suite. I hope that is convenient with you."

"*Merci beaucoup, monsieur*," replied Tom. "Could you move my brother in as well?"

"*Mais oui, mon Colonel*." He turned to his assistant. "Get the colonel's luggage to the Somerset Maugham Suite, then send someone to *Monsieur* Callahan's room to help him move." The man bowed and disappeared.

"*Mon Colonel*, there is a message for you."

Tom opened the envelope, read the message, then stuffed it into his jacket pocket. "I will need wireless Internet access."

"But of course, *mon Colonel*. You have the choice of the hotel Wi-Fi system or using your own secure wireless system."

As they followed the manager towards the suite, Angela said, "I see the Vietnamese Intelligence service has just kicked in."

Tom touched his index finger to his lips. "Patience, my dear."

The Somerset Maugham suite turned out to be an exquisite collection of rooms. Tom thought it somewhat ironic that he would be sequestered in a suite named for a wealthy, well-known chronicler of colonialism and an agent of British Intelligence whose stories had influenced the creation of the fictional James Bond.

Angela was entranced by the rooms. Amused, Tom watched her poking around, then found the phone and ordered tea for three in the courtyard. They adjourned to meet Brian by the courtyard pool.

"The Defense Attaché called me into his office today," said Angela arranging scones on her plate as Tom poured her tea. "He wants you to come to the Embassy."

"Why?" asked Tom.

"I don't know why. That's what he said."

"Call him back and give him my regards. I'm not going to the Embassy."

"Tommy, this is the DATT that we're talking about. He's the ranking DoD guy in Vietnam."

Tom had a great deal of experience dealing with American military attachés around the world; some he had met were superb officers, others were dreadful. Attachés function as accredited military advisors to ambassadors and "observe and report" on military activities of their host countries. Essentially legal and overt spies, they provide useful conduits of military information in both directions. Often they also exercise command and control functions over other military personnel assigned within the countries.

"I know that, Angela. If I go to the Embassy, it will look like I'm here on an intelligence operation and therefore under Embassy control. I'm not either of these."

"The Attaché Office controls all DoD assets in-country, except for my people."

"Well, I don't work for him either. I'm here as a private citizen."

"No, you're not. You're a full bird colonel and you work in the White House as an advisor to the President on Asian and Russian affairs. Definitely not a private citizen."

Tom sighed. "I just want to find my dad."

"You just can't wander around this country, Tommy. This isn't France. There are restrictions on movement."

"I have a hard time believing that the Vietnamese care one iota about Tom Callahan."

"Wrong," said Brian. "They know everything about you, probably right down to your shoe size. Do not underestimate these people, Tom." He sipped his drink. "Have some faith, brother. I've already met with two generals and a slew of colonels. Plus assorted civilian bureaucrats."

Tom laughed. "Is this the Stanford Business School connection at work?"

Brian nodded. "That, and some Asian Rim connections that I made during a couple of our IPOs. You know how networking makes things happen, Tom."

"Get anything concrete out of them?"

"They were pleasant, asked a lot of questions, but very much want to meet with you, the Senior Partner. They're big on rank and status. This is a family matter and you're the Number One Son. Very Asian."

Tom thought for a minute. "Angela, what's your schedule?"

"I leave tomorrow morning at oh-dark-thirty to the F-4 dig. It has moved faster than we anticipated. And yes, you may take me to dinner tonight. I'd love to try the hotel restaurant. It's supposed to be one of the best in Hanoi." She batted her eyes in an exaggerated flirtatious gesture.

"Sorry, can't do it tonight, sweetcakes." He held up the message envelope. "But if you promise to behave yourself and can find a dress that doesn't make you look like a Hooters waitress, I'll take you to dinner with the Foreign Minister and the Vice Minister of National Defense for International Relations."

"How did you manage that?" asked Brian.

"I didn't. Your mother did. And you're coming, too."

"You're joking, Mom pulled this off?"

"Totally serious." He turned to Angela, "Angie, please call the Attaché and ask him to join me for breakfast here in the hotel, say, 0800. Do not say anything about dinner tonight. While you do that, I will scour the Internet. I am in serious need of some information. When you get back here, we'll work out the details."

***

The drive to the residence of the Foreign Minister took thirty-five minutes in the hotel Mercedes, affording Angela and Brian opportunities to show off their knowledge of Hanoi to Tom. Entering the Ba Dinh administrative sector, they made the mandatory drive by the tomb of Ho Chi Minh, which reminded Tom of a simpler version of the Lincoln Memorial in Washington. The evening street traffic felt even livelier than the morning traffic as the limo made its way into the government district.

"Look at all the people in the streets," said Tom. "It's amazing."

"No, it's Tet, the Chinese New Year," said Brian. "People are coming from all over for the celebrations. Lots of feasting, lots of parties."

"One problem with the New Year festivities, Tom" said Angela, "is that the farmers are smuggling in live poultry in violation of the government bans. There's been another outbreak of bird flu and the only way to contain it is to forbid the transport of poultry."

"Well, the Vietnamese people certainly proved their ingenuity during the war. Nice to see that they can also outwit their own government, not just ours."

The Americans were met at the door of the Ministry by a Vietnamese Air Force colonel who escorted them through a large ornate hall into a somewhat more modest room with a long table set for twelve.

Introductions took several minutes. The language of the evening seemed to be French, although several Vietnamese officials who had some English tried to use it. Tom and Brian were at ease while Angela, fluent in Spanish but hopeless in French, smiled and charmed her way through the receiving line.

The Foreign Minister was a gracious man somewhat taller than most Vietnamese. As host for the evening, he made a point of introducing Tom to the Vice Minister of Defense for International Relations and his senior staff, then placed Tom to his right at the head of the table. Immediately, waiters swarmed out of the kitchen carrying platters of exotic food for the guests. Tom smiled to himself as he listened to the Minister, proudly explaining every new dish, just as the admiral had done the night before in Bangkok.

The Foreign Minister said, "I understand that this is not your first time in Asia, Colonel."

"Yes, Minister. Our family spent several years in Japan as I was growing up. I had a tour in Australia, and later one in Japan. My brother had a tour in Japan as well. My mother lived in China as a young girl in the White Russian refugee areas in Shanghai. She speaks Chinese and taught all us kids to speak it, although I have to admit, mine is pretty shaky now."

"Your father was an honorable adversary," said Minister, sounding very much like the army general that he had been. "Unfortunately, we have no records of his capture."

"That's why I'm here, Minister. To see if there can be some review of the records."

"We've already searched the records. Your brother is very persuasive. But we have found nothing other than the fact that he was shot down, probably in the western part of Gai Lai province. There are often difficulties dealing with the administration of the southern provinces."

Tom nodded. "Yes sir, I understand. When my wife and I adopted a baby in Bolivia, we lived in the capital and he was located in another district of the country. It set off all sorts of political fireworks and power struggles. In the end, the President of Bolivia had to step in on our behalf."

The Minister looked Tom over. "I heard there is a great deal more to that story of you and the Bolivian President."

Word certainly does get around, thought Tom. So much for security. He took another bite. "It always amazes me how rumors are so persistent and can even encircle the globe."

"Exactly," said the Minister with a diplomatically suitable deadpan expression. "You realize that your father may have ended up in Cambodia. Most of those contacts ended with our conflict with Cambodia in January, 1979. We did not have good relations with the Khmer people. They destroyed most records as a matter of policy when the criminal Pol Pot came to power in 1975." He dipped a shrimp into a delicious sauce, then looked Tom in the eyes. "I will see what I can do."

"Thank you, Minister."

"You have come at an auspicious time, Colonel Callahan. Our Tet festival is the biggest event of the year, a time for friends, families, and loved ones to come together." He peered over the top of his glasses at Tom. "It is also a time to pay respects to deceased ancestors."

"I pay my respects to my father by finding out what happened to him. In the meantime, Minister," said Tom, "I'd like to fly down to the F-4 dig in Gai Lai. My brother can stay here to work with your people."

"Certainly, Colonel. That can easily be managed." He turned to his aide. "Make the arrangements."

Chapter Eight
Hotel Sofitel Metropole Hanoi

Tom and Brian relaxed in the Parisian sidewalk café atmosphere of the restaurant, an appropriate setting for early morning espresso and croissants. Tom read *Le Figaro* while Brian perused the pink pages of the *Financial Times*. Waiters hovered nearby, smiling and efficient. Tom looked up to see a trio of Caucasians in business suits striding towards them. In the lead, a large, beefy man with a full head of wavy, blond hair. Tom recognized the ambassador from his bio picture on the Embassy website. The second man, middle-aged with close cropped-hair and a slight paunch, was clearly military, masquerading as a diplomat, *ergo* the Defense Attaché. The youngest one looked distinctly familiar.

"Good morning, Mr. Ambassador," said Tom, standing and offering his hand. "This is a surprise."

"Colonel Callahan, this is Colonel Marsh, the Defense Attaché, and this is Gunnery Sergeant Johanssen, the head of our Marine guard detachment."

"Johanssen, good to see you!"

"Thank you, Colonel. It's good to see you again, sir."

"So, a gunny now. Terrific. Well done." Tom looked at the ambassador and Colonel Marsh. "I knew the gunny in Bolivia, back when he was a corporal."

Johanssen gave Tom a big grin, then turned to the ambassador. "The colonel used to take some of the junior Marine guards out in the Embassy C-12, so we could see some of the country. He also took care of us when the Marine House was bombed by terrorists." Johanssen looked back to Tom. "I got a Christmas card from Dave Scher, sir. He told me that after he was medically retired from the bombing, you got him that job in the American Cooperative School in La Paz."

"How's he doing?"

"He and Maria are fine, sir. They have a baby now."

"Well, great. Tell him that our boy is fine as well. We'll be heading to Bolivia next year to show Mikey where he was born. We'll look them up." Tom asked for more coffee and croissants, which appeared nearly instantaneously. The waiters set three more places places and the guests sat down. The ambassador stirred his café au lait.

"Colonel, I'll be blunt. You should not be here."

"Why is that, Mr. Ambassador?"

"Had you gone through State Department channels and asked permission as you are required to do, I would have, regretfully, denied your request."

"I'm not here in an official capacity. I am here as a private citizen."

"Come, come, Colonel. You cannot be a private citizen. Especially in this country."

"Then I'm even gladder that I didn't make the request." He sipped his coffee to help calm his temper. "Out of curiosity, on what grounds would you have denied me entry?"

"There is a fresh outbreak of bird flu. Poultry are smuggled into Hanoi in record numbers for Tet, meaning the virus is everywhere in the city. It's quite dangerous here."

"I've had a vaccination."

"Of course you have. You work in the White House. That sort of proves my point, doesn't it? Some pigs are more equal than other pigs?"

Tom bit back a sharp reply, glanced at Brian, then deliberately tore apart and slowly ate a croissant.

"What do you know of the political situation here?" asked the ambassador.

"I'm not interested in the political situation. I'm just here to find out what happened to my father."

"There are on-going negotiations, delicate politics in flux. I don't want you to interfere with or disrupt those discussions."

"I have no intention of doing so. All I want to do is look into the archives and perhaps see some of the shoot-down locations."

"Colonel, it has been thirty-plus years since anybody heard a thing about your father. There is no Vietnamese casualty list with his name on it, no prisoner list, nothing. He's gone."

"He's gone all right. But the operative phrase is 'no casualty list.'"

"This is my country, Callahan. I give the orders here."

Tom had had enough. "Fine, then go give orders to somebody else. I'm not under your command and never will be."

The ambassador reddened, then stood. "You cannot visit any digs in Vietnam. Those are my orders."

"Really?"

"Really."

The ambassador's companions stood, ready to depart. Johanssen looked distinctly uncomfortable. Tom remained seated and again broke open a croissant and smeared a dab of fresh butter on it. "Interesting. I have not asked for your permission." He took a bite and slowly chewed. "As I understand the rules of these cooperative recovery efforts, the Vietnamese government decides who goes where and for what purpose. I have the Vietnamese government's permission to go anywhere I want, whenever."

"Really?"

"Really."

Watching the ambassador's broad backside exit the restaurant, Brian said, "It seems as if His Excellency the Ambassador does not like you, dear brother."

"Yeah. It did seem that way, didn't it? Usually diplomats are more subtle than that."

"It appears that this particular diplomat is also an asshole. Or am I being redundant?"

Tom looked at his brother. "You, sir, have not a single diplomatic bone in your body. I see why you left the service."

"On Wall Street we don't put up with people like that."

"Oh, please, Brian. You Wall Street types will put up with anything and anyone, as long as they make you lots of money. Wall Street egos make this guy look like a minor leaguer." He laughed. "Yours, for instance."

"Hey, it ain't braggin' if you produce!"

"I rest my case," said Tom and they both laughed again. "Did you know that this particular diplomat just happens to be an ex-POW?"

"No way!"

"Yep. Don't be so surprised. He's not our first former POW ambassador. This guy flew F-4s."

"When did you find out this tidbit about our fat friend? And when did you plan on enlightening me?"

"Last night. The Defense Minister happened to mention it. And it's still pretty early in the day, Brian."

"So why in the world are you so adamant about not cooperating with the ambassador and not going to the Embassy?"

"I didn't come here to be wined and dined by a bunch of State Department flunkies, then led around by the nose wherever they want me to go. I want to get out there and find out what really happened."

"You don't really think there's a conspiracy or a cover-up of live Americans, do you? Our government isn't good at keeping secrets. It's been a hell of a long time, brother."

"I do not *know* if there has been a cover-up—a conspiracy if you will. It could be possible for reasons I can't begin to fathom."

"Tom, there are lots of people who believe in alien abductions. That doesn't mean you have to believe it."

"If you don't think we're going to find Pop, then why the hell are you here?"

"Because you're here, big brother. I want to help you find out whatever we can, to put this behind us, to bury our father. Or at least find out what happened to him. Then all of us, Mom included, can move on knowing that we did everything that we could. Besides," he said with a grin, "I'm really enjoying watching you in action. Last night, the Vietnamese Ministers. And this morning, I've never seen an ambassador outflanked like you just did. Takes real *cojones* to challenge The Man in his own backyard."

Tom made a dismissive gesture. "There's something about him that just doesn't ring true. Either he's got an overly developed ego—something not unique to the State Department, by the way—or he's up to something. Afraid I'll stumble across something."

Brian rubbed his chin. "Maybe."

Tom bent down and produced a gym bag. "Here, take these," he said as he handed Brian three cell phones. "They're pre-paid and untraceable."

Startled, Brian said, "Aren't these what drug lords use?"

Tom nodded.

"Just how close were you to the action down there in Bolivia?"

Tom slipped one phone in his pocket and zipped the bag. "Actually, it was Porter Nelson who told me about using these. He carries them on dangerous assignments when he's afraid his communications could be compromised."

Brian gave his brother a look. "I'm not sure I like your use of the phrase 'dangerous assignment,' Tom."

Chapter Nine
Nelson Residence, Georgetown

Porter Nelson sipped his wine as he prepared dinner. The young Seebass Vineyards Grand Reserve Chardonnay was perfect, exactly the right flavor to complement the Cornish game hens stuffed with lemon that were tonight's main course. He closed his eyes and savored the tastes and the smells wafting about his spacious kitchen.

The moment was lost as the phone rang. He cursed softly and glanced at the caller ID. He hated dinner interruptions. It was an anonymous number. He hesitated; then the investigative journalist in him took over. Anonymous tips had won Pulitzers for smart reporters.

"Hello?"

"Hi, Porter, this is Tom. Got a minute?"

Surprised, Porter glanced at the clock and did the arithmetic on the time differences between Hanoi and Washington. "You're up early, pal."

"Of course. You know me. Three miles every morning."

"Let me guess. Now you're sitting in the hotel gardens, surrounded by bougainvillea plants and sipping espresso."

"Actually, fresh squeezed orange juice and fresh croissants. But we digress, my friend."

"Okay, okay. So what can I do for my favorite fighter pilot?"

"Port, something here's totally irrational. The problem isn't what I'm doing, it's more who I am."

"Why should that matter?"

"That's just it. I don't know. The ambassador flipped out when he met me. First, he was all concerned about my safety, claiming bird flu was going to get me. Next, he tried to intimidate me into leaving. Then he threatened me. He denied me access to the digs."

"So you're stymied. Man, that's tough. All that way for nothing."

"No, actually I already had the Foreign Minister's permission to go anywhere I like."

Porter laughed, delighted. "Nicely done, Colonel! A classic Callahan move. Always ahead of the curve. I'll bet the ambassador's trying to get you declared *persona non grata* as we speak."

"Brian and I had a little altercation with persons unknown on our way over here."

Porter listened as Tom related the shooting at the ski area, the death of the deputy, and the disappearance of the prisoner.

"Remember the feeling you had in Germany a few years back?"

Porter felt a chill. "Yeah," he said, scarcely daring to breathe. Following that feeling in Germany had resulted in the murder of two close friends and the uncovering of a massive Soviet-East German plot to infiltrate the government of the United States.

"Well, I'm having it now and it scares me."

"No kidding. Any particular reason?"

"Nope. Perhaps I'm just paranoid after so long in Washington."

"Hey, just because you're paranoid doesn't mean there ain't someone out to getcha."

"Maybe the problem we found back then was bigger than we thought. I'm wondering if there might be a connection with my shooting and yours."

Porter let out a long breath. It seemed unlikely, but he had seen all sorts of unlikely scenarios materialize. And in Washington, hardly anything was unlikely except finding an honest politician.

"I didn't have much time to do research before coming over here," said Tom. "I'm going to an F-4 dig way down south in the morning. I'll be out of touch for a couple of days. Do you think you might be able to poke around a bit back there?"

"No problem. I'm just sitting on my butt trying to heal... I'm about eighty per cent right now."

"I wouldn't ask if it weren't so weird."

"Listen, buddy, always go with your intuition. I get kicked in the ass when I use my brain, but I win Pulitzers when I go with my gut. If you feel strange, it's probably strange. At least we can check it out."

"Okay. I think you should start with the Big Guy here. If you have time, perhaps a re-look at your first fourteener."

99

A curse ran through Porter's mind. *Callahan knows this isn't a secure line.* Porter scribbled down the clues. As he stalled, he asked, "Do you have lots of friends around you these days?"

"Yes. Everywhere I go."

"Tall ones or short ones?"

"Both."

Interesting. He was being followed by both Americans and Vietnamese. "Remember how I told you I communicated when I was in Europe last time?"

"That's what I'm doing now," said Tom.

"Good. Keep using that. Contact should be at our special time, Eastern." Porter thought some more. "Give me three days. And use our favorite State Department guy."

"Roger that."

"You need to take care of yourself. And remember to check six."

"Always."

Porter hung up, intrigued and worried. Tom Callahan wasn't the sort of man who got spooked.

Porter hurried to complete dinner preparation, then sat at his computer to cruise the Internet. Twenty minutes later, Robbie Robinson rang the doorbell.

Porter ushered him in, gave him a glass of the exquisite wine, and served dinner.

"Porter my boy, you've outdone yourself yet again." A confirmed bachelor, Robinson had somehow never learned how to cook. He was an enthusiastic, and frequent, visitor to Porter's kitchen, willing to try just about anything home-cooked.

"Callahan's spooked," Porter said, and related their conversation. "He wants me to check out the ambassador. Something's fishy in Hanoi. Callahan works for the President and appointed government officials don't usually cross swords with White House staffers. Especially senior ones. Meanwhile, I think you should check out Russia, especially rumors about POWs."

"I don't like this, Porter. I don't think he should be over there rattling cages. Especially now that this new Russian president is running amuck. Nearly everyone in Asia's skittish."

"I don't like it either, Robbie. I don't like the politics of the area, too many old animosities. The Chinese and the Vietnamese haven't been friendly for a long time. Hell, the Chinese invaded Vietnam in 1979. And both are scared shitless of the Russians right now."

Robinson took another bite of the hen and made appreciative sounds as he chewed. "Like a good portion of the world, the Vietnamese think that the United States is too strong, not to mention expansionist. But they also think the same about the Russians and the Russians are a hell of a lot closer geographically than we are. They don't like the Chinese, either, but are willing to play ball with them in order to counter the Russkies." He sipped his wine. "You're right, though. The Chinese are more than a little nervous about the Russians."

Porter cleared away the dishes leaving each man alone with his thoughts for a few minutes. As he served the after dinner liquors, Porter said, "Robbie, you need to know the rest. Tom asked me to re-examine at my first fourteener."

Robinson laughed. "What's a fourteener? A nooner with a teenager?"

"A fourteener, you dirty old man, is a mountain over fourteen thousand feet high. I have climbed all the ones in California and Colorado. Since I grew up in California, my first ascent was in the Sierra Nevadas—Mount Langley, named after the famous American aviation pioneer, Samuel Pierpont Langley. Langley, as in CIA Headquarters, Langley, Virginia."

***

The Vietnam Airlines flight touched down at Ho Chi Minh City's Ton Son Nhat International Airport, or as Tom knew it from his history, Ton Son Nhut Air Base. In 1956, the U.S. built a 7,200-foot runway in Saigon, from which USAF and U.S. Army planes and helicopters flew countless missions over South Vietnam. On April 30, 1975, the last flights of the Vietnam War took off in scenes of chaos watched in living rooms all over the world.

The discrepancy in the airport's current spelling was the result of the Southern Vietnamese dialect *Nhut* versus the Northern Vietnamese dialect *Nhat*. Since the north won the war, Nhat it became. Now Tan Son Nhat International Airport was the busiest airport in Vietnam, handling almost three times the flights of Hanoi's No Bai.

As Tom crossed Terminal 1 to catch his Vietnam Airlines flight to Pleiku, he spotted Angela Davidson towering over the mostly Vietnamese passengers. She greeted him with a smile and a hug.

"Sorry you had to travel down here to meet me, Tommy."

"No problem, sweetcakes. It made the day a bit longer but more interesting. And we can use the flight for you to brief me on the findings so far."

"We've had great weather at the site and we're hoping that it holds a bit longer. We're getting down to the wreckage now. Dr. Borgeson, our assistant anthropologist, is optimistic." She paused. "Tom, we've uncovered enough pieces to confirm that it was an F-4D like your father flew."

Tom digested that piece of information as the twin turboprop AT7 airliner taxied and took off. The short flight to Pleiku was uneventful and provided Tom with an opportunity to get a complete "how goes it" update from Angela about the dig and a closer look at the terrain in this part of Vietnam. They would be driving through the Annam Highlands that stretched north and south in an arc just west of Pleiku and between it and the nearby Cambodian and Laotian borders. Normally the JPAC teams traveled by helicopter, but the Vietnamese helicopter fleet was temporarily grounded due to a recent crash of a Mi-17 helicopter in foggy mountains southwest of Ho Chi Minh City.

They were met in Pleiku by two team member escorts, one American, one Vietnamese, who produced a Russian-made Vietnamese Army truck and loaded Tom's gear. The capital of Pleiku province, Pleiku sported tree-lined streets crowded with three-wheeled taxis and elegant French colonial style buildings interspersed with dilapidated tin-roofed homes. The city bustled with activity and seemed more free-spirited and relaxed than Hanoi.

Leaving the city proper, the terrain quickly gave way to rural Vietnam. The truck headed into the countryside, passed through jungle and the occasional village. The team settled back for the long drive through the sometimes difficult, terrain. They headed in a generally northwesterly direction towards the nearby Cambodian and Laotian borders. As the truck bounced and rattled in the rutted roads, Tom reflected again on the advantage of aircraft in terrain such as this. They arrived at the dig site in late afternoon. Tom was struck by the ordered chaos surrounding the work area. Tents were arranged so the Americans were on one side of the camp and the Vietnamese team was housed on the other. Supplies were stacked and organized for easy access. Tom knew that successful deployments into primitive conditions frequently turned on the quality of the logistics. The JPAC people knew what they were doing; the Vietnamese government typically assigned some of its best people to these missions because of the high visibility and prestige. And Tom knew Angela was a wizard at organization.

Tom had scarcely put his feet on the ground when a trim, almost handsome, Air Force officer approached and saluted. "Colonel, I am Major Roger Carver, the Detachment Two commander. Sir, the ambassador instructed me to tell you that you were not to be allowed access to this dig."

Tom was stunned. "What?" He thought the ambassador was smarter than that. "Major, why don't we take a walk?" The two men excused themselves from the rest of the team and walked slowly around the perimeter of the work area.

"Did the ambassador say this dig or all digs in-country?"

"All of them, but especially this one, sir."

Interesting, thought Tom. Why, especially, this dig? "Did he mention that I have the Foreign Minister's permission to go anywhere I like?"

"No sir, he did not, but Colonel Davidson did."

"Look, Major, I read your official biography online. Very impressive. More important, Angela says that you're one of the good guys. So I will stay out of your way. But this dig is the reason I am in Vietnam. Feel free to report my presence to the ambassador and tell him that I refuse to leave. He can discuss it with me when I get back to Hanoi." He stopped and looked Carver in the eyes. "I give you my word that I have the Foreign Minister's permission to be here. Check it out if you want."

"Colonel, I may not be a fighter jock, but I know who you are." He smiled for the first time. "I have discharged my duty to the ambassador. As one Air Force officer to another, how can I help you, sir?"

"Thank you, Roger." Tom offered his hand. "I would like a walk-through. Then I'll find something to do to keep out of your hair while the excavation continues."

"Pacific Command has funded the building of a school as partial payback to the village. You can help out there if you'd like."

"Great. I helped build some houses in Phoenix for Habitat for Humanity. I'm pretty handy with a hammer. I'll look around the site first, then head down to the village tomorrow morning."

Carver introduced the assistant anthropologist, Dr. Donald Borgeson, a thin, bearded black man on temporary duty from Adams State College in Colorado. Borgeson was clearly in his element as he scurried about the area. He explained that the space being worked was larger than normal because of the supposed low angle of impact. The clearing was staked into grids, worked one at a time. Dikes were built to hold back the groundwater and piles of mud surrounded the dig. Dozens of laborers moved through the site, local farmers dressed in what looked like black pajamas—wearing the ubiquitous conical hats, hired to perform the bulk of the digging. A bucket brigade steadily passed buckets of dirt and mud up the line to be sifted through quarter-inch wire mesh screens. Weeks of work had uncovered what, to Tom, seemed a significant area. As he watched, he was reminded of the pictures he saw in the Vietnam Memorial back in Angel Fire. He was escorted through the storage area where recovered pieces were kept. Most were small, twisted, and useless except to the archeologists. The site had been scavenged long ago for anything useable.

Tom could see that work at the site was controlled and steady and that he needed a broader view of the project. Spotting a nearby hill, he climbed up to the ridge. A constant breeze across the hilltop cooled him as he took in the panorama, listened to the sounds of the jungle, and surveyed the valley. He imagined the plane streaking in, ka-bam! The peaceful jungle shattered by the aircraft smashing into the earth, tearing through the trees, and disintegrating. Tom had investigated a few crashes, even witnessed one in Australia when a close friend and aerobatic performer crashed right at the airfield in front of the entire wing. Crash destruction ranged from light, like a broken landing gear or a bent wingtip, to total destruction, where the aircraft was reduced to unrecognizable pieces of twisted metal. Looking over the valley again, he could barely discern a gash in the foliage that ended at the dig site, a wound that had nearly, but not quite, healed. Somebody here bought the farm. This was a great big F-4 hole in the ground.

The next morning, while Tom helped in the framing of the school, he was summoned to the crash site. He walked through the excavation trenches, made his way over to the grid square, and looked down. Angela and a sergeant were at the bottom of a trench two meters below the surface. She beckoned for Tom to lower himself into the hole. "Look at this, Tommy," she said, pointing to a half-buried piece of twisted metal with two barely legible numbers.

Tom nearly choked. The last two numbers were "68," the last two tail numbers of his father's F-4. He collapsed to his knees and blinked back tears while his world narrowed down to the metal scrap. He slowly traced the numbers with his fingers, then covered his face.

"Tommy, are you okay?" asked Angela.

He tried to speak but nothing came out. He shook his head. Angela knelt next to him and slid her arm across his shoulders He fought back sobs. Now he was now face-to-face with the hard fact of his father's downed aircraft. It was no longer a dark childhood fable. It was reality.

Tom watched the work for two more days, not sure what he wanted the workers to uncover. Was his father in this hole? Typically, MIA families expected or hoped for a full skeleton. That was not going to happen with this kind of crash. A tooth, or shards of bone or skull would be more like it.

Late in the morning on the third day, there was another flurry of activity with a major find. The team probed deeper and uncovered the compressed, twisted remains of the cockpit area. The remaining question was if the cockpits contained intact ejection seats, or showed the scrapes and scorching of the ejection sequence as the Martin-Baker seats launched their occupants into the air. Tom knew about ejection seats. As an exchange instructor pilot with the Royal Australian Air Force, he had survived a low-level ejection from a Mirage III over a dusty gunnery range.

Work continued all afternoon on excavating the forward section of the aircraft. Tom, Angela, and most of the staff gathered around the trench to watch Dr. Borgeson personally scratch through the hard subsoil. He would periodically ask one or another of the team's technical experts to join him in the trench. Finally, he asked Tom and Major Carver to drop in. "Colonel, as you can see, there are no ejection seats here. Therefore, the occupants of this aircraft ejected before the aircraft impacted the ground."

So Pop and his backseater got out. Tom covered his eyes and murmured a brief prayer. His father had been alive going down. Then what? Was he wounded or killed in the ejection? Was he captured and killed by villagers? Was he tortured and killed by Viet Cong? Was he starved? Was he shot?

Or was he still alive somewhere?

***

Brian Callahan sat enjoying the early morning sunshine, surrounded by bougainvillea, his laptop computer, the morning papers, and the remains of a delicious breakfast from the Hotel Sofitel Metropole's exquisite restaurant. Since Tom had disappeared into the Vietnamese countryside, Brian had been working hard at the Foreign Ministry, sorting through dull after-action reports from "The American War." He compensated for an unhappy day's work by starting off the morning enjoying a brisk run, a long hot shower, and a leisurely continental breakfast. Then Elizabeth had called and they had a long chat.

"Bye, Elizabeth. I love you, too."

He disconnected his cell phone and looked up from his paper to see a Vietnamese Air Force officer standing at attention.

The officer saluted. "I am Major Tran. I have been assigned to escort you around Hanoi," he said in fluent French.

Brian made a gesture that vaguely resembled a salute. Great, he thought. Another damned spy to follow me around. "Thank you, Major, but I don't need an escort. I go to the archives and I read all day. Not fun. So I don't need you watching me. Excuse me, *escorting* me."

The major did not move. He gave Brian a look that could have been either hatred or anger. "I don't want to be here, either."

"Oh?"

"My father was killed by you Americans."

Brian stood. "I am sorry for your loss, Major. It seems we have something in common." He offered his hand. Reluctantly, the major shook it. Brian motioned for him to sit and instructed the waiters to serve more coffee and croissants.

"So, who did you piss off?" asked Brian.

"W-what?" said the major, gagging on his coffee.

"Who did you piss off to get stuck with nursemaid-ing me around Hanoi?"

Brian caught the first hint of a smile, but got no answer.

"Hey, Tran, my brother's the big-wig. You can talk to me, I'm only a major. Actually, I'm really a civilian in uniform. I resigned my commission years ago."

"I was chosen because I speak French and Russian."

"*Pochemu zanimalsya v Russii?*" Brian asked.

The major answered in Russian. "I was in Russia for pilot training. I am a fighter pilot as well."

Brian regarded the major with new respect. "That training must have been a bitch. It was hard enough for me in English."

107

The major nodded. "Yes, it was difficult. It was a gift from the Party for my father's service. It allowed me to study abroad and become an officer. It has been good for my family."

"Plus you get to fly jets, right? For me, flying was the ultimate kick in the pants."

The major laughed. "Yes. Much better than pushing a plow." They both laughed.

"So, what did you fly?" asked Brian.

"I flew MiG-21s for ten years, what your NATO calls the Fishbed-J." With pride in his voice he said, "Then I moved up to the Su-27SK Flanker."

Brian knew them both. Even after years of civilian life, he could remember most of the details of many enemy aircraft, the product of long hours of study and combat simulation. "The MiG-21 was a good plane in its day," he said. "A bit of a truck with short legs, but solid. The Flanker is a beauty, wicked fast, too. I've flown against it in exercises with the Indian Air Force."

Major Tran looked surprised. "I was told that you were a money maker, a capitalist, not a warrior."

"That's right," said Brian. "I am a true running-dog capitalist lackey. But before that, I flew the F-15C Eagle for almost six years, all here in Asia. But I never made it to your country. I'm quite impressed with your people." He picked up the *Financial Times*. "So, Tran, look at this. It says here that your country is a big-time producer of offshore oil. Thirty per cent of your national budget is petroleum sales from a joint venture with British Petroleum." He looked up from the paper. "Smart of you guys to bring in the Brits as partners. They certainly know about offshore drilling."

"There are those in our government who favor the Russians because of their oil expertise."

"So I've seen. I've met more than a few admirers of the Russians since I've been here. I also hear that there are those in your government who hate and fear the Russians for their arrogance and their new power."

Tran's eyes narrowed.

"Hey, Tran, relax. I'm not a spy. I am a simple capitalist pig who is here to find out what happened to his father." Brian raised his right hand, "I promise not to put you on the spot like that again. But for the record, I don't trust the Russians. Never have. And my mother's parents were born in St. Petersburg."

Major Tran considered that statement for a moment. "Since I now know that you are an aviator, would you care to visit the Air Museum, Major? We can swing by on our way to the Foreign Ministry archives."

"Great idea! My brother's out in the boondocks breathing fresh air while I sit in a bomb shelter reading through file cabinets." He slapped the table. "Let's do it. On the condition that you call me Brian."

The Vietnamese Air Force museum was an informal affair, open air and tucked away in an average neighborhood, surrounded by a simple chain-link fence. The main museum was dominated by helicopters, some huge Russian ones that Brian had never actually seen before but vaguely remembered reading about. As far as he was concerned, helicopters were in the "target" category. There were multiple MiGs, from 15s to 21s, many with placards describing battles fought, the "heroic" pilots' names, dates of engagements, even tail numbers and types of American planes shot down. Brian looked in vain for the tail numbers of his father's F-4D.

"Tran, the English translations on these placards are really bad. You should talk to the museum directors and fix them. This place is too important to have something sloppy like that."

"My English is not good enough."

Brian said, "I'll help you. In fact, tell you what. I'll help you with your English if you work on my Vietnamese. I speak reasonable Chinese and Japanese, so my brain's wired for tonal languages. I might as well go home with a mental souvenir of my visit here."

The men wandered around the compound, talking aircraft and flying. Tran proudly pointed out various aircraft and filled in details: a captured A-37 that was used to drop bombs on Saigon; an A-1 Skyraider without a propeller, but with folded wings and a flat tire; a cockpit panel from an F-4C; and a captured UH-1 Huey, sporting Vietnamese markings. Brian's favorite was the front section of a MiG-21 set up for

109

visitors to sit in the cockpit. He made Tran take his picture using Brian's cell phone, then e-mailed the picture back to Elizabeth.

At the Foreign Ministry, they settled in to sift through papers brought in by a team of assistants who kept bringing drawers full of documents to stack in front of Brian's workspace. For a solid week, they read through thousands of report stacks searching for any references to U.S. Air Force shoot-downs. It was dull, tedious work. Tran and a host of clerks assisted, but Brian still felt like a medieval monk, locked away, searching for evidence of the Holy Grail.

Classification levels were routinely ignored by the Vietnamese, which provided Brian's only excitement. Brian also kept notes on any other sightings or captures that would be of interest to the JPAC research wizards.

Many of the files were in Russian; some were in French. All the originals were in Vietnamese, which did Brian no good at all. Occasionally he checked with Major Tran about a Russian word or phrase since the text was technical and formal. Brian's Russian vocabulary was more extensive than Tran's and his accent was native, but Tran did know his official Russian government jargon.

Occasionally, they would just talk, about their families, their careers, the weather. Brian persuaded Tran to take him to lunch at his favorite local restaurants. Tran acted as guide and host; Brian paid the check, knowing that what Tran made in a month wouldn't pay Brian's electric bill at home. He treated Tran's wife and eight-year old son to dinner at the hotel restaurant as partial payback for keeping Tran so busy.

At the end of the week, Brian presented Tran with a gift-wrapped box. "Elizabeth sends her regards and wants me to give you this for putting up with me all this time."

Surprised, Tran stammered his thanks as he methodically peeled away the paper, a grin on his face. "It's not necessary, Brian, but thank you."

Brian said, "I remembered that I flew the Su-27 in a flight simulator video game, years ago. I called my wife. Thanks to our friends at FedEx, here it is. This is the updated version with killer graphics. It's in Russian. The air-to-air combat scenes are staged over the Crimea. Pretty realistic, too. So, if you want, you can bring your family for dinner at my hotel again. We'll hook this up to my computer, and show your son what his daddy can do."

Tran turned the box over and over, reading and re-reading all the details like a kid at Christmas. He looked overwhelmed. "This is very kind of you, Brian."

"Not really," Brian said with a chuckle. "I bought two joysticks. I plan on going one-on-one with you and waxing your fanny."

Late in the afternoon of the eighth day of Tom's trip, Brian found himself staring once again at the walls of his small office in the Foreign Ministry, thinking about an early morning phone call from Tom. His brother was heading to another village-with-no-name to investigate yet another reported sighting of an American in the jungle. Brian was increasingly concerned that this mission, which he had dubbed "Tom's Quest" was in danger of becoming "Tom's Obsession."

Brian's reverie was interrupted when one of the Ministry's functionaries, who had been feeding them reports, slipped into the room and, with a small bow, informed Brian that Gunnery Sergeant Johanssen needed to speak with him. Brian liked the gunny, especially after Tom related how Johanssen's quick thinking had saved the lives of at least two Marines after the terrorist bombing of the Marine House in La Paz four years ago. Too bad he had to work for such a prick here in Hanoi.

Brian found Johanssen pacing the capacious foyer.

"What's up, Gunny?" he asked, offering his hand.

"Major Callahan, the ambassador insists on seeing you this afternoon, sir."

"Why does he think I'll come to the Embassy when my brother's already refused?"

Gunny Johanssen looked embarrassed. "Sir, your brother is, well, your brother."

"You mean that he's a White House colonel and I'm not."

"Something like that, sir."

"Well, Gunny, you're going to have to do better than that. I don't have time to argue right now. I'm on my way to a bit of a soirée, if you

111

will. A late afternoon meeting with the senior staff that is a disguised happy hour. You can tag along. We can discuss the ambassador afterwards."

The "soirée" was well under way as Brian led his group into the Ministry reception room. The teak floor, colonial French furniture, lazy ceiling fans, and a massive teak bar gave the room a sense of intimacy, reminding Brian of cozy senior executive haunts in New York. The Foreign Ministry was riddled with military officers, especially at the senior levels. Brian counted five senior officer/diplomats and a few of the defense staff clustered around the bar, mingling with Foreign Ministry professionals. Brian was always amazed at how foreign diplomats sucked down Johnny Walker Black; judging from the number of bottles on the bar, this group was no different. One man, a Lieutenant General Nguyen, whom Brian thought of as a dried-up little gnome, sounded as if he was out in front of the rest by at least two drinks. Nguyen spoke in French, which meant that he either did not care that the Americans heard him, or he was sending a message to them.

"Our country is backsliding into capitalism. The people have been corrupted by the West. They have forgotten the attributes of a true communist state. Contact with the West has had a corrosive effect on the revolution."

Tran was clearly embarrassed, Johanssen angry. Brian bit his tongue and tried to be polite as the old man worked himself into a true communist lather.

"Capitalist economic dogma is everywhere, and weakening the Party. We need more central control, not less!"

Two minutes later, Brian had had enough. "General, you have no idea what you're talking about."

The general took a swallow of his drink, swiveled his head toward Brian and sneered. "What would a capitalist know about true communist economic thought?"

"I know that it has never worked, not even once, anywhere in the world. Ever. It cannot work, either, because it ignores basic human nature. If you really believe what you're saying, you are living in a fantasy world."

112

Nguyen glared at Brian. "We have done well since we defeated you."

Brian shook his head. "Not true, General. After your country won the 'American War,' Vietnam adopted the Soviet communist economic model. You collectivized farms and repressed private businesses. You wrecked the economy and drove tens of thousands of your people away in boats."

The general stood. "They were counter-revolutionaries!"

"Wrong!" Brian held his eyes. "They were some of your best people, the ones who wanted to work, who wanted something better. Those people made it to Singapore, some made it to the United States. They established whole villages, started businesses, sent their kids to some of the best universities in the world. Miraculous results. And all the while, Vietnam's economy was in the toilet. When the Soviets turned off their subsidies because of their own economic disaster, your country nearly imploded. You had famine. You had people dying in the streets." Brian paused. "Vietnam had to institute market-based reforms to turn loose the creativity of your own people. If you hadn't, everyone here would be simply living in a warmer version of North Korea.

"You want to do what all command economies want to do: consolidate power in the hands of the Party elite, meaning you and your buddies. You would annihilate the productive markets so that the country depends more on the government. Or, in reality, the Party. Again, meaning you and your buddies."

"All assets of the State belong to the People. You cannot talk to us like that!"

"Maybe I shouldn't, but I certainly can." Brian started to walk out, then turned back to face the general. "Listen, pal, if you and your commie brothers nationalize any industry or international holdings, Vietnam will become an international pariah in the world money markets. Your country's commercial paper will be worthless, no bond trader anywhere will touch your notes. Then foreign investment here will wilt like an old man's dick. Now that, General, *is* something you probably know all about!"

113

Brian stalked out of the room, trailed by Tran and a shocked Gunnery Sergeant Johanssen.

Tran said, "General Nguyen is a hardliner."

"No kidding."

"His family was killed by the southern criminals aided by your country."

Brian turned to face his friend. "Look, Tran, nearly everyone in your country, north and south, lost someone in that damned war. So did a lot of Americans. That's why my brother and I are here. That's why those teams of ours, American and Vietnamese, are scouring the countryside looking for bones and pieces of planes to help people get on with their lives. We're all in this. We need to get past the past."

He took a deep breath. "Where the hell is my brother?"

Chapter Ten
Near the Vietnam-Cambodian border

Tom Callahan sat in the passenger seat of an ancient Vietnamese Army jeep-like utility vehicle as he and his two Vietnamese escorts snaked their way through the humid haze of the jungle. With the sun well up, they passed through yet another village. The locals paused and stared as the procession motored through. The countryside glowed in the early morning sunshine; carts and small vans plowed along the dirt track; people tending rice dotted the nearby fields; a few high clouds were strewn across the azure sky. Another day in the Asian jungle, gorgeous, he thought, except for the dread of what might be found at the end of the journey.

A sixty kilometer drive over a crowded rutted dirt road was the final leg of the trek to a remote village rumored to shelter an American. Tom watched thunderclouds boil up on the distant horizon, could smell the rain coming. As the vehicle lurched over the rutted streak of a road, he thought that the day would not end well for any aviators in the local area. None of this did anything to improve his temper, ragged now after two days of driving, alone with his thoughts and his fears.

Finally, the trees thinned and they saw the village where the road turned along the edge of the valley. It looked so peaceful now, a collection of huts alongside an irrigation ditch, the ubiquitous rice paddies in the background. The villagers stood and watched in silence as the vehicle proceeded.

The driver stopped in what passed as the village plaza, more of a wide, open area surrounded by a cluster of small houses. Tom gazed around, as curious about the village as the locals were about him. Was his father here in this collection of huts? Or was the rumored American a friend of his father's? Someone who might know what had happened to Sean Callahan? Or was this just another dead end?

An elderly man wearing, what Tom had come to regard as the peasant's uniform of black pajamas stepped forward out of the crowd. Tom's interpreter, a young Vietnamese Air Force lieutenant named

Phan, introduced Tom to the village mayor with much bowing and respect while the entire village moved in to hear the exchanges.

Phan seemed confused by the mayor's answers and apparently repeated his original questions. Heads bobbed and arms waved as villagers crowded around the mayor.

The interpreter took a deep breath, then turned to Tom. "I'm sorry, Colonel. The mayor says that there was an American here for many years but he died three days ago. In a fall."

The news hit Tom harder than he expected. So close. So close!

"Ask the mayor what happened to the body."

Lieutenant Phan said, "Most of the villagers are Catholic. The village has two cemeteries; one Buddhist, one Catholic. The American was buried in the Catholic cemetery. The mayor wants to escort us. So do many of the people. Your American was quite popular in the village."

They were led along a narrow path lined with more villagers to a small cemetery on a nearby rise. Tom stared down at the fresh-turned earth marked with a simple cross, covered with flowers. His emotions churned and he felt light-headed. His legs buckled and he knelt beside the grave. He searched his mind for a prayer and a saint and settled on St. Jude, the Patron Saint of Lost Causes. St. Jude's specialty was "causes despaired of"—certainly this expedition fit the category. Tom had never prayed to St. Jude before, but it certainly seemed appropriate now.

He finished his prayer and settled back on his haunches staring at the grave to sort through his surging emotions and his options. Now what?

Out of the corner of his eye, he noticed a middle-aged woman push her way to the edge of the silent crowd, pulling another, younger, prettier woman with her. She stood, eyes cast down and respectful of his mourning but blocking his exit.

Tom stood, faced the two women, and gave a slight bow. He motioned to Phan and said, "Ask these ladies what they want from me."

The village elder stepped forward and introduced them to Phan. The interpreter looked surprised and confused. Questions flew; the elder became quite voluble.

Phan was embarrassed. "Colonel, the mayor says these women are the American's wife and daughter."

The intensity of his reaction surprised Tom. This is what Porter warned me about, he thought. The past is often better left alone. He fought his emotions and maintained his composure as he regarded the two women. The "wife" was of indeterminate age, about five-foot-two and maybe a hundred pounds, but she had steel in her eyes. The "daughter," who appeared to be about eighteen, had classic Eurasian features, smooth skin, and gorgeous dark eyes.

The woman spoke.

Phan translated, "She says her husband was an American Air Force pilot, shot down and wounded near the end of the war. Her husband's name was Thomas and that his family had come from Ireland."

Tom's father's middle name was Thomas. He stood there in the hot afternoon sun, his stomach churned. Sweat poured off his nose, ran down his neck, and stained his shirt. It was all he could do to keep from puking. Oh sweet Jesus, is this my sister?

The woman stepped closer and slowly, reluctantly, handed Tom a small parcel that contained something she regarded as precious. Tom gave a slight bow of thanks, then slowly unwrapped it.

It was his father's West Point ring.

Oh God! How was he going to deal with this? Another wife for his father? A half-sister for him? He felt like screaming. How could Pop do this to us?

Tom turned the ring over and over in his hand. Something was wrong. He looked closer. Class of 1960! He looked inside the ring. Engraved inside was the name Thomas Anthony Kinkaid.

Wrong class! Wrong Irishman!

Tom's self-control vanished in a flash. He sobbed, then covered his eyes. The Vietnamese woman peered up at him and touched his arm. Tom took another gulp of air and forced himself to calm down. He pulled out his handkerchief and rubbed his face, trying to think.

He turned to Phan. "She knows that this ring was as precious to her husband as it is to us. Give her my thanks for her sacrifice. Tell her that I cannot guarantee that she will get it back, but that I will do my best for her and her daughter. We will send some people here from the United States to talk with them."

An hour later, Tom was in his vehicle, headed back to Hanoi. He had the all-important ring in his pocket, safely wrapped for its journey back to the Western world. It would ignite a firestorm in the States, proof positive that at least one American serviceman had survived, despite repeated denials from the CIA and State Department. Tom wondered how many more Americans might be isolated in the dense Vietnamese jungle.

He would report this finding. Then what? Who had claim on the remains? The United States? The American family? Or the Vietnamese women who had clearly loved the man? Tom remembered the searing pain he had felt when he thought that his own father had had another family. Should that be inflicted upon any unsuspecting Kinkaids back home?

On the other hand, the name Thomas Anthony Kinkaid would now be recognized as perhaps the last casualty of the Vietnam War. He had been dealt a crummy hand, and he'd played it the best he could. Who was Tom Callahan, or anybody else, to say he should have stayed faithful to his American family? The man died without seeing them again. This Vietnamese family probably brought him some joy. Let JPAC make the announcement of the finding and let the chips fall. If there was a problem, so be it.

Still, Tom was troubled by his feeling of relief that this would be a Kinkaid problem, not a Callahan one.

***

Porter Nelson glanced at his watch for the tenth time in five minutes. If Tom Callahan was going to call, he'd call in the next sixty seconds or not at all. He sipped the incredible cabernet provided by his host, Ambassador George Brent. Despite his efforts at self-control, he peeked at his watch again.

"Just like old times, isn't it, Porter?" Brent said with something between sympathy and excitement.

Porter nodded. Ambassador Brent was one of the three people in Washington whom he truly admired, along with Tom and Colleen Callahan. Not quite five years before, the ambassador had sent Tom Callahan into the Bolivian jungles to find and save an unknown and unnamed American journalist, a rescue that Porter felt he could never repay. Later, Porter had helped them uncover a ring of Soviet spies embedded within the United States government, along the way winning his second Pulitzer. Now, it looked as if they were in it again.

The phone jangled; Nelson nearly dropped his wine glass.

"Hello, Thomas. Prompt as always," said Brent. "We were hoping you'd call tonight. Let me put you on speakerphone."

"Hi, Tom, it's Porter."

"And Robbie," chimed in Robbie Robinson.

"Hi, guys."

"We have quite a lot to tell you, Thomas. Perhaps it would be better if you spoke first," said Ambassador Brent.

None of the men interrupted as Tom told the story of the American who had survived in the jungle. "I have the ring in my pocket. Porter, please check out Thomas Anthony Kinkaid's story. If it's true, that should shut up those clowns at Langley and Foggy Bottom."

"Okay. I'll get on it tomorrow morning. Sorry it doesn't get you any closer to your dad, but it does prove our theory, doesn't it?"

Ambassador Brent leaned forward. "Excuse me, Thomas, but what is the significance of a ring from West Point? Wouldn't that mean Kincaid was an Army officer?"

"No, sir. The Air Force was formed from the Army Air Corps in 1947. Many of the original Air Force officers were West Point grads. The Air Force didn't even have its own academy until the first class graduated in 1959. Until then, grads from both West Point and Annapolis could be commissioned in the Air Force, instead of the Army or Navy. My father did. So it seems did Kinkaid."

Ambassador Brent said, "Thank you. Now I understand. Although how Kinkaid managed to hold on to his ring is beyond me."

"Yes, sir. It just shows that the POWs were not just courageous and heroic, they were ingenious as well."

Brent nodded to Porter.

"That will be one hell of a story, Tom. Can't wait to write it. In the meantime, Robbie and I have more stories for you. How much time do you have?"

"I'm out here in the boonies on my way back to Hanoi. Just left the largest village for fifty miles. I had my vehicle pull over so I could make this call on time. Give me everything."

"Tom, this is Robbie. There were certainly Russian interrogators in North Vietnam during the war. Cubans, too, but that's another issue. More important, the Soviets had a trophy group, or *spetsgruppa,* composed of GRU intelligence officers assigned to Vietnam to acquire American combat equipment and arrange for shipment back home for exploitation. We found reports that some Americans were selectively chosen to go along as well to show the Soviets how to use the equipment."

"I knew most of that."

"Yes, but Tom, here's more information to put this all in context."

Robbie paused and looked at Porter.

"Hey, guys, I don't know what it's like back in Washington, but I'm standing here cooking in the jungle."

Porter jumped in. "Tom, you were right. Big Boy, a.k.a. Ambassador Billingsley, is a former POW. Shot down in late 1972 near Cambodia. Guess what type of aircraft."

"F-4s. I knew that. So were a lot of guys."

"No, Tom, guess who was the commanding officer of his unit."

Silence. Then a tentative, "My father?"

"Give the man a shiny balloon. And guess who was along for the ride when your father got shot down?"

"What! No way. The names don't match. Pop's backseater was named Paul Anders."

"Actually, Tom, he was born Paul Billingsley Anders. Both his parents were Minnesota high society. Apparently, Daddy was a hero in

120

WWII, a big-shot Republican, and a number one asshole. After our future ambassador graduated from Yale, Daddy gave him a choice: join the military or be written out of the will. While Big Boy was in Vietnam, Daddy dropped dead from a stroke, so our Yalie had his inheritance waiting when he was repatriated. After cashing the check, he dropped his last name and now uses his mother's maiden name, Billingsley, as his own."

"Son of a bitch!"

"That's what I thought, my friend."

"Why would he keep that from me? And why does he want me out of the country so much?"

"Good questions all, *mon Colonel*. We've had some time to ponder these and other ideas, Tom, and we still have no clue. But it's obvious that he doesn't want you there for some reason... Maybe because he's hiding something?"

"Of course he's hiding something." A pause. "Any records of where he was captured or held? When he got to Hanoi? Did he even get to the Hilton? Where was he interrogated, and by whom?"

"Those records are hazy," said Robbie. "He said he was held in South Vietnam for some weeks, then hustled up the Ho Chi Minh Trail to North Vietnam and turned over just before the repatriation. The debriefers said he had been beaten, but looked pretty healthy otherwise. They attributed his robust appearance to the fact that he had been overweight before he went down and hadn't actually been a prisoner too long."

"Or he was treated pretty well for some reason," said Tom, "then beaten just before being turned back over. For credibility."

Ambassador Brent signaled to Porter that he wanted to speak next. "Thomas," he said, "after Porter's revelations about Anders/Billingsley, I managed to get a copy of his personnel file. He has had a rather spectacular career. Good assignments, excellent evaluations, several prestigious awards, all the right professional schools."

"Let me guess: one or two assignments that he just seemed to fall into, right? Just like your deputy in Bolivia?"

"Precisely."

121

Tom, Porter, and Robbie had uncovered the presence of Soviet "moles" scattered throughout the U.S. government. One of the first was Patricia Pointer, Ambassador Brent's Deputy Chief of Mission (DCM) in the U.S. Embassy in Bolivia. Tom and Robbie had been involved in subsequent FBI investigations that had uncovered several more Soviet, now Russian, agents within the government.

"Which means that our friends in the FBI missed a few moles," said Tom, disgusted.

"It appears so. At least one," agreed Brent.

Tom said, "If Billingsley is what you seem to think, and I am inclined to agree, there is a Russian connection in all this." He paused. "Okay. Great work, guys. You keep digging and I'll keep pushing. We'll see what happens next."

"Yeah. But Tom, this could get pretty nasty," said Porter.

"It will, when I punch out the ambassador."

"Thomas, be careful," said Brent. "Ambassador Billingsley has more contacts in Vietnam than you do. Not to mention the embassy security detail." He paused. "Should I report this to the President?"

"No, George, not yet. He might call me home."

"What about Colleen?"

A pause while Tom thought this over. "Use your judgement, Port. I need to get going now. I don't have much time for a long explanation."

Porter had another thought. "Tom, are they still following you?"

"Yeah. Everywhere I go."

"Tom, remember that there are factions within the CIA and the State Department that are furious that you are over there. Now that the Russians may be tied in, when you return with that ring it's really going to hit the fan. We're talking major scandal, with potential international ramifications."

"It won't be our first, will it, Port?"

Tom snapped the cell phone closed. He fought the urge to throw the damned thing into the ditch half-filled with muddy water that separated him from the men in the jeep. He had rarely been this angry. He needed to get a grip on his temper before he did something really stupid. He crossed the narrow footbridge and turned back towards the waiting jeep. Three steps later, the vehicle exploded in a huge red and orange fireball, followed by a black pillar of smoke. The concussion knocked him off his feet. His body flew backwards, turned over twice, smashed down on the muddy embankment, and slid into the muddy ditch.

Chapter Eleven
Hotel Sofitel Metropole Hanoi

Brian Callahan, sweaty and tired from his early morning run, opened the door to his room. Something was different. He felt a chill, despite his overheated state. Tom had warned him to be careful and taught him some rudimentary, "James Bond-like," spy field craft. By now, Brian was used to being followed around Hanoi, but this was different. This was his *room*.

He scanned the suite and walked carefully through the living area. In his own room, he saw two dossiers on his bed, just like the thousands he had read over the past week.

Where had they come from? Brian looked around again, checked the bathroom and closets. He closed, locked, and bolted the door. Satisfied that there was nobody in the suite, he returned to his bedroom and the dossiers. He picked one up and scanned through the documents. Almost all were in Russian, many with official stamps and signatures. All were classified, some with classification levels that he didn't even recognize. Holy cow, he thought, this is hot. He settled down in his chair and spread the papers on his desk. The documents clearly spelled out Russian involvement with the North Vietnamese military from the early 1960s through the end of the war. Details about Russian units taking equipment and POWs back to Russia, Russian military officers teaching interrogation techniques, even authorizations for active involvement interrogating American POWs. It was a compilation of exactly what Brian had been searching for.

The second folder contained clippings from American periodicals and newspapers, summaries of POW hearings from the Congressional Record, even Internet sites, some of which Tom had told him about, others unfamiliar. Someone or some group in the Vietnamese government was actively tracking American inquiries into the POW issue. "They" were watching who was watching them. Interesting.

These papers had been hidden for decades, even from his now own officially sanctioned eyes. He could be fried for having these classified folders in his personal possession. That realization launched an avalanche of ideas. He looked around. Whoever left these docs could have just as easily shot him instead. Another chill. Oh man, I'm getting paranoid.

His cell phone rang. "Hello?"

"Brian, it's Tom. Have you used this phone?"

"Yeah. Tom, you wouldn't believe what just happened—"

"Go to Number Two phone." The phone went dead.

Brian scrambled for his gym bag to intercept a ringing from deep in his socks. Cursing, he peeled away the clothing. "Hey."

Tom spoke in cryptic Italian. "Someone just tried to kill me."

"How? Why?"

"They blew up my jeep. If I hadn't stopped to make a phone call to Porter, I would have been sailing merrily down the road, then boom! Dead, along with my men. As it was, I landed in a ditch and nearly drowned."

"Jesus, Tom! What's going on? I just got in from a run. Someone was in my room while I was gone. Left a packet of papers, mostly in Russian. Proof, Tom, the Russians were taking equipment and POWs back to Russia."

"That checks with what Robbie just told me. Watch yourself. Here's something else. Ambassador Billingsley's real last name was Anders. He was Pop's backseater."

"What? That son of a bitch!"

"Yeah, my reaction, too, brother. Trust me on this one, Brian. You need to get out of there. Right now. Don't wait even five minutes."

"Where are you?"

"Don't worry about me. I'll be there tomorrow or the next day. You know where to go. Move it, Brian!" The phone went dead.

Brian grabbed his suitcases, threw them on the bed and stuffed in his clothes. Yuck, he thought, I'm all slimy. I'm going to take a shower first. He stripped and took a shower brief enough for even a hard-pressed Academy basic cadet.

Dripping and wearing a towel, he emerged from the bathroom. Gunnery Sergeant Johanssen stood in the bedroom holding a pistol.

Startled, Brian said, "Gunny, what the hell are you doing here? How did you even get in?"

"Where's Colonel Callahan?"

"He's not here. What are you doing in my room?"

Gunnery Sergeant Johanssen did not answer. He looked in the closet, then walked back into the living area. "I need to find the colonel."

"You'll have to go through me to get to him," said Brian, grabbing his pants. He looked closer at the Marine. "Jesus, Gunny, you look like hell. What's the matter?"

Johanssen holstered his Beretta then slumped into a chair.

"I've been up all night." He took a deep breath. "Major, you and your brother are in danger. The ambassador really hates your brother."

"I noticed."

"I overheard him talking to some people in Russian. He didn't think I could understand. He wants you gone, 'taken care of,' he said. And he doesn't care how. I came to warn your brother."

"And you know this how?"

Johanssen leaned forward and ran his hands over his tired-looking face. "Part of my duties are to act as the ambassador's bodyguard. I go with him on trips. Sometimes he tries to slip away from me."

"To meet somebody?"

Johanssen nodded. "So I followed him a couple times. He's not nearly as clever as he thinks he is." He accepted a glass of water from Brian.

"He's met with two different guys that I know of. Both Caucasians. Never seen either of them before. But I seen one of them later at a Russian Embassy function. I think he's Federal Security Service. That's the KGB under a new name, Major." He drained the glass.

"Sir, I worked with your brother in Bolivia for over a year. The things he did for me and my Marines was way past 'above and beyond.' If half the rumors I heard about what he did with Ambassador Brent and the Military Group in Bolivia are true, he's a solid gold hero in my book." His face reddened in embarrassment. "What you said to that

126

Vietnamese general showed me you are as tough as your brother. Your father must have been one hell of a man. I want to help you find out what happened to him."

Oh shit, I am way over my head. "Gunny, my brother trusts you. He says you're one of the good guys and he doesn't say that very often."

Johanssen brightened and sat up straighter.

"I'll have to go with what I think Tom would want." He pulled on a shirt. "Somebody tried to kill him this morning."

"Damn it! See, I told you, Major."

Brian stumbled as he tried to put on his shoes. "Tom told me to get out of here."

"Where are you going?"

Brian paused. "Don't ask."

Johanssen stood. "You said the colonel trusts me. So can you."

Chapter Twelve
Potomac View Condominium - Georgetown

Porter Nelson eased his automobile under the elaborate portico just as Robbie Robinson emerged from the foyer. Robbie took one look at the vehicle, a new silver Aston Martin DB9 Volante convertible, and shook his head in admiration.

"No longer loyal to the folks at Lamborghini?"

"Thought I'd go cross Channel for a try with the British," laughed Porter. "I got a good deal on this one. Jeez, Robbie, I needed some wheels, fast."

"I suspect these are fast wheels," chuckled Robbie. He settled into the leather passenger seat and gave a sigh. "It does feel good, Porter."

"Beats riding the bus, my friend."

The Callahans lived a few miles away in a graceful section of Georgetown renowned for its lavishly restored colonial homes. Porter maneuvered through the quiet, tree-lined streets as the men enjoyed the feel of the new car.

Robinson got out of Porter's car and walked up the drive to the house, a lovely old Georgetown colonial with a five-foot-high brick fence surrounding almost two acres of elaborate gardens filled with old maple and cherry trees.

He studied the house, especially the roof. "Good job. I can't see anything to give it away."

"Give what away?"

"To look at this gorgeous old house you wouldn't know there's a high tech safe room in it."

"What's a safe room?"

Robinson smirked. "The concept is simple enough even for a guy like you, Porter. It's a secure room within the interior of the home, where the family can retreat during a home invasion and summon help. Loaded with multiple access routes to the room, small radio transmitters pre-keyed to the police, and audible alarms to alert even the dumbest intruders that the cavalry is on the way. All this in a house that looks like Thomas Jefferson could walk out the front door at any time. In fact, Old TJ actually lived a couple of blocks from here when he was Secretary of State. Pretty cool, if I do say so."

"How come I didn't know about this room and you did?"

"Because, dummy, it's supposed to be secret. The only reason I'm telling you now is because Tom told me to watch out for his family."

Porter punched in a code; the metal gate swung open and the men walked up the cobblestone path.

The massive oak front door swung open. "Hello, I'm Elizabeth Callahan."

Porter's first thought was that her stunning auburn hair would be perfect for a shampoo commercial. "Hi, I'm Porter Nelson, this is Robbie Robinson. I'm sorry for staring, but I was expecting Colleen."

"She's in the library. I'm just visiting."

Any further attempts at adult conversation were halted as a small whirlwind exploded down the hallway. "Uncle Porter!"

"Hi ya, Mikey!" Porter said as he snatched the boy up and held him over his head. "How's my favorite soccer star?"

Mikey squealed in delight as Porter bounced him up and down.

"Hello, Mr. Robinson," Mikey said, offering his hand over Porter's shoulder.

Elizabeth led them through the foyer and through the massive living room with its high ceilings and many windows that opened out onto the gardens. The tasteful décor was speckled with child clutter: a truck, a stuffed frog, a soccer ball under a side table.

Colleen greeted the men and gently peeled Mikey off Porter's back.

"Mikey, you need to go upstairs for a few minutes while Aunt Lizzie and I talk."

"Please, Mommy. I'll be quiet."

"After we've had our talk, we will call you and we can all have something to eat." She kissed him on his head and scooted him upstairs. "Go play with your new trains."

The adults adjourned to the library, a grand room lined with bookcases up to the ceiling. Tom's massive walnut desk stood off to one side, decorated with a stainless steel model of an F-15C Eagle.

Colleen motioned the men to the leather couch. "It's well after happy hour. Could I offer you a glass of wine? Porter, I opened a bottle of red just for you. Would you do the honors? Elizabeth and I have already started on the white."

Porter loved this part. The Callahans had the best wine cellar he knew of, even better than George Brent, especially when it came to Australian and New Zealand reds. Better than some of Washington's finer restaurants. He carefully examined the bottle Colleen had set out. A 2001 Bald Hills Pinot Noir!

"Colleen, Wine Spectator Magazine voted this the best red wine in the world last year!"

Colleen smiled and nodded.

Porter dug into his pocket and extracted his car keys. He tossed them to a surprised Robinson. "Robbie, old buddy, this is your lucky day. You are now the designated driver."

Porter carefully poured a splash into a glass for Robbie, then a full one for himself. He sat next to Colleen and savored his first experience with a wine he had only read about. Wonderful!

"Thank you both for coming," said Colleen. "I've been worried about Tommy. I haven't heard from him in two days. We have an agreement not to go more than forty-eight hours between phone calls. He called me from a satellite phone from some mountaintop in western Vietnam," she glanced at a clock, "oh, more than fifty hours ago."

"We heard from him last night," said Porter. "Which is why I called you this morning."

"I know. But he didn't call me. That's unprecedented." She set down her wine and leaned forward. "Tell me everything he told you. Don't leave out a word."

Porter glanced at Robbie, then back to the women. "Well, that's why we're here." He related Tom's story of finding a recently deceased American POW in the Vietnamese backwaters and about bringing home the West Point ring. "Tom thinks the ring is a real prize. I checked out the West Point connection. Thomas Anthony Kinkaid was, in fact, a 1960 West Point graduate who was shot down in December of 1972. No mention of him has ever been made by Cambodia, Laos, or Vietnam. He simply disappeared, leaving a big void where his life should have been."

Elizabeth slowly released her breath and sighed. "How sad."

"Wars are like that." Porter sat his wineglass on the side table. "This is going to cause an explosion when it's made public. The difference, between the rumored sightings listed on the Internet or discussions in Congressional hearings and what Tom found, is that Tom is a respected active duty Air Force colonel, an advisor to the President of the United States. And his brother is a well-known Wall Street guru. Everyone wants this story. It'll be front page news for weeks."

"Especially if it's written by a Pulitzer Prize winning journalist?" asked Elizabeth, with a smile. "I particularly liked the part about the well-known Wall Street guru."

Porter grinned and gave a slight bow. "I'll remember to include that in the articles." He turned back to Colleen. "The other bit of information is that we confirmed Ambassador Billingsley's real birth name was Anders. He was Sean Callahan's backseater when they were shot down."

"That wanker!" Colleen exploded. "Excuse my language, but that bloody *wanker*! He's been obstructing Tom at every turn. And now we discover this secret life!"

Robbie spoke for the first time. "Both Tom and George Brent think that Billingsley had a surprisingly successful career in the State Department that parallels careers of several of our identified moles."

"Whoa, hold on, Robbie!" said Porter. "We need to stay away from that subject. Elizabeth's not cleared."

"It's okay, Porter," said Colleen. "Elizabeth is a Callahan now. I've filled her in on what happened in Bolivia."

"Colleen, that is classified up to the Presidential level!"

She shook her head. "Her husband is Tom's brother. They're over there together. And we're here together. Elizabeth needs to know what Brian is involved in because she's involved in it, too. Anyhow, it's done." She swirled her wineglass. "Tommy and George are right. The ambassador is up to something. And he's been turned by the Russians. There's no other explanation."

"Do you think that there is any connection between the attack on you and Ron Minor and the attack on Tom and Brian in Angel Fire?" asked Elizabeth.

Porter glanced at Colleen, then back to Elizabeth.

"Porter, I'm concerned about Brian as well," said Elizabeth. "He has called me every morning since they've been gone. Except he didn't call yesterday or today."

Porter shook his head in resignation at this breach of security. "We don't know if there's any connection, Elizabeth. We have a complex situation here. Some people within our government do not want Tom and Brian to succeed. How far they'd go to stop them is an unknown. There are certainly moles in our government left over from the Cold War, aging, but present nonetheless. Are they under orders to stop Tom and Brian? Or is it somebody else, another group we don't know about? We simply do not know. And finally, there is the question of the Russians.

"All that we have is that ring to show that there was at least one American POW who survived and was left behind. That is bound to chafe some people here. Lots of people."

"I don't care what Tommy told George Brent," said Colleen. "If I don't hear from him by breakfast, I'm calling the President. I don't trust this chap Billingsley or Anders or whatever his bloody name is."

Colleen heard Mikey's running footsteps racing down the stairs. He burst into the library. "Mommy! Mommy! Men are climbing over the back wall!"

"Safe room, everybody!" ordered Colleen.

Robbie leapt to his feet and he drew his Beretta. "I see two in the garden!"

Colleen darted over to the desk. She pushed a button carved into the wood and a concealed drawer slid open. She pulled out a loaded pistol.

"Give me the gun," said Elizabeth. "You and Porter take the boy."

"Can you shoot?"

"Every Okie ranch kid can shoot. Take Porter to the room!" She chambered a round. "Robbie, take that door. I'll take this one." Elizabeth moved towards the rear door. "Run, Colleen! We'll slow them down."

Porter picked up Tom's metal model airplane and launched it through the den window. The glass shattered; the security alarm shrieked. He snatched Mikey and sprinted through the door after Colleen. Two shots exploded as he flew up the steps. A man screamed. Mikey burst into tears. Then more shots. Porter bolted down the hall and through the upstairs sitting room. Colleen slammed her hand on the wall bookcase; it slid to one side. She pulled open the steel reinforced door and Porter darted inside a room about the size of a walk-in closet.

Two video monitors were already powered up. In the split screens, he had eight camera-eye views. Robbie Robinson lay in the library hallway, blood pooled around him. Mikey blubbered and trembled, his dark eyes wide with fear.

Colleen threw a switch. The lights went off. The alarm stopped. "Elizabeth knows this house better than they do. She knows how to get here. Call the cops!"

Clutching the terrified Mikey, Porter grabbed a phone and heard a quiet, calm voice on the other end. "This is Buchanan Security. Do you need assistance?"

"Intruders with guns! We have one man down!"

The voice said, "Please secure your room. We have men on the way."

"Shut the door, Colleen!" ordered Porter.

She shook her head. "I'm waiting for Elizabeth."

He stared at the blacked-out monitors. The house generator kicked in and images flooded the screen. Elizabeth crawled up the steps towards safety. When the lights came on, she jumped up, turned to fire three quick shots, then raced upstairs. She crashed into the wall, bounced around the corner and sprinted into the safe room. Colleen hit the close button after her.

On screen, two black-clad men wearing balaclavas stormed up the stairs in pursuit. As the door slid shut, the men burst into the outer room, guns ready. They unleashed a burst of fire.

Bullets slammed against the ballistic door. "They can shoot pistols at that door all afternoon," said Colleen. "We're safe."

Then the friends clutched at each other in relief. Elizabeth sobbed, "Poor Robbie."

Chapter Thirteen
Hanoi

Tom Callahan walked through the park and onto a main street in downtown Hanoi, looking for one particular cafe. He limped slightly from his bruises but his mind refused to acknowledge the pain. As he turned the corner, he spotted both the café and the ambassador's blond bulk. He was seated facing the street with his back to the building so he could watch the foot traffic along the busy sidewalk while he enjoyed a solitary lunch. Just what a field operative would do. Tom wondered who taught him that. The KGB? The CIA? Tom slipped into the café's side entrance, emerged out the front door and slid in almost directly behind the ambassador without being seen.

"Good morning, Mr. Ambassador. Mind if I join you?" Tom sat.

The ambassador dropped his fork. "What the hell are you doing here?"

"Surprised to see me, Ambassador Billingsley? Or should I call you Paul Billingsley Anders?"

The man colored, but said nothing.

"Somebody tried to kill me yesterday, Paul. And some armed men tried to pay a visit to my brother at the hotel yesterday afternoon. Fortunately, he had already checked out. Curious, isn't it? Both of us in one day?"

Tom motioned a waiter over and ordered a café au lait and a croissant. "Put it on the ambassador's bill," he said to the waiter.

Tom leaned into the man's face and said in a low voice, "Why didn't you tell me you flew with my father?"

"I don't have to tell you anything, you little prick."

"And yet, you could have. It's interesting that you'd choose not to say anything. Not to anybody in all these years."

Tom reached into his pocket and produced the gold West Point ring. "This belonged to one Major Thomas Anthony Kinkaid, United States Military Academy class of 1960. An unknown and unaccounted for POW hidden away in the Vietnamese jungle. He died in an accident last week. I met his wife and daughter."

The ambassador threw down his napkin. "Callahan, you cannot imagine how many problems you are causing. Years of high-level diplomatic work gone down the drain because of your bungling about."

Tom shrugged. "What is undone can be re-done." He took a bite of his croissant and thought for a moment. "The position of the U.S. government is that there are no live POWs. Now, we know that's wrong. What's the problem with discovering the truth, Paul? Don't you want us to find these guys? You used to fly with them, for God's sake."

"'These guys,' as you so quaintly put it, do not exist."

"Wrong. I've seen evidence."

"All you have is a ring. It could have been bought off the Internet, for all you know."

"I've seen a daughter."

The ambassador waved his hand as if to dismiss that argument. "She could be any Eurasian."

"Fine. Let's do a DNA analysis. The JPAC labs in Maryland have DNA samples for hundreds of missing guys. Kinkaid should be easy to arrange."

"No."

"No? What do you mean no?"

"I mean I'm the ambassador and I say no!"

Tom stared at him, then laughed. "You know, Paul, your boss is the President. By coincidence, he's my boss too. Why don't we call him and let him decide?"

"We'll do nothing of the kind! This is bigger than finding your daddy. He's gone and forgotten."

A clamor broke out in the street as a particularly aggressive motor scooter driver caused a near collision. Traffic screeched and halted. Horns beeped and people shouted. Tom waited until the mess was sorted out and the noise level dropped.

"You seem to have problems with my father. Is that because you had problems with your own?"

"Oh, so now you're a psychologist?"

"Not really. But I have some people poking around into your past. One of them is an investigative journalist. He told me about your family and why you changed your name. Also interesting is that the Air Force has no record of your name change. Lieutenant Paul B. Anders simply vanished. How did you manage that?"

The ambassador's florid complexion paled a bit. He took a sip of his beer.

"We've learned a lot about you in the past few days, Paul. For example, apparently your flying squadron had a nickname for you. Minnesota Fats."

"Nobody calls me that!"

"Funny, I just did."

Billingsley/Anders slammed his meaty fist on the table. "Goddamnit, I hated your father."

The ambassador's black Cadillac glided up alongside the café. Gunnery Sergeant Johanssen stepped out and approached the table. He did not meet Tom's eyes. "Is there a problem, Mr. Ambassador?" he asked.

"Not yet, but there might be. Stay right there." The ambassador leaned toward Tom and switched to Russian. "Your father was a coward, Callahan. The last time I saw him, he was crying and sniveling. He crossed over."

"To the Russians?"

"That's what I said." The ambassador had a triumphant look on his face. "The Russians." He switched back to English. "Now, get out of here. I order you out of my country. I am the senior U.S. official in Vietnam and you are hereby ordered out."

"Screw you, fat bastard! My father's no traitor. You're lying. I'm not leaving until I learn the truth!"

"Gunny, arrest this man!"

"Sir, I have no jurisdiction here."

"Then march him at gunpoint to the Embassy and arrest him there."

"Sir, that is illegal. I cannot do that."

The ambassador lunged for the gunny's pistol. The gunny dodged. The ambassador lost his balance and sprawled onto the sidewalk.

Tom stood and threw some bills on the table. "On second thought, I'd rather pay for my own coffee. See you around, Fats."

***

Porter Nelson watched as Colleen Callahan finished giving her statement to the police. He marveled at how calm she was, sitting, holding her sleeping son and refusing to be rushed or intimidated. Elizabeth had also refused to be cowed by the investigators. Instead she demanded that they review the safe room videotapes to verify her story. Even the most skeptical observer could see the armed men chasing her up the stairs.

His own interrogation was not going as well.

"A very complete description of the events, Mr. Nelson," said the detective sergeant. "You seem to have a good eye for details."

Porter didn't like his tone. "I make a living seeing and remembering things other people don't see, Sergeant."

The detective seemed amused, then consulted his notes. "One more time, Mr. Nelson, where exactly were you when the shooting started?"

"I was running up the stairs behind Dr. Callahan."

"So you didn't actually see the shooting?"

"No. I told you Dr. Callahan and I went out one door while Elizabeth and Robbie went out the other doors. Robbie was killed almost immediately. Elizabeth took Colleen's pistol and shot back. And hit one, if not two of the attackers."

"While you were in the safe room."

Nelson could feel his temperature rising. "I carried the boy upstairs, Sergeant."

"Do you know how to shoot, Mr. Nelson?"

"I'm pretty good with an AK-47."

That got the sergeant's attention. Before he could ask another dumb question, Porter said, "I was a war correspondent in Afghanistan. I carried a rifle sometimes; often an AK-47."

"But not pistols?" the sergeant persisted.

"Hate the damned things."

The sergeant nodded and put away his note pad. "Do you have any ideas or guesses who might have done this?"

Porter shook his head. Nothing that you'd believe, buddy, he thought.

"Probably just a robbery gone bad," mused the sergeant.

"May I go now?"

After good-byes and hugs from Elizabeth and Colleen, Porter settled into his car and shook his head. Robbery, my ass. These were assassins, not burglars. The FBI should be all over this.

He drove home the long way, watching his rear view mirror, suspicious of any car that got too close. He made several detours, even drove down one, short, one-way street the wrong way just to spot any tail. Nothing, but he didn't feel any safer. He arrived at his townhouse and parked in the garage, locked the car, and stretched a fabric cover over his new automobile. Inside, he took a loaded and cocked SIG Sauer P250 pistol from a concealed floor safe in his office and walked through his entire home, checking every room, looking for signs of a break in. Returning to the safe, he took out a bundle of passports and riffled through them. He chose three and tucked them in a briefcase, along with a stack of euros and several new credit cards matched to the names in the passports. Then he picked up a black leather computer case complete with a virgin laptop. Using a prepaid cell phone, he called a cab while he packed a single small suitcase. He paid the cabbie off at Union Station, walked through the capacious station, and entered a men's room on the restaurant floor. He pulled a baseball cap from his backpack, changed his coat, then exited and took another taxi to Ronald Reagan Airport. There he merged into the mass of passengers, occasionally checking for a tail. Porter studied the departure board for the next flight to Atlanta and bought a ticket using a pristine credit card.

He spent the thirty minutes before his flight hiding in a bar, watching the local D.C. news. There was no mention of the attack on the Callahan house. Stupid damned cops.

In Atlanta, he took a long looping route to the Lufthansa desk, showed a German passport, and bought a first class ticket to Frankfurt.

Arrival into Germany's largest airport was normally a model of Teutonic efficiency. This descent and landing sequence after the nine-hour flight was complicated by unseasonable weather, gray and wet, which suited Porter's mood exactly. He was the third person to exit the airplane, after a middle-aged man and his twenty-something girlfriend. He presented his German passport to the Immigration officer and was whisked through with a bored *"Wilkommen."* At the cabstand, he let two other passengers in front of him, then took the third taxi. He settled in and tried to enjoy the ride to his hotel. He liked Frankfurt, more properly *Frankfurt am Main*, which translates to Frankfurt on the Main River. It was the largest city in the German state of Hesse, not as pretty as the capital at Weisbaden, but it had been his first taste of Germany when he had flown into the country as a college student many years before.

Porter had grown up hearing stories of Germany from his maternal grandparents who had fled the country in 1939, just ahead of the invasion of Poland. He had been determined to attend a German university and had won a scholarship to *Philipps-Universität Marburg*, or Marburg University. Founded in 1527 in the small city of *Marburg an der Lahn* by Philip I of Hesse, it was the world's first and oldest Protestant university. Marburg was what Porter thought to be the ultimate *universitätsstadt*, or university town, where one in four inhabitants was a student. Life there was awash with rampant hormonal rushes and youthful idealism: sex, drugs, and ideals. Marburg University was very different indeed from his cozy berth at University of California-Santa Cruz. The sex, drugs, and idealism were the same of course, but not the ideas. The quantity, breadth, and scope of the ideas he had been exposed to in Marburg were astonishing in a university nearly five hundred years old, world famous for its philosophy department as well as its chemistry department.

Porter checked into a hotel near the Frankfurt (Main) Hauptbahnhof, Germany's most important rail station, paying with euros. He made a few phone calls on another pre-paid cell phone, then walked a half mile towards downtown, all the while trying to remember the lessons in counterintelligence field craft that Robbie Robinson had tried to drill into him. Ragged clouds scudded across the gray sky spattering intermittent rain.

He ditched the phone in a café trashcan along the way. He watched and listened for anything suspicious, but noticed nothing. He might be safe, though he didn't feel safe. Back in his hotel, he had only a few hours for a nap and a shower. Leaving the hotel, he strolled in the main entrance of the Hauptbahnhof, out a side door, and snagged a taxi back to the airport. He checked the international departures, proceeded to the Lufthansa desk and bought a first class ticket to Hanoi.

Porter's nervousness peaked as he reached the security checkpoint. He saw two airport officials eyeing him. One motioned for Porter to step out of line and follow him. Two more armed security guards appeared and stood behind Porter, blocking his retreat.

"Open the computer, please," ordered the guard.

As he opened the computer case, Porter prayed that the new battery held a charge.

Satisfied that the computer was clean, the guard inspected the contents of Porter's backpack, then waved Porter through.

Porter ducked into the first class lounge and gratefully accepted a cup of coffee from the gorgeous attendant. He sat alone near a window and used every remaining minute of the pre-departure time trying to get his nerves back under control.

As he entered the cabin of the Airbus A340-600, Porter checked to see if there were any familiar faces, people he had seen in downtown Frankfurt, or even Georgetown. Safely airborne, he allowed himself to relax a bit and asked the flight attendant for a half bottle of Prinz von Hessen Extra Brut German *sekt*, a favorite of his that he had often shared with Robbie Robinson. He silently toasted his late friend as he tried to erase the memory of Robbie's body lying in a pool of blood.

Eleven hours later, he changed planes in Bangkok and took a Thai International Airways Airbus 330. He automatically scanned the passengers to look for anyone who had been on the flight from Frankfurt and was stunned to see a familiar face seated directly behind him in first class. And another and another. Then he remembered, this was the scheduled connecting flight between Frankfurt and Hanoi so there should be some of the same passengers. His heart rate wound down to normal.

Two hours later he was on the ground in Hanoi. He cleared customs and immigration using his German passport and grabbed a taxi to his hotel. On the drive, he was fascinated by the colors and the street scenes. Despite being jet-lagged beyond belief, the journalist part of his brain kicked in. He had composed three story leads in his head before he arrived at the Hotel Sofitel Metropole Hanoi. A smiling, maroon-clad doorman rushed to grab his bags and Porter allowed himself to be led into the enormous marble foyer.

He presented his German passport to the clerk and filled in the registration forms. "I'm waiting to meet an *Oberst*—Colonel—Callahan or his brother, Major Callahan. Are they in?"

"Let me check, sir." The clerk took the passport and disappeared into the manager's office.

A dapper, middle-aged man emerged from the office wearing a nametag that identified him as the manager. He placed the passport on the marble countertop and asked in accented German, "You were asking about *Oberst* Callahan, Herr Schneider?"

"*Ja.*"

"You are a friend of his?"

"I have that privilege."

The manager shook his head and pursed his lips. "The oberst and his brother checked out the day before yesterday."

Scheisse, thought Porter. All this way and no Tom. Where the hell could he be now? "Are you sure? I spoke with the oberst only three days ago." The manager shook his head again. Porter fumbled for a business card and handed it to the manager. "If he returns, please let him know that I need to speak with him."

"Of course, sir. In the meantime, I will put you in the suite next to where he stayed."

To help fight his jet lag, Porter took a walk in the hotel's lush gardens, a quick swim, then a long hot shower. Relaxed at last, he walked out of the shower right into a pistol.

"Who are you really, Herr Schneider?" asked the intruder as he thrust the pistol into Porter's face.

Porter instinctively raised his hands over his head. "Who the hell are you? And why are you in my room?"

"I asked first. And I have the gun." The crew cut man smiled a grim smile. "I have a talent for showing up when people are getting out of the shower."

"What are you talking about?" asked Porter, confused as well as acutely aware of his nakedness.

"Never mind." The man stood between Porter and the door. He motioned with the pistol for Porter to move to the center of the room. "What do you want with the colonel?"

"I need to know where he is. There are things he needs to know."

"I don't believe you. Tell me why I shouldn't shoot you right now."

Sweet Jesus, thought Porter. He means it! And he looks like he'd like nothing more. Then his intuition kicked in. "You're Gunnery Sergeant Johanssen! You were in Bolivia with Tom."

Slowly, Porter backed up and lowered his arms. "Listen, man, Tom Callahan saved my life, too. That means something to me just like it does to you. My name is Porter Nelson. I wrote those articles about Tom and the Marine House bombing. You should remember my name if not me."

The gunny looked doubtful. "Then who is Henning Schneider?"

"It's my pseudonym."

"Your what?"

"My pen name, sort of like 'Mark Twain'. I use it when I write articles for European publications. I used it to get out of the States without anybody knowing."

"Why?"

"Can I put on my clothes first?"

The gunny relaxed slightly and motioned for him to get dressed. Porter reached for his pants. "Gunny, the ambassador flew with Tom's father. And somebody tried to kill Tom's wife and son—and Elizabeth Callahan as well. I was there."

"Did Colleen send you?"

Still watching the pistol, Porter shook his head. "She doesn't know that I'm here. She has enough problems. Gunny, I'm a grown up, and a reporter, I don't have to ask anybody for anything."

The gunny gave a little flick of his wrist and the pistol again centered on Porter's face. "Not true," he said. "You have to ask me."

Porter could see right up the barrel of the pistol. "Well, yeah," he conceded. "Okay, I'm asking. Please tell me where Tom and Brian are."

"By the way, the ambassador's missing," said Gunny.

"Missing? What do you mean missing?"

"Missing. As in not here. Gone. Nobody knows where. I was there when Colonel Callahan confronted him about being his father's backseater. It got real ugly real fast. The ambassador told me to arrest the colonel. I swear, if the ambassador'd had my gun, the colonel would be a dead man."

Johanssen holstered his pistol. "Finish getting dressed and we'll go."

"Do you know where they are?"

"No, but I know who does." He motioned Porter towards the door. "And if you're not Porter Nelson, you're in big trouble.

Chapter Fourteen
Callahan Residence - Georgetown

Colleen sat at her desk, trying to plow through some of her correspondence. Nervous tension battered her concentration. Scenes of the recent home invasion kept flooding back. She recalled Winston Churchill's comment that nothing in life is so exhilarating as to be shot at without result. She sighed. Maybe it was exhilarating for old Winnie but all she felt was depression and anger. Paperwork seemed so unimportant at the moment. She needed to gather her family around her. To find her husband.

Unable to sit still any longer, she found a watering can and began to tend to her office plants as she wrestled with the new situation. She heard a yell and the sound of running feet.

"Colleen, I have an e-mail from Brian! They're okay!" shouted Elizabeth as she ran down the stairs to the library, waving a piece of paper.

Colleen reached for the printout.

Elizabeth snatched it back. "Let me read it to you. The important part says 'We're okay and are moving on in our quest.'"

"Where did he send it from?"

"I can't tell. I'm sure it's been routed through servers all over the world."

Colleen nodded. Her work at the World Bank had made her well aware of techniques to sterilize the point of origin of an e-mail or an electronic money transfer. "Yes, I'm not surprised that Brian knows how to do that."

She closed her eyes and gave a short prayer of thanks. She looked at Elizabeth. "But how do you know the e-mail is really from Brian?"

Elizabeth hesitated, "Because he says some private things in it as well."

"Please let me see the whole message."

Face flushing bright red, Elizabeth handed the paper to Colleen.

Colleen glanced through the paper, then read it again. "Sounds like Brian misses you a whole lot." It was her turn to be embarrassed.

"Elizabeth, I am so sorry to intrude. I just had to see for myself." She hugged Elizabeth, then said with a smile, "You're right, though, those are things that a husband would say to a wife, especially a new wife."

Elizabeth was confused, then her face lit up. "Tom, too?"

Colleen laughed outright. "Must be a Callahan thing!"

They both flopped onto the leather couch and laughed so hard they cried. Colleen wiped the tears from her eyes and gasped, "Thank you, Lizzie, I needed that." She sat upright. "I know where Brian is, maybe Tommy as well!"

"Where?"

Colleen went to the bookcase and pulled back a section revealing a wall safe. Opening it, she reached in and took out a prepaid cell phone that Tom had given to her before he left. She riffled through a Washington phone book and wrote down a number. She looked at Elizabeth, put her finger to her lips, and walked outside into the garden to call. Colleen trusted no one now, even though the Secret Service had swept her house for listening devices. After a brief conversation, she hung up and motioned Elizabeth to join her in the garden.

"Change out of your jeans. Something nice and simple, but professional. No heels, we'll be walking a bit."

"Colleen, what's going on?"

"We're going to the Thai Embassy to call Admiral Shinawatra. I didn't want to say any more in the house and I don't want to say anything important in the car. Pretend to chat. Our mother-in-law started things in motion with that e-mail to her friend the admiral, who is also her friend the ex-Foreign Minister. The Thai Embassy is just a few blocks from here." She smiled, "It's near the shopping district over on Wisconsin and M Street. Wonderful stores. We'll use them as a decoy to shake anybody who may be following us."

"Why do we need to go to the Embassy?"

"I need to speak to the Admiral and daren't call from my house."

"But Tom has that secure phone in his office."

"Yes, but secure from whom? It's a U.S. government phone, Lizzie. After yesterday, I don't trust anybody anymore."

"How do you know that we can trust the Thai ambassador?" asked Elizabeth.

"I don't. But right now, I trust the Thai government more than our own." Colleen glanced at her watch. "We have an appointment with the ambassador in forty-five minutes. I'll check on Mikey and let the nanny know where we'll be. Then we'll go."

As Colleen drove, the women talked about the new Italian shoes Elizabeth had seen and whether or not to give up spike heels. The few blocks to *The Shops at Georgetown Park* mall passed quickly. They strode, arm-in-arm, into the stylish mall and wandered through it, going into stores to check out several exciting sales. Colleen stopped three separate times to watch reflections in window glass to see if anyone was following them. Satisfied, the women exited the mall onto Wisconsin Avenue and headed south. Colleen again scanned for a tail. If they were being followed, it was by experts and nothing more could be done about that. They followed Wisconsin Avenue over the C and O Canal, past Grace Street to the five-story brick Thai Embassy.

They showed their identity cards to the security guards, who made a phone call. An aide appeared almost instantly and whisked the women to the Ambassador's office.

"Dr. Callahan! This is indeed a pleasure," said the ambassador with a broad smile, as he rose to shake hands.

"Colleen, please, Mr. Ambassador. This is my sister-in-law, Elizabeth Callahan."

An aide brought a tray of tea and biscuits and departed. The ambassador motioned the women to a leather couch and poured the tea himself.

"Mr. Ambassador, I'll get right to the point. I need to call Admiral Shinawatra on your secure phone."

Surprised, the ambassador said, "May I ask what this is for?"

"I'm sorry, sir. It concerns my husband and his brother. I would like to keep this confidential, but if the admiral approves, you may listen."

"Excuse me, Dr. Callahan, but this is in no way official business."

"You are correct, Mr. Ambassador. If you remember, I did not ask for an appointment to discuss World Bank business. I came here because I need your help and your secure phone to call to your country and locate the admiral."

The ambassador sat back, an unhappy look on his face. He drummed his fingers on the arm of his chair. "I am not pleased with this request. It is quite improper."

"Sir, it may be improper but it is important, I promise you. Perhaps a matter of life or death. Please excuse my bluntness, Mr. Ambassador, but yesterday my house was attacked by men who came to kill me and my son. My husband is missing. I need to know where he is and if he is safe. If necessary, I will call the admiral from a pay phone. I will inform him that I came to you for help but you were most unhelpful." She paused. "I would prefer not to do that."

The ambassador was silent for what seemed to Colleen like a very long time before a small smile appeared on his face. "It seems as though I have an opportunity to, as you say in this country, aid a damsel, or damsels, in distress. As it happens, the admiral is a cousin of mine, distant but related nonetheless. I was planning to call him this week. Why don't I just do that now?" He reached for the teapot. "This may take some time. May I offer you some more tea?"

They gratefully accepted and watched as the ambassador went to his desk and called Thailand on what appeared to be a Thai version of a U.S. Government STU-III secure phone. Several calls and three cups of tea later, he handed her the phone, excused himself and left the women alone in his office.

Colleen gripped the phone. "Hello?"

The admiral's voice was softer than she expected. "Lovely to hear from you, Colleen. Thomas has told me many stories about you and your son."

"Do you know where Tommy is?"

"Why?"

"Our house was attacked yesterday. Fortunately, the attackers didn't do enough research. Instead of a defenseless mother and a four-year-old boy to slaughter, we had guests. Brian's wife, Elizabeth, and two friends were there. Elizabeth shot at least one of the attackers."

"Are you all right?"

Colleen was convinced that she had guessed correctly. He knew where Tommy was. "Yes, sir. We hid in our safe room until the police arrived. But one of our friends was killed."

"I am sorry for your friend, Colleen, but overjoyed that you and your son are uninjured."

"Admiral, I have to talk to Tommy."

"I realize your concern, Colleen. But you need to let Thomas do what he needs to do. He needs no distractions."

"Is he in danger?"

A thoughtful silence. "Thomas is doing what he needs to do. It will not be an easy task. I can only say that he is well protected now."

"Admiral, this is very difficult for both Elizabeth and me. But I will not pursue my other options if you promise me that you are protecting our husbands."

"As I said, Colleen, they are safe."

Chapter Fifteen
Bangkok, Thailand

Tom and Brian sipped tea as they sat under the trees in the admiral's luxurious gardens, surrounded by fountains, bougainvillea, and gorgeous flowering trees they didn't recognize, and listened as the admiral made call after call. Tom tried to deflect his impatience by listening to the phrasing of the one-sided conversation and attempting to decipher the new language. The more he saw and heard of Thailand, the better he liked it. He decided that after this was all over, he wanted to bring Colleen back to experience the culture and the friendly people.

Finally, the admiral hung up the phone and turned to his guests. "It's all arranged. Your plane is scheduled to leave in an hour."

"Do we have enough time to get to the airport?" asked Brian.

A smile split the admiral's rotund face. "The aircraft will experience a mechanical problem which will require it to leave only after you arrive."

The admiral's black limousine headed east carrying the three men towards the airport. They crossed several of Bangkok's famous *klongs* and drove briefly alongside one of the few remaining floating markets. *Klong* was the general name for canals in central Thailand. Bangkok used to have so many *klong*s and floating markets full of boat traffic, people, and merchandise that it was called the "Venice of the East." But now, most of the canals had been paved over for roads that sluiced through the growing metropolis. Just like in London, one of his favorite cities.

"The Chinese are willing to risk helping you," said the admiral, as he poured each man a glass of fresh fruit juice from the limo bar. "You will be met at the airport in Beijing and taken to a secure location to meet with officials of the Foreign Ministry and their military intelligence services."

"They must be really worried about this new Russian president," said Brian.

"Who isn't?" said Tom. "With the price of oil in the stratosphere, Russia has the money to buy anything. Ten years ago, the Russian military was rotting, soldiers not being paid, ships tied up in port, airplanes falling apart, parked on the ramp. Now the president is pouring money into a huge arms buildup."

The admiral nodded. "He's made aggressive moves in and around Georgia, propped up the government thugs in Belarus and the Chinese are nervous about the new forces he deployed into the Indian Ocean and off Japan."

"It's tied up in economics," said Tom. "You should hear Colleen when she gets on this subject. Wow!"

"I am looking forward to meeting both of your families," said the admiral. He looked to Tom. "I spoke to Colleen this morning. She called from our embassy in Washington. She and your son are fine, as is your wife, Brian. Apparently, there was some excitement in Washington. You can get the details from your friend, Porter Nelson. He'll be meeting you in Beijing."

"Really? Why there?"

The admiral took a sip of his juice. "He showed up in Hanoi. Your ever-vigilant gunnery sergeant challenged him at your hotel, then took him to our embassy just as he did with you, Brian. Our naval attaché called me; I told him to have Mr. Nelson placed on one of our military planes. He'll arrive in the afternoon, Beijing time."

"Admiral, we can't begin to tell you how much we appreciate your sticking your neck out like this," said Tom.

The admiral looked stern. "You can begin by calling me 'Uncle,' like I asked." He smiled, then laughed. "You two are so different, but both so much like your father. Smart. Determined, head-strong. True believers."

"Good looking, too," added Brian.

"Perhaps," said the admiral, "but all you Caucasians look the same to me."

As they arrived at the new Bangkok International Airport, security officers met them and two black security vehicles escorted the limo around the glistening terminal—all curved metal and glass—onto the ramp. The convoy pulled up alongside the Thai Air International Boeing 747-400. After quick good-byes from the admiral, Tom and Brian climbed the ladder into the loading chute, and the aircraft purser led them into the spacious first class cabin. After they were seated, the rest of the passengers were allowed to board.

Five hours later, they were on the ground in Beijing. As they deplaned, three Chinese officials approached them, bowed, and motioned for them to follow. Tom and Brian were escorted through immigration and customs without being asked any questions or for any papers. Brian's eyebrows went up at the diplomatic treatment, but Tom merely shrugged. He was here as a private citizen, not as an official of the United States Government. If the Chinese wanted to treat him like a diplomat, fine. What he didn't like was the downside of this treatment. There was no official record of their arrival in China in case anything went wrong. He had to trust the admiral on this one.

They were led out of the terminal into another black limo, this one a Mercedes, and whisked off on a long drive through Beijing. Neither brother had ever visited the city, big and powerful, open and newly peaceful. The drive was not designed as a tour of recent architectural marvels, but meant to get them out of the city as quickly as possible. They passed through several medium-sized towns, then back out into the countryside. Eventually, they arrived at a fenced compound surrounded by trees; they passed through several security checkpoints without being questioned. Tom looked around. Guards everywhere. Uniformed guards and black-suited guards. But the limo was not inspected. Interesting.

The office complex was large and tastefully decorated with exquisite Chinese porcelain vases, sculptures, and watercolors. As he walked through the long hallway, Tom shook his head and chastised himself for not knowing enough about Chinese art; he vaguely remembered reading that Chinese art was now the hottest sector of the international art market. He had no idea which works here was priceless and which were merely valuable. He forced the subject out of his mind. He had to stay focused.

The large conference area was dominated by a massive mahogany conference table. The eight men seated around the table stood when Tom, Brian, and their escort entered the room. Half the men were in uniform, half in civvies. Expensive civvies. These were not just mid-level bureaucrats. He nudged Brian. "These guys are the Chinese varsity."

Brian nodded. "I think they want to help us. Our new 'uncle' has some serious clout in Asia."

The introductions took some time, as the language problem had to be sorted out. Tom's Chinese was passable, but not good enough to have a high-level conversation; Brian's was better due to his recent financial dealings in Singapore. Only the ranking civilian was fluent in English; most of the Chinese officers and senior bureaucrats had some knowledge of English but not good enough to negotiate deals without the ever-present interpreters. Tom's Japanese was fluent, but most Chinese government officials preferred not to speak the language of their centuries-old adversary unless necessary. Tom switched from Chinese to Japanese to English as the occasion demanded.

Brian jumped right in, smiling and shaking hands, working the room as if this were a social event in New York. He threw in some Vietnamese words he had picked up—the Chinese smiled at the effort—then he told a few one-liners in a deliberate mélange of Italian, Spanish, Russian, and Chinese that made them all laugh at the sheer incongruity of the conversation. Tom felt a flush of pride; he saw his brother in a whole new light. Brian was in his element here, brokering a deal. This ability to get people to focus on a single task while maintaining a light atmosphere was part of Brian's Wall Street genius.

The military officer at the head of the table, a major general, stood aside; his seat was taken by a newly arrived civilian. Everyone sat up and paid attention. The atmosphere palpably changed from social to professional.

The civilian addressed the group. "We have been asked to help these men penetrate Russia. We are here to decide how to accomplish that mission. Colonel Callahan, we already have the essential facts, but perhaps you would like to go over them yourself with us."

Tom stood and gave a proper Asian bow. He had made a conscious decision to speak Chinese as he gave a summary of what had happened since the discovery of the fateful photograph up to the finding of Thomas Anthony Kinkaid and the dossiers of classified Vietnamese/Russian documents. "We appreciate your hospitality and for meeting with us. My brother and I understand that you also have similar concerns about the Russians. We are here to explore what information there may be about any missing Americans held inside Russia. Thank you."

As Tom sat down, the senior Chinese civilian, a deputy minister named Zhang said, "Yes, we know about these POW issues and rumors. We have often wondered about your government's position, but felt that it was not our place to raise these issues. We do have reason to believe that there are at least a few American POWs living in the former Soviet Union."

He handed Tom and Brian several dossiers. "Our people have heard stories, rumors. What little hard evidence exists is here in these summaries of our findings over the past three decades."

Briefings continued for the rest of the morning. Bureaucrats shuffled in, gave their presentations and shuffled out. An interpreter sat between Tom and Brian and spoke softly as the briefers elaborated on the information contained in the dossiers. Tom recognized that he was getting a glimpse of the internal workings of the Chinese government that would make a State Department or CIA Asian desk officer dance with delight. The Chinese Intelligence services certainly had been watching the colossus to the north for some time.

During the informal working lunch, Tom and Brian sat alone and pored over the documents, many dating back to the 1960s and '70s. Translations were provided for the more relevant ones, especially the executive summaries and updates presented by individual Intel officers.

"Things are moving right along, Tom," said Brian. "It looks like the Chinese are offering to let us take advantage of their intelligence network to slip into Russia and have a look around."

Tom nodded. "Apparently they're going to help us. Just why is beyond me. The Chinese may have a bulky decision-making process but once they make up their minds they make things happen."

"Yeah, but we just arrived this morning."

"Meaning that they had already decided—for their own reasons—to do something to undermine this new Russian president. This is a political decision, Brian. Nothing, and I mean nothing, like this gets done here without political permission. Remember that the head of the Chinese Military Commission is also the chairman of the Chinese Communist Party."

"So we're just an excuse to stick it to the Russians."

Tom laughed. "Hey, can't beat the timing! It's a calculated risk on the part of the Chinese. The Russian president is perceived as dangerous. As he consolidates his power, he grows, but he does have enemies. Helping us could hurt him. It's the old Sun Tzu maxim of 'the enemy of my enemy is my friend.' You heard the Vietnamese. They're afraid as well. That's why they helped us get here."

"Don't you think the Russians have penetrated the Chinese government?"

"Of course."

"Then they could know what we're doing."

"Hell, Brian, *we* don't even know what we're doing!"

Brian looked Tom straight in the eyes. "We can't put together a plan in a few days. Any covert mission takes excruciatingly detailed planning. Even I know that."

"Well, in the immortal words of George Patton, a good plan executed well today beats an excellent plan next week."

"Yeah, but is this even a good plan?"

"Hey, where's my optimistic brother, Brian?"

"Tom, the Russian government doesn't really care about its international image. It will do whatever it wants. Even if that happens to be shooting a few people. This is serious, pal. You are an active duty colonel and what we're talking about is very nearly a spy mission. This is your Rubicon, brother. If you go into Russia like this, you're done in government."

155

"Jesus, Brian, that's the least of my problems. If I screw this up it could mean a firing squad for any POWs that might still be alive in Russia."

"More to the point, Tommy, if we get caught, Mom might end up missing more than just a husband."

Tom paused. Brian was remorseless; while Tom had avoided this detail, Brian always ticked off all the points of a contract one by one, pro and con. He never overlooked anything. And the thing was, Brian was right. Neither of them was the least bit prepared for this. Studying dossiers and interviewing desk officers was not the same as having expertise in field work. They were totally out of their element. Sure, even if they screwed this up and got nabbed, Tom would probably be okay. His office in the White House probably would protect him—and Brian as well. Maybe.

"Well then," he said, "let's not get caught."

"That, brother, is a deal."

Chapter Sixteen
Chinese Military Compound, near Beijing

The briefings continued into the afternoon. Ideas of how and where to penetrate Russia were floated, discussed, discarded. Maps and satellite photos were tacked to the conference room walls, then taken down and replaced. Documents flowed through the room and across Tom's table. Some translations and analyses were better than others. It seemed the most relevant documents were more thoughtful, as if there had been more time to write them in either English or Russian. The admiral must have given the Chinese a heads up; his fingerprints were on everything. This mission would be doomed without the admiral's considerable influence.

Late in the afternoon, an officer entered the room and spoke briefly in the general's ear. As the officer left, the general turned to Tom. "Colonel Callahan, it seems your friend, Mr. Nelson, has arrived. Perhaps you would care to use my office to catch him up on today's activities."

Tom stretched. "Actually, General, I think a walk in the gardens would be better. We've been inside all day."

Porter was waiting in the large outer office. When he saw Tom, he leapt up and hurried across the room to embrace him. Tom's first reaction was that Porter looked like hell; pale, drawn, with hair and clothing mussed. Tom introduced Porter to his brother and motioned for them to follow him outside. They walked in the extensive gardens while Porter gave them an emotional rundown of the attack on the Callahan residence.

"Those bastards killed Robbie!" he said as he dropped onto a stone bench. Tom slid in beside him and put his arm around his friend's shoulder.

After a long moment, Porter said, "I had to come here to try to help you guys." Then he broke down and cried.

Tom came close to tears himself, thinking of the good people who had died in the past few weeks. Robbie had been a trusted and dear friend. The three men sat in silence, each lost in his own thoughts.

Porter looked up at Tom as he wiped his nose. "This is bigger than we thought, Tom, and I had to tell you in person. Before I left, I called the head of the Secret Service detail and told him what had happened at your house. He said he'd post some agents in and around your home. Maybe the CIA's infiltrated but if we can't trust the Secret Service, we're all screwed."

"Thank you for what you did for my family, Porter. You've been a good friend to us. Colleen adores you."

Porter smiled and sat up straight. "Tom, you know that Colleen is one of my favorite people. She's a wonder." He turned to Brian, "And your wife, pal, is a tiger. You should have seen her in action. She snatched up that pistol and went out and shot one of the bastards."

Brian closed his eyes, crossed himself, then smiled. "She's something, all right."

"You have no idea, Brian." Porter shook his head, still amazed. "Those women of yours may be gorgeous but they're as tough as Navy SEALs. They're the whole package, they even smell smart. I don't know what it is about you Callahan boys, but you sure as hell have great wives."

Both Callahans acknowledged the compliment. Tom looked to Brian. "I think it might be time to get the women out of the States."

"Thailand?"

"That's what I was thinking, Brian. Can Elizabeth leave the gallery for another week or two?"

"Not a problem. Moises can handle it."

"Okay. Send them another of your magic, untraceable e-mails and tell them to get ready. I'll get Uncle on it. He'll love it."

"Uncle?" asked Nelson. "Who is Uncle?"

"That, Porter, is one of the many mysteries that we will unravel for you. A surprise even greater than discovering the secret background of the ambassador."

"By the way, the gunny told me that the ambassador disappeared."

"What! When?" said Tom. "I just saw him two days ago."

"Dunno. Sometime after you and Brian skipped Vietnam."

"They'll find him floating in a *klong* somewhere around Hanoi, I bet," said Tom.

"I hope they do," said Brian. "He must have panicked after your meeting and run to the Russians. They probably had to shut him up."

They walked a few minutes. Tom's emotions were roiling. He blessed the admiral for shielding him from the details of the attack on Colleen and Mikey until now, when Porter could personally assure him that all was well with his family. Getting them to Thailand seemed the best answer.

"So, what's happened to you guys?" asked Porter.

Tom sketched out the details of what had happened to him after the car bomb and the confrontation with the ambassador. Brian fleshed out Tom's statements with the evidence found in the Russian documents, and how he was spirited out of Hanoi on a Thai Air Force C-130.

Porter pointed back at the military compound headquarters. "Why are all these Chinese government people running around here with you two?"

Tom began his explanation of the purpose of the briefings—

Porter exploded. "Tom, what the hell are you thinking? You can't go into Russia without permission."

"Oh, but I have it. The President told me to do whatever I needed to do to relax and take care of my family."

"So, entering a foreign country illegally and possibly as a spy is what you call relaxing?"

"It is taking care of my family."

"Yeah, but somebody in our own government will hang you for it when you get back."

"So what, Porter? This is my father. We have a chance to find out what happened to him. Maybe even find him. What does a career mean next to that?"

159

"Hold on, Tom. That's not what I meant. Wouldn't it be better if I were to go instead of you? I speak pretty good Russian. Nobody'll even notice me. I'm a journalist, I'm supposed to be nosey. If I get caught, I'll just stay alive until you can get the President to work out a deal to get me back."

"That's just what I tried to say to him, Port. Good for you," said Brian. "Tom, buddy, pal, brother, you stay here. Let me go. I'm the ex-cocaine addict, remember? I'm supposed to be off the rails and do crazy things like this. Or let Porter and I go together and you stay here to call the shots with the Chinese."

Tom was tempted. The idea made sense.

Porter took Tom by the shoulders. "One more time, my friend: you can't do this. It's spying, for Christ's sake. It's bad enough if Brian or I get caught. You're an officer. They can shoot you as a spy."

That did it. "Yeah, Port, and they can shoot you, too, if they want. You can come along if you want, but I'm going." He turned on his heel and led them back into the conference room.

They worked until nearly midnight when, exhausted, they were forced to adjourn.

The next morning Tom was up early and went for a quick run through the gardens that surrounded the headquarters building. The guards were very polite but insistent that he be accompanied by another guard, also in running gear. Tom tried his best to lose him but eventually had to concede that he could not. Only after finding out that this particular guard had nearly made the Chinese Olympic track team did his disposition improve.

The Americans joined the Chinese after a quick breakfast, only partially refreshed, and began to deal with the great mass of information that had grown even larger overnight. Tom noted that they had all the talents and resources of the Chinese Intelligence services, all that expertise, at their disposal. The CIA normally took forever to digest all the information it vacuumed up with satellites, listening intercepts, and field agent reports. The problem was almost always the sheer volume of information; the Agency was simply overwhelmed with input, just as they were here. But invariably, the right nugget of information, the key to a successful operation, was buried in all the data. He just had to find it.

They continued the discussions throughout that day and the next. At meals, they met operatives who had actually been inside Russia. Tom and Brian asked question after question. Porter was the only one who had ground time in a combat zone and had experienced sudden terror when surprises could mean death. They tried to bring reality into the planning process, searching for each other's strengths and weaknesses. All three men were action oriented by nature. At the same time, they were detail oriented by training and profession and could plow through immense piles of paper—fact sheets, spread sheets, or just plain data— like an Olympic skier through two feet of fresh powder.

Porter had more experience with ordinary Russians, the eighteen to twenty-year-old conscripts that he had spent time with in Afghanistan. Tom and Brian were more familiar with educated Russians; their Russian was smoother than Porter's and less full of soldier chatter. Slowly, over the endless sessions, a skeleton of an operation began to take shape. More operations people made their appearance as plans were drawn up. The language of the briefings and planning shifted from Chinese to Russian, as more of the Chinese were actually Russian specialists.

Siberia became the most obvious focus. Possible sightings, and rumors of sightings were all examined and collated, then re-evaluated. From that consensus emerged two most obvious candidate locations. The discussions and shared information also showed Tom just how compartmentalized the intelligence world was. The Chinese had all this data and the Americans didn't. Or, maybe did and decided to ignore it. That, in itself, was another sure sign of compartmentalization. If it were generally known within the CIA or even by those military-haters in the State Department that there were some Americans left behind, surely someone would have spoken out, or leaked the information. Tom found it much easier to believe in a cabal of fanatics than that an entire institution was corrupted. He knew too many dedicated men and women like Robbie Robinson within the CIA to believe that the whole Company had gone bad.

161

"Okay, we'll look at what the Chinese propose," said Tom. "We may only get one chance. One target. Anything else is pressing our luck."

"Jeez, Tom, going into any place in Siberia is pressing our luck," said Brian.

Tom ignored him. "This is going to be a maximum effort by the Chinese. They're turning over their assets to help us. We need to be careful not to stumble around in there and burn their guys."

"Or get burned ourselves."

"Brian!"

"Okay, okay." Brian laughed. "But this mission would make Maxwell Smart look as smooth as James Bond."

Even Tom chuckled at that.

Deputy Prime Minister Zhang, whom Tom had pegged as a very high ranking spook, entered the room followed by an aide carrying a briefcase. The Americans stood and bowed. Zhang sat.

The aide placed a dossier in front of each of the Americans. Zhang opened his and began the briefing. "We think that there are two likely places to start: Irkutsk and Chita. They're both mining cities. Both have had POWs or exiles there before." Zhang turned the page and continued. "We recommend you consider Irkutsk first. It is known for its mining and aviation businesses. Most famous is *Irkut*, or the Irkutsk Aviation Industrial Association, set up in 1932. It manufactures the Su-30 family of interceptor/ground-attack aircraft and recently merged with Ilyushin, Mikoyan, Sukhoi, Tupolev, and Yakolev as a new company named United Aircraft Building Corporation."

"Yeah, I read about that merger in the *Journal*," said Brian.

Zhang gave Brian a cold stare; Chinese ministers were not used to being interrupted.

"The city is located on the Trans-Siberian railroad, forty-five miles from Lake Baikal in thick forested taiga and rolling hills. The metropolitan area covers many square miles and encompasses multiple satellite industrial cities.

"Irkutsk was established in 1652 as a center of gold-trading and fur trade. Now mining includes gold and diamonds. Irkutsk has also been a prison for exiles, most notably after the Decembrist Revolt in 1825. By the end of the 19ᵗʰ Century, there was one exiled man in Irkutsk per two locals. The architecture of the Decembrists and other exiles is what made Irkutsk famous. By 1900, it had earned the name Paris of Siberia."

"Okay, I understand Irkutsk. But why Chita?" asked Brian. "I've never heard of it before."

Zhang answered, "From the 1930s to the fall of the Soviet Union, Major, Chita was a closed city because of its military installations and proximity to China. No foreigners were allowed, and few Russians."

He glanced back down to his papers and continued reading. "Chita also has a history of refugees and prisoners. They were capable people and began to expand agriculture and trade. Eventually Chita became a trading center for timber, gold, uranium, and coal. Japanese prisoners of war were also held near Chita. To this day, the influence of the Japanese can be seen in the city center; many of the buildings are Japanese style. These days, since it's on the Trans-Siberian Railroad, many foreigners pass through. It is even brother city to your Boise in Idaho."

"Brother city? You mean sister city?" asked Porter.

"Port, remember the Russians call their ships 'he;' our Navy calls them 'she,'" said Tom. "Same concept—brother city instead of sister city."

Porter thought for a moment. "This summary sounds right to me. Though any POWs in the area probably wouldn't be actually in Chita or Irkutsk themselves. Siberia is almost incomprehensibly huge, guys. It's easy to get lost once you get off the main roads. The minor roads there are worse than awful; you go fifty miles off a main drag and you might as well be on the moon. So a POW could be only a short distance away and still be isolated. You have to remember that all maps were classified documents under the old Soviet system.

"After the Russians pulled out of Afghanistan, I took the Trans-Siberian Express across Siberia to write a series of articles for *Stern*. The Germans are fascinated by Siberia. During WWII, the Soviets stashed hundreds of thousands of German POWs there; more than 300,000 soldiers were captured at Stalingrad alone. When the war ended, POWs trickled back to Germany, but not nearly as many as we thought. Eisenhower wrote that there were tens of thousands unaccounted for. Lots of people in Germany think there could be compounds of leftover German POWs."

"Where do we go first?" asked Brian.

"Chita," said Tom. "Pop's a West Point trained engineer. He could be useful in a mining community."

"Are you saying that if our father is alive, he's a traitor working for the communists?"

"Look, Brian, if he, or any other POW, is alive, he will be working. It's so Russian. Historically, captured soldiers and political prisoners have always been made to work. Read *A Day in the Life of Ivan Denisovich.*"

"I did, Tom, several times—and in Russian."

"Okay, okay, Brian. Point taken. Sorry."

"Then using your logic, Tom, why wouldn't the Russians have our father stashed at an airplane factory or a city with advanced aircraft stationed nearby, like Irkutsk? He was also a test pilot."

"I know." Tom began to pace as he tried to put his feelings into words. "I'm just going with probabilities. If the Russians have any Americans, they would most likely stash them in the boonies where there are fewer prying eyes and fewer chances for them to escape. Aircraft manufacturing or research facilities host too many foreign buying delegations, especially these days."

"Yeah, maybe. But Dad was a graduate of the Air Force test pilot school. By definition, he was one of the best pilots in the world. The Russians would not have been able to resist using him."

"I just don't see Pop working as a test pilot for the Russians. I don't think he'd cooperate. I can see him working in a mine, but I think he'd dig his heels in at overtly aiding their military. He would never be a traitor."

"But we don't know, do we? It's been a long time, brother."

Brian was right, as usual. Tom knew that he was just being stubborn. Brian's instincts were usually right on, but so were his own.

"Tom, you're telling me he would have refused to fly? That he would rather be shot than do what the Russians wanted? Why do you believe this?"

"Because I wouldn't fly," Tom said in a quiet voice.

Brian studied his brother. "You wouldn't, would you?" Brian shook his head. "I only hope that I would have the same courage."

"Don't kid yourself, Brian. You're one of the toughest guys I know."

Porter cleared his throat. "Tom, I only met your mom one time. We had dinner in Athens a couple years ago. She told me story after story about how much you remind her of your father."

He looked at Brian. "I'll go along with Tom on this one. I vote for Chita first."

Brian examined the documents, and pointed to a map. "Chita does have some MiG 29s over at the military airport. That's a good combination of mining and airplanes. Chita it is, then."

Deputy Minister Zhang looked over the tops of his glasses, with the barest hint of a smile, said, "I'm so pleased you approve, young man."

Brian nodded and Zhang graced him with another faint smile. He packed his papers, bowed slightly, and left.

Tom turned back to his brother. "You know, Brian, there are two distinct camps among the Chinese: those who are on our side and those who are anti-American for some reason. Guess which group that guy falls into."

"He didn't seem very enthusiastic."

"Actually, he's the leader of the 'pro-Callahan' contingent here. He's actually spent some time in the States. A lot of this planning came from his department. It probably fits into his grand scheme of causing trouble for the Russians any way he can. So make nice with the minister." Tom reached for another briefing sheet and handed it to Brian and Porter.

"The Chinese think they can get us into Russia via Mongolia as consultants to their delegation to a major mining exposition in the capital."

"Mongolia? Why Mongolia?" asked Porter.

"We have to do this one step at a time. We go to Mongolia to establish our credentials. We can't just beam down somewhere inside Siberia."

"I met with some international investors once in Singapore who were looking at Mongolia," said Brian. "It's an interesting place, apparently. According to them, there are lots of opportunities, especially in the mineral extraction business. Mongolia is off the beaten path, the ultimate boondocks, or under the radar. Pick your own cliché. Most Westerners don't know much about the country. I took an informal poll in my office and not three in ten even knew where Mongolia was."

"So, what's going to be our cover?" asked Porter.

"That, my friends," said Tom, "is the best part."

Chapter Seventeen
Chinese Military Compound - Near Beijing

The conference room was quiet. Most of the staff were taking a late dinner in the compound mess hall and enjoying a well-deserved respite. Only Tom, Porter, Brian, Deputy Minister Zhang, and two other ranking Chinese Intelligence officers were present. They sat after their catered dinner, plates cleared and wait staff retired, determined to conclude the day's efforts.

Tom opened the meeting. "Our Chinese friends have made a couple suggestions that we need to address. I'm inclined to agree with what they've proposed, but we need to go through them together. We have a couple of choices each.

"We are going to two-hop our way into Russia, via Mongolia. There is going to be an annual mining convention at the Misheel Expo Center in the capital, Ulaanbaatar, sponsored by the Mongolian National Mining Association or MINETECH. The Chinese are going to send an official delegation, as will several other countries in the region—the Russians and Australians for example. The Chinese delegation is also scheduled to visit Chita to examine a mine and meet some Russian mining officials after the exhibition. We have permission to attend as consultants to the Chinese delegation."

Tom picked up the briefing documents and handed copies to Brian and Porter. "China is the world's largest producer of coal; domestic coal consumption has more than doubled since 1990. The Chinese are constructing two mid-sized, coal-fired power plants a week, basically adding the equivalent of the entire United Kingdom power grid each year, and they still can't keep up with demand. But Chinese coal mines are grotesquely unsafe; thousands of miners die each year in accidents. That's one reason why we're supposed to be along."

Deputy Minister Zhang spoke up. "The second area where you can help our delegation is in finance. Mongolia is always looking for investors. Our government and several of our companies are looking to invest in Mongolia. One of our largest companies, Sichuan Energy Trust, just raised $8.9 billion to invest in Mongolian coal mines."

"I read about that," said Brian. "It was the largest domestic Initial Public Offering ever floated in China."

"True," said Zhang. "And your résumé regarding finance and the raising of large amounts of capital, Major, is quite impressive. So is yours, Mr. Nelson. Any cover story has to have grains of truth embedded in it, in order to hold together. With Colonel Callahan's help, we've come up with some new identities and titles for all of you."

"Brian," said Tom, "you've been to Panama, you've lived in Italy. You know finance better than anybody in Siberia, so you will be posing as an Italian financial advisor to the Chinese government on potential investment in the Mongolian energy sector. You can certainly pass yourself off as an Italian. If questioned, just start talking cooking or wine and wave your hands around." The Americans laughed; even the Chinese managed small smiles.

"Why the Panama connection?"

"China has been making massive investments in Panama since I was in Bolivia. You could have been brought in to help. You speak Spanish. You've been around. According to the dossier the Chinese have created for you, you're quite a guy."

"I *am* quite a guy, Tom. You know that."

"Modest, too," said Tom with a grin. "As for you, Porter, you're on tap to be, of all things, a journalist!"

"Character actor! You are typecast, son," chuckled Brian.

"Damn!" said Porter. "I was hoping to impersonate a NASCAR driver. I have the persona down pat. I don't suppose that I can get you to change your mind?"

"Nope. You're going to continue in your role as Henning Schneider, stringer for *Der Spiegel* and *Stern.*"

"Well, I speak better German than either of you guys and I even have my own fake German passport," he said. "I'm going on this crazy expedition on one condition: if we get back—"

"When we get back," corrected Tom.

"Okay, when we get back, I want first shot at your father's story: the cover-up, the murders, the whole enchilada."

"Deal," said Tom, "though you'll probably have to fight it through the State Department and CIA."

Porter waved a hand. "Been there before, Tom. I can handle those guys. I'll probably win another Pulitzer, too. No, on second thought, since I'll be writing as a German, I'll shoot for a Henri-Nannen Prize, the highest national honor for print journalism in Germany."

"How about you, Tom?" asked Brian.

"I am an obscure Bolivian mining engineer, specializing in administration and safety issues. China has been spending a lot of time and energy looking for investments in Latin America so it's logical to have a Latin along in the delegation. I probably know more about Bolivia than anybody in Russia."

"Yeah, but you don't know much about mining."

"I recognize that, Brian. I'll fake it, stress to them I'm not an operations guy, just a chair-warming administrative weenie. God knows I've spent enough time doing that in Washington. Anyhow, we just have to get in and get out. Our mission is not to bring anybody home; it's to find proof that there are live POWs still in Russia."

Deputy Minister Zhang smiled, "Colonel, you are a natural for intelligence."

"I'm not an Intel guy," groused Tom. "I am a simple jet jockey who would much rather be doing anything but this."

"You are anything but a simple jet jockey, Colonel."

"But to answer your question, Brian, I visited mines and natural gas fields with Ambassador Brent while we lived in Bolivia. At least I know what earth movers are supposed to do."

"Tom, I worked summers in the molybdenum mine north of Taos while I was in high school. That doesn't make me a miner."

"No, but it's easier to fake it if you have some background. For example, I thought about going in disguised as a *Federal'naya Sluzhba Bezopasnosti* colonel. I can do the arrogant FSB colonel thing; in fact, I could probably win an Oscar for the quintessential arrogant colonel role. I rejected it for a couple of reasons. This isn't an old Clint Eastwood movie. This is real and all it would take these days is one cell phone call back to Moscow to check out my papers and look for my name on the roster of arrogant FSB colonels. And it's a long list. As an aside—and to give you a peek at what we're up against—did you know that of the top one thousand decision makers in Russia today, about seventy-eight percent of them have worked for either the FSB, or it's gone-but-not-forgotten predecessor, the KGB?"

Brian and Porter both shook their heads.

"So," Tom continued, "I figured the chances of me pulling that off for very long were pretty slim. As an engineer, anybody who wants to check me out will have to call to Bolivia; someone from the Russian Embassy in La Paz will have to call over to the Bolivian Foreign Ministry. Everybody there will be out to lunch or siesta, or not able to get back to the Russians for at least a week, and then only to ask for clarification, then another lunch break, etcetera, etcetera and by then we'll be back in Washington, home free."

Brian didn't seem convinced. "I think your Spanish is too pure to be from Bolivia. You sound more like a Spaniard."

"Okay, good point, though not many people in Siberia would know the difference. I'll say that my father was stationed in the Bolivian Embassy in Madrid for my high school years." Tom looked at the Chinese Intel official who nodded and made notations in his fake Bolivian dossier. "I'll have to keep my head down while we're in Mongolia. I spent two years in Australia and wouldn't want to be recognized by a visiting Aussie."

"Yeah, Tom, but you were there as a pilot not an engineer. Nobody at this event will know you."

"It was a high profile job, mate. You won't believe the level of people that I met. And we don't want this operation blown before we even get started. The Chinese have sent the underlings ahead on the train to Ulaanbaatar. We'll fly out tomorrow afternoon with the higher officials."

"Why?" asked Porter.

"First of all, it takes thirty-two-plus hours by train."

"Thirty-two hours?"

170

"It's a long way, Port," explained Tom. "Plus they have to change wheels at the border. In another exercise of sound engineering judgement, the track gauge is different between China and Mongolia; they have to jack the cars up at the border and put new wheels on."

"You're kidding!"

"Nope. They're called bogeys, by the way, and it takes at least six hours on a good day. I'm a U.S. Government bureaucrat; I can't make this stuff up like you journalists."

"Man, I'm not going to have to make anything up on this trip. I can just stick to the facts, nobody will believe them anyhow."

"We will, however, ride the train across Mongolia to Chita and later to Irkutsk, if needed. That's how we should be coming home, too." Tom handed Porter and Brian each a dossier. "This is your homework for tonight. Read these and try to absorb as much as you can. In the morning we'll get our last instructions and any updates."

Brian laughed. "Never in my life did I expect to ride a train across Mongolia. But I guess there will be a few more surprises in store for us on this little adventure." He laughed again. "Sure beats the hell out of selling stocks on Wall Street!"

Zhang glanced around the table one more time. "Any more questions?"

There were none. Zhang made a call and three assistants entered the room, each with a leather briefcase.

"Each of these cases contains a cellular satellite phone, programmed with numbers of each of the other phones plus contact numbers here in Beijing," said Zhang. "You need to memorize the list of speed dial numbers tonight. Tomorrow you will be given additional numbers and some simple code words for your contacts in Ulaanbaatar, Chita, and Irkutsk." He pointed to packets within the cases. "There are your identity papers, except for you, Mr. Nelson.

"All of you have phone numbers to give, in case required for verification of identities. Each of you has a different number. The phones have embedded GPS chips so we can track your movements. Keep your phones with you at all times."

171

Brian carefully examined his phone, which looked like a Chinese knockoff of an iPhone. After some basic instruction on the operation of the phones, he held up the empty case. "Isn't this the part where Q gives James Bond a rocket-propelled pogo stick or something?"

Zhang was not amused. "We have no such toy, Major. However, you'll find that your phones are secure and have Internet." He handed a pair of wire-rimmed glasses to Brian and a pair of black horn-rim glasses to Tom. "Wear these and start growing beards. It's not much of a disguise but it might help."

Tom put on the heavy plastic glasses and laughed. "Just like the glasses issued by the Air Force. We call these 'birth control glasses' because they're so ugly no woman would even talk to you while you wear them."

Brian laughed. "You look like an old photo of Benny Goodman or Buddy Holly."

Tom headed off to meet with the Chinese Foreign Ministry desk officer for Panama. The entire conversation was in Spanish. Tom found Chinese-accented Spanish difficult to understand. The briefing took much longer than it should have because Tom had to keep asking the officer to repeat certain phrases.

The Chinese had been pouring investment capital into both coasts of Panama since before Tom had been stationed in Bolivia. There was growing concern within the U.S. government about security of the Panama Canal; it was interesting to hear the same situation presented from the Chinese viewpoint. Tom was briefed on the details of Bolivian-Chinese government joint ventures in developing Bolivia's eastern gas fields, and China's agreement with Venezuela to build another refinery in China to process heavy Venezuelan crude.

He got further briefings about the Chinese view of politics in Latin America in general and Bolivia in particular. Because of Mikey's Bolivian roots, Tom had stayed in touch with friends and associates in Bolivia and was well aware of the messy political situation there with the new president. Other erstwhile Latin dictators were cussed and discussed.

Brian adjourned for briefings with Finance Ministry officials. He found refuge in the reams of financial documents. He asked for and received details of all government investments in the mining and oil industries within Mongolia. He searched the Internet and found hundreds of documents about international investment and the development of mining infrastructure in Mongolia. He was surprised to see so much attention from the United Nations and the International Monetary Fund. Both organizations had special offices devoted to monitoring Mongolian government financials.

After finishing his briefings on South America, Tom stopped in Brian's room.

"In just a few hours, Brian, me boy, we'll be in the land of Genghis Khan."

"You know, Tom, I don't know a damned thing about Mongolia except what I've learned in the past three hours about finance."

"In that case, little brother, listen and be amazed. Genghis proclaimed himself the 'Ruler of All Those Who Live in Felt Tents' around 1206 and founded the greatest empire ever known, encompassing China, the Middle East, Russia, and Central Asia. His grandson, Kublai Khan, founded the Yuan Dynasty while consolidating the empire during his reign from 1260 to 1294."

"You know, when you do this you really piss me off?"

"Do what?"

"Just happen to know everything there is about any given subject."

Tom laughed, reached into his gym bag and produced a copy of *Fodor's Guide to Mongolia.* He tossed it to Brian. "Yours is in Italian; mine's in Spanish."

Brian caught the book, then gave his brother a gesture known as the finger. "Not that I'm worried or anything," he said, "but who will be watching our back?"

"Don't worry. There will be at least one spook along. When I worked on the Conventional Forces in Europe Treaty, each inspection team that we sent to Europe or Russia had at least one CIA guy masquerading as an accountant or something."

"So who is the spook on this delegation?"

"Don't know. But I hope he's the best guy they have."

Brian sat up and pulled out his laptop. "Look at this. I've been on the Internet all evening."

Tom sat and looked at the screens that Brian had indexed. His own picture and fictitious résumé were posted on a dozen websites. A search on his Bolivian name showed ninety-four hits. The Chinese had put creative and completely bogus articles and references to his Bolivian persona. He clicked on a link. Broken. He tried again, same result. Then a research paper mentioned his contribution in a mine in southern Bolivia; another mentioned a mine in Chile; yet another article quoted him.

Tom Googled Brian's Italian name and Brian's face peered back at him, embedded somewhere within almost twenty different websites and referenced by two hundred more, all bogus. Tom did a search on Brian's Italian name with the same results: many broken links, several mentions, one or two quotes, all entirely fictitious.

"Pretty clever," he said. "They even have bogus broken links to add a little realism to a net search."

"Yeah. I wonder how many times they've used this system before."

"You mean like to provide cover for Chinese Intel guys posing as academics or as businessmen penetrating the United States?"

"Yeah. This just popped up, all neat and damned complete, like they have a template or something to just shoot these bogus résumés and articles out there. They've done it before."

Tom nodded. Interesting. Disturbing.

He left to go pack the few remaining articles that he would need on the trip. They were all traveling light, meaning one suitcase each, plus the leather briefcase that no self-respecting consultant would be caught without. He dawdled, packing efficiently but slowly, not wanting to finish. He knew what he had to do next, but put off the task. Finally, he sat at his desk and reached for a sheet of writing paper. From his briefcase, he extracted an antique fountain pen, a gift from his mother when he'd made colonel. Dark blue lapis lazuli with speckles of gold and a twenty-one carat gold nib, it was one of his most treasured possessions because it had also been her gift to his father when he pinned on his eagles.

He began to write: Dear Mr. President, I regret to inform you—

Chapter Eighteen
Ulaanbaatar, Mongolia

Ulaanbaatar was not an inspiring city, decided Tom, as the Chinese delegation was driven from the airport to the hotel. The view of Mongolia's largest metropolitan area was dominated by unlovely Soviet-era block apartments and low-lying concrete buildings. Construction cranes were everywhere, lending an air of hope as newer, more modern, even sleek buildings peeked up out of the unimaginative skyline. "UB" was living up to its reputation as the "World's Coldest Capital City," the only one with an annual average temperature below freezing. Tom watched some attractive young women, dressed in miniskirts and summer blouses walk along the sidewalk oblivious to the cold, snow swirling around their leather boots.

On the positive side, the sky was clear blue, there was no pollution to speak of, and lots of open spaces. Fewer cars and people gave the city a distinctly laid-back feel. The four sacred mountains surrounding the city were covered by dense pine forest to the north and grassy steppes to the south, dotted with the famous Mongolian felt tents, or *gers*, and their sheep, horses, and cows. The Tuul River flowed through the city, providing more open spaces and vegetation. Directly in front of the hotel was a large plaza dominated by an enormous statue of Lenin. The delegation was bustled inside and soon dispersed to their rooms.

In the elevator, Porter said in Russian, "Oh my God, did you see those women in the lobby? They were gorgeous! Exotic, too. Russian, Asian, blends…wow!"

"Sorry, didn't notice," said Brian.

"Don't give me that. What kind of traveling Italian man keeps his eyes caged?"

"This kind."

"Here we are in Ulaanbaatar, home of beautiful women. I'm stunned."

176

"Well, you're the delegation's only bachelor. Be our guest, Herr Schneider. Good luck with the ladies."

MINETECH hosted its annual exposition of mining machinery and equipment at the Misheel Expo Center, an unremarkable two-story building with skylights and metal siding. The mountainous background gave a rural feel to the urban setting. The parking lot was full of predominately Korean and Japanese cars, but a sizeable number of Russian-made Ladas and Moskvich automobiles were mixed with an abundance of minivans.

Inside, the building was fitted out for the exposition with booths touting mining equipment, machinery, even international financial institutions proclaiming their mining expertise. Suits mixed with hard-hatless engineers and mechanics wearing Carhartt work clothes or the foreign equivalent. He heard languages from all over the globe: Australian-twanged English, Chinese, Japanese, French, Italian, Afrikaans, and German. It seemed everybody wanted to get in on one of the last mining stampedes left as Mongolia opened up for exploitation. Tom steered away from the Australians, stopping at several booths to inquire about specific pieces of machinery, always asking his first question in Spanish, then switching languages as required. He was determined to learn as much as he could about mining.

On the second morning, Porter was everywhere, asking questions and taking pictures, everyone's idea of a nosey reporter. Tom was surprised to see several booths promoting Russian-built mining equipment. He didn't know that Russia was known for making mining equipment; that information hadn't come up in his briefings. He wondered how many other holes there were in his background. Tom bumped into other members of the Chinese delegation and would occasionally step outside to compare notes with them and breathe some fresh air.

Tom and Brian were investigating a New Zealand exploration company's machinery offerings when Brian turned abruptly and headed for the exit. As soon as Tom could detach himself from the earnest young Kiwi salesman, he followed. Brian leaned against the wall, face pale.

177

"Holy cow, that was close! Did you see that guy in a navy blue suit?"

"Sure, why?"

"I spent almost two weeks with that guy putting a deal together in Tokyo a couple years ago. If he had seen me, this Mickey Mouse disguise wouldn't have helped one bit." He laughed. "And I gave you grief for thinking that you'd see someone here who would know you." He laughed again. "Who wudda thunk it? Me, almost literally running into an acquaintance in Ulaanbaatar of all places? It would be much more likely in a brothel in Manila." His face colored as he realized what he had said. He turned to Tom, "And that slip of the tongue is never, I say again never, to be repeated. Especially to the wives."

"Of course, Brian," said Tom. "You know what they always say: 'What happens in Ulaanbaatar stays in Ulaanbaatar.'"

***

The third morning found the Chinese and Russian delegations boarding a Mi-8 twin turbine helicopter for an early, one-hour flight to a working Mongolian open pit coal mine. Tom could not help but think of the chopper in its NATO designation as a "Hip," reverting to his Cold War mentality to see Soviet helicopters as priority targets. This particular Hip was fitted out as a civilian transport, set up with twenty-eight airline seats and a "head" or toilet in the rear. Tom sat by one of the square windows and watched, mesmerized as the flight took them over the wide open spaces of the Mongolian steppe. The single track of the Trans-Mongolian Railroad bisected their route, stretching off into the horizon north and south. The buff-colored sand hills and rocky outcroppings interspaced with broad grasslands were dotted with clusters of gers surrounded by livestock. The grasslands became more prevalent as they headed southeast; the terrain reminded Tom of the Bolivian uplands and parts of New Mexico.

Where there was water, there was life; where there was coal, there was a coal mine. Tom's pilot eyes picked out the smudge of a mine on the horizon, then watched as it grew into an enormous hole that he estimated to be maybe a mile by a half mile. They flew over the terraced levels chopped through the thick bituminous coal seam and slashes in the surrounding earth, which he now knew were referred to as "overburden." The haul road leading up from the crater floor was busy with dozens of trucks hauling coal up to the train loading tipple. The railroad spur ran back towards the Trans-Mongolian Railroad line.

He tried to listen politely to his middle-aged Russian seatmate as he droned on and on about how he preferred open-pit mining to underground mining, especially for coal. Tom nodded and filed that information away as the aircraft approached the helipad and touched down.

The sheer magnitude of the mining operation was impressive. The amount of activity rivaled aircraft and support equipment movements on a large civil airport: dozens of dust suppressing trucks spraying water on the road and the coal bed floor, excavators and huge coal shovels, coal trucks, bulldozers, and support vehicles were everywhere. Tom figured the amount of diesel fuel they must consume would be staggering.

As they disembarked from the helicopter, cold air swirled around them. The dull rumble from the enormous mining equipment was a constant hum in the background as they motored to the mine headquarters for a briefing.

The mine was owned by Galahad Holdings, Ltd, a joint Australian-Canadian company headquartered in Hong Kong, and one of the largest mining operators in the world. These enormous international mining companies were voracious consumers of investor cash, thus the invitation to visit. The tour was designed to impress and seduce potential investors. The mine manager and his staff were ready to encourage the delegations to part with huge sums of money. As such, the briefings were complete and laden with facts and figures, numbers that were second nature to Brian, who peppered the manager with questions for even more numbers. Tom was staggered by the amount of mining concessions—measured in thousands of square kilometers instead of mere acres or hectares—owned by Galahad Holdings just within Mongolia. This mine alone was projected to produce at current or higher levels for another eighty years. Tom found the idea of a multi-generational mine fascinating.

After the briefing, the mine manager led the caravan of vehicles to a spot overlooking the pit to witness a scheduled explosion. The manager pointed across the mine face to a terrace where a series of four-inch diameter holes had been drilled fifty feet deep and packed with a mixture of ammonium nitrate and diesel fuel. At the manager's signal, warning sirens sounded. Another signal and the side of the mine erupted in a rippling series of dull explosions, the sound muted by the sheer distance across the mine. The terrace slid down in an enormous cloud of coal dust. Earthmovers and trucks moved in like scavengers swarming a road kill. Work resumed. All very efficient and profitable.

They loaded up in the mine's fleet of Range Rovers and started the drive back to the heliport. "We are bringing in newer and more fuel-efficient equipment, using the old stuff until it breaks down," said the manager to Tom and Porter. "Like that old Soviet-style bulldozer left over there. That thing is in the way." He pulled to a stop next to the machine. "Just stopped working this morning and our mechanic, who specializes in old equipment, is sick. I need it moved."

Porter opened his door, got out, walked around the machine, then climbed into the seat and pressed the starter. Nothing. He dismounted and asked the manager for a screwdriver, then took off his jacket and tinkered with the engine for a few minutes as the others watched.

"The starter solenoid is shot," he explained to the mine manager. "Happens a lot in these old machines." He flipped a switch. "So, first turn on the master switch, then by-pass the solenoid with the screwdriver, like this." Sparks flew, and the motor turned over and caught, then died. Then caught again. Smoke billowed, and the engine smoothed. "Climb on up," he shouted, as he scrambled into the seat.

Tom and six others clambered up, including the mine manager and four Russians. Porter put the dozer in gear, and drove slowly down the haul road to the equipment area, executives hanging all over the machine, laughing and waving like little kids.

The senior Russian official, a burly middle-aged man named Boris Suslov, clapped him on the back. "Good job, my friend. Where did you learn to work on Russian equipment?"

"I spent six months with the Soviet Army in Afghanistan reporting for European magazines. We had equipment like this."

Suslov put his hand on Porter's shoulder. "Which branch?"

"Three months with armor units, three months with *Spetznatz*."

"My son was *Spetznatz*," said Suslov, voice soft now. "He did not come home."

Porter nodded. "A lot of good men did not come home, my friend."

The flight back was uneventful but it gave Tom another chance to walk through the UB airport terminal that featured a three-story-high mosaic of Genghis Khan, which, according to his guidebook, was made up of some 430,000 pieces of crystal tile. The minibuses picked them up in front of the terminal and deposited them in front of the hotel.

Brian spotted the hotel maître d' and asked about dinner reservations, starting in Italian, then switching to Chinese, and finishing in Russian. Satisfied with the address of a prominent Italian restaurant, he invited several of the Russians, as well as Tom and Porter and a sizeable portion of the Chinese delegation.

Thirty minutes later, the men loaded up the minivans. The *Camerino* turned out to be a modest little Italian restaurant tucked away on a back street. The interior occupied a single long room with a bar at one end. A dark wooden floor, tables with crisp white tablecloths topped with candle-impaled Chianti bottles, and a wall mural depicting the view of what had to be Lake Como completed the ambiance.

"*Buono sera*,"—good evening, said Brian to the maître d'. "We have reservations for twelve." Brian's greeting elicited a flood of Italian from the maître d' as he and Brian exchanged greetings, birthdays, and genealogies on their way to the largest table in the restaurant.

Bustling waiters produced menus. Tom watched as Brian studied his, then motioned the head waiter over to discuss the culinary options. The owner, a robust Italian from the Piedmont region near Turin, recognized a fellow gourmet. Brian was invited to inspect the kitchen and re-appeared with the chef in tow—the owner's wife. They studied the wine list together, Brian conferring with the owner and the chef over each entrée, and debating the pairings of wine with each course. Massive amounts of food arrived in waves. The Chinese took prim little bites of pasta and squinted curiously at the labels of unpronounceable Italian wines, while the Russians had no problem fitting in and having a grand old time. Eventually even the Chinese got into the spirit, or spirits, as Brian's pairing of wines with specific dishes proved to be superb. Empty wine bottles lined the table like miniature Easter Island monoliths.

By sipping his wine and insisting on a clean glass with every new food item, Tom managed to drink only half as much as his tablemates; he was pleased to see Brian discreetly drinking as much mineral water as he did wine.

Suslov put a beefy arm around Brian's shoulders. "I have to visit Italy," he said, voice slurred. "If the food there is as good as this, it must be heaven."

"Italian restaurants travel well," said Brian. "Good food is always appreciated. I eat Italian in London, Panama City, Chicago, even Tokyo. One of my favorite Italian restaurants is in Singapore."

"We have fine restaurants in Chita," said the Russian. "You must be my guests. Then we'll take you to your mine. You are flying to Chita, yes?"

Tom shook his head. "No, we're riding the train. Budget cuts."

Suslov nodded. "Ah, working with governments has a price." He took one last gulp of his wine. "Which mine are you to visit?"

Tom handed him a copy of their itinerary.

The Russian took out his glasses and tried to focus on the unsteady paper. "No, not that mine," he announced. "It's old and boring. You deserve to see some of our new Russian mining technology. I'll get those chair-bound bureaucrats in the Ministry to allow you to visit a different mine."

Back in the hotel, Brian, Tom, and Porter helped load their new friends into the elevator, then took a car up themselves. Slouched against the wall, Porter said, "I'm looking forward to the train ride. I need a couple of days to dry out."

Chapter Nineteen
Los Angeles, California

Colleen Callahan sat in the first class section of the Boeing 777 as the aircraft made its turn over the Pacific onto final approach into Los Angeles International (LAX). The inky blackness of the ocean contrasted with the millions of lights twinkling on the mainland ahead. Mikey's face was glued to the window. She watched his joyous expression reflected in the glass.

"Look at the lights, Mommy!" he said in Japanese.

"Aren't they beautiful, son?"

"Look!" he squealed. "There's a Ferris wheel. Oh, can we go, Mommy? Please?"

"Not this time, darling boy. Remember what I told you about our costumes?"

"Yes, Mommy." His voice dropped to a whisper. "We're trying to trick some people. And we need to behave and get to our next airplane. Right?"

Dressed casually, Colleen wore nothing to attract attention. Jeans, sweater, athletic shoes, no jewelry except her wedding ring, topped off with a brunette wig. Mikey was dressed in his Halloween cowboy outfit, with a big bullrider's cowboy hat and boots. The long black hair that Colleen adored was gone, freshly trimmed back over his ears. Seated two rows back, Elizabeth was also attired in jeans, sweater and a brunette wig.

The captain planted the aircraft on the runway; it bounced twice before settling down. Colleen smiled as she thought about the disparaging comments Tommy would have made at such a poor landing; few pilots measured up to his exacting standards.

Ah, Tommy, where are you? That thought unleashed a torrent of emotions. Brian's cryptic e-mail had suggested the family fly to Bangkok to stay under the protection of Admiral Shinawatra. Both she and Elizabeth had jumped at the idea since neither felt secure in the United States after the attack at the Callahan residence. Neither the police, nor the Secret Service were taking the attack more seriously than an armed burglary gone wrong. Colleen worried that because Tom sensed danger for her, he was probably doing something dangerous himself. She forced that out of her mind; her job now was to get Mikey and Elizabeth to safety in Thailand.

Colleen waited until the cabin was nearly empty before exiting the airplane, then crossed from the domestic arrival terminal to Terminal B, the international departure terminal.

There were five people in the Thai Airways first class check-in counter; Elizabeth was next to be processed. Colleen whispered a reminder to Mikey to pretend not to see her.

"G'day," said Colleen with a smile as she handed her Australian passport to the lovely Thai agent.

"Good evening, Mrs. O'Kelly," she said, reading Colleen's maiden name from the passport. She matched the reservation on her computer screen with the passport. "And this is your son?"

Colleen nodded as she handed over Mikey's Bolivian passport with his birth name of Luis Inocente.

"Why are you traveling alone with your son?"

"My husband is in Tokyo on business. He's flying in later this week. We will return to Sydney together."

"Do you have permission from your husband to take the boy out of the country?"

Colleen handed her a letter, composed that morning and bearing Tom's signature forged by the Thai ambassador and notarized by his secretary.

The agent read the letter, then disappeared into the nearby office.

Two minutes passed—though they felt like an hour to Colleen—before the agent re-appeared accompanied by her supervisor.

He looked her over carefully. "I have to ask you, madam: Why are you traveling alone with your son?"

"I explained this once before."

"It is a U.S. requirement, madam."

"Neither I nor my son is a U.S. citizen. But I have a letter from my husband just to prevent this type of interrogation."

"And your place of residence?"

"We have several, actually. One in Sydney, one in Perth, one in Bangkok, and one in Tokyo. Which one of them will get me on the plane?"

The supervisor looked at the documents, then back to her. "In the passport, you are a blonde."

She drew herself up tall. "Hardly something to disqualify a person from a flight. Do you deny tickets to a man who has grown a beard? Or is it only women you choose to harass?"

"Madam, I am not trying to harass you. I am trying to do my job."

"Is there a problem with my documents?"

"Everything seems to be in order."

"Then why all the questions?" she said. "I would like my tickets and boarding passes, please. In fact, I insist."

He shrugged, handed the papers to the agent and said something in Thai. She nodded, then stepped to her computer and began issuing the tickets.

After struggling through security with Mikey, the car seat, and the backpacks, Colleen located and entered the nearest ladies' restroom. Elizabeth wandered in a few moments later. The women moved to the back and waited for the only other occupant, an elderly woman to leave.

"I'm worried that we weren't as clever as we thought," said Colleen. "I think the word is out that we're trying to leave the country."

"How could that be?"

"I don't know, but I just got the third degree at the check-in counter. I thought they were about to bring out the waterboards." She took a couple of deep breaths. "Let's go with the assumption that somebody is looking for us, probably just me and Mikey. They must not have you on their radar yet because you're so new to the family." She thought a moment. "I think we should split up. You take Mikey. Nobody would expect that. Let's meet at the ladies bathroom nearest the departure gate."

"But they could be watching it," said Elizabeth.

"No, I don't think so. They would think that either we're going to my family in Australia or to Tommy—meaning Vietnam or China, depending on how much they know."

"But we don't know for sure."

Colleen shook her head. "No." She gave Elizabeth a weak smile. "Tommy would call this 'going with the odds.'" She handed Elizabeth the tickets and all her own documents. "I'll head down another concourse, away from our departure gate. If I don't show, get on that plane!"

She caressed Mikey's check and kissed him. "Listen to Aunt Lizzie, sweetie. Do what she says. I'll see you soon." And she was gone.

As Colleen crossed the terminal food court, she forced herself to not look back for a last glimpse of her baby. She paused in front of the departure board and found two flights for China leaving from the same concourse. She noted their gate numbers and headed in that direction. She slipped on her sunglasses to better fit in with the LA crowd, and carefully surveyed the area around her for potential tails.

She noticed two men in suits standing in the open, photographs in hand, studying passengers walking through the departure terminal.

She felt rather than saw someone following her. She turned towards the escalator to try to duck down a level. The two suits changed direction to cut her off. She heard one say, "Excuse me, ma'am." He reached for her arm.

Colleen punched him in the stomach. The man gasped and doubled over. She brought up her knee catching him in the face. She heard the cartilage crush as he half-rolled and went down screaming. Blood spurted from his ruined nose. Colleen half turned on the other man and smashed her elbow in his face. He staggered back and collided with two passengers, nearly falling.

She vaulted over the railing and ran down the moving stairs. She sprinted as fast as she could through the crowds, darting around slow-moving tourists and their baggage, desperate to get away. Shouts behind her. A shot. A man just ahead of her screamed and went down in a heap. Her path was blocked by panicking passengers. She careened off one man, then another.

A blue-uniformed man lunged out of a coffee shop doorway and tackled her. His partner helped wrestle her to the ground. The first officer smashed her face to the floor while the second wrenched her arms behind her back. With one knee digging painfully between her shoulder blades, he slapped on cuffs. Four more cops appeared, pistols drawn, another with an automatic weapon.

Colleen's assailants charged up, both with guns drawn and bloody noses. The first man waved his credentials. "CIA. We'll take it from here."

"No, he's not," Colleen screamed. "He tried to kill me!"

The CIA agent bent down and pulled her up to a sitting position. He yanked off her wig.

She screamed again, "He's a rogue agent. The CIA has no arrest authority—"

He slapped her across the face. "Shut up, you bitch!" A burly, black police sergeant grabbed him by the shoulders and threw him across the concourse. The agent rolled and came up with his pistol pointed at the officer. Five police pistols and an Uzi pointed back. The agent raised his hands, gun pointed up at the ceiling.

"Put the gun down!" ordered the sergeant. The agent started to argue. "Put the gun down! Now!" shouted the sergeant. An officer moved in behind him and took the gun. He ejected the clip, worked the action to clear the chamber, then stuck the pistol in his belt.

The agent closed in on the sergeant. "Her husband is a fugitive. She's going to him. She knows where he is. We need to make her talk. All I need is five minutes alone with her."

"Yeah, I've just seen your idea of persuasion, asshole. Not in my airport you won't. This ain't Guantanamo."

"This is federal, you stupid cop," he shouted. "I'll have your badge for this!"

The police sergeant grabbed him by his shirt. "You shot a citizen in my airport, an innocent man. I don't give a damn about who you think you are. This is my airport and this is Los Angeles, not some jerkwater country. You want the woman, talk to a judge and get a warrant. In the

187

meantime, you get out of my face or I'll arrest your ass. I've got a prisoner and a wounded citizen to attend to." He shoved the agent away.

"Get him outta here. And the other one, too. Take them to the station and turn them over to the Captain. He'll know what to do." Officers jerked both men around and pushed them down the corridor.

A radio crackled. "EMTs are on the way, Sarge," said one of the officers.

"Good. How's our citizen doing?"

"Scared mostly. Lots of blood. It's under control. He'll live, but his vacation's a mess."

The sergeant nodded. "Stay on top of it." He holstered his weapon and knelt down beside Colleen. "Who are you, ma'am?"

"I don't know why these men attacked me. I just defended myself."

"We're going to have to take you in, ma'am. Do you have any identification?"

She shook her head.

Another officer handed the sergeant her backpack. He opened it and pulled out another wig. Then a jacket, shoes, and sunglasses.

"This is a disguise, ma'am. Why were those men trying to kill you?"

She shook her head and said nothing.

He tried again. "What is your name? Where are you from?"

Colleen met his eyes but said nothing.

"Where is your ticket? This is the international terminal. You have no passport, no identification, no money."

She looked up at the corridor clock. Scheduled takeoff was in thirty minutes. Allow another hour for a possible takeoff delay and/or to clear U.S. airspace. Thai Airways was a national flag carrier, so the plane could not be turned around by the FAA even if those CIA wankers managed a warrant and discovered which flight Elizabeth and Mikey were on. Not likely. Her job was to stall for ninety more minutes.

"Thank you, sergeant. You saved my life." She gave him one of her best smiles. "But I'm afraid that I must insist on my rights now. I believe that I am entitled to an attorney and a phone call."

Elizabeth led Mac down the terminal concourse to the departure gate. She looked around for the nearest women's restroom, found a stall, and locked the door. She sat on the toilet holding Mac in her lap. He started to protest. "Shh, Mac," she whispered. "We have to stay here for half an hour."

"This game's no fun, Aunt Lizzie."

"I know, Mac, but we have to do it."

"When am I going to see my daddy?"

"Soon, sweetie, soon, after our airplane ride."

Elizabeth devoutly hoped what she said was true. She had no idea what to expect in the near or any other future. But she had a little boy to protect and she was determined to get him to Thailand safely with as little trauma as possible.

"We need to change our clothes, sweetie." Elizabeth pulled off his cowboy boots, took off his hat and shirt. She opened her backpack and dressed him in jeans, white athletic shoes, a D.C. United soccer jersey, a Washington Redskins satin jacket and a New York Yankees hat. She rolled the boots and cowboy hat up in his old jacket and threw them away in the trash, carefully covering them with dirty paper towels.

She heard the muffled first call for boarding and checked her watch. Quickly, she pulled off her own brunette wig and replaced it with a black one. She reversed her red jacket turning it blue, and put on a blue beret, sunglasses, and blue Crocs. Satisfied, she sat, gently rocking Mac and softly singing him the only lullaby she could remember.

Elizabeth tensed as she heard a disembodied voice made the second and third boarding announcements. God! What could have happened to Colleen?

Mac was getting squirmy. She was afraid he'd call attention to them. There was only so much patience in a four-year-old boy. Where was Colleen? Being late was not like her. Elizabeth had to face up to the possibility that she wouldn't, or couldn't, show. Finally she couldn't stand it anymore.

"Okay, Mac, if I say we can leave now, will you be good and do the pretend game?"

"Where's my mommy?" he pouted, arms crossed.

"I don't know, Mac, but remember what she said?"

"Yes. She said to do what you told me and to behave. But it's really hard, Aunt Lizzie."

"I know it is, sweet boy. But this is really important." She took his face in her hands and looked him in the eyes. "We're going to walk out of here and get on an airplane."

He looked doubtful. "But what about mommy?"

"Mac, this is important. She may be outside already. She might get on just as we do. She might not. If not, we'll have to go on our trip and she'll join us later."

"Promise?"

Elizabeth took a deep breath. "I promise."

"Okay. Mommy said to listen to you, so I will. But I wish she was here."

"Can you do something really funny?"

"What?" said Mac, intrigued.

"Can you sing me the Japanese song your daddy taught you?" She hoped his almond-shaped eyes would fool somebody programmed to look for a Latino child. "Or would you rather to pretend that you're asleep and I'll carry you?"

He considered the question. "Will you carry me if I pretend to be asleep?" She nodded. "Okay, let's do that."

She quickly organized everything so the tickets were handy. Even so, she waddled slowly and awkwardly holding a sleeping toddler, carrying a car seat and both backpacks. As she approached the gate, her heart sank; there were still dozens of economy class passengers waiting to board.

A young man stepped out of line. "May I help you, ma'am?"

Startled, Elizabeth resisted the urge to run. Instead she smiled. "Yes, thank you." She shifted Mac and handed the man the car seat and a backpack. "You are very kind."

"Not really," he said with a grin. "I always look for mothers with kids to help board early. That way, I get to do my Boy Scout good deed for the day and get on the airplane sooner."

They moved through the loading chute and into the first class cabin of the Airbus 340. Elizabeth found the two seats assigned to Colleen and the boy and set Mac in the window seat with his face against the side of the aircraft. She thanked the young man who made his way back into coach.

Elizabeth arranged the contents of Mac's backpack within his reach in the huge first class seat: an iPod loaded with three episodes of *Barney* and two Disney movies; his plastic sippy cup; three books; and a stuffed panda that he insisted upon calling "baby wolf cub." Then she wrapped a blanket around him and leaned over to kiss him. She whispered, "You are a wonderful boy. I am going to tell your mommy and daddy how well you played this game. Thank you, sweetie."

The eighteen-hour, overnight flight was the longest of her life. Where was Colleen? What should she expect in Bangkok? Who to call? Where was Brian?

She gazed out the window and saw only her own reflection.

Chapter Twenty
Ulaanbaatar, Mongolia

The next day, minivans carried the Chinese delegation to the stately UB train station for their appointment with the Trans-Mongolian Railroad. Uniformed porters piled the luggage on trolleys and followed as the delegation members made their way through the crowd of backpackers, Mongolian families—some in traditional dress—and international businesspeople. Tom was again surprised at the number of languages and ethnic groups represented in Ulaanbaatar.

Tom had ridden more than a few trains in the developing world and knew first-hand the uneven quality of service. He was relieved at the condition of these sturdy German-built train cars, well maintained and clean. The Chinese had Brian and Porter in the same first class berth while Tom had the connecting berth. Each cabin had bench seats and a small table. Two porters lived aboard each first class car and took care of the travelers and the car. They magically appeared, helped the travelers settle in, and even provided steaming cups of strong black tea and sugar cookies.

Porter and Brian joined Tom in his cabin as their train car crept through the train yard. Headed by two locomotives for safety purposes as it traveled through the wide open north, the train jostled back and forth through the switches and banked turns, past long strings of coal cars parked on rail spurs awaiting their delivery to the power station. Pungent smells of cooking permeated the car. Outside the city, the speed picked up as they sliced through the Mongolian countryside heading north towards the Russian city of Ulan-Ude and the junction with the Trans-Siberian Railroad.

Tom opened his bag and took out a Chinese-made electronic bug detector, a small box slightly bigger than a pack of cigarettes, and flicked a switch. No warning lights flashed or audible warnings sounded. Relieved, he gave the others a thumbs-up. "The berth is clean."

Porter said, "Ours checked out, too. That could mean that either we've escaped detection so far or the Russians know about us and are just waiting for us to get to Russia before arresting us."

"Or just that we're on our way to Russia," said Tom. "We're committed now."

"We should be committed," grumbled Brian, "for even considering this crazy escapade."

"What we're scheduled for, Brian, is to meet Suslov and the Russians at Chita, look around a bit, go to at least one mine, either the one on the official itinerary or the new one Suslov says is more interesting. Then over to Irkutsk and check out at least one mine there."

"So explain to me again why the Russians are so interested in the visit of a Chinese mining delegation," said Porter.

Tom glanced out the window as the train made a sweeping turn out of the rail yard, the vista revealing a broad expanse of gers crowded together on the outskirts of the city. "It makes economic sense as well as political sense. Geographically, Chita and Irkutsk are much closer to Beijing than to Moscow. A couple of years ago, Russia and Mongolia signed a new agreement to boost cross-border trade and to remove customs hurdles at designated checkpoints. This also made Russian-Chinese trade easier. Then, using petro-dollars, the Russian president bought controlling interest of the top Mongolian copper producer. Suslov told me that the president is on the prowl for more investments. That's why there was a Russian delegation at the MINETECH convention.

"Right now, he's looking at building an oil pipeline from Russia to China through Mongolia. The Russians need the Chinese market and the Chinese need Russian oil as well as Russian markets. Mongolia is sort of caught in between and is in a great position to exploit the needs of both China and Russia. Everybody wins—but only with new treaties and protocols. Thus, the need to host delegations like the one we're attached to. You still with me, Port?"

"That all makes sense, Tom. But it's all economics. What's the political angle?"

"The Russian Constitution limits the president to two consecutive four-year terms. This president is in his last year of his second term. He appointed his successor who has already been approved. The successor then named him prime minister. Last week, they announced a proposed constitutional amendment to increase the term of office for the president to six years. It will pass. That would mean the current president would be allowed to become president again after his four years as prime minister. Therefore, he would be in more-or-less complete power twenty out of twenty-four years.

"The key point is this: he's using petro-dollars to invest in expanding other moneymaking commodities and the oil pipeline. He's leveraging everything he has while simultaneously pumping up his defense budget. Using those new profits, he will expand his armed forces until there will be no country in Asia, maybe anywhere that can stand up to the new Russia."

"He'll be President-for-Life, essentially a twenty-first century *tsar*," breathed Porter.

Tom nodded. "I think that's how he sees himself."

"Jesus, Tom. Does anybody else know this?"

"The President of the United States."

"What?"

"I wrote him a letter before we left China."

"What?"

Tom laughed. "Porter, you're a journalist. You're supposed to ask more penetrating questions than 'What?'"

"Okay. What else did you say to the President?"

Tom looked out the window at the rough terrain. The past twenty years had passed so quickly. Faster than he had imagined they would. He had always thought there would be more. He sighed. What was done was done. "I resigned."

"What? I mean: What compelled you to go to such extremes?"

"Before we left China, I wrote the President and resigned."

"Brian, did you know about this?"

"I resigned as well."

Porter looked confused. "Can you even resign by mail?"

"I did. And retired from the Air Force."

"Can you really do that?"

"The Chief of Staff of the Air Force is my godfather. He was also my father's wingman when he was shot down. So, yeah, I can. And did."

"Your rank could have saved your ass if we got caught."

"Porter, you and Brian were right. This is my quest, not the President's."

"So now he listens!" Porter threw his hands in the air and shook his head. "I had gotten used to the idea that the President was somehow backing this mad expedition."

"That's the problem. He's not, nor is anybody in our government." Tom settled back into his seat. "I feel like this is the right way."

"Tom Callahan, you are either the most honorable man I've ever met or the dumbest."

"Or both," chimed in Brian.

"Okay, assuming you're right and all this somehow works out," asked Porter. "How are we going to make contact if we see anyone who might be American?"

"First answer: we're not here to make contact, we're here to find evidence of POWs. Second answer: I don't know. We'll have to improvise. Maybe push them into a closet or an empty office and start talking."

"Man, this plan sounds like Amateur Hour," said Brian.

"Bush league stuff," echoed Porter with a smile.

"Seat of the pants," said Brian.

"Candid Camera," said Porter.

"Pull it out of your ass," said Brian.

"Okay, okay," said Tom, laughing. "I get the idea. Anybody have a better plan?"

"Nope," said Brian. "You're the brains here, brother mine. We lackeys await your orders."

The men settled back into their seats. The landscape flashing past, their windows was very different from the terrain to the south of UB. This was not the Gobi Desert. The land became more complex and rougher. Stunted steppe vegetation huddled the south-facing slopes right up to the ridges, changed to forest on the north-facing slopes. They passed through multiple valleys, some wide, some not. Strong winds buffeted the train as they headed north and a thin film of sandy dust permeated the train cars.

Brian dialed up his satellite phone and the men studied satellite images of the Mongolian north on the small screen. The web mapping service offered hybrid options; Brian superimposed the road/railroad image onto the satellite photo. They tracked the rail line and the only paved road from Ulaanbaatar to the Russian border, and noted even the small cities along the route to Russia: Gusinoye, Djida, and Naushki. The Mongolian mountains stood out, as did forests that reached down from Siberia's vast taiga ecosystem.

They switched trains in Ulan-Ude with a minimum of confusion and delay. The ride on the Trans-Siberian Railway east from Ulan-Ude initially followed the Uda River. Rising terrain to the north, an open valley stretched off to the south as they traveled west to east, then southeast through narrow valleys and rising landforms on both sides. Low clouds extended as far as they could see and touched the tops of the rising hills to the west. Finally, the land flattened out a bit and they could see signs of Chita, "The City of Exiles," capital of the Zabaikal Region. It was also the main transport junction in the east of Russia, home to a federal highway, the Trans-Siberian mainline, and the newly-refurbished Chita International Airport. The train moved slowly through the rail yards past hundreds of parked railcars loaded with logs.

The cavernous Chita train station was a large brick and concrete building, plain but efficiently laid out, topped with a tower and a gilded dome. The delegation was met in the lobby by several members of the local mining authority, as well as two middle-aged men from the Chinese consulate in Chita. To reach their buses, they crossed a plaza crowded with people, and through a biting wind and flurries of snow.

The bus made its way through the city, affording Tom a chance to get a feel for the area. While not exactly depressing, the architecture was decidedly Soviet; concrete block apartments that appeared universally five stories high, as if the local building code limited structures to five stories. There was little imagination, no doubt a residual effect of being a city closed to foreigners—and most Russians—

for decades. The numerous statues of Lenin scattered about only served to accentuate the "Soviet-ness" of the city. As they made their way towards the town center, some of the buildings took on a vaguely Japanese look; buildings with slightly upturned roof corners and spacious, intricate rock gardens, courtesy of the former Japanese POWs. Tom decided that the painted wooden houses and vegetation would help make Chita attractive enough in the summer, but it was not particularly eye-catching in the winter.

"My friends!" Suslov's voice boomed across the hotel lobby as they entered. "Welcome to Chita!" He bear-hugged each in turn, starting with Porter. Suslov introduced his companions, Dimitry Popov, a stocky man with a bushy black moustache and a hard-bitten look. Tom decided Popov was classic FSB counterintelligence. Grigori Kozlov was slightly built, with an innocent face; he looked like a clerk, and was almost certainly FSB. Tom felt his heart lurch. Game time.

Suslov took charge. "The bellhops will take your bags to your rooms. Let's go have a drink and talk about tonight." He dragged the men across the hotel lobby into the smoky hotel bar and found a table.

After the first toast, he said, "The old coal mine that you are scheduled to visit just had an underground fire. Sixteen miners dead." His voice took on an odd tone and a pained expression passed over his face. Tom noticed his gnarled hands and guessed that Suslov had, as a young man, worked in the mines. Those dead men were probably like his brothers, or now as an older man, his own sons. Tom felt the same pain reading about aviators or young soldiers dying in combat. "Right now, the mine is in chaos," continued Suslov. "Obviously you cannot see the daily activity of the mine but you'll get a good view of our emergency actions. Tomorrow we leave early and spend one day there. Then we will see what I can arrange. Agreed?"

Heads nodded. Tom stood and said, "I think a toast to the fallen miners is in order." All the men stood and, after a moment of reflection, drank a toast to the fallen.

"And tonight, my friends," said Suslov, as he sat back down, "you will experience Russian food the way God Himself ordained it. I made reservations at the Potemkin restaurant. It has the most beautiful dining rooms in the city. It's unpretentious but, as the saying goes, pretty as a Fabergé egg. A dance floor with live dancers. And the food!" He closed his eyes in rapture as he kissed his fingers.

The group was driven to dinner at the Potemkin. The Chinese and Russian delegations melded into one giant group as they made their way towards the three large tables that had been reserved next to the dance floor. The air was thick with cigarette smoke. Russian folk music played in the background. Tom recognized *Capriccio Espagnol,* one of his favorites. Judging from the empty vodka bottles decorating the tables, many of the patrons had been there a while.

Suslov took charge and ordered *zakuski* (hors d'oeuvres) so everyone could try a variety of tastes and textures. Tom recognized them all from the table of his maternal grandparents: *assorti rybnoye* (assorted cold smoked fish); *pod shurboy* (cured herring and vegetable cake); *selyodochka* (cured herring); and his favorite, *buzhenina* (spiced roast pork). Some were quite spicy and thirst-provoking, thus *zakuski* were always accompanied with copious amounts of vodka—not that Russians needed excuses to drink vodka.

The meals arrived, a medley of fiery dishes that required more vodka. Conversation buzzed as they drank toast after toast. Kozlov sat across from Tom but spent most of his time talking to Brian. He seemed intrigued by Brian's résumé and travels.

Kozlov's questions were drowned out as the second dance act started. The tunic-clad, leather-booted dancers began their slow rhythmic movements, eventually breaking into the classic boot-slapping, Cossack-style dance famous the world over. The audience clapped and cheered as the dancers leapt and pranced.

Then the lights came up and the dancers went into the audience to find "volunteers" to join them on stage. Several of the Chinese were "invited" and pulled up on stage. Two attractive female dancers appeared at the delegation table and pulled Brian and Tom to their feet. On stage, Tom did a few stretches and feigned doing calisthenics to the laughter of the audience. He took off his glasses and handed them to one of the dancers, a buxom blonde. She put them on, then waved them over her head and stashed them in her low cut blouse. Loud whistles and laughter from the raucous and more than slightly drunk crowd.

The music started and both Tom and Brian began the slow steps. The audience joined in and started clapping in time with the music. Both men knew the dances; they had been taught by their grandfather and had performed together since they were small children. They clicked their heels and spun through multiple turns; they linked arms and pranced across the stage, duplicating the moves of the Russian dancers. As the music sped up, they dropped together into the squat position, kicking one leg out after another, twirling faster and faster. The music ended; the crowd was on its feet, cheering and clapping. Sweaty and winded, Tom held Brian's hand aloft and they bowed together. Delighted, the Russian dancers surrounded them and pounded their backs. Tom could hear Suslov and the rest of the combined delegation whistle and cheer.

An American voice carried over the background noise. "Colonel! Colonel Callahan! Hey, what are you doing here?"

It took every bit of self-control to keep from turning towards that voice. Tom grabbed the buxom blonde dancer and twirled her around twice, lifting her off the ground. Then he took a knee in front of her to mime begging for his glasses. The blonde played to the audience by pretending to search in her blouse but came up empty-handed. She plumped up her breasts and searched again. Nothing. She mimed inviting Tom to search for himself. The crowd liked that even more.

He had to get those glasses back. He had to get off that damned stage and out of the spotlight. He turned to the crowd and made a "What the hell?" gesture then pulled her elastic bodice out and stuck his face between her breasts. The crowd roared its approval. Finally he reached in and rescued the glasses, which he held aloft in triumph. He put them on, kissed the dancer, and jumped down from the stage away from the loud American voice.

He made his way through the cheering patrons, who pounded him on the back. Tom tried to smile as he searched frantically for an escape.

The voice followed, "Hey, Colonel. It's Bill Wilder, mayor of Boise, Idaho. We went skiing last year."

199

Before Tom could react, Brian intercepted Wilder and grabbed his hand, "*Signore*, come dance." He dragged the protesting Wilder onto the stage where he was engulfed by the other dancers and patrons who were eager to join the fun.

Tom returned to his table, sat down, and threw back another shot of vodka. The entire Russian delegation, except Kozlov was now on the stage. Tom forced himself to sit still, and looked around as if nothing was amiss. Kozlov was staring at him, a curious look on his face. Tom met his eyes and held up his empty glass in a salute. Then he leaned towards the chief of the Chinese delegation and told him that he needed to go back to the hotel.

Tom walked through the dining room, collected his coat, heart racing, body taut. He commanded himself to be calm. He took regular breaths and slowed his pace. He paused to look at an elaborate icon in a niche along the wall near the front door. His near-panic subsided to a controllable level. His mouth was dry, his shirt soaked. He had a raging thirst.

It was dark outside. A few cars were parked along the street. A young couple was necking in the adjoining doorway. The buildings along the street were quiet and dark. The air was surprisingly cold, or else his senses were turned up. He imagined being followed by men in the shadows, but resisted the urge to look over his shoulder.

He walked to the nearest cross street, better lit and busier. A taxi stopped to discharge a passenger. He shouted to the driver, then ran to the car, jumped in, and gave the driver his hotel name and address. The cab made a U-turn; as the headlights panned across the road, Tom thought he caught a glimpse of a man running after him.

***

"*Per favore, signore*—please, sir—come with me," Brian gently pulled the confused Bill Wilder through the crowd, down a hallway, and out into an alley.

Brian spun around, slammed Wilder against the brick wall and punched him as hard as he could in the solar plexus. The air whooshed out of Wilder and he bent double. Brian yanked him upright and slammed him against the brick wall, his forearm pressed against Wilder's windpipe, hard enough to hurt but short of crushing it.

"Do I have your attention, Mr. Mayor?" he said in Italian accented English.

The terrified man's eyes bulged and he couldn't breathe. Brian relaxed his hold a bit.

"One sound and I will crush your windpipe. You will die slowly and painfully. Understood?"

Wilder struggled to nod.

"What are you doing here? This is a long way from Idaho."

"I'm a guest of Chita," Wilder gasped. "Boise is the sister city of Chita."

Damn, thought Brian. Of all the times and all the places. This drunken bastard's going to blow Tom's cover and get us all thrown into a gulag.

"You need to keep your mouth shut in there. You have made a mistaken identification."

"But—"

Brian leaned harder on Wilder's throat to cut off speech. "No buts, *signore*...you have made a mistake. Understood?"

Wilder's eyes bulged as he gagged again. He looked confused and scared. Even in the cold air, sweat trickled down his face. He tried to nod.

"Do you know of the Italian Mafia, *signore*?

Wilder nodded.

"The Russian Mafia makes the Italian Mafia look like boy scouts. That man you have misidentified as an American is here to work with the Russians. If you get in their way, it will get ugly very fast. It will not be your fault, but you will still be dead."

Wilder groaned.

"They know you're from Boise. They can find City Hall...they will track you down and kill you no matter how many cops you have at your service. Is that clear?"

"But—"

"I said no buts. Got that?"

Wilder tried to nod but could only muster a moan.

"I will let you go," said Brian. "You may return to your tour group. You will keep your yap shut. Got me?"

"Yes," he stammered.

"If anybody asks what you thought you saw, you will say that you made a mistake, that you were drunk, it was the restaurant lighting, anything you want, but you will say you made a mistake. Is that clear?"

Wilder nodded.

"I am trying to save your life. Do not lie to me. You are a politician. Lying is second nature to you, almost like breathing. Let me emphasize that you, and probably your entire family, will die if you make even one tiny little slip. I suggest, Mr. Mayor, you come down with a tummy ache or something tonight and decide to cut short your visit to Chita. Go home. Tomorrow."

Wilder raised his hands in a gesture of surrender.

Brian said, "I will release you now and go inside. In two minutes you may come in. Tell your friends that you needed some fresh air, then leave the restaurant."

Brian slowly relaxed his hold on the stricken man who collapsed to his hands and knees. Then walked away. Behind him he could hear the sounds of retching.

Chapter Twenty-one
Suvarnabhumi International Airport
Bangkok, Thailand

As the aircraft taxied into the gate, Elizabeth tried to send one last text message to the only contact number she had in Thailand. She hoped it got through, though she had no bars and her phone was dying.

She let everybody else off ahead of her, hoping to be lost in the shuffle. Mac was bouncing in the seats, totally wound up after spending twenty-four of the past twenty-seven hours in airplanes.

As she bent down to gather her things, Mac escaped through the door and ran down the loading ramp. "Mac!" she called, nearly frantic.

"Oh, ho! What have we here?" said the young man from Los Angeles as he grabbed Mac's arm and hauled him in. "Not cool, running from your mom, my man."

Elizabeth caught up and took Mac back. "Thank you, again. He's just so wound up from sitting."

"No problem," said the young man. "He's just doing what we all would like to do. Would you like some more help?"

"No, thank you," she said, suddenly nervous. "I can manage."

She corralled Mac and tried to reorganize her carry-on baggage, then her thoughts for what to tell the immigration people.

There was nobody waiting for her in the arrival area. That seemed to her a good news/bad news situation. The good news was that no men with guns were there to arrest her; the bad news was that Admiral Shinawatra wasn't there to greet her and help her with all the baggage and the now-rampaging Mac, not to mention tracking down Colleen. Surely a man as powerful as the admiral would have an airport pass to meet a plane.

Dragging her baggage and the car seat down the terminal concourse, she was struck by how different everything seemed in Thailand. She had never been to Asia. She had not traveled much, a couple trips to Cancun and one lucky buying trip to Paris for her boutique. So far, Bangkok was different. Very different. The people looked different; the architecture was different; the letters of the alphabet were different. Signs and posters were in Thai, German and some, thank goodness, in English. All at once it seemed overwhelming.

All her plans had rested on being met by the admiral or some of his people. She entertained the idea of checking into a hotel and simply looking up the admiral in the phonebook. Then she noticed an advertisement for a restaurant that listed the address as Shinawatra Avenue. Another sign said greetings from Prime Minister Shinawatra. So much for that idea. Was everybody in Thailand cousins?

The line at immigration was long. Elizabeth inched her pile forward as a sour-looking little man processed the passengers in front of her.

She presented the passports to the immigration official. He flipped through her passport, stopping at the photo. He looked up at her, then back to the photo. Unsmiling, he looked back at her, a frown on his face. He pointed at the picture and started to say something.

Mac plopped himself down at her feet and let out a wail. "I'm tired, Aunt Lizzie. I want Mommy!" And burst into tears.

The immigration officer, startled at the noise, stood up and looked down over the counter. Mac wailed louder. Elizabeth bent down and wiped away the tears. She picked him up and turned to face the official.

He smiled and held up three fingers. "I hab tree. All boy." He pointed at Mac. "He tired."

Elizabeth smiled, too. "I just have one. He's very tired, sir. Could we go?"

He nodded and he slapped official stamps in both passports. Then he reached out to stroke Mac's back, gave her a slight bow and beckoned to the next in line.

She tried to push the baggage with her feet down the hall and over to one side to get out of the way, still trying to comfort a sobbing Mac. After a few minutes of crying and comforting, Mac appeared ready to try for their next hurdle: customs.

They found the carousel that had Thai Airways TG 795 above it and waited with the other passengers as the carousel went round and round. Thirty minutes later, the carousel was still empty.

That did it.

Elizabeth pulled off her backpack and dropped to her knees. She took off her jacket and stuffed it in the backpack, yanked off her black wig and shook her head. Her auburn hair cascaded down to her shoulders. She rubbed her scalp with her fingertips and shook her head again. It felt so good. If she was going down, she was going down as Elizabeth Callahan, not some mousey creature.

Mac studied her transformation. "Does this mean the pretend game is over?"

"We're going to a hotel, Mac."

"Is there a pool?"

"You bet, sweet boy. You can help me by behaving a little while longer, then we'll go swimming."

"Yay!" He jumped up and down and clapped his hands. Then he hugged her neck. "I'll help, Aunt Lizzie. I can carry my backpack."

The luggage finally arrived. Mac found a luggage trolley and they loaded it up for the long walk to customs. The customs officials took Elizabeth's declaration form and waved her through. She exulted in this small triumph as she and Mac passed through the automatic double doors from customs into the terminal.

The Suvarnabhumi Airport terminal is the second largest in Asia; the arrival area that opened before them was enormous, swarming with people. Her heart sank. Nobody seemed interested in them. Travel agents and drivers stood at the doors, waving signs with names. Elizabeth read them all, hoping for a welcome. The admiral should be here or have sent someone for us, she thought. She looked around one more time, taking in the colorful vistas showing through the massive glass walls, the splashy artwork, enormous posters of temples and beaches.

She straightened her shoulders and let Mac push the trolley to a bank of telephones connected to the hotels advertised along one wall. The poster for the Novetel Suvarnabhumi Airport Hotel, nearby and four stars caught her eye. She began to read the long list of amenities, got no farther than "pool" and picked up the phone. Reservation made, she smiled down at the anxious boy by her feet and pointed at the picture of the hotel. "This is it, Mac." He gave her a big smile.

The air outside was warm, humid and it wasn't even breakfast time yet. She peeled the satin jacket off an already sweaty Mac, stuffed it into his backpack and then wrestled his arms back through the straps. Two of the huge, white Mercedes airport buses roared past.

A black limousine pulled close, its windows tinted. Hairs on the back of her neck stood up. She had never thought of a limousine as sinister before, but she watched the car glide silently through a cluster of taxis like a barracuda through a school of reef fish. She moved up a few yards; the limousine followed.

She snatched up Mac, sat him on the baggage trolley, and tried to cross the road to the hotel shuttle bus pick-up area. The limo moved again, slipped through traffic, and pulled up alongside them.

The rear window rolled down exposing a pudgy brown face of indeterminate age. "Elizabeth?"

Chapter Twenty-two
Headquarters of Federal Security Service
Chita, Siberia

Grigori Kozlov sat at his desk and reviewed the facts. He hated these delegation surveillance taskings. He knew that the FSB's Counterintelligence Service (SHR) was suspicious of each and every one, but he remained unconvinced that a delegation of Chinese miners would attempt to steal state secrets. Still, industrial espionage was a growth business and he might as well accept the fact. Chita's mining operations were impressive, thus attractive to spies. At least this delegation included some interesting additions with the inclusion of more than the usual amount of non-Chinese.

Kozlov was annoyed by the German journalist, Henning Schneider. He hated journalists in general because they were nosy, poking into things they had no business questioning. He also hated Germans; his grandfather and great-uncle had been killed at Stalingrad during the Great Patriotic War. Turning on his computer, a gift from his father, a FSB Major General, he logged onto the Internet. He did a search on Henning Schneider and discovered an extensive library of articles. After an hour of reading, mostly articles about Afghanistan, he was slightly mollified by the tone of the pieces. Many were critical of the politics of the invasion—as was Kozlov himself—but Schneider was clearly pro-soldier and told stories of heroic actions by individual soldiers while maintaining an aloof view of the macro efforts of the Soviet Army.

Kozlov was suspicious of the Bolivian. The Russian knew something of the politics of the region. The progressive president of Bolivia was reaching out to China, desperate for foreign investment to offset the losses of revenue from the Americans who were gradually cutting off funding. The Bolivian certainly didn't look like his idea of what a Bolivian should look like, but during his Internet search, Kozlov discovered that most of the upper class Bolivians looked as European as Kozlov did. No wonder the native Indian president was so popular with the Indian peasants. There were not as many Internet references to the Bolivian, but he did have some professional credentials and experience.

What really intrigued Kozlov was the behavior of the boorish American mayor at the Potemkin restaurant, acting as if he knew the Bolivian, and calling out his name. Kozlov had followed the Bolivian outside and seen him enter a cab. By the time he returned to the restaurant, the American was gone. Either of those actions would have been suspicious; together they were worthy of investigation. Kozlov looked at the vodka glass carefully wrapped in his handkerchief. He would have the FSB lab check it for the Bolivian's fingerprints and submit them to Moscow, along with photos taken by the hotel's security cameras. FSB labs could run those photos through their computerized facial recognition systems to see if there was a match. Who knows, he might get lucky.

He glanced at his watch. The delegation was on its way to the coal mine to watch rescue efforts; he would talk to the Bolivian at dinner. Right now, the American was at his hotel. Kozlov decided that it was time to ask him a few questions.

***

Tom peered out the window as the Mi-8 helicopter circled the mine twice. The housing area and the small town squatted just southwest of the underground mine, near where the river sliced through the taiga.

The mine area itself was a dirty gash of older buildings, heaps of coal, and heavy equipment, nothing at all like the open pit mine in Mongolia. Railroad tracks led off to the south with cars lined up in both directions, some full of coal, others returning for another load.

After the second helicopter landed, the delegation was shuttled to the headquarters building where a command post was set up. It was small and crowded, but strategically located with windows that overlooked the mine's central area. Exhausted rescue teams staggered in and out of the mine entrances. The entire atmosphere was tense and dark.

The mine supervisor briefed them that there had been an explosion and fire, probably due to an insufficient volume and velocity of air that allowed a buildup of methane. The explosion and fire engulfed and cut the escape route of the miners. A massive roof fall and secondary explosion killed more miners including almost an entire rescue party; one man survived and made it to the surface. The first reports said sixteen dead; that number grew to twenty-five as the day wore on.

Crowds gathered at the entrances of the mine, waiting for news of their friends and family trapped below. A temporary morgue was set up nearby. Stolid, tough Russian wives, gray and shapeless in their thick winter clothing, huddled together for warmth as they waited for news.

A sudden stir in the crowd as stretchers were brought to the surface. The crowd surged towards the mine entrance. Several women dissolved into grief; others clustered around them for support. Tom could hear wailing through the thick glass of the headquarters building. He felt useless, a voyeur as the blackened bodies were carried past.

"Time is the enemy for the men trapped below," said the stoic Suslov. He sat behind them, gripping the arms of his chair as if they were the gunwales on a lifeboat. Even in advancing middle age, he was a powerful man. Now though, his face seemed more fleshy and his eyes mournful, unlike the man who had danced and drunk until midnight the night before. "What you're seeing is the old Soviet Union. The mining sector is highly politicized, probably the most politicized sector of our economy, which of course leads to intense government oversight and control—the president himself watches us."

"This mine was built decades ago to maximize production. Regrettably, at the expense of safety and worker's living conditions. I have worked my whole life to prove to the government bureaucrats that a safe environment is cost-effective—fewer accidents, fewer shutdowns. It is good business, besides being the right thing to do." He pointed to the chaos outside. "This is what I wanted to prevent."

Suslov eased himself out of his chair and commandeered the mine manager's adjacent office and made a series of phone calls. He spoke quietly at first, then louder and more emphatically. He re-emerged and shouted orders at the Russian delegation staff, who disappeared. He turned to the Chinese group.

"Come, I've bludgeoned the chair warmers at the Ministry into granting you access to our newest mine, a diamond mine that no outsiders have ever visited. You must take that image back to your countries." He paused and pointed out the window. "Not this one."

***

Grigori Kozlov poured himself a fresh cup of coffee, took a sip and pondered again the situation of the Chinese delegation. He had gone to talk with the American, Bill Wilder, at his hotel only to find the man had checked out. A couple of phone calls confirmed that he had taken the morning's first plane out of Chita International Airport, a direct flight to Ulaanbaatar, and onward to Beijing—not even transiting Moscow where Kozlov could have had him stopped and questioned. Almost as if Wilder were trying to escape from something in Siberia.

Kozlov did not believe in coincidences. Something wasn't right here. Why would a man on a free trip to Chita abruptly claim sickness and vanish?

What was it that Kozlov heard him call out at the restaurant? Kal something. And something through all the background noise that sounded like a title. Sounded like kel-nel. He looked into his English dictionary. Kernel? A piece of grain. Why would he call him that? No, not kernel, he remembered his courses on western military structure, colonel, as in rank! How the hell do you spell that in English? He cursed his sketchy grasp of the language and leafed through his dictionary, trying different combinations of sounds and letters. Here it is, colonel. Damned French derived words; no wonder it had such a strange spelling. Yes, he thought, colonel. So, why that?

Kozlov sat back in his chair to consider this new detail. An American politician in Chita sees a colonel whom he knows well enough to address by name. The colonel, then, must be an American. If he knew him as colonel, what does that mean?

Where was the politician from? Kozlov went back to his notes: Idaho. The man was the *mehr*—mayor—of Boise, however that was pronounced. What is a Boise like? And why was he here? Ah, Chita is brother city with Boise. He turned back to his computer. Oh, Boise was big, much bigger than Chita, if you count the entire metropolitan area.

Okay, then why would he know a colonel? Are there any military bases around Boise? He studied the Internet graphics. Ah! Mountain Home Air Force Base. Satisfied, he decided to go with the idea of an Air Force colonel from Mountain Home. What kind of base is this Mountain Home? He searched the Internet again. He studied the pictures and recognized the aircraft as the infamous F-15 fighter.

Now why would an American Air Force colonel—presumably an F-15 fighter pilot—be in Chita. And with the Chinese? Is he a spy? What do we have here that the American colonel would be looking for? Kozlov knew that there were many fighter bases in Siberia: Dzhida; Bada; Domna, all nearby. There were even some MiG-29s on alert at Chita International Airport but the MiGs were old airplanes, even he knew that. Wouldn't a spy want to penetrate the military district headquarters at Novosibirsk? Was there a secret base nearby? Kozlov shook his head and stared at the wall. This made no sense.

He found that his mouth was dry and his pulse was racing. It was beyond his comprehension. His father said the difference between a major and a general was intuition and the force of personality to follow through. Let's go with this, he thought. Suspend disbelief, as the FSB instructors said over and over again. Assume that this is true. Action. The next step is action.

Where was the delegation now? He checked the clock, then looked back at the itinerary. He placed a call to Dimitri Popov, his deputy, who was assigned to accompany the delegation to the coal mine.

"Are they still at the mine?"

"No, sir. They left earlier than planned due to the fires at the mine. They flew in a helicopter to the new diamond mine northeast of Chita."

"Why didn't you go?"

"One of our helicopters was commandeered to fly some injured miners back to Chita this afternoon. There wasn't enough room for everybody in the second one. They were supposed to come back for me,

211

but the weather crumped. I'll get to them after the morning fog here burns off."

Damn, Kozlov thought. But it couldn't be helped. If Popov had pulled rank to get on the helicopter, everyone would have known he was FSB.

Kozlov had to make a choice now: submit his report through channels and risk having it reviewed and second-guessed until next month, or call his father and get somebody to look at it today.

It really wasn't much of a decision. The stakes were too great to rely on the system. He tried to organize his thoughts before calling his father on his private line. He *knew* very little. He suspected quite a lot. What he did know was that he needed advice. It was, as the Americans said, way above his pay grade.

His father would want to know what he had done. The fingerprints and the photos were already at the FSB archives. They should be routed to the Department of Military Counterintelligence, perhaps the Directorate of Aviation. These tasks needed a higher priority.

His father could do that.

His father answered before the second ring.

"Good morning, General. This is Chita calling."

"Damn it, Grigori, I told you never to call me here unless it was important."

"Father, think of me as just another major with a report for you."

"A major with my private number?"

"This is an official call, sir."

"Okay, Major. Go ahead."

Kozlov related the events of the past twenty-four hours, his suspicions, and what he had already done on his own authority.

"You say this man speaks good Russian?"

"Like a member of the aristocracy."

"How would a Bolivian learn good Russian?" mused General Kozlov. "I will send an e-mail to our FSB man in the Washington embassy. Perhaps one to the air attaché as well."

Kozlov checked the clock and did the math. "It's early there, Father."

"Even better. It will do them good to get out of bed," the general chuckled. "To remind them that they still serve the people." He paused. "Good work, Major."

"Sir, I hope that I'm wrong."

"So do I."

"It seems so unreal. What would he be looking for?"

"Siberia holds many secrets, Grigori."

Chapter Twenty-three
Vitim Diamond Mine - Siberia

Tom gained a new appreciation for the immensity of Siberia as the M-8 Hip helicopter flew from the coal mine to the newer, cleaner, diamond mine. A glance at his satellite phone gave him GPS coordinates but those numbers meant little in the midst of this vast taiga. The forest spread to the horizon in all directions. According to his research on the Internet, the extensive Siberian forest covered an area larger than the continental United States. They flew for more than ninety minutes without seeing more than a river and a few narrow dirt roads, almost that entire time without any sign of human beings. Occasionally, in Bolivia flying the embassy Beechcraft C-12 over incredibly remote areas and high places in the mountains, Tom had experienced the same sensation. Just about the time he had convinced himself that no human had ever seen this particular bit of Bolivia, he would pass over a house or a cultivated field carved out of the jungle or along a mountain ridge.

The mine manager, Sergei Andropov, met them and showed them to their lodgings. Tom couldn't help but think of the accommodations as the Russian version of Bachelor Officer's Quarters: long buildings with sparsely furnished rooms and shared bathrooms. He had spent many a night in such quarters at military bases around the world. The earnings for this particular mine were not going into any creature comforts for the staff that he could see.

The mine area was surprisingly open. Before dinner, the delegation was given some time off and permission to walk about the above ground portion of the facility. Tom, Brian, and Porter split up to cover more territory. Tom studied the ten foot chain link fence that surrounded the mine facility. His initial impression was that the reason the compound was fenced was to keep out nasty things like wolves, not keep people in. He remembered Porter's words about Russian gulags in the taiga where the land itself was the prison. Security personnel were not obvious, but Tom had no doubt there were security guys lurking somewhere. Every military unit in the old Soviet Union had had its political officers and secret police, always linked into the KGB somewhere. He was sure that it wasn't much different now. Mines were too important not to be secure, perfect for sequestering foreigners.

It was nice not being followed by that FSB Neanderthal, Popov, who was stuck back at the coal mine. The snow had stopped but the darkening clouds had dropped even further; there would be no more flights tonight; the weather report for tomorrow promised more of the same.

The mine layout reminded Tom of military bases—efficient yet austere. Arrow-straight roads, carved from the forest, linked buildings with the processing plant. The towers of the process and treatment plant were connected by conveyors. Apart from those structures sat what he thought of as the headquarters building, flanked by an administrative complex. In the distance stood housing units built for the workers; some women and children wandered about. He flashed back to the bereaved families at the coal mine and he squeezed his eyes shut. He had to focus on the present.

In the morning, the weather was, if anything, worse. After breakfast, the delegation filed into the headquarters building where Andropov, a large man much like Suslov, but smoother, a bit more sophisticated, waited.

"We are not used to having guests here," he said. "In fact, other than official inspections, you are our first outside delegation." He smiled. "I thought that since you are all involved with mining that we would simply head down the mine and I'd just talk on the way. You people don't need briefing slides." At that, his staff handed out hard hats and coveralls. "I would apologize for the weather, but this is fairly typical of the conditions that we have to work under. Russians are used to this."

Tom smiled to himself at this nationalist tweaking of the Chinese delegation. Andropov was a company man and was probably going to play the company song.

The tour of the mine took the entire day. Andropov accompanied them down the decline into the mine. The tunnels carved into the living rock were surprisingly well lit; workers dressed in blue coveralls, black knee high boots, and hard hats passed by. Miners used semi-automated production drill rigs to drill into the rock and pack the holes with explosives. The explosions created "stopes" or underground rooms supported by pillars of standing rock. The ore was loaded into "load-haul-dump" or LHD vehicles, which were computer controlled en route to the dump area.

The underground surroundings of the naked rock walls reminded Tom vaguely of the Cheyenne Mountain complex outside of Colorado Springs. During the Cold War, the United States and Canada hollowed out a huge, atomic, bomb-proof area under the mountain for the headquarters of the North American Air Defense system. Very modern, very leading edge, just like this mine. Continuing his sales pitch to the Chinese, Andropov made a point of identifying Russian-made equipment scattered throughout the mine.

Tom stood behind Andropov as the rest of the delegation filed into the underground Treatment Recovery Control Center. Before they could enter the room, a mining engineer ran up and handed a clipboard to Andropov. He scanned through several layers of paper, asked a couple of questions and nodded, signed one sheet, and handed the clipboard back to the engineer.

In the control center, Andropov seemed surprised and annoyed to see five operators sitting behind the consoles monitoring operations. He pointed at the two older men and angrily signaled to the security guards who hustled the senior operators out of the chamber.

The underground treatment recovery control center proved to be as up-to-date as the rest of the mine. It was well-lit, clean, and spacious, with curving walls covered with green flat LCD panels showing flow of material and status at each point along the production process. Glistening wood wainscot surrounded the work areas. By Russian standards, it was an impressive setup compared to the rest of the mine, luxurious in fact, which indicated to Tom the importance attached to the center's functions. This was a room where thinking and imagination were required and even honored.

Andropov glowered at the remaining operators, who ducked their heads and got back to work. He turned back to the delegation and forced a smile. "This is the nerve center of the mine where we make things happen." He strode over to the wall and pointed to a diagram on one of the screens. "Here is the main shaft which we started five years ago; the shaft was commissioned six months ago. It's a small mine, but it has proven itself, the results are much better than predicted. Our reserves are sufficient for another forty-seven years at current rates of production, about 2.5 million carats per year." He walked to another wall covered with a large-scale map of the entire mine area. "We will have about 1,300 employees when we are at full capacity. We will eventually have to build a small town to support the mine's activities right here," indicating an area to the east of the mine. He used the video panels to illustrate his points as he gave a detailed description of the mining process that showed the flow of material, equipment, and people.

That evening, Andropov hosted the delegation at a dinner in the dining facility. Tables were laden with food, Russian music played from some small but remarkably efficient speakers, and groups of people were knotted in conversation. Vodka bottles appeared early and stayed late.

Brian was at his finest, telling jokes, laughing, challenging the Russians to vodka drinking games. Andropov was right in the middle, arm draped across Porter Nelson's shoulders, another admirer of Porter's Afghan adventures with the Soviet Army. Everyone smoked, another reason to move to the edge of the room. No one paid any attention to Tom, who stood with his back to the wall and sipped vodka as he observed the scene. He noticed several of the control center operators, but only the younger ones. Something about that bothered him but he couldn't decide what it was. The party dragged on; the food was good, the vodka plentiful. Lots of people joined in, mostly executives. No one was eager to leave the warm comfort of the dining hall for the freezing temperatures and blowing snow outside.

Tom casually put on his coat and eased into the darkness. Initially, he headed back towards his quarters in case he was being followed but no one had noticed his departure. He took a deep breath, then detoured to the admin building, his footsteps muffled by the snow. The front door was unlocked and he slipped in. The building was empty. A couple of lamps on unattended desks provided the only lighting in the gloomy main area.

The weather had effectively isolated them from the rest of the world. No electronic communication. Tom found himself alone in a nearly empty building in a nearly empty land, at night, in the weather, looking for clues to a decades-old mystery. Great.

He walked through the building. Perhaps he could find some of the older men to ask some questions. Something was not right about Andropov's abrupt dismissal of them.

An overhead light clicked on. A harsh Russian voice shouted, "What the hell are you doing here?"

Chapter Twenty-four
Los Angeles

Colleen sat in the shade of an umbrella as she sipped her tea. The surrounding gardens were lush with brilliant flowers everywhere. A fountain bubbled near the enormous white house, framed against a brilliant blue sky. Mikey laughed as he ran around kicking his favorite soccer ball. Elizabeth passed the ball back to Mikey, who took the shot and scored in the small goal set on the grass. The four-year old ran around the yard in celebration, pulled off his shirt just like a professional soccer star, and slid on his knees across the lawn.

He saw a stick on the grass and ran over to investigate. When he picked it up it started to sway in his hands. To Colleen's shock it wasn't a stick, it was a snake! Mikey walked toward her, holding the snake as it writhed in his hands.

"Put down the snake, Mikey."

"You're in my place," he said, shoving the snake at her. "Move!"

"Mikey, put down the snake!"

He pushed it at her face. "Move your ass!"

Colleen awoke with a start—on a bench in a dreary Los Angeles jail cell.

"Move," said a large woman towering over her. "You're in my spot."

Colleen sat up. "There are plenty of places."

"I told you that one's mine. Move it, blondie!" She tried to pull Colleen off the bench.

Colleen pushed back. "Leave me alone!"

The woman grabbed Colleen's arm and yanked. Colleen reached across her body, grabbed the woman's wrist, and twisted her arm. The woman yelped and bent over as Colleen stood, then gently but firmly pushed on the arm and slowly forced the woman to the floor.

"Look, I don't want to hurt you or anybody else. I just want to be left alone."

The cell lights flashed and a jailer appeared.

219

"Jane Doe," she said, pointing at Colleen, "let her go. The lieutenant wants to see you. Now."

A female detective escorted Colleen upstairs into a large room and motioned her onto a bench. The room was filled with police who bustled about or sat at their desks writing reports or making phone calls. She was universally ignored. Colleen sat back on the uncomfortable bench. She was dirty, sore, and she knew she stank, but anything was better than being in that holding cell. The detective returned and pointed her into an office, then closed the door behind her. The spacious room had large windows that provided a lovely view of Los Angeles. Behind the walnut desk sat a man poring over a stack of reports. He looked up, smiled, and stood. He was middle-aged, with short dark hair, not bad looking, dressed somewhat better than Colleen expected for a cop. After all, this was LA!

"Good morning, Jane Doe, or should I call you Dr. Callahan? I am Lieutenant John Nichols." He smiled as he offered her his hand, then motioned her to one of the leather chairs next to his desk. "Yes, we now know who you are. What we don't know is why you're here and why people tried to kill you in our airport."

Colleen sat. "Could you tell me what day and time it is, please?"

He pointed to a digital clock on the credenza. "It's eight in the morning, Dr. Callahan." She read the display again and did the calculations. The plane was on the ground in Thailand. She breathed a quick prayer of thanks.

"Forgive me," he said. "Coffee?" She nodded and smiled her thanks as he handed her a cup. She took a sip; seldom had coffee tasted so good.

Lieutenant Nichols settled back into his chair. "You know some important people, Dr. Callahan. I've been on the phone with Ambassador Brent at the State Department twice this morning. He's demanding your release. He said you called him last night."

She grinned. "Well, when you only get one call you might as well make it count."

"You've caused quite a bit of turmoil around here, Dr. Callahan."

"Why is that, Lieutenant?"

"The two men who attacked you have disappeared."

"What? They shot an innocent bystander and got away with it?"

"They knocked out one of my men and escaped. We're still looking for them."

A polite knock on the door, it opened. In walked a sandy-haired, athletic-looking man in a dark suit and white shirt that marked him as either FBI or Secret Service. "Excuse me, Lieutenant Nichols, Dr. Callahan. I'm Agent Larry Leahy, Secret Service." He showed them his credentials. "I need to ask her a few questions, Lieutenant."

Nichols motioned him to a seat.

"Dr. Callahan, I'm here as a friend," said Leahy.

"Forgive me, Agent Leahy, but my world has been turned upside down recently," said Colleen. "I need to verify who you are."

"Fire away."

"Do you know Steve Severance?"

"Yes. We worked together in counterfeiting a few years back. He's on the Presidential Detail now. He's actually why I'm here."

She raised an eyebrow.

"The Secret Service is quite small, Dr. Callahan. Everybody knows everybody."

"How small?"

"I'm afraid that's a secret. That's why we're called the Secret Service." Leahy's lame attempt at a joke seemed hysterical after what Colleen has just been through.

"Do you mind if I call Steve to verify that?"

Leahy handed her his Blackberry. "Be my guest."

Colleen handed it back, not yet trusting this clever young man. "Lieutenant Nichols, may I use your phone please to call Washington?"

She dialed the White House switchboard. "This is Dr. Colleen Callahan. May I speak to Special Agent Severance, please?"

A gruff voice answered almost immediately. "Severance."

"Steve, this is Colleen Callahan."

The voice changed to one of concern. "Colleen, how are you? Are you okay?"

"I spent the night in a Los Angeles jail. How good could I be? I'm putting you on speaker." She punched a button and hung up the receiver. "I am with Lieutenant John Nichols, LAPD, in his office. Larry Leahy's here as well. Larry says he knows you."

"Hello, Lieutenant. Larry. Colleen, Larry's one of the good guys. George Brent called me this morning about you. What the hell is going on?"

She mentally blessed George Brent, not for the first time. "Two men accosted me in the LA airport. They identified themselves as CIA."

"What do you mean 'accosted?'"

"They grabbed me. Tried to 'arrest me.' I broke one man's nose, and ribs of the other bloke. They actually chased me and shot at me."

"In the airport?"

"Yes."

"An overreaction for a simple broken nose, don't you think?"

"They tried to pull the federal agent card on the LAX cops, but it didn't work."

"Good for the cops. The federal card works on television but not so well in the real world."

A pause. "Where were you going? And why incognito?"

"I can't tell you on this line, but I think there's a connection with what went on at my house last week."

"You mean the burglary?"

"It was no burglary, no matter what the D.C. Police say. Those men came in shooting. Robbie died there, Larry"

"That's what Ambassador Brent said."

"I have no proof, but that's why I had to get the hell out of the country."

"Okay, Colleen, go with Larry and call me on a secure line from his office."

She paused. "No, I don't think that's best either. I have somewhere else in mind."

"Where?"

The door opened again. A middle-aged man dressed in an expensive suit pushed his way in, followed by an Oriental man.

"My name is Anderson. I'm an attorney. I have been retained to represent Dr. Callahan," he announced, handing Leahy and Lieutenant Nichols his business card. He turned to Colleen. "George Brent sends his regards." Anderson motioned forward his colleague. "This is Narong Kasit, the Thai Consul here in Los Angeles."

Kasit bowed, then offered his hand to Colleen. "Lovely to meet you, Mr. Kasit," she said.

"Our mutual friend sends his regards," Kasit said with almost no trace of a Thai accent. "He has instructed me to help you in any way I can." He paused. "He said to tell you that both your packages arrived safely. They are in excellent condition."

Colleen covered her face and sobbed. Finally! With Mikey and Elizabeth safe in Bangkok with the Admiral, she could concentrate on getting out of here. And finding Tommy. She took several deep breaths and gathered herself. Each man hastily pulled out a handkerchief and offered it to her. She took Anderson's, carefully wiped her eyes and returned it with a smile. She stood and hugged Kasit. "Thank you."

Anderson looked at Leahy and Nichols. "I think my client has answered all the questions that she's going to."

Colleen waved him silent. She walked to the desk and leaned over the phone. "Steve, I'll talk with Larry on the condition that nobody interferes with me getting on a plane today for wherever I want to go."

"Okay, Colleen. As long as the cops in LA agree."

"Get them to agree. I know how persuasive you chaps in the Secret Service can be."

"Well, I guess the presence of Mr. Kasit clears up the mystery of where you're going."

Colleen looked around the room and studied the men. She had to decide whom she could trust and what she should say.

"Lieutenant Nichols, could you get me my things? I need my backpack."

The pack must have been in the outer room because it appeared almost immediately. She asked for a knife and slit open the back panel where she had concealed her American passport. "This is still valid."

Kasit said, "Dr. Callahan, why don't I take your passport to my office, process your visa, and return it to you at, say, the Los Angeles Airport this evening prior to your boarding our Thai Airlines flight to Bangkok?"

"That would be lovely," said Colleen as she handed him the passport. "Thank you ever so much."

"What about her safety?" objected Leahy. "I could arrange an escort on a U.S. registered airline."

"The United States is not the only country that employs sky marshals, Agent Leahy." Kasit stood and gave a slight bow. "I expect that you all have things to discuss. I will return to my office. If you need me, Mr. Anderson has my cell phone number." He bowed again to Colleen. "Until this evening, Dr. Callahan."

"If you need a secure phone, we have one in our communications center, thanks to our friends in the Department of Homeland Security," said Lieutenant Nichols.

"Excellent," said Colleen. "We can talk with George Brent." She leaned towards the desk phone. "Steve, be a dear and call George. Let him know we will be calling him via secure phone."

Lieutenant Nichols led the way to the comm center. While he obtained the phone key from the safe, the others settled into chairs around the phone.

"How well do you know George Brent, Mr. Anderson?" asked Colleen.

"Please, my associates call me Robert."

"And what do your clients call you?"

"Clients who are friends of George Brent can call me anything they want, but please call me Bobby."

"How well do you know George Brent, Bobby?"

"George and I go way back. Roommates at the Tufts University Fletcher School of Law and Diplomacy. We wanted to join the Foreign Service and help bring peace and prosperity to the world."

"What happened?"

"George took the Foreign Service exam and aced it. I decided that financial prosperity and the Foreign Service were mutually exclusive and decided to go into law instead."

"George hasn't done so badly financially. He seems quite comfortable, actually."

"That's because I handle his investments," Anderson said with a chuckle.

Nichols set up the phone and departed. Colleen dialed the number from memory. Brent answered on the first ring.

"Good morning, Colleen. How are you?"

"Much better, thanks to you."

"So where are Elizabeth and Mikey?"

"Thailand."

"Where's Tom right now?"

"I don't know."

"Please, Colleen, I need to know."

"George, I really have no idea. But I will call you when I find out. I should know once I get to Thailand."

"I fear that things are getting out of hand, Colleen. We need to go to the President."

"Are you sure?

"Yes. In retrospect, we should have done so after the attack on your house. Somebody murdered Ron Minor, Robbie Robinson, then tried to kill Porter, Tom, and you since Tom started this POW quest. The President doesn't even know about the POW deniers in the CIA and State Department. We should have also told the President where Tom was going and what he was doing. Nobody seems to know where Tom is right now. You haven't heard from him in over a week—this from a man who normally calls you every single day he's away. All we know is that he is no longer in Vietnam."

"Now you have me more worried than I already was, George."

"I'm sorry, my dear, but this is exactly why I have to talk with the President."

"Do you think there's a connection between all these events?"

"Most certainly, though I couldn't prove it in court. We need to find Tom and Brian. And soon."

"Bobby," said Brent, "are you there?"

"Here, George."

"I need you to fly to Washington tonight. We're going to meet with the President as soon as he returns from his European trip. You read people better than anybody I've ever known. You've seen Colleen, watched her while she spoke. Are you convinced that she's telling the truth?"

"She's my client, George!"

"No, get past that, Bobby. Do you believe Colleen?"

"As bizarre as it all is, yes I do."

"That's why I want you here to meet with the President."

"Okay, George. I'll call you before I leave."

Colleen stood. "Now that we have settled all that, gentlemen, I am going shopping for some clean clothes and getting myself a room at the airport Hilton until my flight." She could hardly wait to slip into a long hot bath.

Leahy spoke up, "I'll detail a female agent to accompany you until your flight."

Colleen nodded. "I think that would be best." She clapped her hands in delight. "Tomorrow I get to see my son!"

Chapter Twenty-five
Vitim Diamond Mine - Siberia

The next day the weather was foul, even worse than the evening before. The Chinese delegation gathered at the dining hall for breakfast. The mine operations officer announced that Andropov was tied up. The Russian senior staff melted away, leaving the Chinese delegation on its own for the day.

After a quick meal, Tom caught Brian's eye and motioned to the door. They timed their exit from the dining hall so they hit the door at the same moment and joined with Porter outside. The men walked towards the fence and traced the perimeter. It was snowing and bitterly cold.

"Find anything suspicious? Or even interesting?" Tom asked.

"What we have here," said Porter, "is the initial cadre, specialists that the Russians brought in to get the mine up and running. Now that things are smoothing out, the Russians are about to ship them off, probably next month to another site up near the Arctic Circle where the cadre will start the whole cycle again by opening another new mine."

Brian wiped snow from his glasses. "Tom, if our father is a mining engineer now, this is exactly the kind of operation where they'd use him. If he hasn't retired already."

Tom shook his head. "I don't think our father is the kind of guy who retires. Plus, Russians tend to work longer than most. The Politburo is full of guys in their seventies, and even a couple in their eighties."

"You know, the older guys in the recovery room were probably part of that cadre," Brian said. "Why were they kicked out of the room? Why didn't Andropov want us to see them?"

"Good question," said Porter. "To add to that, there's this one old man I came across over in the operations building. Wears an eye patch over his right eye. He seemed more than casually interested in me. Watched me the whole time I was in the area."

Tom said, "He wasn't at the party. Come to think of it, the two old guys we saw Andropov kick out of the recovery control room weren't there either. I wonder why."

"Maybe they're working tonight," Porter offered.

"Maybe," Tom said. "Or maybe Andropov has a reason for not wanting us to see or talk to those guys. We know he's not happy with us being here this morning. We were supposed to fly out yesterday."

"Hey," protested Porter. "It's the weather, not our choice."

"I know that, they know that, but it's awkward anyhow."

"They sure as hell don't know what to do with us this morning," laughed Brian.

"Well," said Porter with a gesture towards the low clouds and blowing snow, "it's a good bet that nobody will be here today to pick us up."

"How about you, Tom," Brian asked. "Find anything?"

"They nabbed me."

"What?" said Brian. "How? When? Who?"

"In the admin building. I thought it was Andropov himself. Good thing it wasn't. I almost fouled my pants. I talked my way out of it, told them I got disoriented in the snow, got cold, and ducked into the building to get warm again before heading back to the barracks. They bought it, but I don't want to get caught again."

"Frightened, Tom?" asked Brian.

"Yeah," he admitted. "Yeah, I am." Tom paused as he remembered the sick feeling he had when the lights switched on. "But we're here and damn it, we've got to see this through. If not for us, then for Mom."

"I never thought I'd ever hear you say that you were frightened of anything," said Brian.

"Believe it, brother. The stakes are too damned high here for my blood." He forced his hands into his jacket pockets. "I'll check the ops building again before dinner and look for Porter's mysterious one-eyed man. Brian, you look into the finance building. Porter, you keep doing your investigative journalist thing. You're supposed to be nosey. Maybe somebody will let something slip.

"Okay guys, let's go have a wander. Be conspicuous," he ordered, "hide in plain sight and don't do anything dumb like I did last night. Try to find any of those old guys. See what their story is."

Tom headed for the admin and mine safety offices. Over the next three hours, he visited every office he could, asking questions, being friendly and expressing admiration for the professional setup of the mine offices. After lunch, he asked for and got an escorted tour of the above ground processing and treatment buildings.

Darkness fell early in Siberia this time of year. The snow continued to blow. Tom found his way through the gloom to the operations building. Again the door was open and most of the staff gone to dinner. Tom made his way through the hallway lined with shelves, stacked with books and what appeared to be ore samples. He heard voices coming from a back room and slowed. He was discouraged; he had now been in every building where he had access. But no one-eyed man.

Then he saw him, standing against the far wall, scoping him out. Tom felt the hairs on his neck stand up. The man was older, probably late sixties or early seventies with short gray, almost white hair, slightly stooped, and almost as tall as Tom. But it was the way he carried himself and stared directly into Tom's eyes that riveted Tom's attention.

The man gave Tom a thumbs-up. Tom instinctively returned the gesture. With a start, he hoped he hadn't just made some sort of Russian dating signal. A romantic interlude with a horny Russian miner wasn't one of his immediate priorities.

He stared at the man; he had a strange familiarity. Tom's heart raced. Could it be him? Could it be this simple?

He had to do something before someone else showed up. How to signal this man who was now looking at some charts stapled to a bulletin board. Get his complete attention? There has to be a better way than this kabuki dance. Ah! He had a flash of inspiration.

He frantically searched his pockets and pulled out the lapis lazuli fountain pen he had used to write the President and end a chapter in his life. It was the pen his mother had given his father when he made colonel and passed on to Tom. Tom took a deep breath. This was the moment he had been dreaming about all his life, but his feet were heavier than stone blocks. What if his father didn't want to be found? What if he were a traitor and didn't want to come home or even acknowledge Tom's existence? What if he turned him in?

Tom Callahan had done many brave things in his life. He had flown combat; in fact, he was one of the most decorated fighter pilots on active duty. Yet taking those steps across the room took more courage than he had ever had to muster before. A bead of perspiration ran down his face as he felt his legs carry him slowly and deliberately towards the one-eyed man.

The miner glanced around as if checking for intruders, then back to Tom. A shadow of a smile flicked across his face. His good eye widened in surprise as Tom approached and held out the pen. He took the pen from Tom's fingers. He studied it, then looked back to Tom's face. The one blue eye burned a hole through him. Tom hesitated, then forced himself to speak. "Pop? General Callahan, is that you?"

The man didn't respond. He looked at the pen again, then at Tom.

"We've come to get you, Pop."

Still no response.

Desperate, Tom said, "Pop, Mom wants you to come home. Your wife, Barbara."

Something changed in the old man's face. He smiled, then said, "Barbara."

"Pop, we don't have much time. You've got to recognize me! Look at my face!"

The old man grabbed Tom and dragged him into a side room. "Tommy? Is it really you? You were just a little boy."

Tom's throat went dry. He could hardly breathe. He managed a strangled, "Pop, it's been a long time."

Sean Callahan grabbed Tom and hugged hard, his fingers digging into Tom's arms. "At last! At last!" he said, voice husky with emotion. He looked Tom in the eyes. "And your mother?"

"She's fine, Pop. She's waiting for us. We've got to get you out of here."

"And your sister?"

"She's fine Pop. Married, two kids. Lives near Seattle."

"And Gregory?"

"He died, Pop. Fifteen years ago. But Brian's with me."

"Brian? Your brother? Here?"

"Yes, come on! We've got to get you out of here tonight. We can talk later."

"No."

"What do you mean no? There's a train tomorrow afternoon from Chita to Ulaanbaatar. I'll get us a compartment."

"No, there are more of us!"

"What? More of who?"

"There are four of us. Americans. Two Air Force, two Army. Plus families."

"Families?" Not another Thomas Anthony Kinkaid situation! He felt sick to his stomach. "You?"

His father scowled. "Not me, Tommy."

Tom's nausea gave way to anger. "Pop, your family needed you. I needed you."

Sean Callahan took Tom's face in his hands and looked him in the eyes just as Tom did with his own son when he had to say something very important and needed his total attention. Tom almost sobbed.

Sean said, "Son, I know that. I tried eight times to escape. Every few years, the Russians would get careless. I would escape; they would catch me. Finally, they moved me to Siberia. They even showed me on a map where I was. I was hundreds of miles from any village. Nothing but open wilderness. That is what Russians have done to their prisoners for centuries. Sent them to Siberia where they cannot escape. No need for guards. They dared me to escape.

"Then they moved me here with the other Americans. I couldn't fly since I'd lost my eye and none of the others were pilots. But I have a plan."

"What?"

"In case a rescue team ever showed up. I would have risked it by myself but not with the families. Now the other men have wives, children, even two grandchildren. Once the babies started showing up, it was impossible for me to escape by myself. I have told the men to be ready to leave at any time."

231

"What about the women and children?"

"They have to come, too. If the men leave, they will be ripped apart by the FSB."

Tom closed his eyes and leaned against the door. He only had false papers for his father. How in the world were they going to get out of a prison camp in Siberia with kids?

"Pop, I don't know how to do this."

Sean Callahan smiled at Tom, the same slightly crooked smile Tom had seen peering at him from hundreds of photographs his mother still displayed in her house in Taos or stored in treasured photo albums. "Don't worry, son. I have a plan."

"To get everybody out?"

Sean nodded. "Can you fly? Are you a pilot?"

"Yes, sir, both Brian and I are fighter pilots."

He laughed out loud. "Of course you are! My sons!" He hugged Tom again. "First, we need a bus to take us to Chita. Then get the families. I know our compound. I know where all the families are and all the work schedules."

"Pop, the FSB's watching me."

"They watch everybody." Sean bit his lip as he thought. "I'll get the families."

"What if they can't come? Or won't?"

"Leave that to me."

"What do Brian and I do?"

"Where are you staying?"

"In the mine executive quarters. I'm traveling under false papers with the Chinese delegation. I'm supposed to be a Bolivian mining engineer. Brian's an Italian financial wizard."

"Very clever," Sean said. "You boys must take after your mother."

"But some Americans are in Chita," said Tom. "One of them recognized me. He has a big mouth and he was full of vodka, talking way too loud in a restaurant. I think the FSB spooks picked up on it. They may have figured out that I am really Colonel Tom Callahan, United States Air Force."

232

"A colonel? Good for you. And Brian?"

"He's a reserve major. Pop, we can't just chit chat! We've got to get moving. Tonight. The bad weather should help us get a head start."

"Okay, I'll get the bus and the others. Do you know how to find the west entrance?"

"Yes, sir."

"I'll meet you there at midnight. That'll give the staff time to get drunk and fall asleep." They looked at each other. Tom did not want this moment to end. Sean hesitated. "Could I keep the pen?"

Chapter Twenty-six
West Entrance - Vitim Diamond Mine

Tom Callahan stood in the snowy darkness with his brother and Porter Nelson. It was past midnight and Sean Callahan was late. Tom glanced down at his watch. It was exactly two minutes since the last time he checked.

"Relax, Tom. He'll be here," said Porter.

"And you base that on what?" snapped Tom.

Porter took the sarcasm with easy grace. He put his hand on Tom's shoulder. "If your dad is anything like what your mom says he is, he'll be here."

"Sorry, Port. I'm really uptight."

"No problem, buddy. In your shoes, I'd be nearly berserk."

"He said midnight, right?" said Brian. "The west entrance?"

"Yes, Brian. Midnight. Right here."

Tom bit back another sarcastic reply. Something had changed. He sensed movement off to the north. Then heard the low growl of an engine. He looked at Brian and Porter. They had turned to face north as well. It wasn't his imagination.

A small Mercedes bus running without lights emerged from the night gloom and snow. Brian grabbed Tom and they jumped up and down.

Sean bounced down the bus steps, a big grin on his face. He headed straight for Brian. "My son," he said as he wrapped his arms around him. Both men held on tightly. Sean pulled back, staring at Brian. "You look like your grandfather, Vasily. I would have recognized you anywhere, even with that silly beard."

"And you look like Tom and Greg," said Brian with a catch in his voice. "Dad, it's great to see you after all this time." They hugged again.

Tom cleared his throat. "Okay, gents, we have to get moving." He pulled Porter forward. "Pop, this is Porter Nelson. He's a great friend and the guy responsible for us being here."

Sean pushed aside Porter's outstretched hand and hugged him hard. "Thank you," he said. "This is a debt that I can never repay."

"No thanks are necessary, sir. It's been a privilege to know your family," said Porter.

"Okay, guys. We need to get out of here," said Tom. "Pop, how many people do you have?"

"Fourteen. Nine adults, five children."

Tom sucked in his breath. "Wow."

Sean winked at Tom. "Don't worry, Tommy. Everything is going according to plan. Let's go!" He tossed the keys to Tom. "You drive."

"Me? I don't know the way."

"You got here didn't you?"

"We flew in on choppers; Mi-8s."

"You came for us, no? Where are your maps? Don't you know the way?"

Tom shook his head. "Pop, you don't know how to get to Chita?"

"I've only been here two years. I go to Chita once every six months by a different route each time."

Tom looked at his friends. They were shocked into silence. Sean seemed to wilt before their eyes, from a confident, even ebullient, older gentleman to a depressed old man.

Some rescue! This was a disaster, even worse than not having found his father. They, he actually, Tom had to admit, had raised everyone's expectations. The POWs and their families had been ripped out of their comfortable lives at the mine, expecting him, Thomas Patrick Callahan, to lead them like Moses to new and better lives. And he didn't even have a bloody map.

Tom racked his brain. "Brian! Your sat phone!"

Brian smacked his forehead. "Of course!" He fumbled through his pockets and pulled out the phone. He punched it on, then entered some new commands. The men huddled around Brian, heads almost touching as they peered at the glowing screen.

"Where are we now?" asked Brian, talking to himself. The first screen showed a view of Russia suitable for an astronaut. Brian stroked the screen with his fingers to zero in on Siberia, then Chita Oblast, then Chita city.

"What are you doing? How are you doing that?" asked a dumbfounded Sean Callahan. "That's impossible!"

"Satellites, Pop," answered Tom.

"How is this possible? This is magic!"

"Yes, sir, it is. And it's going to get us out of here," said Tom. "Stop! Brian, back up a screen." He pointed. "There! That's the mine complex, that's where we are. See that corner and those buildings?"

"Yeah."

"Okay, Pop, see that?"

"Jesus, Mary, and Joseph! That's the admin building. And the operations building. From outer space!"

Tom looked at his father and laughed. "Why, General Callahan. I am shocked. Shocked I am at your language. I certainly hope that you didn't swear like that around your Russian friends."

"I didn't have any Russian friends," said Sean in a quiet voice. "Just captors."

"Sorry, Pop." Tom pointed at the screen. "Show us the way out of the mine area past the fence and we'll head down this road."

Sean nodded. "I can do that. Let's go."

The group boarded the bus, full of people wrapped in blankets, small suitcases between their feet. Fourteen people huddled in the seats, fourteen pairs of eyes drilled into Tom—the men excited, the women worried, the children scared.

"This is my son, Colonel Thomas Callahan; my son, Major Brian Callahan; and their friend, Porter Nelson," announced Sean. "They have come to take us to the United States."

"Actually, Dad," said Brian, "Tom works for the President of the United States. Or did."

"What? You told me that you were a colonel."

"Pop, it's not important. We need to go."

"He resigned to come get you," finished Brian.

"Is that true?"

"Pop," said Tom, glaring at an unrepentant Brian, "we need to get going."

Tom slid into the driver's seat. Brian and Sean took the seat behind his and Porter slid down the aisle to an open seat. Guided by Sean's directions, Tom drove through the open gate and into the Siberian night. Once clear of the mine complex he felt secure enough to turn on the headlights.

The passengers were a jumble of emotions. The children found refuge in sleep as they typically were at this time of night. The women held their babies and spoke softly among themselves, the men expectant but trying to remain calm. In the rearview mirror, Tom could see Porter, surrounded by the men, answering rapid-fire questions as they drove through the night. Tom tried to put himself in the minds of those men, abandoned and forgotten by their country but refusing to believe it, clinging to hope of rescue or escape through decade after decade in the frozen gloom of Siberia.

They groped their way through the taiga in near-total blackout conditions. The Siberian forest had seemed endless to Tom when he was flying above it; it was much larger now that he was actually down in it. At times he had to slow to a crawl in low gear in the blowing snow. There were no road signs of any kind. No signs of life, either. Only trees and more trees. The primitive road had no shoulders, trees lurched out of the forest right up to the edge of the road. Tom tried to balance the need for speed with the need to drive only as fast as conditions permitted. It was white-knuckle driving.

They passed through birch groves, over narrow river crossings, slowed to a crawl through a bog. Tom was surprised by some stone outcroppings and a tumble of broken granite slabs and the sheer number of hills they traversed. Tom knew the taiga constituted about five million of Siberia's ten million square miles; he felt that he had driven through about half of them.

Suddenly, they reached an intersection.

"Which way, Brian?"

"Dad, look!" said Brian. He spread his fingers over the phone, and backed off two screens to get their location to higher definition.

237

"Prekrastno!"—marvelous, breathed Sean. "Magic."

Brian nodded to Tom. "That looks like the shortest way to Chita." He studied the screen.

"You know, brother, we're not actually all that far from the city. It just seems like we are."

"Keep talking, pal. It feels to me like we're on the dark side of the moon."

Gradually, the road got a little wider and better plowed. They passed several isolated houses. Several more turns and the road opened up even more.

Hours passed. Tom struggled with the effects of the long drive. Then the sky began to brighten a little and they could see the glow of city lights reflected under the clouds. Houses appeared more frequently. His optimism meter started to rise. Maybe this crazy quest was going to work out after all.

Chapter Twenty-seven
Russian Embassy, Washington, D.C.

Colonel Arkady Romanov sighed as he took his chair behind his desk. He had just returned from a three-day blitz of American pilot training bases, a tour set up by the Department of Defense for foreign attachés. He had once again seen graphic evidence why the U.S. military in general, and the U.S. Air Force in particular was such a dreadnaught: they trained and trained and trained. He couldn't even imagine how big the American training budget was, but he was sure that it exceeded the Gross National Product of half the world's nations.

He was particularly impressed with the Euro-NATO Joint Jet Pilot Training (ENJJPT) program at Sheppard Air Force Base in Wichita Falls, Texas where NATO trained a sizeable portion of its fighter pilots. A fighter pilot himself, Romanov had met NATO pilots ten years his junior with more fighter hours than he had managed to accumulate. How could the Russian Air Force hope to contend with the NATO threat if they could not meet and defeat the NATO air forces? He had written and pleaded and pounded desks in the Ministry of Defense to get more flying for his pilots. Finally, the new president was listening and more training funds were pouring into the Russian military, but it would take years to catch up with the West. Still, Romanov had made a difference; something good had come from this damned desk job far away from his beloved MiGs.

He tore himself away from his daydream to a sealed envelope marked "Urgent" in his in-basket. *Chyort!* He swore to himself. His assistant should have taken care of this yesterday but was confined to bed with a bout of pneumonia. Romanov opened the envelope. Inside was a two-page, classified message accompanied by several grainy but legible photos. He studied the photos then read the message, looked at the photos again, re-read the message, and felt his heart rate accelerate. He swore again, checked the wall clock display of Moscow time, shook his head, and called the phone number on the message.

"General Kozlov, this is Colonel Romanov, Air Attaché in Washington. Sorry to disturb you at home, sir, but the message was marked 'Urgent.'"

"Yes, Colonel? This is an unsecure line."

"I know this man, the man in your message."

"Are you positive?"

"I recognize him, General. I had dinner with him two months ago. Colonel Thomas Callahan, USAF."

"Does he speak Russian?"

"Like a nobleman. His maternal grandparents were White Russians, exiled to China. He's an advisor to the President of the United States, a decorated combat fighter pilot. He cannot be where you think he is."

There was a pause. "Are you absolutely sure of this, Colonel?"

"I'd bet my career on it."

"You just have, Romanov."

Major General Kozlov gathered his notes and dialed the number of his commanding officer, Colonel General Alexy Petrovich. "We have a problem in Siberia."

"Come," said Petrovich. "I will be waiting."

"Yes, sir."

Kozlov drove the six blocks to Petrovich's residence. An FSB guard met him at the car and escorted him to the General's study. The General, in pajamas and robe, shook Kozlov's hand and offered the obligatory bottle of vodka.

Kozlov related his son's investigation in Chita, and his conversation with Romanov.

"What is this American doing in Siberia, masquerading as a Bolivian?"

Kozlov shrugged. "That is the question, isn't it?"

"His name again?"

"Callahan."

"You say he speaks Russian?"

Kozlov nodded. "His mother's parents were Russian, his father was a decorated war hero shot down in the Vietnam War—"

240

Colonel General Petrovich blanched. "What did you say?"

"His mother—"

"No, his father!"

"Was a brigadier general fighter pilot. Shot down in late 1972—"

"Damn!" Petrovich slammed his fist on his desk. "That man must be caught!"

"Why?"

"Just do it! He must not leave Russia." He pointed at the secure phone in the corner of the study. "Call your son. Now! Have him arrest that spy. And everybody with him."

Chapter Twenty-eight
Near Chita, Siberia

Sean Callahan grew animated, stood upright and pointed as he recognized the Chita environs. "We're doing it!" he said with a grin. He clapped Brian on the shoulder.

Tom turned onto a major road, much better construction, but it still seemed to be designed and maintained by sadistic engineers. Multiple stoplights were placed haphazardly; plastic cones marked off lanes for no apparent reason. There were only a few other vehicles on the road, but they blasted by the bus as if driven by maniacs on amphetamines.

Brian said, "Tom, the airport is up ahead about three miles."

Tom followed the signs to the airport and Sean guided him around to the poorly lit industrial side. Security was non-existent. Chita had been free too long; security guards were used to foreigners, buses, and early morning departures.

"Where is everybody?" asked Brian.

"The airport only has some roving guards who prefer to stay in their guard shacks or their cars. Budget problems, I think," Sean said.

"We know about that, don't we, Brian?"

They turned out onto the ramp. Tom drove very slowly. The ramp was in almost total darkness; the early morning fog made it a very dangerous place. He almost hit several pieces of equipment parked seemingly at random.

"Where's the plane?" asked Tom.

"Over there," pointed Sean.

Tom looked. Parked near the commercial loading area was an enormous biplane that he recognized as an Antonov An-2 Colt.

"Behind the Colt?"

"No, it is the Colt."

Tom slammed on the brakes, waking everybody on the bus. "You mean we're going to fly out of here in an An-2 Colt, the world's oldest airplane? That's your plan?"

"The world's oldest airplane? No, this one was built about 1970."

"A *biplane*?"

"I know the plane, Tommy. I drink with the pilots sometimes when they fly into the mine. They tell me things. I memorized the details. I have a checklist."

"Where?"

Sean tapped his head. "Don't worry, son, we can do it."

"I'm glad you're so confident, Pop."

"Actually, Tom, the Colt is officially the world's *largest* biplane," said Brian. "I parachuted out of one with the German Army when I was a cadet. It's slow but dependable; very common around the Warsaw Pact countries during the Cold War, sorta like a communist Gooney Bird. The engine is a legal Wright Cyclone knockoff. Nothing too complicated."

"Just great," muttered Tom.

"C'mon, Tom, we're the Flying Callahans. We can pull this off if anyone can."

Tom studied his brother's face for a moment wondering what precipitated this sudden burst of confidence.

He stared down the ramp. The wind had picked up, dissipating the early morning fog. The ceiling had lifted a bit, almost to takeoff minimums.

"Okay, let's go take a look."

He parked close to the aircraft. Tom, Brian, and Porter followed Sean to the plane and watched as he opened the fuselage door. The plane was set up like an airliner with seats for twelve passengers.

"Not enough seats," said Tom. "Pop, you'll ride up in the cockpit with Brian and me. Porter, grab the first seat aft of the cockpit. Kids will have to ride in laps." He looked down the aisle. "Hope the head works better than in most Russian airplanes," he muttered.

"Porter, go park the bus behind the hangar while we try to get this beast ready to fly. Have everybody go pee, but hurry. Then get everybody on board and strapped in.

"Brian, hop in the co-pilot's seat and see if you can find me a runway layout on your sat phone. When we fire up this beauty, it's going to make a hell of a racket and wake everybody from here to the city. Even Russian rent-a-cops will know something's up."

He looked at his father. "Okay, Pop. We're here. Now it's up to you to get us to Mongolia."

***

The bedside phone screamed in Major Grigori Kozlov's ear. He groped for it in the darkness, cursing and stupid from sleep. In his business, early morning calls were never good news.

"Kozlov," he barked.

"Grigori," said his father, all business. "You were right. The man in the photos, the man you saw is an American Air Force pilot named Callahan."

"What—?"

"Wake up, damn it!"

Kozlov swung his legs out of bed and stood up. "Okay, Father, I'm awake. He's an American Air Force officer. So he's a spy. Why is he here?"

"Arrest him and find out. In fact, arrest everyone in the delegation. Colonel General Petrovich nearly had a heart attack when I told him. The American's father was a general shot down in Vietnam."

"Why is this Callahan interested in a Siberian mine?"

"Think, Grigori."

Kozlov mentally reviewed the events of the past two days. "We have American prisoners? Here in Siberia?"

"Gulags were invented in Siberia." The General paused. "Just do it, Major. This comes from the top."

"Yes, sir—"The phone went dead.

Kozlov snatched up his bathrobe and hurried into his small den. He opened a safe and took out the classified folder that contained copies of everything he had on the Chinese delegation. He dialed the phone number of the mine switchboard.

"This is Major Kozlov. Get me the mine manager. Now!"

Andropov came on the line. "This is Kozlov. Orders from Moscow. Get your security detail out of bed and arrest the Chinese delegation, especially the Westerners, if they're still there. Call me at my office when it is done."

Kozlov hit the speed dial for his duty officer. "This is Kozlov. Get everybody in. I'll be there in fifteen minutes."

Eighteen minutes later, as Kozlov ran up the stairs to his office, the phone was ringing. The duty officer answered and handed the phone to Kozlov. Andropov said, "I ordered a search of the mine area, Major. You were right. The three non-Chinese are gone."

Kozlov swore. Why hadn't he listened to his instincts? "Anybody else?"

"What do you mean, anybody else?"

"Why do you think these spies were in your mine? They're looking for defectors, you idiot! Go check everybody on the mine staff. Take a head-count, then call me on my cell phone. And Andropov, get the number right the first time."

Chapter Twenty-nine
Chita Kadala Airport

Tom stood on the still dark tarmac beside the enormous biplane, its huge engine poking out in front like an elephant's trunk. If Pop had to steal an airplane, why couldn't he have picked something more normal, like the Siberian Airlines Boeing 737 they had seen by the entrance to the tarmac, something that would shorten the odds of getting caught. And where was Pop now?

His father appeared from behind the hangar.

"Where have you been?" said Tom. "I had to strap some of your people into their seats. The women are scared to death without you here."

"I had one more thing to do. Let's get moving, Tommy."

"So what's the plan from here, Pop? Where are we going?"

"There's a dirt strip about fifty miles over the Mongolian border. I have the heading and distance. There's a Non-Directional Beacon on the field that we can use to find it."

Tom nodded, then pointed at the Colt. "How do we do the pre-flight?"

"Everything's ready to go, son," said Sean. "The pilots always pre-flight the aircraft after the last flight of the day so they don't have to do it in the morning."

Tom nodded. "What we U.S. Air Force types would call 'cocking the aircraft,' like when it's on alert."

Sean nodded and chuckled. "Exactly, except here it's because the pilots like to drink and carry on late and don't feel like going through the ritual of thirty or forty minutes of reading a checklist when they're hungover."

"In that case, I think I'll take a nice thorough Air Force walk-around, if you don't mind. Why don't you go forward with Brian and see if the switches seem to be in the proper positions?"

***

Kozlov sent two men to set up roadblocks with the local cops. His driver brought his official car around and Kozlov and his last agent jumped in. "To the train station!" he ordered. His cell phone rang. "There are four operatives missing," said Andropov. "All foreigners in our cadre."

"Foreigners?"

"Yes, foreigners. Involuntary visitors, if you get my meaning. Plus three families. Fourteen total, plus the three spies. Gone. They took a white Mercedes bus."

Kozlov swore again. These men are truly desperate. Nobody can drive out of Siberia. They must have another plan. Father said the "Bolivian" was a military pilot! These men are pilots! Kozlov banged on the driver's headrest. "To the airport!"

"But, Major, there are no flights this early."

"They're hiding somewhere nearby."

***

Tom was intrigued by the An-2, nicknamed *Annushka* or "Little Annie," although the frigid Siberian early morning darkness was hardly the time to be learning about a new aircraft. He had only seen this type airplane once, two years before at the Farnborough Air Show in England. The pilot had demonstrated the Colt's Short Takeoff and Landing (STOL) characteristics by landing it in less than two hundred feet. Tom had little doubt he could fly the Colt—he had flown dozens of different aircraft types. It might not be pretty or pass a check ride, but he could get them to Mongolia, even through this crummy weather. He started at the tail, pulling the chocks from under the tail wheel and removing the locking boards on the enormous rudder. He continued around the plane's right side. It was a big mother for sure, twice as tall as he was. Fat wings. Interesting flaps and slats. It would be nice to have a copy of the Pilot's Notes so he could understand the mechanics as well as the aerodynamics of this machine. He pulled the chocks from the right wheel, and noted the big oil pan under the enormous engine. He stood in front of the plane and looked up at the cockpit bay windows through the monster four-

247

bladed propeller. Getting thumbs-up from Brian that switches were off, he carefully pulled the prop counterclockwise enough to clear any hydraulic locks and to flush any oil trapped in the bottom of the cylinders.

A car with airport markings on the door drove by, slowing as it passed the Colt. The driver studied the aircraft and looked at Tom, then reversed course. As he drove away, he pulled out a cell phone and made a call. Tom continued around the left wing, pulled the chocks for the left wheel, gave a nonchalant wave to the man in the car, then climbed in and pulled the door shut.

Climbing into the left-hand pilot's seat, he said, "I think we've been spotted, boys. No more time for study."

Brian pointed to a rectangular hole in the instrument panel. "Bad news, Tom. The plane's on a red X for nav equipment. No weather flying."

"Oh man, this just keeps getting better and better."

"Tell me about it," said Brian. "Instrument flying is out, but the ceiling has lifted a bit with the sunrise. I think I can get us out of here, using my sat phone for navigating."

Tom looked at his father. "Any ideas, Pop?"

"How good are you at low level?"

"Pretty damn good, thank you very much."

"Then I suggest we use the taxiway for takeoff… and get the hell out of Dodge."

Tom looked at his father. "'Get the hell out of Dodge?' Did you really say that?" He looked at Brian. "Our father's back, brother!" They slapped high fives and laughed.

"Pop, it's great to have you here. Now, how do I start this beast?"

"It seems complex, but isn't really. I'll be your third arm." He pointed. "I've already done the Before Start checklist. We're ready to start. Prop control—low pitch; mixture—pull back for full rich; fuel master lever—open." They marched through the memorized checklist, Sean's instructions crisp and clear.

Whining and protesting, the massive engine turned over and over, then fired on the last feeble kick of the prop. "Keep pumping the wobble pump!" ordered Sean. He played with the throttle as the engine tried to roar into life. Smoke enveloped the aircraft and engine noise filled the air. "Lots of oil accumulates overnight in a Colt."

"No kidding!" said Tom.

They nursed the big radial engine until it began to smooth out. Sean called out the critical Before Taxi and Before Takeoff items, checking gauges and directing Tom's actions as the engine warmed up. "Remember, the brakes are air operated and make strange noises."

"Any other pearls of wisdom, Mr. Test Pilot, before we launch?"

"It tends to weathervane into the wind because of the large tail. The leading edge slats are on large rubber springs and retract automatically at about forty knots."

"And you have how many flights in this machine?

"Never been in one. Usually they fly me in 737s."

"Terrific. Let's go!"

Chapter Thirty

Kozlov strained his eyes to make out details of the airport area. The fog was lifting but he could only make out dark lumps as equipment winked in and out of the mist.

His agent's cell phone rang. "Sir, a security guard reports unusual activity around the industrial aviation side."

"What kind of activity?"

"He said it looked like a group of people was boarding the An-2 Colt over in the industrial area."

"Of course! They're stealing a plane! Call the tower. Stop all takeoffs!" He smacked the driver. "Go! Go! Go!"

The driver stomped on the accelerator and the car skidded around the last turn towards the fenced security area and slammed through the police checkpoint barrier.

"There they are!" Kozlov pointed and the driver accelerated on a line to block the plane from the taxiway.

The Colt staggered around its first turn.

"We've got them!" he shouted. "Oh, shit! They're taking off on the parking ramp! Impossible!"

***

Inside the Colt, Brian monitored the instruments. "Compass erected," he said. "Instruments aligned. Runways are 11/29. Suggest Runway 29. Oh, Jesus, here come the cops! Turn right now!"

Tom brought the power up and tried to turn out of the parking area; the plane staggered around the turn, tires protesting.

"Gently, Tommy," coaxed Sean.

Outside, trucks rushed down the taxiways to cut them off from the runways.

"Another change, guys," said Tom, eyeing the vehicles. "We'll use the ramp for takeoff. We're outta here. Set the flaps, Pop."

Tom brought the power up again and the plane vibrated from the thousand horsepower engine. The airplane accelerated slowly because of the extra passengers.

"Tom!" shouted Brian and pointed at the trucks.

The Colt rumbled ahead, directly at the trucks. Tom eyed the rate of closure. He held the wheel forward to help the acceleration, then rotated the aircraft to barely clear the trucks. Cheers erupted from the passenger compartment. Brian gave Tom a thumbs up.

Tom kept the Colt low over the taxiway to pick up some speed before turning out of the airport confines. His only goal now was to reach Mongolia before the Russians could react and shoot them out of the sky. He played with the yoke, trying to get a feel for the aircraft; it was very different from a fighter, but not so different from some of the older planes he had flown around Arizona.

"Which way, Brian?"

Brian pointed. "That way, down the valley. It'll take us southwest. Initial heading about two-two-zero degrees. Stay low and belly out as far along the western edge of the valley as you can. There's an air force base right along the railroad tracks at Drovyanaya. We don't want to overfly it and wake up the Russian cavalry."

"Drovyanaya? No kidding? They used to have ICBMs based there, SS-19s and 24s."

Brian looked over his shoulder at Sean and rolled his eyes. "There you go, Dad. Your son, the colonel. He just can't turn it off."

Tom ignored him. "The Russians have fighters stationed all over this area so watch out."

"We shouldn't have to worry about MiGs from Chita," said Sean.

"How do you know? There were MiG-29s on the ramp."

"Because I put machine bolts into the intakes of the alert birds."

"So, they shredded their engines on start? Pop, you are a genius!"

"I told you, I've had a lot of time to plan this."

The narrow valley extended generally southwest with rising terrain all around. Tom flew just under the clouds to maximize forward visibility. He had no idea of where he was relative to power lines and antenna towers. Their flight path snaked along the valley's edge as he avoided built-up areas, generally staying west of the river as it meandered through the valley. Gradually, the clouds forced the aircraft lower and lower as the terrain to the west rose to meet the clouds; ditto to the south.

Turbulence picked up, bouncing the aircraft enough to be uncomfortable. Crying from the passenger area and the smell of vomit permeated the cabin. Even Tom's iron stomach felt queasy. He looked back through the open cockpit door. Porter Nelson walked up and down the aisle, trying to calm people.

Tom passed the flying duties over to Brian and tried to relax his aching muscles for a few moments. He scrolled through several screens on Brian's sat phone to try to get a good mental picture of their flight options. Nothing looked very good. They were cruising at only 125 knots, painfully slow for pilots used to flying Air Force jets. They didn't have far to go in a straight line to Mongolia, but they couldn't fly in a straight line due to the weather. They would simply have to pick their way through the valleys and ridges while trying to bend their flight route around to the south and Mongolia. Twice they had to reverse course and try an alternate route; both times, Tom heard cries of protest from the rear.

"Look, Brian, there's a city over there."

"That should be Sokhondo."

"Yeah, according to the satellite map there's a big road, the M-55, which bends off to the northwest up to Ulan-Ude."

"Talley-ho the M-55!" said Brian.

"Good. That checks. Now we need to work more south or southwest."

"Can't. The clouds are on the deck. Gotta go northwest. Dad, what's the range on this crate?" asked Brian.

"Five hundred fifty-nine miles."

Brian passed the controls back to Tom and made some rough measurements on the sat phone screen. "Man, oh man, we're going to be cutting it close. No way will we get to Ulaanbaatar."

"I'll be happy if we get to the first town south of the Mongolian border," said Tom.

"That would be Suche Baatar, first stop of the Trans-Mongolian Express in free territory."

Brian studied his sat phone, then leaned over to show his father. "Look, Dad. We should be able to pick up the railroad tracks from Ulan-Ude, south to Mongolia, over here somewhere. If we go west far enough, we'll cross them. Then we just fly down the tracks to Mongolia and freedom."

Tom tried to keep the aircraft on a westerly course, to save time and gas as they snaked their way through valleys and over ridges. Visibility in the valleys was relatively good, but the clouds descended lower as they worked their way west. Tom was forced to fly lower and lower, sometimes just skimming the ridges. All three men in the cockpit strained their eyes looking for the best flight path. Gradually, the ridges seemed to pull farther apart with houses and cultivated fields more prevalent.

"Looks as if we're near what passes for civilization in Siberia," said Brian. "We should be seeing tracks—Jesus!"

Pylon towers appeared out of the gloom. High power wires drooped down to snatch the Colt from the sky. Tom instinctively dove the aircraft; the wires flashed by overhead.

"Whoa, good job, brother," said Brian. "I'm glad the folks in the back didn't see that."

"I wish I hadn't seen it," breathed Tom as they descended down the windward side of the ridge into the valley. "Makes me wonder how many more there are out there."

"Good thing we're going slow. Those power lines would have snagged us in the F-15."

"I wouldn't be doing this if I were in the Eagle," said Tom.

Two more ridges later, they dropped into a broad valley, intensively cultivated. Fields and farming communities ran together. The cloud base was irregular; Tom had to drop even lower.

"Train tracks, Tom!" called out Brian.

Tom stood the Colt on its wing and honked it around to the south to keep the tracks in sight.

"Whoa, there's a passenger train," said Brian. "Just ahead." They flew down the tracks and over the train. The airflow from the cars made the flying a little bumpy as the Colt gradually passed the train.

"Wow, we actually can go faster than a Russian train. What an accomplishment!"

"Hey, we're making good time."

"The clouds seem to be lifting," said Sean.

"I'd be happy if we had clouds all the way to the border," said Tom. "Just in case there are bad guys out looking for us."

"You think there are?"

"Do you expect the Russians to just let us go?"

"Sure, why not? We'll give them their airplane back. I'll even pay for the gas we used."

"Doesn't work that way, Brian, and you know it."

An explosion off the right wing rocked the aircraft. Screams from the back of the plane.

"Missile!" shouted Brian. "Break left!"

Tom went to full power, rolled the aircraft on its left wing, and pulled it around hard, rolling out heading back up the tracks. He flew as low as he dared, less than ten feet off the ground. Railroad ties flashed by as he tried to keep the wingtips out of the trees on either side of the narrow cut.

Tom risked a glance towards the explosion. "Someone's out there. Find him fast or we're goners." A swept-wing plane flashed by.

"There!" said Brian. "Su-24s—at least one."

"Damn! At least they're not MiGs. If they were, we'd be dead right now. Better missiles on MiGs."

"Fencers?" asked Sean. "They're still flying Fencers?"

"Yes, sir. They're supposed to be replaced starting next year."

"You know these airplanes? Do you know their flight characteristics?"

"Pop, we're fighter pilots. Of course we do."

"I am finally believing that you are fighter pilots and not just my baby boys."

"Keep your eyes peeled, Pop. They're looking for us. Fencers have guns."

"Eyes peeled; I haven't heard that expression for a long time. But of course for me, it's keep my *eye* peeled."

"Okay, Tom," said Brian. "What's the plan? Why are we flying north?"

"We're heading back to the train. Not even Russians will shoot at us if we're near the train."

"The Colt can fly at less than 42 knots," said Sean. "That should help keep station over the train."

"How do you know?"

"I told you. I drank with their pilots, asked them questions and memorized the answers. Every pilot I know flies the Colt. They say it can't be stalled, that you can ride it down in what they call a parachute glide, around thirty knots."

"Hey!" said Brian, "I know both you guys are legends and have ice water in your veins, but my heart's about to explode. We have people screaming and puking in the rear. Let's cut out the Auld Lang Syne and fly the bloody aircraft!"

Sean looked at Tom. "Is he always this excitable?"

"Pretty much. He's a real detail guy. Made a fortune on Wall Street."

Sean patted Brian on the shoulder. "It's good to have you here, son."

"The train!" said Brian.

They could see the nose of the engine as it barreled straight at them, closing rapidly. Tom carefully gauged the rate of closure, and pulled up a bit and slid out to the east in anticipation of another course reversal. He advanced the throttle to full power and pulled up, kicked in left rudder and turned the Colt left through one hundred eighty degrees, rolling out directly over the last of the train cars.

Sean clapped his hands in delight. "Well done, Tommy!"

Tom took his right hand off the yoke and flexed his fingers several times. Sweat ran down his face. He took several deep breaths. "So if they aren't from Chita, where are they from?"

255

"Probably Irkutsk."

Tom checked the clock. "We've been airborne nearly two hours. Unless these are a second wave, they've been up for a while."

"They won't have much time left on station to figure out how to get us!" said Brian.

"With any luck," said Tom. "Brian, how would you do this if you were the Russians?"

"Fencers are wicked fast on the deck. I'd make a high-speed pass right over us. Try to drive us into the ground with wake turbulence."

"Me too—watch out, here he comes!"

Tom slammed the throttle to the stop. "Pop, full flaps!" He abruptly pulled up into the path of the Fencer. The Colt's leading edge slats automatically extended as the speed fell away. The airplane shot up like an elevator. The Russian pilot pulled up sharply to avoid a mid-air and disappeared into the stratus clouds. Its wake turbulence slammed into the Colt, rolled it on its side, and drove it towards the ground. Tom fought for control of the bucking airplane and recovered just before they smashed into the train beneath them.

"Good job, Tom!" said Brian. "I bet no Fencer pilot has ever seen that counter maneuver before."

"It'll only work once, though," said Tom. "What's next?"

"Oops, there goes the train!" said Brian, looking out his side window. "The engineer must have been ordered to stop."

"Damn it!" said Tom. He could see the train sliding backward beneath him despite his hanging the Colt on its prop, flying as slow as he could manage. Out his side window, he caught a glimpse of the border town. So close! Full throttle, he tried to will the clumsy Colt to accelerate—

"Tom, two o'clock! His wingman's making a gun run!"

The Fencer arced down on them like a falcon on a pigeon. Only one hope. Tom dropped the nose and descended until his wheels straddled the tracks. He flew the aircraft as slow as he could, now sliding towards the attacking Fencer, trying to place his left wheel on the right track. Surely the Fencer wouldn't take the shot, and risk shooting up the rails right in front of a moving passenger train.

"Give it up, you Russian asshole!" shouted Brian.

Tom focused all his attention on precision flying, forced the Colt as low as possible and lined up as close to the tracks as he could. One wheel touched down, softly. Tom could feel the tire start to spin, then stop again as he leveled off about a foot off the ground.

Brian gave a running commentary. "Still coming...Still coming...he's pulling up...he's pulling off target...you did it, Tom! And we're almost in the city! Damn it! Here comes the other one...He's heading in...No, he's pulling up...We're too close to the city...too many witnesses!"

Brian clapped Tom on the shoulder. "Tom, you did it. The second one is rejoining on the leader. They're heading home. We made it!"

"It's not over yet, Brian. Let's get across the border before something else goes wrong."

The Russian border town of Naushki was bigger than Tom had anticipated. He drove the airplane as hard as he could towards the center. No winking of muzzle flashes, no missiles. They were across Naushki in minutes, everyone in the plane was staring down at the last bit of Russia. As they crossed the fences demarcating the border, a ragged cheer broke out in the passenger compartment. They crossed into Mongolia and set a course over the tracks heading south.

Brian sat back in his seat, arm stretched across the cockpit, hand resting on Tom's shoulder. "I suggest that we go as far south as we can, oh brother mine, to the next town in Mongolia if possible, some distance away from the border anyway. Just to discourage the Russians from thinking about a cross-border raid to 'liberate' the plane and recapture the escapees."

***

The Colt sat in a field about three miles north of Darhan, some sixty miles inside the Mongolian border on the road to Ulaanbaatar. The passengers stood in family groups beside the Colt, weeping and laughing. Two of the women knelt and kissed the ground, then kissed Tom and Brian.

"I never thought I'd say this, but I am actually glad to be back in Mongolia," said Brian.

"Yeah, but now what?" said Tom. "Somebody's going to have walk into town and alert the Mongolian authorities."

"Not to worry, big brother. We should have a ride soon."

"What do you mean?"

"The Chinese are sending a helicopter for us. Probably the same Mi-8 that the Mongolians used to fly us to the coal mine."

"How do you know this?"

"I sent a text message to our contact in Ulaanbaatar. You were busy at the time, evading marauding Russians."

Tom was dumbfounded. "You lunatic! What were you thinking? We could have died back there!"

"Nah, Tom. Luck of the Irish and all that."

Tom looked at his father. They all started laughing, then Sean pulled his two sons to him in a giant hug. Tears ran freely down his cheeks. "We really are the Flying Callahans."

Chapter Thirty-one
Genghis Kahn International Airport
Ulaanbaatar, Mongolia

The flight in the Mi-8 helicopter, bearing Tom and the rest of the American and Russian "escapees" back to Ulaanbaatar, took just under forty-five minutes, a bit longer than Tom had estimated, but there were some adverse winds. The pilot set up for a landing on the far side of the airport, away from the civilian terminal. A Mongolian Foreign Ministry representative and several officials from the Chinese Embassy led them from the aircraft into a hangar where they found a hastily arranged reception area. There were two tables covered with food and drink and a rest area roped off in the rear of the hangar with couches and cots for the children.

Two hours later, they boarded a bus and were driven across the airport to an Air China Boeing 737. Tom led the group up the airline steps directly into the empty aircraft while Porter and Brian each carried a small child and helped herd the confused but willing passengers. When the last one entered the airplane, Tom nodded to the purser who shut the aircraft door and signaled the cockpit crew. Tom took his seat across the aisle from his father and Brian as the engines began to turn. The plane taxied and swung onto the runway, engines spooling up for takeoff. The passengers sat quietly, glued to the windows as the plane accelerated. When the aircraft broke ground and the wheels started retracting, a loud cheer erupted. Tears flowed and exultant fists were raised in relief and celebration.

Tom sat back in his seat, knowing that this flight was only the first of many steps these people were going to have to take to re-join Western society. Exhaustion took over and he nodded off to the vibrations of the plane.

The approach into Beijing Capital International Airport was routine flying for the pilots but anything but routine for the passengers. They were stunned by the enormous size of the city as it passed off the right wing. They gaped at the spectacular lattice and glass international terminal, until recently the largest terminal in the world. The aircraft taxied to a gate where they were met by still more Foreign Ministry officials and some Chinese Army officers who led the passengers to an underground concourse. Luggage trolleys were produced to ease the walk and were loaded with the passengers' pitiful belongings. After several corridors and more turns, they emerged into a parking area where a military bus was waiting for them.

As they drove through downtown Beijing, the Chinese guide gave a running narration of the sights of the city to the rapt group. This was the first large modern city that the Americans had seen in decades, and the first that some of the Russians had ever seen. Exhaustion forgotten, the bus bubbled with excitement.

They arrived at the same military compound where the expedition began and were met by Deputy Minister Zhang Chin, multiple Chinese officials, and three Chinese army colonels and their wives. The Russian-speaking colonels were paired with the American officers and each American and his family was led away to a special suite that would function as the family's quarters for their stay in China.

Deputy Minister Zhang singled out Sean Callahan. "General, it is an honor to meet you, sir."

Sean bowed. "Thank you, Minister. You cannot imagine how much of an honor it is to be here. Thank you for your kindness and the help you have extended to my people and to my sons."

"General, your sons were quite determined, but I expect you know that already." He smiled. "Would you like to continue speaking Russian, or perhaps you would prefer English?"

"I would prefer English, if you don't mind."

"Excellent. I rarely get to practice. When I was a junior minister, I spent a year at the University of Oklahoma to improve my English." He chuckled, "Boomer Sooner!" then laughed outright. "I don't get to say that very often." He made a small bow. "General, I have taken the liberty of setting up a small dinner. Would you, your sons, and Mr. Nelson do me the honor of joining me after you clean up?"

Forty minutes later, they settled into an exquisite and intimate executive dining room. Waiters swooped in flourishing trays of delicious food. Tom realized that he was not only exhausted, but famished. After a welcoming toast, Zhang said, "General, I assume that you were told what is in store for you and your people?"

"Yes, Minister," said Sean. "Your assistant on the bus explained that you would assign each of us escort officers. I understand that we will be getting physicals tomorrow, followed by briefings and de-briefings."

Zhang said, "Just so. We are trying to duplicate your own government's Operation Homecoming of your fellow POWs in 1973. Your people need to be updated on the social and political changes of the past few decades. And the wives and children will need assistance adjusting as well."

Brian said, "From what I've seen, these guys have been isolated so long it'll take months to get them caught up on current events alone." He looked embarrassed. "Sorry, Dad."

"No, no, son. You're right. There's so much to learn. I feel like a cave man waking up in the twenty-first century."

"Minister, what is going to happen to the rest of your delegation back in Russia?" asked Tom, trying to shield his father from further embarrassment.

"They were arrested of course, as accomplices," Zhang said, voice matter-of-fact.

Tom looked at Brian. "We were afraid of that."

"The Russian president will be furious," said Porter.

"What now, Minister?" asked Tom.

"We have demanded the Russians return our delegation," said Zhang. "They will refuse. We will remind the Russian government that there are thousands of Russian citizens currently in Mongolia and China. They will still refuse, to save face, but it will give them pause. Eventually, we will announce an agreement; our delegation will be quietly returned, followed closely by a large purchase of Russian mining equipment." He took a sip of his tea, then gave the Americans a slight smile. "Which we had decided to do anyway."

"You are assuming that the Russian president will stay rational."

"That is where your President enters the picture."

Tom nodded. "My second phone call after dinner will be to Washington. My wife comes first."

Zhang turned back to Sean. "General, I have taken the step of calling your good friend Admiral Shinawatra. He has relayed the news of your escape to your family." He turned to Brian. "Your wife is in Bangkok, as is your wife and son, Thomas. They will be expecting calls soon." He chuckled. "As a married man myself, I recommend that you don't disappoint them."

When Tom and Brian led their father back to his quarters, he linked his arms through theirs. "I still can't believe that we're here, together," he said. "I've dreamed about this so much." He hugged both of them, as if touching them would prove that this was no dream. "My boys, my beautiful boys," he said through tears.

"We know what you mean," said Brian, tears streaking his face. "I can't believe it, either. Dad, the whole idea was Tom's and don't let him tell you otherwise."

Sean hugged Tom again, then motioned for the men to sit. He took a chair facing them. "Okay, boys, I don't want to learn about current events. I want to hear Callahan events. I want to know everything. Tell me about your mother, tell me what it was like growing up, where you lived, where you went to school. About your sister, your brother, about your families, your careers. Everything!"

***

Tom returned to his spacious suite and sat on his bed. He picked up the phone and asked the compound operator to connect him with the Admiral's home outside Bangkok. A servant answered; Tom asked for Colleen. "Hi, Darlin'."

"Tommy, is it really true? You found him?"

"Yes. He's here. Brian and I talked him to sleep, reliving our lives." He sobbed. "It was one of the greatest pleasures of my life."

A pause. "You can do anything, can't you, husband of mine?"

"Hold on, sweetheart. This trip took a lot of people. Brian and Porter are as much to blame as I am. Not to mention the Chinese. Without them, we would have gotten nowhere."

"Don't forget Uncle."

"Especially Uncle," said Tom. "Colleen, Pop only has one eye, but otherwise he's fine physically. In fact, remarkably fit."

She hesitated. "How is he mentally?"

"He's fine. Has a major guilt complex, though, about leaving us alone for so long. And the thing is, he tried over and over to escape. That's how he lost his eye."

"When can we come to Beijing?"

"Give us a few days to get organized."

"Oh."

He heard the disappointment in her voice. "Sweetheart, these people need a little time to get oriented. There's just so much territory to cover, nobody even knows where to start. For example, Pop has been badgering Brian about how his sat phone works. He's fascinated by the video games. Like a teenager."

"Then Mikey will have a new playmate."

"Now that's something Pop will enjoy," said Tom. "Where's Babushka?"

"Your mother is on her way to Bangkok as we speak. She'll be landing in about three hours. She insisted on coming out herself to be with us. She doesn't know about your father yet. Oh, Tommy, this is so wonderful!"

"If Babushka wants to talk to me, I'm available. Right now, I need to call the President."

"George Brent has an appointment with him in the morning, Washington time," said Colleen. "I spoke with George about two hours ago." She spent ten minutes filling Tom in on details of the attack on their residence, her arrest in Los Angeles, and Brent's intention to bring the Russian trip to the President's attention.

Tom's emotions roller-coastered as he learned of the dangers his family had faced in his absence. "You're right, Colleen. I'm in no mood

263

to listen to politics. I might say something that I shouldn't. I'll call George instead of the President. Let him handle it."

"Good idea," said Colleen. "This is where George shines. He and the President go back a long way."

"Okay, we'll try to keep the lid on things here. I just had dinner with a Chinese deputy minister. The Russians will not take this 'defection' well. Sooner or later, it's going to hit the fan. When it does, I'd rather be here with the family than in Washington." He paused. "In fact, I'd rather be with family than anywhere. Period."

Chapter Thirty-two
Washington, D.C.

"How dare you do this to me!" the President shouted at George Brent, thumping the arm of his chair.

"Mr. President, you told Tom to go do the best for his family—"

"I didn't tell him to illegally enter another country. He was a spy, for Christ's sake. He could have started a war."

"Some people in the United States government condemned his father to stay a prisoner of war for thirty-plus years," said Brent in a somber tone. "Somebody—waving CIA identification, mind you—tried to kidnap his wife in Los Angeles, shot at her in an airport! Somebody tried to kill his wife and son, not to mention Porter Nelson, his best friend, in what now looks suspiciously like a U.S. government operation. And you expect him to do nothing?"

The President glared at him for a long moment, then shifted his withering gaze to Bobby Anderson who sat, ashen faced, next to Brent.

"Mr. President," continued Brent, "you are merely the latest in a long line of Presidents who have been misled by your own government about these POWs. Callahan had information indicating that there may have been American prisoners in Siberia. Information provided, not by our country, but by three Asian ones. He acted on it rather than bringing it back here, maybe having someone leak it to the Russians, and having those prisoners disappear."

"Don't give me that. Past Presidents won't be taking the heat for this. I will."

"What heat? From whom? Four POWs—American servicemen—have been returned from captivity. This should be cause for celebration. You can say that you had suspicions that the CIA and State Departments were wrong. Not liars, but simply misguided in their beliefs and that you authorized Callahan to investigate. That's called leadership in my book."

"I should court martial Callahan."

George Brent took a deep breath and let it out slowly. "You have his faxed letter of resignation in your desk drawer. I've seen it. Even

265

after a court martial, you'd still have four POWs living in Beijing that the U.S. government turned its back on. What do you intend for them? Charge them with desertion? Slip in a covert team to assassinate them? And their families?"

"Don't you talk to me like that!"

"Then don't say things like that."

Another angry glare. "Be very careful here, Mr. Ambassador."

Brent leaned forward, locking eyes with the irate man across the desk. "I started serving this country when you were still in high school, young man. I swore an oath, not to the President, not to the State Department, but to the Constitution. You and I had an agreement. I would always—every single time—tell you what you needed to know. Not, I repeat, not tell you what you wanted to hear. So don't give me this 'I'm the President and You're Not' bullshit. You want to fire me, fine. Go ahead." He stood. "Come on, Bobby. We're done here."

"Sit down!" shouted the President, jumping to his feet.

Brent ignored him and was nearly to the door when the President said in a quieter voice,

"Please, George, come back and sit down. Please stay, Mr. Anderson... Bobby."

Brent turned. "The same rules?"

The President came out from behind his desk and offered his hand. "Yes, the same rules. You say what needs to be said. No restrictions." He motioned the men to a couch and sat in a chair opposite them.

Brent sipped his now cold coffee and met the President's eyes. "Four years ago, Tom Callahan saved tens of thousands of American lives. Now he's brought us a new level of cooperation from the Chinese, a fantastic opportunity. He deserves credit, not threats."

The President leaned forward, elbows on his knees. "What about the Russian president?"

"Initially, he will react just as you did—he'll be furious. Then cooler heads on his staff will prevail. Eventually—and soon, I hope—he'll come to realize he has the same escape that you have—somebody else committed this atrocity in the government before his time. He will apologize for the past wrongdoings, etcetera. After that, he should pull in his horns and play nice on the international scene. Remember that he has the Chinese to deal with as well. They have just sent him a very pointed message."

"Is that what you are, George?" said the President with a trace of a smile. "A cooler head?"

"Let's just say a different head, one out of the line of fire."

"What now? Where do we go from here?"

"You mean regarding our little group?" asked Brent.

The President glanced at Anderson, then nodded.

"There is always Brian Callahan."

"The brother? What about him?"

"He's smart as hell, speaks Russian, and has been through the wringer on this trip. He has contacts all over the financial world. He knows about the moles. Tom brought him in on it. And I agreed. Off the record, Colleen knows as well. As does Brian's wife."

The President threw his hands in the air. "Jesus Christ! That is one of the most closely guarded secrets of this administration. Doesn't anybody follow the rules around here?"

"We need people we can trust," argued Brent. "Robinson's dead. Tom wants to stay with his father. That leaves me, along with Nelson. I suggest we bring in Bobby here to help. I've known him for forty years and trust him more than any other single individual."

"What do you know about moles, Bobby?"

"Not a damned thing, Mr. President. I thought they were just some kind of rodent until George told me that he, and this small group, have been searching for moles in our government for the past four years. If you'll have me, I'd be honored."

The President offered his hand. "Welcome aboard, Bobby." Then he turned back to Brent. "Did the Callahans put you up to this?"

"No. I haven't talked about this with them. But I'm sure I can sell it to Brian. Porter Nelson and I can bring Brian up to speed pretty fast. He is as dedicated as Tom—he just doesn't know it yet. He'll do whatever he can to root them out."

"And if he can't?"

"He will call the person he trusts the most for help."

The President looked thoughtful, then smiled the first smile of the day. "His brother!"

George Brent nodded. "Right now, Tom Callahan doesn't want to save the world, he just wants to live in it with his father and enjoy the rest of his father's life, surrounding him with love, attention, and grandkids." He shrugged. "But in six months, a year, who knows?"

Chapter Thirty-three
Beijing, China

The next afternoon found Tom and Brian in the ornamental gardens, surrounding the military compound. They were quiet as they studied the topiary figures, the gorgeous flowers, and the small stream that ran between the rock sculptures.

"I finally got in touch with Lisa," said Brian.

"And how is our sister?"

"Spring Break starts in a week. She'll fly here—or Bangkok—depending on where we are. With the kids."

"Our ambassador has called here several times."

"Can't blame him. Somebody's going to leak this."

"Then the President's really going to be smoked. He's going to have a knock-down drag-out with the Russian president. The United Nations will be hoppin', that's for sure. We need to get him to listen and let Porter get out the real facts."

"Hey, Tom, everything worked out. I don't see why Washington won't be happy about this."

"That's not the way it works, pal. Nobody is more anxious to settle a score than an embarrassed politician. And do not ever forget that the Russian president is, first and foremost, a politician." Then he added, "As is our own President."

Brian shrugged. "At least we got Pop out."

They watched their father pacing the veranda at the edge of the gardens, checking his watch, and looking out for the arrival of his family.

Tom said, "He's as nervous as a doolie before his first mixer."

Brian laughed. "True. I remember my first semester at the Academy after doolie summer trying to re-acquaint myself with female companionship. I nearly hyperventilated trying to talk to women for the first time in three months. Imagine what it's like after thirty-plus years." Brian nudged Tom as their father checked his watch again, then turned to stare down the road for the limousine that would deliver his wife. They both laughed again. "So, I thought we had agreed that this reunion wasn't going to take place until tomorrow or the next day. What happened?"

"When was the last time you told Mom she couldn't do something and got away with it?"

"Good point," conceded Brian, laughing. "Is everything set?"

"Yep. I talked to the ladies. Mikey's going to make the first move. Then Mom, then our wives. We're going to give the parents as much privacy as they want, but be available for support if the reunion goes off the rails."

Thirty minutes later, Tom stood with his brother and his father on the garden veranda, facing the long driveway. The Chinese government limousine, bearing the Callahan family from the airport, stopped precisely in front of the stairs leading up to the gardens. A Chinese soldier appeared and opened the door. Colleen and Elizabeth stepped out, then Mikey exploded from the vehicle, a stuffed tiger in his arms. He broke into a run up the long flagstone stairway, making quick work of the distance between them. He stopped in front of Sean and held up the tiger.

Sean kneeled and said, "Is this for me?"

"Yes. Babushka said you were like a tiger, so I bought this for you. With my own money!"

"What's his name? I don't know any good names for tigers."

"Tony, of course."

"Tony-Of-Course? What a strange name for a tiger!"

"No, *Tony*! Just Tony the Tiger." He giggled. "You're silly!"

"Okay, Tony the Tiger it is." Sean tucked the tiger under his arm. "Thank you, son."

Mikey nodded and studied Sean's face. He reached out and gently touched Sean's cheek under the eye patch. "I don't think you look like a tiger. I think you look like a pirate."

"Arghh, matey," said Sean.

Mikey laughed, put his arms around Sean's neck, and continued to study him from close range. "What should I call you? Grandpa or *Dyedushka?*"

"What do you want to call me?"

"Well, you're my only grandpa now. But Babushka said you could help me learn Russian like my daddy so maybe Dyedushka."

Sean nodded. "Now, what do I call you: Mikey or Mac?"

"You're my Dyedushka. You can call me anything you want."

"Well, since you're my only grandson, I'll call you *vnook.*"

"I know that word! Babushka says that to me sometimes."

Tom swooped in, snatched up Mikey and planted a loud kiss on his neck. "Okay, pal, why don't you give me a big hug and introduce me to your mother while your Dyedushka talks with Babushka?"

Tom glanced at the women patiently waiting by the limousine. Colleen and Elizabeth wore Asian-cut silk dresses that fit like gloves with high Mandarin collars and bright flower patterns. Trust Colleen to find a custom dress shop in a foreign country on a day's notice. His mother wore her hair swept up and a white dress that he had never seen before adorned with a gorgeous silk scarf. He realized with a start that he hadn't seen his mother in anything but paint-splattered jeans and floppy shirts for at least ten years.

Colleen and Elizabeth flanked Barbara Callahan as she began her walk up the stairs, then turned and joined their husbands. Barbara paused just in front of Sean.

"Should I say that you haven't changed a bit?"

"Barbara, I am ashamed that I was away from you so long. Can you forgive me?"

"Tommy told me that you tried to escape many times."

"I never gave up."

"I knew you wouldn't, my darling."

"It took our sons to make it happen."

"They're both like you: talented, bright, and stubborn."

"And very much in love with their wives."

"Must be a Callahan thing," she said, voice trembling.

He took her face in his hands. "You are so beautiful."

"Sean Callahan, I'm almost seventy years old. You've not only lost an eye, you've lost your mind. I am many things, but I am certainly not beautiful."

"You are to me."

She studied his face, then slowly placed her hands on his hips.

"May I kiss you?" he asked.

"I flew here all the way from Albuquerque. You better kiss me!"

He gently kissed her forehead, then her eyes. His lips moved slowly across her cheeks then found her mouth. Her arms circled his waist and she pulled him closer.

When they separated, he laughed as he slid one arm around her shoulders and stroked her graying hair. Together they laughed and hugged and cried.

Brian led Elizabeth to Sean and said, "Dad, this is my Elizabeth. She's our own family Annie Oakley." Elizabeth blushed, and slid into Sean's arms.

"Brian exaggerates, Dad."

Sean hugged her. "I don't think so. At least not in this case. I am looking forward to getting to know you, young lady."

Tom introduced Colleen. Sean looked her up and down. "So this is the famous Colleen. Tom's told me stories of your many exploits." Sean hugged her, then turned to Tom, "What was that phrase you used to describe Colleen, son? A kick-ass brainiac?"

Everybody laughed. Sean said, "Looks like the whole family's in agreement, Colleen. I will remind myself to be careful around you."

"Pop, you have no worries from me. Now, Babuska, she's a different story. I am in awe of her."

Sean reached for Barbara and kissed her cheek again. "So am I."

Mikey jumped up and down, chanting, "What about me? I want a kiss!"

Tom stood in the sunshine, looking at the happy group and thinking of how complicated life could be and how different their lives had turned out from their dreams. And yet, the quest was over. This dream was just beginning.

Epilogue
Siberian Forest

An older man, bristling with hoarfrost and stooped with years, opens the door of his one-room, hand-hewn log cabin and carries an armload of wood to the stove, his breath steaming in the frigid air. He stokes the fire, and rubs his hands together as he warms himself. After a few minutes, he shuffles into the corner that he uses as a tiny kitchen, prepares his dinner of hard bread, cheese, and a bit of turnip and eats at a small rough plank table.

After he cleans up from his meager meal, the man limps over to a battered dresser and, after much pushing and shoving, slides it away from the wall. On his knees, he pulls up a floorboard, reaches down and removes a box, which he carefully places on the table. He opens it and removes a small, crudely made American flag. He stands the flag upright, smoothes the wrinkled material, then backs away from the table and stands at attention.

After a moment he salutes. In a voice raspy from decades of breathing frozen Siberian air, he begins to speak: "The American Fighting Man's Code of Conduct. Article One: I am an American fighting man. I serve in the forces which guard my country and our way of life. I am prepared to give my life in their defense. Article Two: I will never surrender of my own free will—"

The End

About the Author

Brinn Colenda is a graduate of the United States Air Force Academy with a B.S. in Political Science. He has advanced degrees in economics and business, and had a post graduate fellowship at the Hoover Institution for War, Revolution, and Peace at Stanford University.

While in the USAF, Brinn served in a variety of flying and staff assignments around the world from Southeast Asia to Bolivia. He was an instructor pilot with the U.S. Air Force, the German Air Force, the Dutch Air Force, Great Britain's Royal Air Force, and was awarded command pilot wings by the Bolivian Air Force. He retired as a Lieutenant Colonel.

Brinn serves on the Angel Fire Village Council. He spends time skiing in the mountains of Northern New Mexico with his wife and three college-age sons and he pursues his love of writing. He has published articles in professional journals and his local weekly newspaper. His first novel was a political/military thriller, *The Cochabamba Conspiracy*. *Chita Quest* is the sequel.